GUSTAVE FLAUBERT was born in Rouen in 1821, the son of a prominent physician. A solitary child, he was attracted to literature at an early age, and after his recovery from a nervous breakdown suffered while a law student, he turned his total energies to writing. Aside from journeys to the Near East, Greece, Italy, and North Africa, and a stormy liaison with the poetess Louise Colet, his life was dedicated to the practice of his art. The form of his work was marked by intense aesthetic scrupulousness and passionate pursuit of *le mot juste;* its content alternately reflected scorn for French bourgeois society and a romantic taste for exotic historical subject matter. The success of *Madame Bovary* (1857) was ensured by government prosecution for "immorality"; *Salammbô* (1862) and *The Sentimental Education* (1869) received a cool public reception; not until the publication of *Three Tales* (1877) was his genius popularly acknowledged. Among fellow writers, however, his reputation was supreme. His circle of friends included Turgenev and the Goncourt brothers, while the young Guy de Maupassant underwent an arduous literary apprenticeship under his direction. Increasing personal isolation and financial insecurity troubled his last years. His final bitterness and disillusion were vividly evidenced in the savagely satiric *Bouvard and Pécuchet,* left unfinished at his death in 1880.

madame bovary

GUSTAVE FLAUBERT

A New Translation by
MILDRED MARMUR

The trial of Madame Bovary
Translated by Evelyn Gendel

With a Foreword by
MARY McCARTHY

(Revised and Updated Bibliography)

A SIGNET CLASSIC

NEW AMERICAN LIBRARY

A DIVISION OF PENGUIN BOOKS USA INC., NEW YORK
PUBLISHED IN CANADA BY
PENGUIN BOOKS CANADA LIMITED, MARKHAM, ONTARIO

Library of Congress Catalog Card Number: 88-84090

Ⓒ

SIGNET CLASSIC TRADEMARK REG. U.S. PAT. OFF. AND FOREIGN COUNTRIES
REGISTERED TRADEMARK—MARCA REGISTRADA
HECHO EN DRESDEN, TN, USA

SIGNET, SIGNET CLASSIC, MENTOR, ONYX, PLUME, MERIDIAN
and NAL BOOKS are published *in the United States* by
New American Library, a division of Penguin Books USA Inc.,
1633 Broadway, New York, New York 10019,
in Canada by Penguin Books Canada Limited,
2801 John Street, Markham, Ontario L3R 1B4

FIRST PRINTING, JULY, 1964

21 22 23 24 25 26 27 28 29

PRINTED IN THE UNITED STATES OF AMERICA

To
Marie-Antoine-Jules Sénard

Member of the Paris Bar
Ex-President of the National Assembly
Former Minister of the Interior

Dear and Illustrious Friend:
Permit me to inscribe your name at the head of this book and above its dedication, for it is to you, above all, that I owe its publication. In the course of your magnificent defense, my work has acquired for myself something of an unforeseen authority. Please accept, then, my grateful homage, which, however great it may be, can never achieve the height of your eloquence and your devotion.

Gustave Flaubert

Paris, 12 April 1857

Foreword

When Flaubert made his famous statement—"Madame Bovary is me"—he was echoing one of his favorite authors, Cervantes. According to the story, Cervantes was asked on his deathbed whom he meant to depict in Don Quixote. "Myself," he answered. In Cervantes' case this must have been true, quite simply and terribly, whether or not he ever said it. In Flaubert's the answer was an evasion. He was tired of being asked about the "real-life original" of his heroine. In fact, there *was* one; there may even have been two. First and most important was Delphine Delamare, née Couturier, the wife of a village doctor in the Bray region in Normandy, not far from where Flaubert lived. In 1848 she took poison, leaving behind her an unpaid bill from a circulating library in Rouen; the Delamares' furniture was sold at public auction to satisfy her creditors. Her case was in the newspapers, and Flaubert's friends had suggested it to him as the subject for a novel, on the writing-course principle of "Write about what you know." When *Madame Bovary* appeared in 1857, Dr. Delamare, like Charles Bovary, had died of grief, but the other principals were still living: Rodolphe, Léon, the servant Félicité. And many years later, in the village of Ry—the original of Yonville L'Abbaye—Delphine Delamare's smart double curtains, yellow and black, were still talked about by her neighbors. Today her house is gone, but her garden is there, the property of the village pharmacist, who displays in his shop what purports to be Monsieur Homais's counter. The real Monsieur Homais was probably legion. Flaubert is said to have spent a month

vii

while writing *Madame Bovary* in a hotel at Forges-les-Eaux studying the local pharmacist, a red-hot anticlericalist and diehard republican whom he had already spotted and banded, but he is also said to have had his eye on other atheistical druggists, birds of the same feather, in the neighborhood.

In short, *Madame Bovary* revived a scandal that had been a nine-days' wonder in the locality, and Flaubert no doubt was sick of the gossip and somewhat remorseful, like most authors, for what he had started. At the same time, as an author, he must have resented the cheapening efforts of real life to claim for itself material he had transmuted with such pain in his study; even in her name "Delphine Delamare" sounds like a hack's alias for Emma Bovary. The gossip was not silenced by his denials. In 1905 Félicité, aged seventy-nine (her real name was Augustine), was still giving interviews about her mistress to literary critics. Even now the village of Ry is recognizable to readers of the novel; a small sign identifies the inn as the original of the Lion d'Or; Rodolphe's château is pointed out on a nearby road. Beyond the village there are the meadows bordering the stream, poplar trees, and many cow bridges made of old planks like the one Emma (or Delphine) used to cross going to meet her lover. After *Madame Bovary*, the figures in the Delamare story must have spent their lives as marked men. "Rodolphe," a veritable Cain, emigrated to America, then came back and killed himself on a Parisian boulevard, possibly from remorse. This cannot have been part of Flaubert's intention. And the gossip, as always, must have been wrong some of the time. What if the gentleman everyone insisted was Rodolphe had been only an innocent neighbor who could not stand the publicity?

The net has been cast wider. A second model for Emma has been found in the life of Flaubert's friend the sculptor Pradier, who made the pretty ladies, Lille and Strasbourg, that sit on pedestals like halted patriotic floats on the Place de la Concorde. A "memoir" of this woman, written out in an illiterate script by her confidante, a carpenter's wife, had fallen into Flaubert's hands. Did he use it? Louise Pradier was good-looking, silly, extremely unfaithful to her husband, and up to her neck in debt; she consoled herself by promises of suicide, though in fact it was her husband who died suddenly, like Charles Bovary, killed by the discovery of his wife's character and the bills she had run up. This does not prove that she "sat for" Flaubert, but bohemian gossip may have said so; she may have thought so herself. Louise Pradier was living when *Madame Bovary* came out.

This endless conjecturing on the part of the public is the price paid by the realistic novelist for "writing about what he knows." With *Salammbo* and *The Temptation of St. Anthony,* there was no occasion for Flaubert to issue denials. But *Madame Bovary* was fraught with embarrassment for its author, and not only, it would seem, for the reasons already given. For example take the following. Dr. Delamare studied with Flaubert's father, the surgeon, in Rouen, and he was a poor student; these facts are established. Dr. Delamare, being dead, could not be hurt by the book. But there was someone else who could. Flaubert's brother, Achille, was a doctor. He did a bad operation on their father; gangrene developed, and Dr. Flaubert died. A little later Flaubert's sister Caroline died of puerperal fever; it is not clear whether this was Achille again, but Flaubert in a letter described sitting up with Caroline's body while her husband and a priest snored. Just like Emma's wake. Flaubert remembered those snores. Did he remember the medical murder of his father when he wrote about Charles's operation on the clubfooted inn boy —the most villainous folly in the book? A novelist is an elephant, but an elephant who must pretend to forget.

On the one hand, Flaubert declared *he* was Emma. On the other, he wrote to a lady: "There's nothing in *Madame Bovary* that's drawn from life. It's a *completely invented* story. None of my own feelings or experiences are in it." So help him God. Of course, he was fibbing, as is clear from his more intimate correspondence. Like all novelists, he drew on his own experiences, and, more than most novelists, he was frightened by the need to invent. When he came to do the ball at Vaubyessard, he lamented. "It's so long since I've been to a ball." If memory failed, he documented himself, as he did for Emma's school reading, going back over the children's stories he had read as a little boy and the picture books he had colored. If he had not had an experience the story required, he sought it out. Before writing the chapter about the agricultural fair, he went to one; he consulted his brother about clubfoot and, disappointed by the ignorance of Achille's answers, procured textbooks. There is hardly a page in the novel that he had not "lived," and he constantly drew on his own feelings to render Emma's.

All novelists do this, but Flaubert went beyond the usual call of duty. Madame Bovary was not Flaubert, certainly; yet he became Madame Bovary and all the accessories to her story, her lovers, her husband, her little greyhound, the corset lace that hissed around her hips like a slithery grass snake as she undressed in the hotel room in Rouen, the blinds of the cab that hid her and Léon as they made love. In a letter he made clear the state of mind in which he wrote. That day he had been doing the scene of the horseback ride, when Rodolphe seduces Emma in the woods. "What a delicious thing writing is—not to be you any more but to move through the whole universe you're talking about. Take me today, for instance: I was man and woman, lover and mistress; I went riding in a forest on a fall afternoon beneath the yellow leaves, and I was the horses, the leaves, the wind, the words he and she spoke, and the red sun beating on their half-closed eyelids, which were already heavy with passion." It is hard to imagine another great novelist—Stendhal, Tolstoy, Jane Austen, Dickens, Dostoyevsky, Balzac—who would conceive of the act of writing as a rapturous loss of identity. Poets have often expressed the wish for otherness, for fusion—to be their mistress' sparrow or her girdle or the breeze that caressed her temples and wantoned with her ribbons—but Flaubert was the first to realize this wish in prose, in the disguise of a realistic story. The climax of the horseback ride was, of course, a coupling in which all of Nature joined in a gigantic throbbing *partouze* while Flaubert's pen flew. He was writing a book, and yet from his account you would think he was *reading* one. "What a delicious thing reading is—not to be you any more but to move through the whole universe you're reading about. . . ."

Compare this, in fact, to the rapt exchange of platitudes between Léon and Emma on the night of their first meeting, at dinner at the Lion d'Or:

"... is there anything better, really, than sitting by the fire with a book while the wind beats on your windowpanes and the lamp is burning?"

"Isn't it so?" she said, fixing him with her large black eyes wide open.

"One forgets everything," he continued. "The hours go by. Without leaving your chair you stroll through imagined landscapes as if they were real, and your thoughts interweave with the story, lingering over details or leaping ahead with the plot. Your imagination confuses itself with the characters, and it seems as if it were your own heart beating inside their clothes."

"How true! How true!" she said.

The threadbare magic carpet, evidently, is shared by author and reader, who are both escaping from the mean provincial life close at hand. Yet *Madame Bovary* is one of a series of novels—including *Don Quixote* and *Northanger Abbey*—that illustrate the evil effects of reading. *All* reading, in the case of *Madame Bovary,* not simply the reading of romances. The books Emma fed on were not all trash by any means: in the convent she had read Chateaubriand; as a girl on the farm she read *Paul and Virginia.* The best sellers she liked were of varying quality: Eugène Sue, Balzac, George Sand, Walter Scott. She tried to improve her mind with history and philosophy, starting one "deep" book after another and leaving them all unfinished. Reading was undermining her health, according to her mother-in-law, who thought the thing to do was to stop her subscription to the lending library in Rouen. It ought to be against the law, declared the old lady, for circulating libraries to supply people with novels and books against religion, that mock at priests in speeches taken from Voltaire. Flaubert is making fun of Madame Bovary senior, and yet he too felt that Emma's reading was unhealthy. And for the kind of reason her mother-in-law would give: books put ideas in Emma's head. It is characteristic of Flaubert that his own notions, in the mouths of his characters, are turned into desolate echoes—into clichés.

Léon too is addicted to books, as the passage cited shows. *He* prefers poetry. But it is not only the young people in *Madame Bovary* who are glamorized by the printed page. Monsieur Homais is another illustration of the evil effects of reading. He offers Emma the use of his library, which contains, as he says, "the best authors: Voltaire, Rousseau, Delille, Walter Scott, the *Literary Echo,* etc." These authors have addled his head with ideas. And Monsieur Homais's ideas are dangerous, literally so; not just in the sense that Madame

Bovary senior, meant. An idea invading Monsieur Homais's brain is responsible for Charles's operation on the deformed Hippolyte. Monsieur Homais had read an article on a new method for curing clubfoot, and he was immediately eager that Charles should try it; in his druggist mind there was a typical confusion between humanitarian motives and a Chamber of Commerce zeal. The operation is guaranteed to put Yonville L'Abbaye on the map. He will write it up himself for a Rouen paper. As he tells Charles, "an article in the paper gets around. People talk about it. It ends by snowballing." This snowballing is precisely what is happening, with horrible consequences yet to come. Thanks to an article in the press, Hippolyte will lose his leg.

The diffusion of ideas in the innocent countryside is the plot of *Madame Bovary*. When the book ran serially, Flaubert's editors, who were extremely stupid, wanted to cut the clubfoot episode: it was unpleasant, they said, and contributed nothing to the story. Flaubert insisted; he regarded it as essential to the book. As it is. This is the point where Monsieur Homais interlocks with Emma and her story; elsewhere he only talks and appears busy. True, Emma gets the arsenic from his "caphanaum"—a ridiculous name for his inner sanctum based on the transubstantiation controversy—but this is not really the druggist's fault. He is only an accessory. But when it comes to the operation, Monsieur Homais is the creative genius; it is his hideous brainchild, and Charles is his instrument. Up to the time of the operation, Monsieur Homais could appear as mere comic relief or prosaic contrast. But with the operation the affinity between apparent opposites—the romantic dreamer and the "man of science"—becomes clear. Monsieur Homais is not just Emma's foil; he is her alter ego.

For the first time they see eye to eye; they are a team pulling together for Charles to do the operation and for the same reason: a thirst for fame. And both, in their infatuation with a dream, have lost sight of the reality in front of them, which is Charles. He surrenders to the dazzling temptation they hold out to him. What is it, exactly? The temptation to be something other than what he is, a slow, cautious, uncertain practitioner who is terrified to set a simple fracture. Charles has got nothing out of books; he cannot even stay awake after dinner to peruse a medical text. He accepts his ignorance innocently as his lot in life and takes precautions to do as little harm as possible; his pathos as a doctor is that he is aware of being a potential danger to his patients. Yet when Hippolyte's clubfoot is offered him, he falls, like Adam, urged on by the woman and the serpent. After the operation, Charles's limitations are made public, and the touching hope he had, of securing Emma's love by being different from what he is, is lost to both of them. This is the turning point of the book. Emma has met resistance in Charles, the resistance of inert reality to her desire to make it over as she can change the paper in her parlor. In furious disgust she resumes her relations with Rodolphe, and from then on her extravagances have a hysterical set aim— revenge on Charles for his incompetence.

Both Emma and Monsieur Homais regard themselves as confined to a sphere too small for their endowments—hers in sensibility, his in sense. Emma takes flight into the country, where the château is, into the town; Monsieur Homais's solution is to inflate the village he lives in by his own self-importance and by judicious publicity. It must be remembered that if Emma is a reader, Monsieur Homais is not only a reader but a *writer*—the local correspondent of the *Rouen Beacon*. That is, they represent the passive and active sides of the same vice. No local event has *happened* for Monsieur Homais till he has cast it into an epic fiction to be sent off to his paper; for Emma, less inventive, nothing happens in Yonville L'Abbaye by definition.

Emma surely felt that she had nothing in common with the grotesque pockmarked druggist in his velvet cap with the gold tassel; he was the antithesis of refinement. But Monsieur Homais was attracted to her and sensed a kindred spirit. He expressed this in his own way: "She's a woman of great parts who wouldn't be out of place in a subprefecture." Homais is a textbook case of the Art of Sinking in prose, and this is the comic side of his hobbled ambitions; he would like to be a modern Hippocrates, but he is a druggist —halfway between a cook and a doctor. He is bursting with recipes; he has a recipe for everything. At the same time, he would like to turn his laboratory, which is a kind of kitchen, into a consulting room; he has been in trouble with the authorities for playing doctor—practicing medicine without a license.

Emma's voluptuous dreams in coarser form have tickled the druggist's thoughts. He takes a fatherly interest in Léon, his lodger, seeing the notary's clerk as a younger self and imagining on his behalf a wild student life in Paris, with actresses, masked balls, champagne, and possibly a love affair with a great lady of the Faubourg St. Germain. He is dreaming à la Emma, but aloud, and he lends his dream, as it were, with a show of philanthropy to Léon. This is double vicariousness. In practice, Monsieur Homais's dissipations are more thrifty. When he goes to Rouen for an outing, he insists that Léon accompany him to visit a certain Bridoux, an apothecary who has a remarkable dog that goes into convulsions at the sight of a snuffbox. The unwilling clerk is seduced by Monsieur Homais's excitement into witnessing this performance, which seems to be the pharmacist's equivalent to a visit to a house of ill fame; and Léon knows he is committing an infidelity to Emma, who is waiting impatiently in "their" hotel room for him. In fact, between Emma and Homais, there has always been a subtle rivalry for Léon, and this betrayal is the first sign that she is losing. Léon is turning into a bourgeois; soon he will give up the flute and poetry, get a promotion, and settle down. As Léon is swallowed by the middle class, Monsieur Homais emerges. By the end of the novel, he has published a book, taken up smoking, like an artist, and bought two Pompadour statuettes for his drawing room.

Bridoux's dog is an evil portent for Emma; he has been heard before, offstage, at another critical juncture, when Emma falls ill of brain fever, having received the "fatal" note from Rodolphe in a basket of apricots. Homais, to whom love is unknown, blames the smell of the apricots and is reminded of Bridoux's dog, another allergic subject. For Yonville L'Abbaye grief and loss only release a spate of anecdotes; similar instances are recalled, to reduce whatever has happened to its lowest common denominator. This occurs on the very first night the Bovarys arrive in Yonville; Emma's little greyhound has jumped out of the coach coming from Tostes, and Lheureux, the draper, her nemesis-to-be, tries to console her with examples of lost and strayed dogs who found their masters after a lapse of years. Why, he had heard of one that came all the way back from Constantinople to Paris. And another that did a hundred and twenty miles in a straight line and swam four rivers. And his own father had a poodle that jumped up on him one night on the street, after twelve years' absence. These wondrous animals, almost hu-

man you might say, are a yipping chorus of welcome to Yonville L'Abbaye, where everything has a parallel that befell
someone's cousin, and there is nothing new under the sun.

Emma's boredom and her recklessness distinguish her from
Monsieur Homais, who is a coward and who creates boredom around him without suffering it himself. Yet Emma is
tiresome too, at least to her lovers, and she would have been
tiresome to Flaubert in real life, as he well knew, because her
boredom is a silly copy of his own, and she is never more
conventional and tedious than when she is decrying convention. She and Léon agree that membership in a circulating
library is a necessity if you have to live in the provinces
(he also has a music subscription), and they are both wholly
dependent on this typical bourgeois institution. The lending
library is a central metaphor of *Madame Bovary* because
it is the inexhaustible source of *idées reçues*—borrowed ideas
and stock sentiments that circulate tritely among the population.

But for Flaubert all ideas become trite as soon as somebody expresses them. This applies indifferently to good ideas
and bad. He makes no distinction. For him the lending library is an image of civilization itself. Ideas and feelings as
well get more and more soiled and grubby, like library books,
as they pass from hand to hand. The curé's greasy thumb-
print on Christian doctrine is just as repulsive as Monsieur
Homais's coffee stain on the philosophy of the Enlighten-
ment. The pursuit of originality is as pathetic as Emma's
decorating efforts. Similarly with the quality called sincerity.
If it exists, it is inarticulate, preverbal, dumb as an ox or
as the old peasant woman who is awarded a medal at the
agricultural fair for fifty years of meritorious service. The
speech of presentation annihilates fifty years of merit—a
life—in a flash by turning it into *words*.

From his own point of view, this renders Flaubert's efforts
in his study as unavailing as Emma's quest for a love that
will live up to her solitary dreams. Words, like lovers, have
the power of lying, and they also, like lovers, have a habit of
repeating themselves, since language is finite. Flaubert's horror of repetition in writing (which has been converted into
the dogma that you must never use the same word, above
all the same adjective, twice on a page) reflects his horror
of repetition in life. Involuntary repetition is banality. What
remains doubtful, though, is whether banality is a property

of life or a property of language or both. In Emma's eyes, it
is life that is impoverished and reality that is banal, reality
being symbolized for her by Charles. But Charles is not
banal; Rodolphe and Léon are banal, and it is exactly their
banality that attracts her.

Rodolphe is superior to Léon in that his triteness is a cal-
culation. An accomplished comedian, he is not disturbed
at the agricultural fair by the drone of the voice awarding
money prizes for animal flesh, manure, and flax, while he
pours his passionate platitudes into Emma's fluttered ears.
"Tell me, why have we known each other, we two? What
chance has willed it?" His view of Emma is the same as the
judge's view of a merino ram. She is flesh, with all its
frailties, and he is an expert in flesh. Yet Rodolphe is trite
beyond his intention. He is wedded to a stock idea of himself as a sensual brute that prevents him from noticing that he
actually cares for Emma. His recipes for seduction, like the
pomade he uses on his hair, might have been made for him
by a pharmacist's formula, and the fact that they work pro-
vides him with a ready-made disillusionment. Since he knows
that "eternal love" is a cliché, he is prepared to break with
Emma as a matter of course and he drops a manufac-
tured tear on his letter of adieu, annoyed by a vague sensation that he does not recognize as grief. As for Léon, he is
too cowardly to let himself see that his fine sentiments are
platitudes; he deceives himself in the opposite way from
Rodolphe: Rodolphe feels something and convinces himself
that it is nothing, whereas Léon feels nothing and dares not
know it. Even his sensuality is timid and short-lived; his
clerkly nature passively takes Emma's dictation.

Emma does not see the difference. She is disappointed in
both her lovers and in "love" itself. Her principal emotions
are jealousy and possessiveness, which represent the strong,
almost angry movement of her will. In other words, she is
a very ordinary middle-class woman, with banal expectations
of life and an urge to dominate her surroundings. Her character is remarkable only for an unusual deficiency of natural
feeling. Emma is trite; what happens to her is trite. Her
story does not hold a single surprise for the reader, who
can say at every stage, "I felt it coming." Her end is inevitable, but not as a classic doom, which is perceived as
inexorable only when it is complete. It is inevitable because it is ordinary. *Anyone* could have prophesied what

would become of Emma—her mother-in-law, for instance. It did not need a Tiresias. If you compare her story with that of Anna Karenina, you are aware of the pathos of Emma's. Anna is never pathetic; she is tragic, and what happens to her, up to the very end, is always surprising, for real passions and moral strivings are at work, which have the power of "making it new." In this her story is distinct from an ordinary society scandal of the period. Nor could any ordinary society prophet have forecast Anna's fate. "He will get tired of her and leave her," they would have said of Vronsky. He did not. But Rodolphe could have been counted on to drop Emma, and Léon to grow frightened of her and bored.

Where destiny is no more than average probability, it appears inescapable in a peculiarly depressing way. This is because any element in it can be replaced by a substitute without changing the outcome; e.g., if Rodolphe had not materialized, Emma would have found someone else. But if Anna had not met Vronsky on the train, she would still be married to Karenin. Vronsky is *necessary*, whereas Rodolphe and Léon are interchangeable parts in a machine that is engaged in mass production of human fates. *Madame Bovary* is often called the first modern novel, and this is true, not because of any technical innovations Flaubert made but because it is the first novel to deal with what is now called mass culture. Emma did not have television, and Félicité did not read comic books in the kitchen, but the phenomenon was rampant in every Yonville L'Abbaye, and Flaubert was the first to note it.

Mass culture in *Madame Bovary* means the circulating library and the *Rouen Beacon* and the cactus plants Léon and Emma tend at opposite windows, having read about them in a novel that has made cactuses all the rage. It means poor Charles's phrenological head—a thoughtful attention paid him by Léon—and the pious reading matter the curé gives Emma as a substitute for "bad" books. It means the neoclassic town hall, with its peristyle, and the tax collector at his lathe, an early form of do-it-yourself. One of the last visions Emma has of the world she is leaving is the tax collector in his garret pursuing his senseless hobby, turning out little wooden imitations of ivory curios, themselves no doubt produced in series in the Orient for export. She has run to Binet's attic from the notary's dining room,

which has simulated-oak wallpaper, stained-glass insets in the
windows, a huge cactus, a "niche," and reproductions of Steuben's "Esmeralda" and Schopin's "Potiphar." Alas, it is like
Emma to stop, in her last hours of life, to *envy* the notary.
"That's the dining room *I* ought to have," she says to herself. To her this horrible room is the height of good taste,
but the blunder does not just prove she has *bad* taste. If the
notary had had reproductions of the "Sistine Madonna" and
the "Mona Lisa," she would have been smitten with envy
too. And she would have been right not to distinguish, for in
the notary's interior any reproduction would have the same
value, that of a trophy, like a stuffed stag's head. This is
the achievement of mass-produced culture.

In Emma's day, mass-produced culture had not yet reached
the masses; it was still a bourgeois affair and mixed up, ironi-
cally, with a notion of taste and discrimination—a notion that
persists in advertising. Rodolphe in his château would be a
perfect photographic model for whiskey or tobacco. Emma's
"tragedy" from her own point of view is her lack of purchasing power, and a critic might say that the notary's dining room simply spelled out the word "money" to her. Yet
it is not as simple as that; if it were, Emma's head would
be set straighter on her shoulders. What has happened to
her and her spiritual sisters is that simulated-oak wallpaper,
say, has become itself a kind of money inexpressible in terms
of its actual cost. Worse, ideas and sentiments, like wallpaper, have become a kind of money too and they share
with money the quality of abstractness, which allows them
to be exchanged. It is their use as coins that has made
them trite—worn and rubbed—and at the same time indistin-
guishable from each other except in terms of currency fluc-
tuation. The banalities exchanged between Léon and Emma at
their first meeting ("And what music do you prefer?" "Oh,
German music, which makes you dream.") are simply coins;
money in the usual sense is not at issue here, since both
these young people are poor; they are alluding, through those
coins, to their inner riches.

The same with Rodolphe and Emma; the same with nearly
the whole cast of characters. A meeting between strangers in
Madame Bovary inevitably produces a golden shower of platitudes. This shower of platitudes is as mechanical as the
droning action of the tax collector's lathe. It appears to be
beyond human control; no one is responsible, and no one

can stop it. There is a terrible scene in the middle of the
novel where Emma appeals to God, in the person of the curé,
to put an end to the repetitive meaninglessness of her life.
God is preoccupied and inattentive, and as she moves away
from the church, she hears the village boys reciting their
catechism. "What is a Christian?" "He who being baptized
... baptized ... baptized ..." The answer is lost in an echo
that reverberates emptily through the village. Yet the question, although intoned by rote, is a genuine one—the fundamental question of the book—for a Christian means simply
a soul here. It is Emma's demand— "Who am I? What am
I to do?"—coming back at her in ontological form, and
there is no reply.

If this were all, *Madame Bovary* would be a nihilistic
satire or howl of despair emanating from the novelist's study.
But there *is* a sort of tongue-tied answer. That is Charles
Bovary. Without Charles, Emma would be the moral void
that her fatuous conversation and actions disclose. Charles,
in a novelistic sense, is her redeemer. To her husband she
is sacred, and this profound and simple emotion is conta-
gious.

He is stupid, a peasant as she calls him, almost a devoted
animal, clumsy, a dupe. His broad back looks at her like a
platitude. He has small eyes; he snores. Until she reformed
him, he used to wear a nightcap. Weeping beneath the
phrenological head, he is nearly ridiculous. He is nearly
ridiculous at the opera, where he complains that the music
is keeping him from hearing the words. "I like to know where
I am," he explains, though he, of all people, does not
know where he is in the worldly way of knowing what is
going on under his nose. His next blunder, at the opera,
is to spill a glass of orgeat down the back of a cotton spin-
ner's wife. He has no imagination, Emma thinks, no "soul."
When they find the green-silk cigar case that must belong
to the viscount, on the way home from the ball at Vaubyessard, Charles's only reaction is to note that it contains
two smokable cigars.

Yet this provincial, this philistine is the only real romantic
in the novel—he and the boy Justin, Monsieur Homais's down-
trodden apprentice, who dreams over Emma's fichus and
underdrawers while Félicité irons in the kitchen. These two,
the man and the boy, despised and rejected, are capable of
"eternal love." Justin lets Emma have her death (the arsenic)

because he cannot refuse her, just as Charles lets her have
her every desire. The boy's passion drives him to books, instead of the other way around: Monsieur Homais catches him
reading a book on "Married Love," with illustrations. Justin
is only a child and he weeps like a child on Emma's grave.
Charles is a man, a provider, and he has a true man's solici-
tude for the weaker creature. He sheds tears when he sees
Emma eat her first bread and jam after her brain fever. This
heavy, maladroit man is a person of the utmost delicacy of
feeling. If he is easy to deceive, it is because his mind is
pure. It never enters his head that Emma can be anything
but good.

He first meets her in the kitchen of her father's farm-
house. He has been waked up at night to go set Farmer
Rouault's leg, in a scene reminiscent of a genre painting—
"Fetch the Doctor." A succession of genre scenes follows
that evoke the Dutch masters of light—Vermeer and Pieter de
Hooch: Emma making the bandage, pricking her fingers with
the needle, and putting them into her mouth to suck while
the doctor watches; Emma in the kitchen sewing a white
stocking, darting her tongue into a liqueur glass of curaçao;
Emma in the farmyard under a silk parasol. Charles's senses
are heated as she cools her cheek against her palm and
her palm against the great andirons, and his mind is buzzing,
like the flies crawling up the empty cider glasses, as he
looks at her bare shoulders with little drops of sweat on them.
He is a man, and she is a young lady; his bewilderment
and bewitchment arise from this fusion of the sensual and the
sacred. For him marriage with Emma is a sacrament, and
the reader never sees him in the act of love with her, as
though Charles, ever tactful, reverently drew the bed curtains.

Why did she marry him? Flaubert does not really say.
"To get away from the farm" is not enough. Would she
have married Monsieur Homais if he had come courting?
There are a number of questions about Emma's inner life
that Flaubert does not ask. But thanks to Charles, the answer
does not matter, because to him the whole thing is a mystery,
and like the mysteries of faith to be accepted with holy
joy and not puzzled over. For Charles Emma is a mystery
from start to finish. The fact that she ministers to his comfort, prepares charming little dishes, takes care of his house
and his patients' accounts, is a part of the ineffable mystery

of her sharing his bed. The reader is persuaded by Charles's unquestioning faith, to the point where Emma's little gewgaws—her watch charms, her monocle, her ivory workbox, the blue-glass vases on her mantelpiece, her silver-gilt thimble—partake of her seductiveness. More than that, these acquisitions, seen through Charles's vision, do just what an advertiser would promise: they give Emma *value*. Thus Charles is not only Emma's dupe but also the dupe of commerce. And yet it works; the reader is convinced that Emma is somehow *better* than, say, Madame Homais—which is not true.

Through Charles, Emma acquires poetry. But he could not possibly put into words what she means to him; and if he could have articulated a thought on the subject, he would have declared that *she* had brought poetry into his life. This is so. There was no poetry with his first wife, the widow. Emma's beauty, of course, is a fact of her nature, and Charles has responded to it with worship, which is what beauty—a mystery—deserves. This explains why Charles, though quite deceived by Emma's character, is not a fool; he has recognized something in her about which he *cannot* be deceived.

Charles, like Farmer Rouault, is dumbly rooted in the organic world, where things speak in a simple sign language. A turkey says "Thank you" every year for a cure, like a votive offering, and two horses in the stable say that business is doing well. Flaubert is not sentimental about the peasantry, yet he prefers Nature and those who live with her and come to resemble her—as old couples come to resemble each other—to the commercial people of the town and the vulgar aristocrats of the châteaus, toward whose condition the tradespeople are aspiring. The peasants still have the virtue of concreteness, and their association with the soil and its products guarantees that they are largely, so to speak, homemade. Emma brings her freshness from the cider presses of the farm, which she hates.

The country people in general are at a kind of halfway stage in the process of evolution from the animal kingdom to Monsieur Homais. The farm men who come to Emma's wedding are seen by the author as collections of strange, out-of-date clothes hung on frames of flesh and bones—tailcoats and shooting jackets and cutaways and stiff shirts that have been kept in the wardrobe all year round and issue

forth only to go to weddings and funerals, as if by themselves. These grotesque animated garments, each with a
strong personality, have as absurd a relation to their owners
as the queer cap Charles wears on his first day at school.
The new cap, which is like a recapitulation of the history of headgear, is an uncomfortable, ill-fitting, false self
donned for a special occasion—Charles's introduction to
civilization, learning, book culture. The country boy does not
know what to do with the terrible cap, any more than how
to give his full name, which he pronounces in a queer
way, as though it too were extraneous to him, a humiliation
that has been stuck to him and that he cannot get rid of,
just as he cannot put the cap down. A name is a label. Witness the penmanship flourishes of Monsieur Homais's names
for his children: Franklin, Athalie, Napoléon. . . .

Many novels begin with the hero's first day in school, and
Charles is the hero of the book that, characteristically for
him, bears someone else's name. *Madame Bovary* starts with
his appearance among his jeering schoolfellows and ends with
his death. Charles is docile. It does not occur to him to
rebel. His mother, his teachers, his schoolmates, and finally
the widow make a citizen of him. They equip him with a
profession, for which he is totally unfitted but which he
wears, like the cap he has been given, mildly and without
protest. He did not choose to be a doctor; he did not
choose his name; he did not choose the widow. The only
thing in life he chooses is Emma. She is his first and last
piece of self-expression. Or not quite the last. When she is
taken away from him, his reverence and gratitude to the
universe turn to blasphemy. "I hate your God!" he bursts
out to the curé, who is trying to console him with platitudes.
"Still the spirit of rebellion," the priest answers with an
ecclesiastical sigh.

Now at first glance this appears to be an irony, since
Charles has never rebelled until that moment against anything,
let alone God. But Flaubert's ironies are deceptive, and what
sounds like an irony is often the simple truth, making a double irony. The priest is right. From the very beginning, Charles
has been an obstinate example of passive resistance to the
forces of the time and the milieu. A proof of that is that,
in all his days, he pronounces only one platitude. His love
for Emma is the deepest sign of that obstination. He loves her

in the teeth of circumstance, opinion, prudent self-interest, in the teeth even of Emma herself.

This passive resistance of Charles's, taking the form of a love of beauty, seems to come from nowhere. There is nothing in Charles's history to explain it: a drunken father, a dissatisfied mother, a poor education, broken off for lack of money. Add to this a very middling I.Q. No program for human improvement could be predicated on Charles's mute revolt against organized society. He is a sheer accident, nothing less than a placid miracle occurring among the notaries and tradesmen, the dyers and spinners of the textile city of Rouen, where he hankers, unobtrusive, uncomplaining, for his country home, which was no arcadia either. He is a revelation, and at the same time his whole effort is to escape detection, to hide in his fleshly envelope like some hibernating animal. Moreover, his goodness (for that is what it amounts to) has no practical utility and will leave no trace behind it. As a husband he is a social handicap to Emma, and his mild deference probably contributes to her downfall; a harsher man might have curbed her extravagances so that she would not have been obliged to commit suicide. After his death, his little girl is sent to work as a child laborer in a cotton mill; he has not even been able to protect his young. His predecessor, the Polish exile (another romantic?), at least left behind him *in situ* the bower he made to drink beer in on summer evenings, but the only reminder of himself Charles leaves in Yonville L'Abbaye is Hippolyte's stump and two artificial legs, one for best—bought by Emma—and one for every day. Was he drawn from life? Or did Flaubert make him up as a consolation to himself? All that can be said is that Charles Bovary is a possibility that cannot be ruled out even from a pessimistic view of the march of events.

MARY McCARTHY

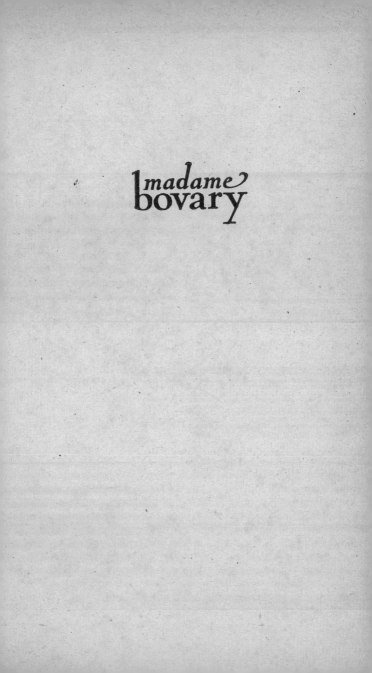

madame
bovary

PART I

I

We were studying when the headmaster came in, followed by a new boy, not yet wearing a school uniform, and a monitor carrying a large desk. Those of us who had been sleeping awoke, and we all stood up as if we had been interrupted in our work.

The headmaster motioned to us to sit down again; then, turning toward the teacher, he said in a low voice, "Monsieur Roger, here is a student I'm placing in your charge. He is starting in the fifth. If he does well, he will advance into the upper school, where he belongs at his age."

Keeping himself in the corner behind the door so that you could hardly see him, the new arrival was a country boy, about fifteen years old and taller than any of us. His hair was cut straight across his forehead like a village choirboy's; he looked sensible and very shy. Although he was not broad shouldered, his black-buttoned green suit seemed tight under the arms, and it revealed through the slits in his cuffs a pair of red wrists accustomed to going bare. His blue-stockinged legs emerged from yellowish trousers held up by suspenders. He wore heavy hobnail shoes, badly polished.

We began to recite our lessons. He concentrated with all his might, as attentive as if he were listening to a sermon, not even daring to cross his legs or lean on his elbow; and at two o'clock, when the bell rang, the teacher had to tell him to line up with us.

We were in the habit of throwing our caps to the floor on entering the classroom in order to free our hands. From the doorway you had to throw them under the bench as soon as

27

you entered so that you would hit the wall and raise a lot of dust. This was "the thing to do."

But either the new boy had not noticed this game or he didn't dare attempt it; he was still holding his cap on his knees when the prayer was over. It was one of those hybrid hats, in which you could find elements of a busby, a lancer cap, a bowler, an otterskin cap, and a nightcap, one of those poor concoctions whose mute ugliness contains depths of expression like the face of an imbecile. Egg shaped and stiffened with whalebone, it began with three circular sausage-like twists, then alternate diamonds of velvet and rabbit fur, separated by red bands; then came a sort of bag ending in a cardboard-lined polygon covered with complicated braiding from which a small crosspiece of gold threads dangled like a tassel at the end of a long, too thin cord. It was a new hat: the visor gleamed.

"Stand up," said the teacher.

He stood up; the cap fell. The entire class began to laugh.

He stooped down and picked it up. His neighbor made it fall again by poking it with his elbow. He picked it up a second time.

"Get rid of your helmet," said the teacher, who was a witty man.

There was a burst of laughter from the students. It rattled the poor boy so much that he didn't know if he should keep the cap in his hand, leave it on the floor, or put it on his head. He sat down and placed it on his lap.

"Stand up," said the teacher, "and tell me your name."

The new boy stammered some unintelligible name.

"Once more!"

The same garbled syllables were heard, drowned by the hoots from the class.

"Louder," shouted the teacher, "louder!"

The new boy, now mustering up all his courage, opened an abnormally large mouth and, as if he were calling someone, shouted at the top of his voice the word: *Charbovari*.

Pandemonium broke loose, rose to a roar punctuated by piercing shrieks (they shouted, howled, stamped their feet, and kept repeating *Charbovari! Charbovari!*), then subsided to isolated sounds, died down with great difficulty, and flared up again suddenly on one bench along which there were still some muffled giggles, sputtering like a badly extinguished firecracker.

However, by dint of a shower of threats, order was slowly restored in class, and the teacher, who had managed to grasp the name of Charles Bovary by having it dictated, spelled out, and read over, immediately ordered the poor devil to sit in the dunce chair at the foot of the lecture desk. He started toward it, then hesitated.

"What are you looking for?" asked the teacher.

"My ca-a-p," the new boy said timidly, looking anxiously around.

"Five hundred lines for the whole class!" shouted in a furious voice, like Neptune's "*Quos ego,*" stopped a new outburst. "Quiet!" continued the angry teacher, wiping his forehead with a handkerchief that he had pulled from under his cap. "As for you, new boy, you will write the verb *ridiculus sum* twenty times."

Then, in gentler tones: "You'll find that cap of yours. No one's stolen it."

The room was calm again. Heads were bent over notebooks, and the new boy sat still for two hours, behaving in exemplary fashion despite the fact that from time to time a wad of paper launched with a penholder would hit him square in the face. He would merely wipe it off with his hand and remain motionless, his eyes lowered.

In the evening, during the study period, he pulled his cuff guards from his desk, arranged his meager possessions, and ruled his paper carefully. We noticed that he was working very diligently, looking all the words up in the dictionary and taking a lot of pains. The even temper he displayed was undoubtedly what kept him from being sent down to the lower class, for while he knew the rules passably, he had absolutely no grace in his style. The priest of his village had started him on his Latin, his parents having kept him out of school until the last possible moment in order to save money.

His father, Monsieur Charles-Denis-Bartholomé Bovary, ex-aide to a surgeon major, had been implicated about 1812 in some conscription scandal and had been forced to leave the service. He then exploited his personable appearance to acquire a dowry of sixty thousand francs offered by a hosier for his daughter, a girl who had fallen in love with his good looks. A handsome, boastful fellow, jingling his spurs, with sideburns trimmed to meet his mustache, fingers always adorned with rings, and clothes in lively colors, he seemed to combine the looks of a warrior with the easygoing ways of a traveling salesman. After the marriage he lived on his wife's fortune for two or three years, eating well, sleeping late in the morning, smoking huge porcelain pipes, never coming home in the evening until after the theater, and frequenting cafés. His father-in-law died, leaving very little. He was furious about it, took a fling at manufacturing, lost a bit of money, and then retired to the country, where he hoped to make the land pay off. But since he understood as little about farming as he did about calico, since he rode his horses instead of working them, drank his cider in bottles instead of selling it in barrels, ate the choicest poultry in his barnyard and greased his hunting boots with his pigs' lard, he soon realized that it was better to give up any hope of profit from that quarter.

He managed to rent, for two hundred francs a year, a sort of lodging, half farm, half country home, in a village on the border between Picardy and Caux. Unhappy, consumed with regrets, filled with resentment against fate and envy of his fellow men, he shut himself away at the age of forty-five, disgusted with mankind, he claimed, and determined to live in peace.

His wife loved him madly at first; she showed her love with a thousand gestures of servility, which estranged him even further from her. Once lively, expansive, and generous, she had become difficult, shrill voiced, and nervous as she grew older, like uncorked wine which turns to vinegar. At first she suffered in silence when he spent evenings running after all the village trollops, only to be brought back to her late at night, dead drunk, from various places of ill repute. Then her pride asserted itself. But she still said nothing, stifling her rage with a mute stoicism that she was to maintain until her death. She kept herself busy with various things, mainly business matters. She consulted the lawyers, or the magistrate, remembered when bills fell due, obtained postponements. At home she ironed, sewed, washed, kept an eye on the workers, and settled their accounts, while the master of the house, without a worry in the world, perpetually sunk in a sullen torpor from which he roused himself only to make insulting remarks, remained by the fireside smoking and spitting into the ashes.

When she gave birth to a child, she had to send him out to nurse. After he was brought back home, he was spoiled like

a prince. His mother stuffed him with candies; his father
let him run around without shoes and, aping the philosophers,
even claimed it was all right for him to run around nude,
like a young animal. In opposition to her maternal instincts,
he conceived the notion of a manly childhood, which he
tried to impose on his son; he wanted the boy brought up
austerely, Spartan fashion, in order to develop a strong constitution. He sent him to bed in an unheated room and taught
him to gulp down large amounts of rum and shout insults at
church processions. But the child, mild tempered by nature,
responded badly to his efforts. His mother was always dragging him around with her; she would cut out paper dolls
for him, tell him stories; and involve herself in endless mono-
logues full of melancholy humor and baby talk. In the lone-
liness of her life she lavished all her thwarted ambitions on
this childish head. She dreamed about important positions,
could already see him grown up, handsome, witty, a successful civil engineer or magistrate. She taught him to read and
even to sing two or three little ballads, accompanying him on
her old piano. But Monsieur Bovary, caring little about education, kept saying that none of this was worth the trouble.
Would they ever have the money to support him in the government schools, buy him a post, or set him up in business?
Besides, "If a man has enough nerve, he'll always succeed
in the world." Madame Bovary bit her lips, and the child
wandered about the village.

He would follow the farmhands and scare off the crows
by throwing clumps of earth at them. He ate the blackberries
growing along the ditches, minded the turkeys with a stick,
pitched hay during harvesttime, and ran through the woods.
He played hopscotch under the church porch on rainy days
and begged the sexton to let him ring the bells on holidays
so that he could pull on the heavy cord with all his might
and swing along as the bell clanged.

And so he grew like an oak. His hands developed strength,
his complexion a healthy color.

When he was twelve, his mother arranged for him to begin his studies. The parish priest was given the assignment.
But the lessons were so short and so badly organized that
they did no real good. They were given in haste at odd moments in the vestry, while he remained standing, between a
baptism and a burial; or sometimes the priest would send for
his pupil after the Angelus, when he didn't have to go out.

They would go up to his room and settle down; the gnats and moths would fly around the candle. It would be warm, and the child would doze off; and the good priest, folding his hands over his belly, would soon start snoring with his mouth agape. Other times, when the curé, returning from administering the sacrament to some ailing soul, chanced on Charles running wild through the countryside, he would call him, lecture him for a quarter of an hour, and take advantage of the occasion to make him conjugate his verbs at the foot of a tree. The rain or some passerby would interrupt them. In general he was rather pleased with the boy, even saying that the "young lad" had a good memory.

Charles's education could not stop there. His mother was firm about it. Ashamed, or rather, worn out, his father gave in without a fight, and they waited one more year until the boy had made his first Communion.

Six months more went by; the next year Charles was finally sent off to school in Rouen toward the end of October, at about the time of the Saint-Romain fair. His father even accompanied him.

None of us now can remember anything about him. He was a mild-tempered boy who played during recess, worked in study periods, listened in class, slept soundly in the dormitory, and ate heartily in the dining hall. His local guardian was a man who had a wholesale hardware business on the Rue Ganterie. The guardian took him out one Sunday a month, after the store was closed, sent him for a walk down to the quay to look at the boats, then took him back to school by seven, before supper. Every Thursday evening he wrote a long letter to his mother in red ink and sealed it with three wafers; then he skimmed his history notebooks or read an old volume of the philosopher Anacharsis that happened to be in the study hall. When he went out walking, he would chat with the servant who, like himself, came from the country.

He managed to stay in the middle of his class by working very hard; once he even won an "honorable mention" in natural history. But at the end of his third year his parents took him out of school to study medicine, convinced that he could win his school degree by studying on his own.

His mother chose a room for him on the fourth floor of a house that belonged to a dyer she knew. It overlooked the Eau-de-Robec. She made arrangements for his room and board, bought furniture—a table and two chairs—and sent him an old cherrywood bedstead from home. She also purchased a small cast-iron stove and enough wood to keep her poor child warm. She left after a week, having given him a thousand lectures about being on his best behavior now that he was going to be left to his own devices.

The courses that were listed on the bulletin board terrified him: anatomy, pathology, physiology, pharmacology, chemistry, botany, clinical medicine, and therapy, not to mention hygiene and materia medica, all names of whose etymology he was ignorant and that loomed like majestic shadows in temple doors.

He understood nothing. No matter how hard he listened, he just couldn't grasp the subject. Yet he worked hard, he acquired bound notebooks, went to all his lectures, did not miss one single class. He managed his daily assignment of work like a millhorse who trots around in blinkers, unaware of what he is grinding.

To save him money, his mother would send some baked veal by the carrier each week. He would lunch on it in the morning when he came back from the hospital, stamping his feet against the wall as he ate. Then he had to run off to his lessons in the lecture hall or at the hospital and would return home later through the maze of streets. After the meager evening meal his landlord gave him, he would climb back up to his room and start working again, his damp clothes steaming on his body before the glowing stove.

During the lovely summer evenings, at the hour when the warm streets are empty and the maids play shuttlecock on the doorsteps, he would open his window and look out, leaning on his elbow. The river, which makes this section of Rouen a poor version of Venice, flowed below him, yellow, violet, or blue beneath its bridges and its railings. Workmen leaning over the edge would wash their arms in the water. Skeins of cotton dried in the air; they were suspended on poles projecting from the lofts above. Opposite, above the rooftops, the red sun was setting in the unclouded expanse of sky. How good it must be back home under the beeches! And he would open his nostrils wide, trying to breathe in the good country air that did not reach him.

He grew thin and tall, and his face acquired a sort of mournful expression that made it almost interesting.

Gradually, out of indifference, he managed to forget all

his resolutions. Once he missed his hospital round, the next day a class. Enjoying his idleness, he did not go back.

He formed the habit of going to the café and acquired a passion for dominoes. To be cooped up each evening in a filthy public room in order to click small sheep bones marked with black dots on the marble tables seemed to him a precious act of liberty that heightened his self-esteem.

It was an initiation into the world, an access to forbidden pleasures. When he entered he would place his hand on the doorknob with an almost sensual joy. So many of his repressed feelings expanded; he learned songs by heart and sang them to entertain the women present, developed a taste for Béranger, learned how to make punch, and finally how to make love.

Having neglected his studies, he completely failed the test for health officer. And he was expected home that very evening to celebrate his success!

He set out on foot and stopped at the village outskirts, where he asked someone to summon his mother; he told her the whole story. She made excuses for him, blamed the failure on the unfairness of the examiners, and cheered him up a bit, taking it on herself to arrange matters. Only five years later did Monsieur Bovary learn the truth; by then he accepted it as ancient history. Moreover, he was unable to accept the fact that a son of his might be a fool.

So Charles went back to work and prepared unceasingly for his examination. He memorized all the questions beforehand and passed with a decent grade. It was a happy day for his mother. They celebrated with a big dinner party.

Where would he practice? In Tostes. There was only one old doctor there. Madame Bovary had been watching out for his death for a long time, and the good soul had barely expired when Charles moved in across the street as his successor.

But it was not enough to have raised her son, arranged for him to study medicine, and discovered Tostes for him to practice in. He needed a wife. She found him one: the widow of a Dieppe bailiff, who was forty-five years old and had an income of twelve hundred pounds.

Although she was ugly, thin as a rail, and had as many pimples as the springtime has buds, Madame Dubuc was not lacking in suitors. In order to achieve her goal Mother Bovary had to overcome them all, and she even frustrated quite cleverly the intrigues of a pork butcher whose suit was being supported by the priests.

Charles had hoped for better days following his marriage. He assumed he would be freer to choose his own actions and spend his money as he pleased. But his wife was the ruler; he had to watch what he said and didn't say in public, eat fish on Friday, dress as she prescribed, and harass the patients who didn't pay. She would open his letters, spy on his whereabouts, and listen behind the partition when there were women in his consulting room.

She had to have her chocolate every morning and constantly demanded various services. She complained incessantly about her nerves, her chest, her moods. She couldn't stand the sound of footsteps; if he went away she couldn't bear solitude; if he hovered near her it was surely in order to see her die. When Charles came home in the evening, she would extend her long thin arms out from under the sheets, twine them around his neck, and make him sit down on the edge of the bed in order to begin telling him her worries; he was forgetting her, he was in love with someone else! She had been rightly forewarned that she would be unhappy; and she would end by asking him for some medicine for her health and a bit more love.

II

One night at about eleven, they were awakened by the sound of a horse stopping right at their door. The maid opened the attic window and spoke for some time with a man below. He had come for the doctor; he had a letter. Nastasie shivered as she went down the stairs; she unlocked the door and drew all the bolts. The man left his horse and walked into the house, following right behind the maid. He pulled a letter, wrapped in a piece of fabric, from his gray-tasseled woolen cap and gingerly presented it to Charles, who propped his elbow on the pillow to read it. Nastasie held the lamp near the bed. Madame remained facing the wall out of modesty and showed only her back.

The letter, sealed with a dab of blue wax, begged Monsieur Bovary to come immediately to Les Bertaux to set a broken leg. Now, it is a good fourteen miles from Tostes to Les Bertaux by way of Longueville and Saint-Victor. The night was dark. Madame Bovary was afraid some accident might befall her husband. Therefore it was decided that the stableboy would go ahead of him. Charles would leave three hours later, when the moon would be visible. They would send a boy to meet him, show him the road to the farm, and open the fence gates for him.

About four A.M. Charles, well wrapped in his cloak, set out for Les Bertaux. Still drowsy from the warmth of sleep, he let himself be rocked by the gentle trot of his horse. When she stopped of her own accord before the holes surrounded by thornbush that are dug at the ends of the furrows, Charles would awake with a start and, quickly remembering the broken leg, try to recall all the fractures he knew. The rain had stopped. Daylight was starting to appear. Birds virtually motionless on the branches of the leafless apple trees were ruffling their tiny feathers in the cold morning wind. The flat countryside stretched out as far as the eye could see, and the clusters of trees surrounding the farms made regular patches of dark purple against the large gray surface that blended at the horizon into the dull tone of the sky. Charles would open his eyes from time to time; then, his mind tiring, and falling asleep against his will, he soon entered into a sort of drowsy state in which his recent sensations mingled with memories. He saw himself as two people at one and the same time, student and husband, lying in his bed as he just had been, and crossing an operating room as in the old days. The warm smell of poultices blended in his head with the fresh odor of dew; he heard the iron rings tinkling on the curtain rods of the ward beds and saw his wife sleeping. As he passed through Vassonville, he noticed a boy sitting on the grass at the edge of a ditch.

"Are you the doctor?" the child asked. And, at Charles's answer, he picked up his wooden shoes in his hand and began to run ahead of him.

As he rode along, the doctor gathered from his guide's talk that Monsieur Rouault must be a very prosperous farmer. He had broken his leg the evening before, coming home from a Twelfth Night celebration at a neighbor's. His wife had died two years ago. There was no one with him but his daughter, who helped him keep house.

The ruts were becoming deeper. They were approaching Les Bertaux. The little boy slipped through a space in the hedge and disappeared, then came back to the edge of a court-yard to open the gate. The horse skidded on the wet grass. Charles bent his head to pass under the branches. The watch-dogs in the kennel barked and pulled at their chains. As he entered Les Bertaux, his horse became frightened and stumbled.

It was an impressive farm. In the stables, over the open doors, big workhorses could be seen feeding leisurely at their new mangers. A large dunghill extended along the buildings; liquid manure oozed from it and, among the hens and turkeys, five or six peacocks, considered luxuries in Caux farmyards, were foraging on top. The sheepfold was long, the barn high ceilinged, with walls smooth as a woman's hand. In the shed there were two large carts and four plows complete with their whips, shafts, and harnesses. The blue wool fleeces were becoming soiled from the fine dust falling from the lofts. The yard, its trees planted equidistant from one another, sloped upward, and the gay cackle of a flock of geese came from the pond.

A young woman in a blue wool dress trimmed with three flounces came out to the threshold of the door to re-ceive Monsieur Bovary, and she invited him into the kitchen, where a large fire was blazing. The farmhands' dinner was boiling around it, in small pots of varying sizes. Some damp garments were drying inside the fireplace. The shovel, tongs, and the nozzle of the bellows, all huge, shone like polished steel, and an abundant supply of kitchen utensils hung along the walls, reflecting here and there the clear flame of the hearth, mingled with the first rays of the sun that were piercing through the windowpanes.

Charles went up to the second floor to see the patient. He found him in his bed, perspiring under the covers, his cotton nightcap thrown far from the bed. He was a short, heavy man of fifty, with white skin and blue eyes; he was bald on the forepart of his head and wore earrings. On a chair at his side he had a large decanter of brandy, from which he kept pouring himself drinks to keep his spirits up, but as soon as he saw the doctor, his excitement subsided, and instead of swearing as he had been doing for the last twelve hours, he began to moan feebly.

It was an extremely simple fracture, with no complications whatsoever. Charles couldn't have wished for an easier one. Then, remembering the bedside manners of his teachers, he comforted the patient with all sorts of kind words—medical caresses like the oil used on scalpels. A bundle of laths to be used for splints was brought up from the cart shed. Charles selected one from the pack, cut it in pieces, and planed it with a piece of broken glass while the maid was ripping sheets to make bandages. Mademoiselle Emma, the daughter, was about to sew some pads. Her father became impatient when it took her too long to find her workbox. She made no comment. But as she sewed she pricked her fingers and then put them into her mouth to suck them.

Charles was surprised at the whiteness of her nails. They gleamed, were finely tapered, cleaner than Dieppe ivories, and almond shaped. Her hand was not attractive, however, perhaps not white enough and slightly dry at the knuckles; also, it was too long and lacked softness in its outlines. Her real beauty was in her eyes; although they were brown, they seemed black because of the lashes, and she would look at you frankly, with bold candor.

The bandages in place, the doctor was invited by Monsieur Rouault himself to "have a bite" before leaving.

Charles went downstairs to the dining room on the ground floor. Two settings, with silver goblets, had been laid on a small table at the foot of a large bed with Turkish figures printed on its cotton canopy. An odor of iris and damp sheets emanated from the tall oak cupboard facing the window. On the floor, in the corners, were sacks of grain stacked upright. This was the surplus from the nearby granary, connected by three stone steps. A charcoal portrait of Minerva in a gilt frame, on the bottom of which was written in Gothic lettering, "To my darling Papa," served as decoration for the room. It hung on a nail in the middle of a green wall whose paint was scaling off from the effects of saltpeter.

At first they discussed the patient, then the weather, the cold spells, the wolves roaming the fields at night. Mademoiselle Rouault did not like the country at all, especially now that she was almost solely responsible for the care of the farm. As the room was chilly, she shivered a little while eating. This caused her full lips to part slightly. She had a habit of biting them when she wasn't talking.

She wore a white, turned-down collar. Her black hair was parted down the middle. The two sections, so smooth that each seemed to be one solid mass, were separated by a thin part that curved downward slightly along with the curve of the head. Barely revealing the tip of the ear, the hair was gathered behind in a thick bun with waves at the temples, which the country doctor was seeing for the first time in his life. Her cheeks were rosy. She wore a mannish-style tortoiseshell lorgnon tucked in between two buttons of her bodice.

When Charles, after going upstairs to say good-bye to Monsieur Rouault, came back into the room before leaving, he found her standing up, forehead pressed against the window, looking into the garden, where the bean props had been knocked down by the wind. She turned around.

"Are you looking for something?" she asked.

"My riding crop, please," he answered.

He began rummaging on the bed, behind the doors, under the chairs. It had fallen to the ground between the sacks and the wall. Mademoiselle Emma saw it and leaned over the sacks of wheat. Charles dashed over out of courtesy, and as he extended his hand in the same gesture, he sensed his chest brush against the back of the girl bending beneath him. She stood up with a blush and looked at him over her shoulder as she gave him his crop.

Instead of returning to Les Bertaux three days later, as he had promised, he appeared the very next day, then regularly twice a week, not counting the unscheduled visits that he paid from time to time as if by accident.

Everything was going well. The injury was healing properly, and when, at the end of forty-six days, old man Rouault was seen trying to walk by himself in his room, people began to consider Monsieur Bovary a very talented man. Old Rouault said that he wouldn't have been treated better by the most prominent doctors of Yvetot or even of Rouen.

As for Charles, he didn't try to ask himself why he came to Les Bertaux with pleasure. Had he thought about it he would no doubt have attributed his zeal to the seriousness of the case or perhaps to the fee he anticipated from it. Was that the reason, however, why his visits to the farm came as a delightful change to the dull occupations of his

life? On those days he arose early in the morning and
left at a gallop, urging his horse on; then he would alight
to wipe his feet on the grass and pull on his black gloves
before going in. He liked to see himself arrive in the court-
yard, to feel the gate giving way against his shoulder
and the rooster crowing on the wall, the farmhands coming
to meet him. He loved the barn and the stables; he liked
old Rouault, who would keep patting his hand while calling
him his savior; he loved the sound of Mademoiselle Emma's
small wooden shoes against the scrubbed kitchen tiles; their
high heels increased her height a little, and when she walked
in front of him, the wooden soles, lifting up rapidly, would
make a sharp clack against the leather of the boot.

She would always walk him back to the first step of the
porch. If his horse had not yet been brought around, she
would remain there. They had said good-bye to each other
and were no longer chatting; the fresh air would envelop
her, blowing the little wisps of hair on her nape in all
directions or moving over her hips the strings of her apron,
which were twisting like streamers. One time during a thaw,
moisture was trickling from the tree bark in the yard; the
snow on the roofs of the buildings was melting. She stood
on the threshold, then went to fetch her parasol and opened
it. The sun came through the dove-colored silk parasol, its
rays moving over the white skin of her face. She smiled beneath it at the mild warmth of the season, and you could
hear drops of water, one by one, falling on the taut-stretched
silk.

During the first weeks that Charles frequented Les Bertaux, his wife did not fail to keep herself informed about
the patient. She had even chosen a lovely white page for
Monsieur Rouault in the double-entry account book. But
when she heard that he had a daughter, she sought information; and she learned that Mademoiselle Rouault, brought up
in a convent of the Ursuline order, had received, as they
say, a good education—as a result, she knew dancing, ge-
ography, drawing, tapestry weaving, and piano playing. It was
just too much!

"So that's the reason he looks so radiant when he goes
to see her," she told herself; "that's why he puts on his new
waistcoat, at the risk of soiling it in the rain. Oh, that woman!
That woman!"

And she hated her instinctively. At first she contented herself with allusions. Charles didn't understand them. Then, by casual comments that he let pass for fear of a storm; finally, by point-blank insults, to which he did not know how to reply. Why did he keep going back to Les Bertaux if Monsieur Rouault was well and those people hadn't even paid yet? Aha! It was because there was someone there, someone who knew the art of conversation, an embroideress, a person of wit. That was what he liked; he needed city girls! And she resumed her attack: "Rouault's daughter, a city girl! Come now! Their grandfather was a shepherd and they have a cousin who barely escaped being haled into court for some misdeed he committed during an argument. It's not necessary to show off so much or appear in church on Sunday with a silk dress like a countess. Besides, that poor man who would have found it quite hard to pay his bills without last year's rapeseed crop!"

Charles stopped going to Les Bertaux, out of inertia. Heloise had made him swear, his hand on his prayer book, that he would no longer go there—after many sobs and kisses and a great explosion of love. So he obeyed; but the boldness of his desire protested against the servility of his conduct, and with a sort of naïve hypocrisy, he concluded that his being forbidden to see her gave him the right to love her. And besides, the widow was skinny; her teeth were elongated; she wore in season and out a small black shawl the ends of which reached down between her shoulder blades; her angular body was encased in straight, narrow dresses, too short, that revealed her ankles with the ribbons of her big shoes crossed over gray stockings.

Charles's mother came to see them from time to time, but at the end of a few days the daughter-in-law seemed to infect her with her own sharpness. Then, like two scissors, they would cut into him with their comments and their observations. He was wrong to eat so much! Why always offer a drink to the first comer? How stubborn not to wear flannel!

At the beginning of spring, a notary of Ingouville, the holder of the Widow Dubuc's money, ran off one fine day, taking along with him all the funds in his custody. Heloise still had, it is true, her house on the Rue Saint-François plus a share in a boat valued at six thousand francs; and yet, out of all that fortune, about which so much noise had been made, nothing but a bit of furniture and some old clothes had turned up in the Bovary household. It was necessary to look into the matter. The Dieppe house turned out to be mortgaged down to its foundations; God alone knew what she had deposited with the notary, and the share in the boat did not exceed three thousand francs. So the good lady had lied. In his exasperation, Monsieur Bovary senior smashed a chair against the paving stones and accused his wife of having caused their son's unhappiness by harnessing him to such an old workhorse, whose harness wasn't worth its skin. They went to Tostes. There were explanations, scenes. Heloise, in tears, threw herself into her husband's arms and begged him to defend her against his parents. Charles tried to speak on her behalf. They became angry and left.

But the damage was done. Eight days later, as she was hanging out the wash in the yard, she began to spit up blood. The next day, while Charles had turned his back to her in order to draw the curtain, she said "Oh God!" sighed, and passed away. She was dead! How strange!

When services at the cemetery were over, Charles came back home. He found no one downstairs; he went up to the first floor, into her room, and saw her dress still hanging at the foot of the alcove. Then, leaning against the writing desk, he remained lost in a sad reverie until evening. She had loved him, after all.

III

One morning old Rouault came to pay Charles for setting his leg: seventy-five francs in forty-sou pieces plus a turkey. He had heard about his misfortune and consoled him as best he could.

"I know what it is," he said, patting him on the shoulder; "I was also like you. When I lost my poor wife, I would go into the woods to be all alone, I would sink down at the foot of a tree and cry or call out to God to tell him all sorts of foolish things. I wanted to be like the moles I saw in the branches, with worms crawling in their bellies. In a word, dead. And when I remembered that others at that very moment were holding their beloved wives in their arms, I would beat my stick into the ground with fury. I was half crazy. I stopped eating. The mere idea of going to the café repelled me. You wouldn't believe it. And then, slowly, as one day followed another, springtime replaced winter, and autumn summer, it dwindled away bit by bit, crumb by crumb. It went away, and disappeared. It went inside, I mean, because you always retain something deep down, a sort of heaviness here, in the chest. But since we all share that fate, we mustn't let ourselves waste away hoping to die because others are dead. You must cheer up, Monsieur Bovary; it will pass! Come visit us. My daughter thinks about you quite often, you know. She says that you're forgetting her. Spring is almost here. You can shoot a rabbit in the warren. It will distract you a bit."

Charles heeded his advice and returned to Les Bertaux. He found everything exactly as it had been five months before. The pear trees were already blossoming, and good-natured Rouault, back on his feet now, was all over the place, making the farm that much livelier.

He believed it his duty to lavish all possible attention on the doctor because of his recent bereavement: he told him not to take his hat off, spoke to him in a low voice as if he had been ill, and even pretended to become angry that the food prepared for him wasn't a bit lighter than that for the others—such as small pots of cream or stewed pears. He would tell him stories. To Charles's surprise, he would hear himself laugh, but the sudden thought of his wife would make him gloomy. Then they would serve coffee and he would no longer think about her.

He thought less about her as he became accustomed to living alone. The new pleasure of independence soon made solitude more bearable. He could change his eating hours now, come or go without explanations, and stretch out over the entire bed when he was very tired. So he coddled and pampered himself and accepted the consolations that were offered him. Besides, his wife's death had not served him badly in his profession, since people had repeated for a month, "The poor young man. How sad." His reputation had spread, his clientele increased. And he went to Les Bertaux whenever he felt like it. He felt an undefined hope, a vague happiness. As he brushed his sideburns in front of the mirror, he found his face more pleasing.

One day he arrived there about three o'clock. They were all out in the field. He entered the kitchen but didn't see Emma at first. The shutters were closed. The sun's rays, coming through the wooden slats, became long thin stripes that shattered upon contact with the furniture and quivered on the ceiling. Flies were climbing up the glasses that had been set out on the table. They buzzed as they drowned in the leftover cider. The daylight coming in through the fireplace made the soot on the hearth look like velvet and turned the cold ashes slightly blue. Emma sat sewing between the window and the fireplace. She wasn't wearing a shawl and he could see tiny drops of perspiration on her bare shoulders.

As was the custom in the country, she asked him if he would like a drink. He refused. She insisted and finally suggested, with a laugh, that he take a glass of liqueur with her. She went to look for a bottle of curaçao in the cupboard, reached for two small glasses, filled one to the top, poured just a bit in the other, and brought it to her mouth after they had touched glasses. Since it was almost empty, she leaned back to drink, and with her head tilted, lips pouting in readiness and neck extended, she laughed because she wasn't tasting anything, and the tip of her tongue, passing between her finely formed teeth, licked the bottom of the glass daintily.

She sat down again and picked up her work, a white cotton stocking she was mending. She sewed with her forehead lowered and said nothing. Charles was also silent. A gust of air blew in under the door and scattered a little dust over the tiles. As he watched it float along, he could only hear the pounding inside his head and the far-off cry of a hen laying an egg in the barnyard. Emma would occasionally cool her cheeks by placing her palms against them, then she would cool the palms against the metal knobs of the big andirons.

She complained that she had been suffering from dizzy spells since the beginning of the season and asked if ocean bathing would help her. She started chatting about the convent, Charles about his school. It seemed easy to talk. They went up to her room. She showed him her old music notebooks, the small books she had received as prizes, and the oak-leaf wreaths lying forgotten at the bottom of the wardrobe. She spoke to him again about her mother, and about the cemetery, and even showed him the flower bed in the

garden from which she picked flowers the first Friday of
every month for her grave. But their gardener didn't understand a thing about his job. You just couldn't get good
servants! She would adore living in the city even if only in
the winter, although the country was possibly even more
boring in the summer because of the long days. Her voice
reflected her various topics of conversation; it would be
clear and sharp or, suddenly becoming listless, would drag
out its inflections until it ended almost in murmurs, and she
would be talking to herself. Sometimes the voice would be
joyous, and naïvely she would open wide her eyes; then the
eyelids would droop, she would look terribly bored, and
her thoughts would wander.

On the way home in the evening Charles analyzed everything she had said, trying to remember it all, to complete the
meaning, to become acquainted with that portion of her life
she had spent before he met her. But he could never imagine her differently from the way he had seen her the first
time, or as the girl he had just left. Then he wondered
what would become of her if she got married. And to
whom? Alas! Her father was quite rich and she was so
lovely! But Emma's face kept coming back before his eyes,
and something monotonous, like the sound of a spinning top,
hummed in his ears: "Suppose you did get married! Suppose you did!" He couldn't sleep that night. His throat was
constricted, dry. He arose to take a drink from his water
jug and opened the window. The sky was filled with stars.
There was a warm wind blowing. Dogs were barking in the
distance. He turned his head in the direction of Les Bertaux.

Thinking that, after all, he wasn't risking anything, Charles
made up his mind to propose when the occasion presented
itself; but each time that it did, the fear of not finding any
of the right words kept his lips sealed.

Old man Rouault would not have been sorry to be rid
of his daughter, who was of little help to him in the house.
Inwardly he forgave her, feeling that she was too intelligent for farming—an accursed occupation in which one never found a millionaire. Far from having made a fortune at
it, Rouault kept losing money each year. Although he excelled in the marketplace, where the wily bargaining amused
him, he was not at all suited for actual farming and the
running of the household. He was not generous with his

money but spared no expense for anything having to do with his personal life: he wanted to be well fed, sufficiently warm, and comfortably bedded down. He liked his cider full bodied, his legs of lamb rare, and his coffee well mixed with brandy. He ate his meals alone in the kitchen, facing the fire, on a small table that was brought to him preset, as in the theater.

Also, having noticed Charles blushing in his daughter's presence—which meant that one of these days he would be asked for her hand in marriage—he thought about the matter in advance. He found Charles rather puny and not the sort of son-in-law he had hoped for; but he was reputed to be of steady character, thrifty and well educated, and he would surely not haggle too much about the dowry. And so, since old man Rouault was going to be forced to sell twenty-two acres of his property, since he was heavily in debt to the mason and to the harnessmaker, since the winepress shaft had to be repaired, he told himself, "If he asks me for her, I'll consent."

At Michaelmas Charles came to spend three days at Les Bertaux. The last day passed like the preceding ones. He kept putting the matter off from one quarter of an hour to the next. Monsieur Rouault set him on his way. They were walking along an empty road and were about to say good-bye. It was the moment. Charles gave himself until they reached the hedge and finally, after they had passed it, murmured, "Sir, I would like very much to tell you something."

They stopped walking. Charles said no more.

"Tell me your story! Don't I know it all?" Rouault said, laughing affectionately.

"Father Rouault—Father Rouault," Charles stammered.

"I couldn't ask for anything better," the farmer continued. "And although the little one no doubt agrees, we have to ask her anyway. You go along. I'll go home now. Now listen carefully; if it's yes, you won't have to return, because people might notice, and besides, she'll be too excited. But so that you won't worry, I'll open the window shutter all the way. You'll be able to see it if you turn around and lean over the hedge." And he went off.

Charles tied his horse to a tree. He stationed himself in the path and waited. A half hour went by, then he counted nineteen minutes on his watch. Suddenly there was a noise against the wall: the shutter had been turned out; the catch was still rattling.

He was at the farm at nine the next morning. Emma blushed when he entered, but tried to smile a little to hide her confusion. Old man Rouault kissed his future son-in-law. They postponed discussing financial arrangements. They had time enough, since the marriage couldn't with any decency take place before Charles's mourning period was over, and that was around springtime of the following year.

So they waited for the winter to pass. Mademoiselle Rouault busied herself with her trousseau. Part of it was ordered in Rouen, and she herself made some shifts and nightcaps, copying them from borrowed fashion patterns. During Charles's visits to the farm, they would talk about the preparations for the wedding, wonder what room to prepare the dinner in, dream about the number of dishes they would need and what they would serve.

Emma wanted to get married by torchlight at the unusual hour of midnight, but old man Rouault could not understand this notion at all. And so a wedding took place, to which forty-three people came and sat at the table for sixteen hours. It began again the next day and continued to a lesser extent the following days.

IV

The guests arrived early in their vehicles: one-horse carts, two-wheeled charabancs, old cabriolets lacking hoods, and delivery vans with leather curtains. The young people from the nearest villages came in wagons in which they were standing in rows, holding on to the rails to keep from falling, moving at a trot and jolted about. They came from twenty-five miles off, from Goderville, Normanville, and Cany. All the relatives from each side had been invited; they had made up with estranged friends; they had written to long-lost acquaintances.

From time to time, whiplashes could be heard from behind the hedge. Soon the gate would open and a cart would

come in. Galloping up to the foot of the steps, it would stop
short and pour out its passengers, who would exit from
each side rubbing their knees and stretching their arms.
The ladies, in bonnets, wore city-style dresses, gold watch
chains, capes with the ends tucked into their belts, or small
colored scarves attached in back with a pin and revealing
the napes of their necks. The boys, dressed like their fathers,
seemed uncomfortable in their new suits (many of them
were wearing boots for the first time in their lives). At their
sides you could see, not breathing a word, in the white dress
of her first Communion lengthened for the occasion, some
cousin or older sister, ruddy faced, bewildered, hair greased
with rose pomade, and terribly frightened of soiiing her
gloves. Since there weren't enough stableboys to unhitch all
the horses, the gentlemen rolled up their sleeves and attended
to it themselves. They wore, according to their social position, suits, frock coats, jackets, or waistcoats; good suits,
which received all the care of the family and left the closet
only for solemn occasions; frock coats with large tails floating in the wind, cylindrical collars, and pockets as big as
sacks; jackets of coarse cloth, usually worn with caps that
had copper rims on the visors; very short waistcoats, with
two buttons in the back as close together as eyes and
tails that looked as if they were carved from one piece of
wood by the carpenter's ax. Still others (but these people,
obviously, would be eating at the lower end of the table)
wore holiday blouses, with collars turned down over the shoulders, backs gathered in tiny pleats, and a very low waistline
marked with a sewn-on belt.

And the shirts bulged over the chests like breastplates.
Everyone was freshly shorn, ears sticking out of heads.
All were close shaven; some, having risen before dawn, and
not seeing clearly how to shave, had diagonal gashes under
their noses or, along the jaws, skinned-off areas the size of
three-franc pieces, which had been inflamed by the open
air on the way and which, with their pink patches, gave a
marbled effect to all those fat, white, shiny faces.

The mayor's chambers being a mile or so from the farm,
they went there on foot and came back the same way after
the ceremony at the church. The procession, at first holding
together like a colored scarf waving in the countryside, all
along the narrow path winding through the fields of un-
ripe corn, soon grew longer and separated into different

groups, many lagging behind to chat. The fiddler led the way with his violin decorated with ribbon rosettes; the bride and groom followed, then relatives and friends in no special order, and the children stayed in the rear, enjoying themselves by plucking the ears of young oat shoots or by playing games and hiding. Emma's dress, too long, was dragging a little at the bottom; she would stop once in a while to pick it up, and then, delicately, with her gloved fingers, she would pull off the blades of wild grass and thistle burrs while Charles would wait with empty hands until she had finished. Old Rouault, a new silk hat on his head and the cuffs of his black suit covering his hands up to his fingernails, offered his arm to Madame Bovary senior. As for Monsieur Bovary senior, feeling contempt for all these people, he had come dressed simply in a single-breasted frock coat of a military cut and was telling off-color jokes to a fair-haired young farm girl. She curtseyed and blushed and didn't know what to answer. The other wedding guests talked about business matters or played little pranks on one another, anticipating the gaiety in advance. By listening carefully one could still hear the fiddler scraping away as he continued to play along the road. When he noticed that they were far behind him, he stopped to catch his breath, waxed his bow thoroughly with resin so that the strings would respond better, and then began to walk again, raising and lowering the neck of his fiddle in order to keep good time for himself. The noise of the instrument frightened the little birds away.

The table was set in the cart shed. On it there were four sirloins, six chicken fricassees, some stewed veal, three legs of lamb, and, in the middle, a fine roast suckling pig, flanked by four pork sausages and cooked with sorrel. In the corners there were decanters filled with brandy. The bottled sweet cider was frothing thickly around the corks, and all the glasses had already been filled to the brim with wine. Huge platters of yellow custard that quivered at the slightest movement of the table had the initials of the new couple traced on their smooth surface in arabesques of sugared almonds. They had gone to Yvetot to find a baker for the pastry and the nougats. As he was a newcomer to the area, he taken special pains; and he brought for dessert with his own hands a layered cake that elicited loud hurrahs. The base was a square of blue cardboard representing a temple with porticos and colonnades, and there were stucco statuettes all around it in niches papered with gilded stars; then, on the second tier there was a turret of Savoy cake, surrounded by tiny fortifications in angelica, almonds, raisins, and orange segments; and finally, on the top layer, which was a green meadow on which there were rocks with candied lakes and boats of hazelnut shells, you could see a small Cupid, poised on a chocolate swing whose two posts ended in two real rosebuds, representing finials, at the summit.

They ate until evening. When they grew too tired of sitting, they went for walks in the yard or played a game of quoits in the barn, then came back to the table. Toward the end, a few fell asleep and snored. But everyone revived during coffee; they sang, performed feats of strength, lifted weights, played a game called "went under your thumbs," tried to lift carts on their shoulders, made coarse jokes, kissed the women. The horses, gorged to the nostrils with oats, could barely be squeezed into their shafts when it was time to leave late in the evening; they kicked and reared and broke their harnesses, while their masters swore or laughed; and all night long in the moonlight there were runaway carriages galloping along the roads, plunging into ditches, jolting over tall piles of stones, and bumping into the embankments, with women leaning out of the doors to grasp the reins.

Those who remained at Les Bertaux spent the night drinking in the kitchen. The children had fallen asleep under the benches.

The bride begged her father to be spared the customary wedding-night jokes. Nevertheless, a fishmonger cousin of theirs (the same who had brought a pair of soles as a wedding gift) was about to spit water through the keyhole when old Rouault arrived just in time to stop him, and explained to him that his son-in-law's dignified position did not permit such impertinences. The cousin gave in only reluctantly to these arguments. Inwardly he accused Rouault of being conceited, and he went to join in a corner four or five other guests who, having by chance received the end cuts of meat several times in a row while at the table, had also decided that they had been badly treated and were whispering guardedly against their host and wishing him evil.

Madame Bovary senior had not unclenched her teeth all day long. She had not been consulted about her daughter-in-law's dress, nor about the wedding arrangements. She went

to bed early. Her husband, instead of following her, sent off
to Saint-Victor for some cigars and smoked until daybreak,
all the while drinking grogs of kirsch, a mixture unknown
to the company, which raised him even higher in their es-
teem.

Charles was humorless; he did not shine during the evening. He replied stolidly to the witty remarks, puns, double-
entendre jokes, compliments, and broad remarks that they
seemed to feel called upon to direct at him from the soup
course on.

The next day, however, he seemed to be a new man. It
was he who could have been taken for the virgin of the night
before, rather than the bride, whose self-control gave no
opportunity for conjecture. Even the most daring jokesters
were silenced, and they looked at her with bewilderment when
she passed near them.

But Charles hid nothing. He called her "my wife," spoke
to her in familiar terms, asked everyone where she was,
sought her everywhere, and frequently drew her into the
yard, where he could be seen from afar, between the trees,
putting his arm around her waist, leaning toward her as he
walked, and burying his face in the tucker of her bodice.

Two days after the wedding the couple left: Charles could
not stay any longer because of his patients. Old Rouault sent
them home in his trap and accompanied them himself as far
as Vassonville. There he kissed his daughter one last time,
stepped down from the wagon, and headed home. When he
had gone about a hundred steps he stopped, and as he saw
the trap moving off into the distance, its wheels in the
dust, he gave a mighty sigh. Then he remembered his
own marriage, his youthful days, his wife's first pregnancy.
He too had been very happy the day that he brought her
home from her father's house, when she rode behind him
on the horse, trotting over the snow; for it was Christmas-
time and the country was all white. She held him with
one arm; the other carried her basket. The wind was
blowing the long lace ribbons of her Norman bonnet. They
occasionally flew into her mouth, and when he turned his
head he would see near him, on his shoulder, her little pink
face smiling at him silently beneath the gold disk of her head-
dress. She put her fingers next to his chest from time to time
to warm them. How far away all that was! Their son would
now be thirty! Then he looked behind him and saw nothing on

the road. He felt sad, like an abandoned house. In his head, which was still in a fog from the effects of the feast, tender memories mingled with sad thoughts; for a moment he felt like taking a walk near the church. As he was afraid, however, that this would make him even sadder, he went straight home.

Monsieur and Madame Charles arrived at Tostes at about six o'clock. The neighbors stationed themselves at the windows to see their doctor's new wife.

The old servant introduced herself, greeted Emma, apologized that dinner was not yet ready, and invited Madame to become acquainted with her home while waiting.

V

The brick front was flush with the street, or rather the highway. Behind the door hung a narrow-collared coat, a bridle, and a black leather cap; in a corner on the ground was a pair of leggings still covered with dry mud. To the right was the parlor, that is, the room where they ate and sat. Canary-yellow wallpaper, set off along the upper edge by a garland of pale flowers, quivered all over on its badly hung canvas underlayer; white calico curtains, red bordered, were crossed along the windows; and on the narrow mantelpiece a clock with a head of Hippocrates shone resplendent between two silver-plated candlesticks with oval-shaped globes. Charles's consulting room was on the other side of the hall, a small room about six feet wide, with a table, three regular chairs, and an office chair. The volumes of the *Dictionary of Medical Sciences,* uncut but with bindings that had suffered in the successive hands through which they had passed, adorned almost by themselves the six shelves of a pine bookcase. The smell of browned butter penetrated the wall during examinations, just as in the kitchen one could hear the patients coughing in the consulting room and pouring out their life stories. Next, overlooking the stable yard, came a large ramshackle room that had an oven and now served as woodshed, wine cellar, and storeroom; it was full of scrap iron, empty barrels, discarded farm tools, and a quantity of other dusty objects the purpose of which was impossible to guess.

The garden, long and narrow, was laid out between two clay walls lined with apricot trees, as far as a thorny hedge which separated it from the fields. In the middle there was a slate sundial on a stone pedestal; four flower beds planted with scrawny rosebushes were set symmetrically around the more utilitarian vegetable patch. Under the spruce trees at the very back was a plaster cast of a priest reading his breviary.

Emma went up to the bedrooms. The first was completely unfurnished, but the second, which was the nuptial chamber, had a mahogany bed in a red-curtained alcove. A box trimmed with shells adorned the chest of drawers; on the secretary, near the window, there was a bouquet of orange blossoms tied with white satin ribbons in a water bottle. It was a marriage bouquet, the other one's bouquet! She looked at it. Charles noticed her glance, picked it up, and took it to the attic, while Emma, seated in an armchair (her things meanwhile were being set down around her), thought of her wedding bouquet, which was packed away in a box, and drowsily wondered what would happen to it if by chance she died.

She kept herself busy the first days, thinking about changes in the house. She took off the candlestick globes, had new wallpaper hung, the staircase painted, and benches built in the garden all around the sundial; she even asked how she could obtain a fountain stocked with fish. Finally her husband, knowing that she liked to go out for drives, found a second-hand carriage that, when it was fitted with new lanterns and mudguards in padded leather, almost resembled a tilbury.

So they were happy and without a care in the world. A meal together, a walk in the evening along the highway, a movement of her hand over her hair, the sight of her straw hat hung on the window latch, and many other things as well that Charles never suspected could be pleasurable, now constituted the continuity of his happiness. In bed in the morning and side by side on the pillow, he looked at the sunlight on the blond down of her cheeks, which were half covered by the scalloped edges of her nightcap. Seen so near, her eyes seemed to him to have grown larger, especially when she blinked her eyelids several times in a row while waking

up; black at night and dark blue in the daylight, they seemed
to have successive layers of color, which, darkest at their
deepest, became lighter as they approached the surface. His
own eye became lost in their depths and he saw himself
reflected in miniature as far as his shoulders, with his scarf
tied around his head and the top of his opened nightshirt. He
would get up. She would place herself at the window to see
him go off and remain with her elbow on the ledge, between
two geranium pots, dressed in her robe, which floated loosely
around her. In the street, Charles would buckle his spurs
on at the mounting block, and she would continue to talk
to him, all the while plucking with her mouth some morsel
of a flower or greenery, which she blew toward him and
which, fluttering and floating, making semicircles in the air
like a bird, would, before falling, become caught in the
badly groomed mane of the old white mare standing motionless at the door. Charles, on horseback, would throw her a
kiss; she would answer with a wave and shut the window.
He would go off. Then, along the highway, stretching out
like an endlessly long ribbon of dust, along the empty roads
over which the tree branches bent low, in the paths whose
corn reached as high as his knees, with the sun on his shoulders and the morning air in his nostrils, his heart filled with the
joys of the previous night, his spirit calm, flesh content, he
went off pondering his happiness like those who after dinner
still savor the taste of the truffles they are digesting.

What good things had happened to him until now? Were
his school days good, when he remained locked between
those tall walls, alone in the midst of schoolmates richer or
smarter than he, whom he amused by his accent, who made
fun of his clothes, and whose mothers came to the visitors'
parlor with cakes in their muffs? Was it good later on, when
he was studying medicine and never had a purse full enough
to pay for a dance with some little working girl who might
have become his mistress? Or still later, when he lived fourteen months with the widow whose feet in bed were as cold
as ice? But now he possessed for life this lovely woman
whom he adored. For him the universe was bounded by the
circumference of her silk petticoat; and he reproached himself for not loving her enough. He wished he could see her
again; he would return in a hurry, climb the staircase, his
heart pounding. Emma would be getting dressed in her room;

he would arrive silently, kiss her on the back, she would give
a startled cry.

He could not keep himself from constantly touching her
comb, her rings, her shawl; sometimes he would give her big
smacking kisses on her cheeks or a row of little kisses all
along her bare arm from the tips of her fingers up to the
shoulder; and she would push him away, half smiling, half
annoyed, as one treats a bothersome child.

Before she had married she thought she was in love. But
the happiness that should have resulted from this love had
not come; she must have deceived herself, she thought.
Emma sought to learn what was really meant in life by the
words "happiness," "passion," and "intoxication"—words that
had seemed so beautiful to her in books.

VI

She had read *Paul and Virginia* and dreamed about the
bamboo cottage, the Negro Domingo, and the dog Fidèle,
but most of all about the sweet friendship of some dear
little brother who gathers ripe fruit for you in huge trees
taller than steeples or who runs barefoot over the sand,
bringing you a bird's nest.

When she was thirteen, her father took her to the city
to enter her in the convent. They stopped at an inn in the
Saint-Gervais section, where they were served their supper
on painted dishes depicting Mademoiselle de La Vallière's
story. The explanatory legends, interrupted in several places
by knife scratches, accorded equal glory to religion, the
delicacy of the heart, and courtly pomp.

Far from being bored in the convent, she was happy at
first in the company of the kind sisters who, to amuse her,
would take her into the chapel, which was connected to the
refectory by a long corridor. She played very little during
recess periods and understood the catechism well; and it was
she who always answered the vicar's difficult questions. Living thus, without ever leaving the drowsy atmosphere of the
classroom and among these white-faced women wearing ro-

saries with copper crosses, she succumbed peacefully to the
mystic languor emanating from the fragrances of the altar,
from the freshness of the font and the glow of the candles.
Instead of following the Mass, she looked at the pious vignettes edged in azure in her book, and she loved the sick
lamb, the Sacred Heart pierced with sharp arrows, and poor
Jesus stumbling as He walked under His cross. She tried to
fast one entire day to mortify her soul. She attempted to
think of some vow to fulfill.

When she went to confession, she would invent trivial sins
in order to prolong her stay there, on her knees in the shadow, hands clasped, her face at the grill as the priest whispered above her. The references to fiancé, husband, heavenly
lover, and eternal marriage that recur in sermons awakened
unexpected joys within her.

In the evening, before prayers, some religious selection
would be read at study. During the week it was a summary
of Abbé Frayssinous's religious-history lectures and on Sunday,
for relaxation, passages from *le Génie du Christianisme*.
How she listened, those first times, to the sonorous lamentation of romantic melancholy being echoed throughout the
world and unto eternity! Had her childhood been spent in
an apartment behind a store in some business district, she
might have been receptive to nature's lyric effusions that ordinarily reach us only via the interpretations of writers. But
she knew the countryside too well; she knew the lowing
of the flocks, the milking, and the plowing. Accustomed to the
calm life, she turned away from it toward excitement. She
loved the sea only for its storms, and greenery only when
it was scattered among ruins. She needed to derive immediate
gratification from things and rejected as useless everything
that did not supply this satisfaction. Her temperament was
more sentimental than artistic. She sought emotions and not
landscapes.

There was an old maid who came to the convent for one
week every month to work in the laundry. Protected by the
archbishop because she belonged to an old aristocratic family ruined during the Revolution, she ate in the refectory
at the good sisters' table and would chat with them for a while
after dinner before returning to her work. The girls would
often steal out of class to visit her. She knew the romantic
songs of the past century by heart and would sing them
softly as she plied her needle. She told stories, brought in

news of the outside world, ran errands in the city, and
would secretly lend the older girls some novel that she always kept in the pocket of her apron, of which the good
creature herself devoured long chapters between tasks. It
was always love, lovers, mistresses, persecuted women fainting in solitary little houses, postilions expiring at every relay,
horses killed on every page, gloomy forests, romantic woes,
oaths, sobs, tears and kisses, small boats in the moonlight,
nightingales in the groves, gentlemen brave as lions, gentle
as lambs, impossibly virtuous, always well dressed, who wept
copiously. For six months, at the age of fifteen, Emma
soiled her hands with these dusty remains of old reading
rooms. Later, with Walter Scott, she grew enamored of historic
events, dreamed of traveling chests, guardrooms, and minstrels. She wished that she had lived in some old manor,
like those long-waisted ladies of the manor who spent their
days under the trefoil of pointed arches, elbows on the
rampart and chin in hand, watching a cavalier with a white
feather emerge from the horizon on a galloping black charger. During that period she had a passion for Mary Stuart
and adored unfortunate or celebrated women. Joan of Arc,
Héloïse, Agnès Sorel, La Belle Ferronnière, and Clémence
Isaure blazed for her like comets over the murky immensity
of history, on which, still standing out in relief, but more
lost in the shadow and with no relationship to each other,
were Saint Louis with his oak, the dying Bayard, a few vicious crimes of Louis XI, a bit of the Saint Bartholomew
Massacre, Henri IV's plume, and the continuing memory of
the painted plates praising Louis XIV.

In the ballads she sang in music class there were only
tiny angels with golden wings, madonnas, lagoons, gondoliers
—gentle compositions that enabled her to perceive, through
the foolishness of the style and the weaknesses of the music,
the attractive fantasy of sentimental realities. Several of her
friends brought to the convent keepsake books they had received as gifts. They made a great to-do about hiding
them. They would read them in the dormitory. Handling
their lovely satin bindings delicately, Emma would focus
her dazzled eyes on the names of the unknown authors,
who usually signed their pieces "count" or "viscount." She
would tremble as she breathed gently on the tissue paper
covering the illustrations. It would lift in a double fold and
then fall back gently against the page. Behind a balcony

balustrade there would be a young man in a short coat holding tight in his arms a girl in a white dress with an alms
purse on her sash, or anonymous portraits of English ladies
with blond curls who looked at you with bright eyes
from under their round straw hats. Some were relaxing in
their carriages, gliding through parks while a greyhound
jumped in front of the team being led at a trot by two
small postilions in white breeches. Others, dreaming on sofas
near an opened letter, were gazing at the moon through
an open window half draped by a black curtain. The naïve
ones were revealed with a tear on their cheek, feeding a
turtledove through the bars of a Gothic cage or smiling, head
to one side, and pulling daisy leaves with their tapered
fingers, which curved like pointed slippers. And you were
also there, you sultans with long pipes, swooning with delight
in bowers in the arms of dancing girls! You giaours, Turkish
sabers, fezzes! And you especially, pale landscapes of fab-
ulous lands, which often show us at one and the same
time palm trees and evergreens, tigers to the right, a
lion to the left, Tartar minarets against the horizon, Roman
ruins in the foreground, and camels crouching; the whole
framed by a well-kept virgin forest with a large ray of perpendicular sunshine shimmering on the water upon which,
like white gashes on a steel-gray background, swans are
swimming into the distance.

And the lampshade, attached to the wall above Emma's
head, shed light on all these tableaux of the world that
passed before her one after the other in the silence of the
dormitory to the sound of rumbles in the distance of some
late fiacre still rolling down the boulevards.

She cried a great deal the first days after her mother's
death. She had a memorial picture made with the dead woman's hair, and in a letter that she sent to Les Bertaux,
all filled with sad reflections about life, she asked to be
buried in the same tomb when she died. Her father thought
she must be ill and came to see her. Emma was inwardly
pleased to feel that she had achieved at her first attempt
this rare ideal of pallid existences that mediocre hearts never achieve. She let herself glide into Lamartinian meanderings,
listened to all the harps on the lake, to the songs of the dying swans, to all the falling leaves, the pure virgins rising
to heaven, and the voice of the Eternal reverberating in the
valleys. She tired of this, didn't want to admit it, con-

tinued first out of habit, then out of vanity, and was finally surprised to find herself soothed and with as little sadness in her heart as wrinkles on her forehead.

The good sisters, who had been so sure about her vocation, realized with great astonishment that Mademoiselle Rouault seemed to be eluding their influence. They had, in fact, lavished on her so many prayers, retreats, novenas, and sermons, had so well preached the veneration that is owed to saints and martyrs, and given so much good advice about bodily modesty and the salvation of her soul that she responded as do tightly reined horses; she stopped short and the bit slipped from her teeth. This temperament, positive in the midst of its enthusiasms, which had loved the church for its flowers, the music for the romantic lyrics, and literature for its passion-inspiring stimulation, rebelled before the mysteries of faith in proportion to her growing irritation against the discipline, which was antipathetic to her nature. When her father came to take her from the convent, they were not sorry to see her go. The Mother Superior even found that toward the end Emma had become quite irreverent toward the community.

Back home Emma amused herself at first by taking charge of the servants, then she began disliking the country and missed the convent. When Charles came to Les Bertaux for the first time, she felt quite disillusioned, having nothing more to learn, nothing more to feel.

But the uneasiness at a new role or perhaps the disturbance caused by the presence of this man, had been sufficient to make her believe that she finally felt that marvelous passion that until now had been like a huge pink-winged bird soaring through the splendor of poetic skies. She could not believe that the calm in which she was now living was the happiness of which she had dreamed.

VII

Yet sometimes she thought that these were the most beautiful days of her life—the honeymoon, as it was called.

To savor its sweetness, it would have doubtless been necessary to go off to one of those sonorous-sounding countries where the first days of married life are languorously spent. Behind the blue silk shades of the mail coaches they would slowly climb up steep roads, listening to the song of the postilion being echoed through the mountain together with the sound of goat bells and the muffled roar of a waterfall. At sunset they would inhale the scent of the lemon trees by the shores of the gulfs; then, in the evening, on the terraces of the villas, alone, fingers intertwined, they would gaze at the stars and dream. She felt that certain places on the earth must produce happiness, just as a plant that languishes everywhere else thrives only in special soil. Why couldn't she be leaning her elbow on the balcony of a Swiss chalet or indulging her moods in a Scottish cottage with a husband dressed in a black velvet suit with long coattails, soft boots, a pointed hat, and elegant cuffs!

She might have wanted to confide all these things to someone. But how do you describe an intangible uneasiness that changes shape like a cloud and blows about like the wind? Words failed her—as well as the opportunity and the courage.

If Charles only suspected, if his gaze had even once penetrated her thought, it seemed to her that a sudden abundance would have broken away from her heart, as the fruit falls from a tree when you shake it. But as their life together brought increased physical intimacy, she built up an inner emotional detachment that separated her from him.

Charles's conversation was as flat as a sidewalk, with everyone's ideas walking through it in ordinary dress, arousing neither emotion, nor laughter, nor dreams. He had never been curious, he said, the whole time he was living in Rouen to go see a touring company of Paris actors at the theater. He couldn't swim, or fence, or shoot, and once he couldn't even explain to Emma a term about horseback riding she had come across in a novel.

But a man should know everything, shouldn't he? Excel in many activities, initiate you into the excitements of passion, into life's refinements, into all its mysteries? Yet this man taught nothing, knew nothing, hoped for nothing. He thought she was happy, and she was angry at him for this placid stolidity, for this leaden serenity, for the very happiness she gave to him.

Sometimes she would draw. Charles was always happy

watching her lean over her drawing board, squinting in order to see her work better, or rolling little bread pellets between her fingers. As for the piano, the faster her fingers flew over it, the more he marveled. She struck the keys with aplomb and ran from one end of the keyboard to the other without a stop. The old instrument, with its frayed strings, could then be heard at the other end of the village if the window were open; and often the bailiff's clerk passing over the highway, bareheaded and in moccasins, would stop to listen to her, his sheet of paper in his hand.

On the other hand, Emma did know how to run the house. She sent patients statements of their visits in well-written letters that didn't look like bills. When some neighbor came to dine on Sundays, she managed to offer some tasty dish, would arrange handsome pyramids of greengages on vine leaves, serve fruit preserves on a dish, and even spoke of buying finger bowls for dessert. All this reflected favorably on Bovary.

Charles ended up by thinking all the more highly of himself for possessing such a wife. In the living room he pointed with pride to her two small pencil sketches that he had mounted in very large frames and hung against the wallpaper on long green cords. People returning from Mass would see him at his door wearing handsome needlepoint slippers.

He would come home late, at ten o'clock, sometimes at midnight. Then he would want something to eat, and Emma would serve him because the maid was asleep. He would remove his coat in order to eat more comfortably. He would report on all the people he had met one after the other, the villages he had been to, the prescriptions he had written, and, content with himself, would eat the remainder of the stew, peel his cheese, bite into an apple, empty the decanter, then go to sleep, lying on his back and snoring.

Since he had been accustomed for a long time to wearing a nightcap, his scarf would not stay put around his ears, and in the morning his hair was all disheveled about his face and whitened by the down from his pillow, the ties of which would become undone during the night. He always wore heavy boots, which had at the instep two thick folds slanting obliquely toward the ankles whereas the rest of the upper continued in a straight line, as taut as if stretched on a wooden leg. He said that it was "good enough for the country."

His mother approved his economy. She came to visit him

as before, after some violent battle at her home. Yet, she
seemed rather prejudiced against her daughter-in-law. She
found her "a bit too haughty for their station in life";
wood, sugar, and candles were consumed "as if it were a
great mansion" and the amount of charcoal that was burned
in the kitchen would have sufficed for twenty-five meals!
She arranged Emma's linens in the cupboards and taught her
to keep an eye on the butcher when he delivered the meat.
Emma accepted the lessons; Madame Bovary lavished them.
And the words "daughter" and "mother" were exchanged all
day long, accompanied by a tiny quivering of the lips, each of
them offering gentle phrases in a voice trembling with anger.

During Madame Dubuc's day, the old woman still felt
herself the favorite. But now Charles's love for Emma seemed
to her desertion, an encroachment on that which belonged to
her; and she observed her son's happiness with a sad silence
like a ruined person who watches, through the windowpanes, people sitting around the table of his former home.
She would recall her exertions and her sacrifices to him in
the form of reminiscences, and comparing them to Emma's
neglectful habits, would conclude that it was not reasonable for him to adore her in such an exclusive way.

Charles didn't know what to say. He respected his mother,
and he loved his wife boundlessly. He considered the former's
judgment infallible but found the other irreproachable. When
his mother had left he would try timidly, and in the same
terms, one or two of the milder observations he had heard
her make. Emma would show him in but few words that he
was mistaken and send him off to his patients.

And yet, in line with the theories she admired, she wanted
to give herself up to love. In the moonlight of the garden
she would recite all the passionate poetry she knew by heart
and would sing melancholy adagios to him with sighs, but
she found herself as calm afterward as before and Charles
didn't appear more amorous or moved because of it.

After she had several times struck the flint on her heart
without eliciting a single spark, incapable as she was of
understanding that which she did not feel or of believing
things that didn't manifest themselves in conventional forms,
she convinced herself without difficulty that Charles's passion
no longer offered anything extravagant. His effusions had become routine; he embraced her at certain hours. It was one

habit among others, like the established custom of eating dessert after the monotony of dinner.

A gamekeeper, having been cured by Charles of a chest inflammation, had given Emma a small Italian greyhound; she would take it out to walk since she went out occasionally in order to escape for a moment and not have the eternal garden with the dusty road constantly before her eyes.

She would go as far as the Banneville beech grove, near the abandoned pavilion that forms an angle of the wall at the side of the fields. Sharp-edged leaves from the reeds would be scattered through the vegetation in the ditch.

First she would look all around to see if anything had changed since her last visit. She would find again, in the same places, foxglove and wallflowers, beds of nettles surrounding the huge stones, and patches of lichen along the three windows whose perpetually closed shutters were rattling away on their rusty iron bars. Her thoughts, at first unfocused, wandered at random like her greyhound, who ran around in circles through the countryside, yapping at yellow butterflies, chasing shrewmice, and nibbling the poppies on the edge of a wheat field. Then her thoughts would start to crystallize. She would sit on the grass into which she would dig the tip of her parasol with brief thrusts and would ask herself: "My God, why did I get married?"

She would ask herself if there might not be a way, by other combinations of fate, to meet some other man, and she tried to imagine what these unrealized events, this different life, this husband she did not know, would be like. None of them resembled her present husband. He might have been handsome, witty, distinguished, attractive, as, doubtless, were all the men her old friends from the convent had married. What were they doing now? In the city, with the street noises, the hum of the theaters, and the lights of the ballroom, they were living lives in which the heart expands, in which the senses blossom. But her life was as cold as an attic with northern exposure, and boredom, that silent spider, was spinning its web in all the dark corners of her heart. She remembered the days on which prizes were distributed, when she climbed to the platform to receive her small wreaths. With her braided hair, white dress, and openwork shoes, she had a gentle manner, and when she was back in her seat the gentlemen leaned over to compliment her. The courtyard was filled with carriages; the people said good-bye to her

through the windows; the music master greeted her as he
passed by with his violin case. How far it all was! How far!

She signaled to her greyhound, Djali, took her between
her knees, passed her fingers along the long delicate head,
and said: "Come kiss your mistress; you have no worries."

Then as she looked at the melancholy expression of the
graceful animal, who was slowly yawning, she softened and
spoke aloud to her, as to someone in need of consolation.

Sometimes there were gusts of wind, breezes from the
sea, that, rolling over the entire plateau of the Caux country
all the way into the fields, carried with them a salty freshness. Close to the ground the rushes whistled and the
beech leaves rustled, while their tops, continually swaying,
kept up their deep murmuring. Emma tightened her shawl
around her shoulders and arose.

In the avenue between the trees a green light filtered by
the foliage lit up the moss that was gently crackling under
her feet. The sun was setting; the sky was red between the
branches, and the uniform trunks of trees planted in a
straight line seemed a dark colonnade standing out against
a golden background. Fear came over her, she called to
Djali, went rapidly back to Tostes by the highway, collapsed
into an armchair, and did not say one word the entire evening.

But toward the end of September something extraordinary
happened in her life; she was invited to Vaubyessard, to the
home of the Marquis d'Andervilliers.

The marquis, secretary of state during the Restoration,
seeking to reentér political life, was preparing his candidacy
for the office of deputy well in advance. He distributed a
great deal of wood during the winter and was always eloquently demanding new roads for his district in the General
Council. During the hot weather he had an abscess in his
mouth that Charles had miraculously cured with a touch of
the lancet. The clerk he sent to Tostes to pay for the operation reported that evening that he had seen some superb
cherries in the doctor's little garden. Now, cherry trees did
not grow well in Vaubyessard; the marquis asked Bovary for
a few slips, made it a point to thank him in person, noticed
Emma, thought she had a pretty figure and a manner not
at all like a peasant's, so much so that he did not feel he
was going beyond the bounds of condescension nor on the

other hand that he was making a mistake by inviting the young couple to the château.

One Wednesday at three o'clock, Monsieur and Madame Bovary set off in their buggy for Vaubyessard with a large trunk attached in the rear and a hatbox set in front on the dashboard. Charles also had a bandbox between his knees.

They arrived at nightfall, just as the lamps in the park were being lit to illuminate the way for the carriages.

VIII

The château, of modern construction, in the Italian style, had two projecting wings and three front entrances. It was spread out at the back of an immense lawn on which several cows were grazing between clumps of large, evenly spaced trees while groups of shrubs, rhododendron, syringa, and snowballs projected their unequal tufts of foliage along the winding sandy road. A stream passed under a bridge. Through the haze could be seen the thatch-roofed buildings scattered across the meadow. This latter was set in between the gentle slopes of two tree-covered hills. In the groves behind the house, set on two parallel lines, were the coach houses and stables, sole remains of the old, demolished château.

Charles's carriage arrived at the middle flight of steps; servants appeared; the marquis came forward, and offering his arm to the doctor's wife, he led her into the foyer.

It was high ceilinged and paved with marble tiles, and the combined noise of steps and voices echoed in it as in a church. A staircase faced it, and to the left a gallery overlooking the garden led to a billiard room, from which you could hear the ivory balls clicking as soon as you approached the door.

As she was crossing it to get to the drawing room, Emma noticed the serious-faced men, chins set over cravats folded high and all wearing decorations, standing around the table. They would smile silently as they hit with their cues. On the dark wood panels were large gilded frames with names written

in black letters on their lower borders. She read: "Jean-
Antoine d'Andervilliers d'Yverbonville, Count de la Vaubyessard, and Baron de la Fresnaye, killed in the battle of
Coutras, October 20, 1587." And on another: "Jean-Antoine-
Henri-Guy d'Andervilliers de la Vaubyessard, Admiral of
France and Knight of the Order of St. Michael, wounded
in the battle of La Hougue-Saint-Vaast, May 29, 1692, died
at La Vaubyessard, January 23, 1693." Those that followed
could barely be made out because the light from the lamps,
directed on the green cloth of the billiard table, left the
rest of the room in shadow. It turned the hanging canvases
brown and highlighted only the cracks in the varnish; and
from all the large gilt-edged black squares only some lighter part of the painting would emerge here and there—a pale
forehead, two eyes staring at you, wigs unfurling over the
powdered shoulders, red suits, or perhaps the buckle of a
garter at the top of a fleshy calf.

The marquis opened the drawing-room door; one of the
women arose (the marquise herself), came forward to meet
Emma, and sat her down beside her on a small settee, where
she began to chat amiably, as if she had known her a long
time. She was a woman of about forty, with handsome
shoulders, an aquiline nose, and a drawling voice; she wore a
simple lace shawl that fell back in a point over her chestnut
hair. A fair-haired young woman was sitting beside her in a
high-backed chair, and gentlemen with tiny flowers in their
lapels were talking to the ladies gathered around the fireplace.

Dinner was served at seven. The men, who outnumbered
the ladies, sat down at the first table, in the hall, and the
women were placed at the second, in the dining room with
the marquis and the marquise.

As she entered, Emma felt herself enveloped in a warm
atmosphere, a mixture of flower scent and the aroma of fine
linens, of well-seasoned meat and truffles. The candles in the
candelabra played their elongated flames over the silver platter covers; crystal pieces misted over reflected each other
with pale glimmers. There were bunches of flowers set in a
line along the entire table, and in the wide-bordered dishes
napkins folded in the shape of bishop's miters held small
oval-shaped rolls.

The red claws of the lobsters hung over the dishes; huge
pieces of fruit were piled on each other in openwork baskets;
the quails still bore their plumage; clouds of steam kept ris-

ing; and the butler, in silk stockings, knee breeches, white cravat, and frilled shirt, solemn as a judge, passing the already carved platters between the guests' shoulders, would make the piece you selected jump with one flick of the knife. On the large porcelain stove with its copper fittings, a statue of a woman draped to the chin stared steadily at the roomful of people.

Madame Bovary noticed that several of the women had not put their gloves in their wineglasses.

At the upper end of the table, alone among all the women, there was one old man eating, bending over his well-filled platter with his napkin knotted in back like a child, drops of sauce dribbling from his mouth. His eyes were bloodshot and he wore a small pigtail tied with a black ribbon. It was the marquis' father-in-law, the old Duke of Laverdière, once favorite of the Count d'Artois in the days of the Marquis de Conflans's hunting parties in Vaudreuil; it was said he had been Marie-Antoinette's lover between Messieurs de Coigny and de Lauzun. He had led a thoroughly debauched life, filled with duels, wagers, and abductions, had run through his fortune and been the terror of his entire family. A servant behind his chair was shouting into his ear the names of dishes that the old man would point to with his finger, mumbling. Emma could not keep herself from staring at the slack-mouthed old man as on someone extraordinary and august. He had lived at Court and slept in the bed of queens!

Iced champagne was served. Emma shivered all over at the prickly sensation in her mouth. She had never seen pomegranates before nor eaten pineapple. Even the granulated sugar seemed to her whiter and finer than elsewhere.

After dinner the ladies went up to their rooms to get ready for the ball.

Emma dressed with the meticulous care of an actress making her debut. She arranged her hair as the hairdresser had suggested and pulled on the *barège* dress that had been spread out on the bed. Charles's pants were too tight around the stomach.

"The shoe straps are going to be in my way when I dance," he said.

"Dance?" she asked.

"Yes."

"You're out of your mind! They'll laugh at you. Stay in

your place. Besides, it's more suitable for a doctor," she added.

Charles said no more. He paced up and down the room waiting for Emma to finish dressing.

Her back was turned to him, and he looked at her reflection in the mirror between the two candles. Her black eyes seemed even blacker. Her hair, gently puffed toward the ears, gleamed with a bluish luster; a rose in her chignon was trembling on its fragile stem. It had artificial dewdrops at the tips of its leaves. She wore a pale saffron-colored dress, set off by three bunches of pompon roses mingled with greenery.

Charles went over to kiss her on the shoulder.

"Let go of me!" she said. "You'll wrinkle my dress!"

A violin flourish and the sounds of a horn could be heard. She descended the staircase, restraining herself from running.

The quadrilles had begun. More people were arriving, jostling each other. She stationed herself on a settee near the door.

When the quadrille was over, the floor remained free. Groups of men stood and chatted while the liveried servants brought in large trays. Along the row of seated women, painted fans were fluttering, bouquets half concealed smiling faces, and gold-stoppered perfume bottles were being turned in half-opened hands whose tight white gloves revealed the shape of the fingernails and hugged the wrists. Lace trimmings, diamond brooches, and bracelets with lockets trembled on bodices, sparkled on breasts, jingled on bare arms. The hairdos, securely arranged and twisted at the napes, were crowned with clusters or bunches of forget-me-nots, jasmine, pomegranate blossoms, wheat ears, or cornflowers. The mothers, sitting quietly in their places, wore red turbans and frowning expressions.

Emma's heart was beating a bit faster when, her partner holding her by the tips of his fingers, she took her place in line and awaited the fiddler's stroke to begin. But the emotion soon disappeared, and swaying to the rhythm of the orchestra, she glided forward, moving her neck lightly. A smile came to her lips at certain delicate strains of the violin during its solo moments; you could hear the clinking of gold coins dropping onto the card tables in the next room; then everything began at once, the cornet emitted a loud blast, feet fell in measure, skirts swirled out and rustled against each other, hands joined, then separated; the same eyes that lowered before you looked up again at yours.

Several men (about fifteen) between twenty-five and forty years of age, scattered among the dancers or chatting at the entrances, distinguished themselves from the crowd by their family resemblance despite the differences in their ages, dress, and facial features.

Their clothes, better made, seemed of a finer cloth, and their hair, made to gleam by more refined pomades, was brought forward in curls toward the temples. They had the complexion of wealth, that whiteness that is accentuated by the pallor of porcelain, the sheen of watered satin, the varnish of fine furniture, and that is nurtured by a diet of exquisitely prepared food. Their necks turned in relaxed manner over low-folded cravats, their long sideburns fell over turned-down collars; they wiped their lips with elegantly scented handkerchiefs embroidered with large monograms. Those who were beginning to age looked young, and a certain maturity lay over the faces of the young ones. The calm of daily satisfied passions showed in their indifferent glances, but their gentle manners did not completely mask that special brutality that stems from their relatively easy conquests, the handling of thoroughbred horses and the company of fallen women, in which the muscles are flexed and vanity sated.

A few feet from Emma a gentleman in a blue coat was talking about Italy with a pale young woman wearing a pearl necklace. They were praising the size of the pillars at St. Peter's, Tivoli, Vesuvius, Castellamare, and the Cascine; the roses of Genoa; the Colosseum in the moonlight. Emma listened with her other ear to a conversation full of words she did not understand. In the center of a group was a very young man who had beaten Miss Arabelle and Romulus the week before and won two thousand louis by jumping a ditch in England. One man was complaining that his racers were getting fat; another, about the way a printing error had garbled his horse's name.

The air in the ballroom grew heavy; the lights were fading. People began moving toward the billiard room. A servant climbing on a chair broke two windowpanes; at the noise of the shattered glass, Madame Bovary looked round and saw some peasants, their faces pressed to the window, staring at her from the garden. Then the memory of Les

Bertaux came back to her. She saw the farm again, the muddy pond, her father in a smock under the apple trees, and she saw once more herself in the dairy skimming the cream from the milk cans with her finger. But in the splendor of the present hour, her past life, so clear until now, was disappearing completely, and she almost doubted that she had lived it. She was here, and outside the ballroom there was merely shadow cast over all the rest. She ate a maraschino-flavored ice, which she held in her left hand in a silver-gilt shell, and half closed her eyes, the spoon between her teeth.

A woman near her dropped her fan as a man danced by. "Would you be so kind, Monsieur," the woman said, "and pick my fan up from under the sofa?"

The gentleman kneeled down, and as he reached out, Emma saw the young woman's hand throw something white, folded into a triangle, into his hat. The gentleman picked up the fan and held it out to the woman respectfully; she thanked him with a nod and began to sniff her bouquet.

After supper, at which many Spanish and Rhine wines were served, along with bisque and cream-of-almond soups, Trafalgar puddings, and all sorts of cold meats, surrounded by jellied molds, quivering on the plates, the carriages began going off, one after the other. By pulling the muslin curtain away from the corner one could see the light of their lanterns gliding through the night. The settees began to empty; there were still some card players; the musicians moistened the tips of their fingers on their tongues; Charles was leaning against a door, half asleep.

The cotillion began at three in the morning. Emma did not know how to waltz. Everyone was waltzing, even Mademoiselle d'Andervilliers and the marquise; there remained now only the château guests, about a dozen people.

One of the dancers, familiarly addressed as viscount, whose extremely low-cut waistcoat seemed molded on his chest, came a second time to invite Madame Bovary, assuring her that he would lead her and that she would manage well.

They began slowly, then moved more rapidly. Everything was turning around them, the lights, furniture, paneling, and the floor, like a disk on a pivot. Passing near the doors, the hem of Emma's dress flared out against her partner's trousers; their legs intertwined; he looked down at her, she raised her eyes to him; a numbness overcame her, she stopped.

They started again and the viscount, with a more rapid movement, swept her away, disappeared with her to the end of the gallery, where, out of breath, she almost fell and for one moment leaned her head on his chest. And then, still turning, but more gently now, he led her back to her place; she leaned back against the wall and put her hand before her eyes.

When she opened them again, there was a woman seated on a stool in the middle of the floor with three dancers on their knees before her. She chose the viscount and the violin struck up again.

They were stared at. Up and down they went, she with her body held rigid, chin down, and he always in the same pose, holding himself erect, elbow rounded, face jutting forward. How she could waltz! They continued for a long time and tired out the others.

People chatted a while and after the "good nights," or rather "good mornings," the house guests went to sleep.

Charles dragged himself upstairs, clinging to the banister; his legs "couldn't stand up another minute." He had spent five solid hours standing near the tables watching the whist games without understanding a thing about them. And so he heaved a great sigh of relief when his boots were finally removed.

Emma wrapped a shawl around her shoulders, opened the window, and leaned out.

The night was black. A few drops of rain were falling. She breathed in the humid breeze that was refreshing her eyelids. With the ball music still humming in her ears, she was trying to stay awake in order to prolong the illusion of this luxurious life that she would have to abandon in a short while.

Day broke. She looked at the château windows for a long time, trying to guess which were the bedrooms of the various people she had noticed the night before. She would have liked to know about their lives, to enter into them, to become involved with them.

But she was shivering with cold. She undressed and snuggled between the sheets against Charles, who was asleep.

There were a lot of people at breakfast; the doctor was amazed that no liquor was served. Later Mademoiselle d'Andervilliers picked up what was left of the rolls in a basket to carry them to the swans on the lake, and they went for a walk in the hothouses, where exotic plants bristling with hairy leaves rose in pyramids beneath hanging vases, which, like over-crowded serpents' nests, dropped long, twisted green tendrils over their edges. The orangery at the far end led via a covered passage to the outhouses. The marquis took Emma to the stable to amuse her. Above the basket-shaped racks, porcelain plaques bore the horses' names in black. When they passed by, each animal stirred in its stall and clicked its tongue. The floor of the saddle room glistened like a drawing-room floor. Coach harnesses were set in the middle on two revolving columns and the bits, whips, stirrups, and curbs were all lined up along the wall.

Meanwhile, Charles went to ask a servant to ready his buggy. They brought it around to the front, and when all their luggage had been packed in, the Bovarys took leave of the marquis and marquise and headed back to Tostes.

Emma said nothing and watched the wheels turn. Charles, seated on the edge of the seat, was driving with his arms outstretched, and the small horse ambled along between its oversized shafts. The slack reins hitting its crupper grew moist with its lather, and the box roped on behind kept making loud, steady thuds against the body.

They were on the heights of Thibourville when suddenly some horsemen passed before them, laughing, with cigars in their mouths. Emma thought she recognized the viscount; she turned around and saw nothing on the horizon but heads moving up and down in rhythm with the uneven cadence of the trot and gallop.

Half a mile later they had to stop to tie a cord around the breech band, which had broken. As Charles took one last look at the harness, he saw something on the ground between the horse's legs; and he picked up a cigar case edged with green silk and emblazoned with a coat of arms in the center as on a coach door.

"There are still two cigars inside," he said. "They'll be for tonight after dinner."

"You smoke?" she asked.

"Sometimes, when I have the chance."

He put his find in his pocket and whipped the horse.

Dinner was not ready when they arrived home. Madame became furious. Nastasie answered with insolence.

"Get out!" Emma said. "You brazen creature! I'm sending you away!"

For dinner there was onion soup with a bit of veal cooked
in sorrel. Facing Emma, Charles said, rubbing his hands together with a contented look: "It feels good to be home
again!"

They could hear Nastasie crying. He was rather fond of
the poor girl. In the old days when he had been a widower,
she had kept him company on many an empty evening.
She was his first patient, his oldest acquaintance in the district.

"Have you sent her away for good?" he said finally.

"Yes. Who's stopping me?" she answered.

They warmed themselves in the kitchen while their bedroom was being readied. Charles began to smoke. He smoked
with his lips puckered, spitting every minute, recoiling at
each puff.

"You'll make yourself sick," she said disdainfully.

He put his cigar down and ran off to gulp down a glass
of cold water from the pump. Emma, seizing the cigar case,
threw it hastily into the bottom of the cupboard.

The next day was long. She walked about in her garden,
passing back and forth over the same paths, stopping in front
of the flower beds, the fruit-tree trellises, the plaster curé,
staring with bewilderment at all these once familiar things.
How far away the ball already seemed! Why should there
be such a distance between yesterday morning and tonight?
Her trip to Vaubyessard had made a gap in her life like one
of those great crevices that a storm sometimes carves out in
the mountains in a single night. She resigned herself, however; reverently she packed away in the chest of drawers
her lovely dress and even her satin slippers, whose soles had
yellowed from the floor wax. Her heart was like them; the
wealth had rubbed off on her, something that would never be
erased.

And so the memory of the ball became a preoccupation for
Emma. Every Wednesday she would say to herself on awak-
ing: "Ah! A week ago today—two weeks ago—three weeks
ago, I was there." Little by little the faces blurred in her
memory; she forgot the quadrille tunes; she no longer saw
the livery and the rooms so clearly; some of the details
faded away, but the regret remained.

IX

Often, when Charles had gone out, she would take the green silk cigar case out of the cupboard from between the piles of linen where she had left it.

She would look at it, open it, and even sniff the lining. A blend of verbena and tobacco. To whom did it belong? To the viscount. Perhaps it was a gift from his mistress. It had been embroidered on some rosewood frame, a delicate item hidden from all eyes. Presumably it had taken up many hours, during which the soft curls of the pensive worker had fallen over it. A breath of love had passed through the meshes of the canvas; each stitch of the needle had fixed a hope or a memory, and all these threads of intertwined silk were but the continuation of the same silent passion. And then the viscount had borne it off with him one morning. What had they spoken about while he was standing near the fireplace with the large mantelpiece between the vases of flowers and the Pompadour clocks? She was in Tostes. He, he was in Paris now—Paris!

What was it like, that city? What a marvelous name! She would repeat it under her breath to make herself feel good; it resounded in her ears like a cathedral bell; it blazed before her eyes on the labels of her cosmetics jars.

At night, when the fishmongers in their carts passed in front of her windows singing the *Marjolaine*, she would awake and tell herself, as she listened to the noise of the iron-rimmed wheels dying away rapidly as they left the area. "They'll be there tomorrow!"

And she would follow them in her thoughts, climbing hills and descending them, crossing villages, moving over the highway by the light of the stars. And away off in the distance there was always some obscure spot where her dream expired.

She bought a plan of Paris, and moving the tip of her finger on the map, she would wander about the capital. She would go up boulevards, stop at each corner between the

street lines, in front of the white squares that signified houses. Toward the end she would shut her tired eyes and see
in the shadows the gas jets of carriages flickering in the
wind, with the lowered tailboards unloading their passengers
amid great tumult in front of the theaters.

She subscribed to *The Workbasket*, a woman's magazine,
and to *The Sylph of the Salons*. She devoured all the reviews
of opening nights, races, and soirees, without missing a single
one; she would become interested in a singer's debut, in
the opening of a store. She knew the latest fashions, the ad-
dresses of good tailors, the days for the Bois or the opera.
She studied descriptions of furniture in Eugène Sue's books;
she read Balzac and George Sand, searching in their writings
for vicarious satisfaction of her own desires. She would even
bring her book to the table and turn the pages while Charles
spoke to her as he ate. The thought of the viscount came
back to her continually as she read. She would create liaisons
between him and the fictitious characters. But the circle
of which he was the focal point gradually widened out, and
the halo emanating from his face spread further out to
illuminate other dreams.

Paris, more vast than the ocean, glistened in Emma's eyes
in a silver-gold atmosphere. The crowded life that bustled
in this tumult was nevertheless divided into parts, acted out
in distinct tableaux. Emma saw only two or three, which
obscured all the others and that alone represented all
humanity. The world of ambassadors trod over gleaming par-
quet floors, in salons paneled with mirrors, around oval tables covered with gold-fringed velvet cloths. There were
dresses with bustles there, vast intrigues, anguish dissimulated
under smiles. Then came the society of duchesses. There you
were pale, arose at four in the afternoon; the women,
poor darlings, wore English lace at the bottom of their petticoats, and the men, with unrecognized talents beneath futile
exteriors, rode their horses to death at every outing, went to
Baden for the summer season, and married heiresses when
they had finally reached their fortieth year. In the private
rooms of restaurants where you dine after midnight, the
motley crowd of men of letters and actresses laughed in the
candlelight. That world was as prodigal as kings, full of
ideals, ambitions, and fantastic dreams. It was an existence
above the others, between heaven and earth, in the midst
of the elements, something sublime. As for the rest of the

world, it was lost, shadowy, and ill-defined, as if it did not exist. Besides, the closer things were, the more she turned her thoughts from them. Everything that immediately surrounded her, the dull countryside, imbecilic petty-bourgeois people, the mediocrity of existence, seemed to her an exception in the world, an unusual accident in which she found herself trapped, while beyond it the immense world of happiness and passion extended itself as far as the eye could see. In her yearnings she confused the sensualities of luxury with the joys of the heart, the elegance of convention with delicacy of sentiment. Didn't love, like the Indian plants, need cultivated land, a special temperature? Sighs in the moonlight, long embraces, tears flowing over forlorn hands, all the fevers of the flesh and languors of tenderness, did not separate themselves from the balcony of the great castle which was full of leisure, of boudoirs with silken shades, thick rugs, filled flower stands, and a bed mounted on a platform, nor from the glistening of precious stones and the lace ornaments of livery.

The postboy who came to groom the mare every morning crossed the corridor in his sockless feet in thick wooden shoes. His smock was filled with holes. This was the groom in knee breeches with whom she had to content herself! Once his work was done, he would not come the rest of the day because Charles would put the horse into the stable himself when he came home, unsaddle her, and adjust the halter while the maid brought a bucket of straw and threw it, as best she could, into the manger.

To replace Nastasie (who had finally left Tostes in tears) Emma took into her employ a young girl of fourteen, an orphan with a sweet face. She forbade her to wear cotton bonnets, taught her it was necessary to address people in the third person, to bring a glass of water on a saucer, to knock on doors before entering, and to iron, to starch, and to dress her. She wanted to make her into a lady's maid. The new girl obeyed without a murmur in order not to be sent away, and since Emma usually left the key in the buffet, Félicité would take a small supply of sugar each evening, which she would eat in bed all by herself after having said her prayers.

Sometimes during the afternoon she would go off to chat with the postilions across the way. Emma would stay upstairs in her chambers.

She would wear a dressing gown, entirely open, which revealed a pleated chemisette with three gold buttons between the challis lapels of the bodice. Her belt was a large-tasseled rope, and her tiny garnet-colored slippers had a cluster of wide ribbons that spilled all over the instep. She had bought herself a blotter, a writing case, a penholder, and envelopes, even though she had no one to write to. She would dust her shelves, look at herself in the mirror, take a book, and then let it fall onto her knees while she dreamed between the lines. She wanted to go traveling or return to live in her convent. At one and the same time she wanted to die and to live in Paris.

When it rained or snowed, Charles would direct his horse over the shortcuts. He would eat omelets at farm tables, put his hand into humid beds, receive full in the face the tepid spurt of bloodletting, listen to death rattles, examine the bedpans, and tuck in a great deal of dirty linens; but every night he would come home to a glowing fire, the table set, the furniture arranged comfortably, and a charming woman, neatly dressed, smelling so fresh you wondered where the fragrance came from and whether it wasn't her skin lending the scent to her petticoat.

She charmed him by a number of elegant gestures. Sometimes it was a new way of cutting paper sconces for the candles, a flounce that she changed on her dress, or the extraordinary name of some quite simple dish that the maid had spoiled but that Charles swallowed with pleasure down to the bitter end. In Rouen she saw some women wearing charms on their watches; she bought charms. She wanted two large vases of blue glass on her fireplace, and awhile later, an ivory workbox with a vermeil thimble. The less Charles understood those elegant touches, the more he responded to their attraction. They added something to his sensual pleasures and to the sweetness of his home. It was as if gold dust were being spread all along the narrow path of his life.

He was in good health and looked well. His reputation was quite established. The country people adored him because he wasn't conceited. He would pat the children, never entered a café, and otherwise inspired confidence by his good morals. He was especially successful with catarrhs and chest diseases. Being quite afraid of killing his patients, Charles hardly prescribed anything but sedatives, occasionally an

emetic, a foot bath, or leeches. It wasn't that he was afraid
of surgery. He bled people frequently, like horses, and he
had "one hell of a fist" for extracting teeth.

Finally, "to keep up to date" he subscribed to the *Medical
News,* a new journal whose prospectus he had received. He
would read a little from it after dinner, but the warmth
of the room, combined with his digestion, made him fall
asleep within five minutes, and he would stay there, his chin
propped up on both his hands and his hair falling in fringes
down to the lamp base. Emma would look at him and shrug
her shoulders. Why wasn't she at least married to one of
those silent, impassioned men who work at their books all
night and who, finally, at the age of sixty, when rheumatism
sets in, wear a string of decorations on their badly made
black suits? She would have liked the Bovary name, which
was hers, to be famous, to see it displayed in the bookstores,
repeated in newspapers, known by all of France. But Charles
had no ambition whatsoever! A doctor from Yvetot, with
whom he had recently found himself in consultation, had
insulted him slightly, at the very bed of the patient, in front
of the assembled relatives. When Charles told this to her
that evening, Emma became furious at the other doctor.
Charles was touched. He kissed her on the forehead with a
tear in his eye. But she was exasperated with shame and
felt like hitting him. She went into the hallway to open the
window and breathe in some fresh air to calm herself.

"What a sad creature! What a sad creature!" she said to
herself in a low voice, biting her lips.

She was beginning to feel more irritated with him in general. As he grew older he acquired some crude habits:
during dessert he would whittle the corks of empty bottles,
pass his tongue over his teeth after eating; he made a gulping
noise at every mouthful as he swallowed his soup; and as he
began putting on weight, his eyes, already small, seemed to
sink in toward his temples because of his puffy cheeks.

Emma would sometimes tuck the red border of his undershirt into his waistcoat, straighten his cravat, or throw away
worn gloves that he was about to put on. This was not, as
he assumed, for him; it was for herself, for her own
ego, out of nervous irritation. Sometimes, too, she told
him about things she had read, a passage from a novel, for
example, a new play or an anecdote about high society that
was being reported in the paper. Charles was someone after

all—an ever-available ear, an everready source of approval.
She confided enough in her greyhound! She would even
have confided in the fireplace logs and in the clock pendulum.

Deep down within her she was waiting for something to
happen. Like sailors in distress, she gazed at the solitude
of her life with despairing eyes, seeking some white sail
in the far-off haze of the horizon. She didn't know what this
change would be, what wind would bring it to her, toward
what shore it would take her, whether it was a launch or a
triple-deck ship, laden with anxiety or filled to the port-
holes with joy. But each morning when she awoke she hoped
for it that day, and she would listen to every noise, leap
out of bed, be amazed that it hadn't come; then, at sunset,
growing continually sadder, she would look forward to the
next day.

Spring returned. She felt stifled at the first warm spells,
when the pear trees blossomed.

From the beginning of July she counted on her fingers
how many weeks remained before October, thinking that the
Marquis d'Andervilliers would perhaps give another ball at
Vaubyessard. But September passed by without one letter or
visit.

After the distress of this disappointment, her heart once
more remained empty and the succession of identical days
began again.

Now they were going to succeed each other one after the
other, always the same, innumerable, and bringing nothing!
Other people's existences, as dull as they were, at least
had the chance of something happening. Some occurrence
would occasionally bring about a series of ups and downs
or a change of scene. But it was God's will that nothing
should happen to her. The future was a totally dark corridor
with a solidly locked door at its end.

She gave up her music. Why play? Who would listen to
her? Since she would never be able to play in a concert on
an Érard piano, in a velvet gown with short sleeves, tapping
the ivory keys with her light fingers, feeling an ecstatic
murmur, like a breeze, waft around her, it was not worth it
to be bored studying. She left her drawing portfolios and
tapestry in the cupboard. What for? For what reason? Sewing irritated her.

"I've read everything," she told herself.

And she would sit heating the tongs or watching the rain fall.

How sad she was when they rang Vespers on Sunday. She would listen in an attentive stupor to each cracked chime of the bell. A cat, walking slowly across the rooftops, would arch its back against the pale rays of the sun. The wind was blowing clouds of dust along the highway. Once in a while a dog would howl in the distance and the bell would continue its monotonous, evenly spaced ringing, which faded off into the countryside.

Then people would emerge from the church. The women in polished clogs, the farmers in new smocks, the little children skipping bareheaded in front of them—all were going back to their homes. And until nighttime five or six men, always the same ones, would remain playing quoits in front of the main entrance of the inn.

It was a cold winter. The windowpanes were covered with frost each morning and the milky white light coming through them sometimes did not change all day long. They had to light the lamp by four o'clock.

In good weather she would go down to the garden. The dew on the cabbages formed a silvery lace with long transparent filaments stretching from one to the other. There were no birds singing, everything seemed asleep, even the straw-covered espalier and the vine beneath the wall coping looked like some large, ailing serpent. As you neared it, you could see wood lice with many feelers crawling about. Under the spruce trees near the hedge the sculptured curé in the three-cornered hat reading his breviary had lost his right foot, and the plaster on his face peeling off from the frost had left white patches.

Then she would go back, shut the door, stoke the fire, and wilting in its warmth, feel even more heavily the boredom that was overcoming her again. She would have gone to chat with the maid, but was held back by a sense of propriety.

Every day, at the same time, the schoolmaster in a black silk cap would fold back the shutters of his house and the village policemen would pass by, wearing his saber strapped over his shirt. Morning and evening the mail horses, three at a time, would cross the street to water themselves at the pond. Occasionally the bell of a tavern door would tinkle; and when there was a wind, you could hear creaking on their two rods the wigmaker's small copper basins, which served as a sign for his store. The store was decorated with an old-fashioned print of women's fashions glued to a pane and a wax bust of a yellow-haired woman. The wigmaker also lamented his unfulfilled talent, his lost future, and dreamed of a shop in a big city, Rouen for example, on the quay, near the theater. He would walk back and forth all day long, from the church to the city hall, waiting for customers. Whenever Madame Bovary would look up, she would see him there, like a guard on sentry duty, with his cap pulled over one ear and his heavy woolen jacket.

Sometimes in the afternoon a man's head would appear at the living-room window: bronzed face, black sideburns, and a slow, gentle, gleaming, open smile. Then a waltz would begin on an organ; in a miniature drawing room, dancers as tall as a finger (women in pink turbans, Tyrolean peasants in jackets, monkeys in black coats, gentlemen in knee breeches) would turn repeatedly around the armchairs, sofas and end tables, and be reflected in the bits of mirror held together at their corners by strips of gold paper. The man would turn the handle, look to the right, to the left, and toward the windows. From time to time, while directing a long jet of dark saliva toward the curbstone, he would lift the instrument, its heavy strap tiring his arm, with his knee; and sometimes languid and slow, sometimes joyous and fast, the music from the box would grind out across a pink taffeta curtain held by a copper clasp shaped like an arabesque. The tunes were those that were being played in the theaters, sung in drawing rooms, danced to in the evening beneath lighted chandeliers—echoes from the world that reached as far as Emma. Never-ending sarabands whirled in her head, and like a dancing girl on a flowered carpet, her thoughts leaped with the notes, swinging from dream to dream, from sadness to sadness. When the man had received a little money in his cap, he would pull an old blue wool cover down, slip his organ onto his back, and go off with a heavy step. She would watch him until he disappeared.

Mealtime was the worst of all in that tiny room on the ground floor, with the smoking oven, the creaking door, the damp walls, and the moist flagstones; all the bitterness of her existence seemed to be served up to her on her plate, and the steam from the boiled beef brought up waves of nausea from the depths of her soul. It took Charles a long time to eat; she would nibble a few hazelnuts, or leaning on her elbow, would amuse herself by drawing lines on the oilcloth with the tip of her knife.

She was neglecting everything in the household now, and her mother-in-law, when she came to spend part of Lent in Tostes, was amazed at the change. She who had been so fastidious and delicate before now spent entire days without dressing, wearing gray cotton stockings, using candle ends for light. She kept saying that it was necessary to economize since they were not rich, adding that she was quite content, very happy, that she liked Tostes very much, and making other similar statements that silenced her mother-in-law's objections. She seemed as disinclined as ever to follow the older woman's advice, and once when Madame Bovary senior took it into her head to claim that masters should watch over their servants' religion, Emma answered her with such an angry look and cold smile that the good woman did not meddle any more.

Emma was becoming difficult and capricious. She would order certain dishes for herself and not touch a thing. One day she would drink only fresh milk, and the next, dozens of cups of tea. Often she would refuse to go out, then she would feel stifled, fling open the windows, dress in light garments. After she had roundly scolded her maid she would give her presents or send her to the neighbors', just as she would sometimes throw all the coins in her purse to the poor, although she was far from softhearted or especially responsive to others' feelings, like most people of country stock, who always retain something of the callousness of their fathers in their souls.

Toward the end of February old man Rouault, in gratitude for his recovery, brought with his own hands a superb turkey to his son-in-law. He remained in Tostes three days. Since Charles was with his patients, Emma kept him company. He smoked in his bedroom, spat on the andirons, spoke of farming, calves, cows, poultry, and the town council, so much so that she closed the door when he left with a feeling of relief that surprised even her. Moreover, she was no longer hiding her distaste for everything and everyone; and she began to express very odd opinions sometimes, condemning things that were generally approved and approving perverse and immoral things. This often caused her husband to stare at her.

Would this misery last forever? Would she never be out of it? She certainly deserved as much as all those women who were living happily. She had seen duchesses at Vaubyessard who had clumsier figures and more common manners than she, and she cursed God's injustice; she would lean her head against the wall and cry; she envied tumultuous lives, masked balls, and insolent pleasures with all the mad distractions they probably offered and that she had never known.

She became pale and suffered heart palpitations. Charles gave her valerian and camphor baths. Everything he tried seemed to irritate her more.

Some days she would talk with feverish abandon. These moments of exultation were suddenly succeeded by sullen moods in which she remained silent and motionless. Then she would revive herself by splashing the contents of a flask of eau de cologne over her arms.

Since she was constantly complaining about Tostes, Charles assumed that her illness was due to some local cause, and the idea taking hold, he thought seriously about setting up his practice elsewhere.

Then she started drinking vinegar in order to lose weight, contracted a small dry cough, and lost her appetite completely.

It meant a lot to Charles to abandon Tostes after four years' residence and at the moment "when he was beginning to take root." But if it was necessary! He took her to Rouen to his old professor. It was a nervous disorder; she needed a change of air.

After looking in every direction, Charles heard that there was a substantial market town named Yonville-l'Abbaye, in the Neufchâtel district, whose doctor, a Polish refugee, had run off the week before. So he wrote to the local pharmacist inquiring about the population, the distance from the nearest doctor, how much his predecessor had earned per year, etc. The answers were satisfactory and he decided to move toward spring if Emma's health did not improve.

One day, as she was straightening up a drawer in preparation for moving, she pricked her fingers on something. It was an iron wire from her wedding bouquet. The orange blossoms were yellow with dust and the silver-bordered satin ribbons were fraying at the edge. She threw it into the fire. It flared up faster than a dry straw. Then it looked like a red bush on the ashes, slowly disintegrating. She watched it burn. The little cardboard berries burst, the brass wires twisted, the braiding melted; and the shriveled paper petals fluttered on the grate like black butterflies, then flew up the chimney.

When they left Tostes in the month of March, Madame Bovary was pregnant.

PART II

I

Yonville-l'Abbaye (so named because of an old Capuchin abbey even the ruins of which no longer exist) is a small town about twenty-five miles from Rouen, between the Abbeville and Beauvais roads, at the bottom of a valley watered by the Rieule. This is a small stream that empties into the Andelle after working three mills near its mouth. It contains a few trout that boys enjoy fishing for on Sundays.

You leave the highway at La Boissière and continue straight on until you reach the summit of Leux Hill, at which point the valley appears. The river crossing it divides it into two distinct regions; everything on the left is pasture, everything on the right is farmland. The meadow stretches out beneath several rolling hills and joins, behind them, the Bray pasturelands, while on the east the plain climbs slowly, becoming wider, spreading its gold-colored grainfields as far as the eye can see. The water flowing at the edge of the grass divides the colors of the meadows and the fields with a streak of white and makes the countryside resemble a large spread-out cloak with a velvet collar edged with silver braid.

At the end of the valley appear the oaks of the Argueil forest and the steep slopes of Saint-Jean Hill, streaked from top to bottom by long, uneven, red tracks. These are traces of rain, and their brick-red tones, cutting finely over the gray color of the mountain, come from the iron particles contained in the springs that flow in the surrounding area.

This is the border area of Normandy, Picardy, and the Île-de-France, a bastard section where the language is without accent as the scenery is without character. It is here that the worst Neufchâtel cheeses of the entire district are made. Here, too, farming is expensive because a lot of manure is needed to enrich the crumbly soil filled with sand and pebbles.

Until 1835 there was no proper road to Yonville; but about that time the local government built a byroad connecting Abbeville and Amiens that sometimes is used by wagoners going from Rouen to Flanders.

Nevertheless, Yonville-l'Abbaye has remained stagnant despite its new outlets. Instead of improving its cultivable land, the farmers cling stubbornly to pasture despite the decrease in value, and the lazy little town turning away from the plain has continued its automatic growth toward the river. You can see it from afar, sprawling out along the bank like a cowherd taking a siesta at the edge of the water.

At the foot of the hill, past the bridge, is a road planted with young aspens that leads in a straight line to the first houses of the area. These are enclosed by hedges and set in the center of yards filled with scattered buildings, winepresses, cart sheds, and distilleries placed under thick trees whose branches support ladders, poles, and scythes. The thatched roofs, like fur hats pulled down over the eyes, cover nearly one third of the low windows (which have bulging panes adorned with a knot in the center, like the base of bottles). An occasional scrawny pear sapling leans on the plaster wall diagonally crossed by black joists. In the ground floor doorways a small revolving gate keeps out the chicks who come to peck at the brown bread crumbs dipped in cider. As you walk on, the yards become narrower, the houses are closer together, the hedges disappear; a bundle of ferns swings from a window at the end of a broomstick. There is a blacksmith's forge and then a wheelwright's shop with two or three new carts outside obstructing the road. Then, through an opening in the wall, you can see a new house in the middle of a circular lawn on which rests a Cupid with a finger in his mouth. Two cast-iron urns are set at each side of the front steps and a coat of arms gleams on the door. This is the notary's home, the finest in the area.

The church is across the street, twenty feet farther down, on one side of the square. The small cemetery around it, enclosed by a wall waist high, is so filled with graves that the old stones sunk into the ground form a continual pavement marked off in equal squares by the grass pushing up in be-

tween. The church was rebuilt in the last years of the reign
of Charles X. The roof's wooden arch is starting to rot on
top and there are occasional black holes in the blue color.
Above the door, where the organ would be, is a loft for the
men, reached by a spiral staircase that creaks under their
wooden shoes.

Daylight coming through the plain glass windows slants
across the benches lined up perpendicular to the walls;
the occasional straw mats nailed to them have large lettered
signs below them: "Monsieur So-and-So's Bench." Further
down, where the nave narrows, the confessional box is bal-
anced by a statuette of the Virgin, dressed in satin, with a
tulle veil sown with silver stars on her head, and her cheeks
a deep purple like some Sandwich Islands idol. Finally at the
back there is a replica of the Holy Family, sent by the minister of the interior, which dominates the high altar between
four candlesticks. The pine choir stalls have remained un-
painted.

The marketplace, which consists of a tiled roof supported
by about twenty pillars, takes up about half of the Yonville
square. The town hall, on the corner next to the pharmacist's house, was built "to the plans of a Paris architect" and
is a sort of Greek temple. It has three Ionic columns on the
ground floor and a semicircular gallery above that ends with a
pediment occupied by a Gallic cock leaning with one foot
on the constitution and holding in the other the scales of
justice.

But it is Monsieur Homais's pharmacy, facing the Golden
Lion Inn, that most attracts the eye. Especially in the evening
when his lamp is lit and the red and green apothecary jars
in his window send their colors across the sidewalk. Then
through them, as in Bengal lights, the pharmacist's shadow
can be seen as he leans on his desk. From top to bottom his
house is papered with signs written in script, round hand and
in block letters: "Vichy, Seltzer, and Barèges Waters; Purify-
ing Agents; Raspail Medicine; Arabian Racahout; Darcet's
Lozenges; Rengault's Salve; Bandages; Bath Preparations;
Medicinal Chocolate; etc." And the sign that stretches the
entire width of the store announces in gilded letters:
"Homais, Pharmacist." At the rear of the shop, behind the
large scales on the counter, the "Laboratory" can be seen
above a glass door in the middle of which the name "Ho-

mais" appears once more in gilded letters against a black background.

There is nothing else to see in Yonville. The street, the only one, is as long as a rifle bullet's range and has a few stores on either side; it stops short at the road bend. If you leave it on the right and follow along the foot of Saint-Jean Hill, you will soon reach the cemetery.

In order to enlarge it during the cholera epidemic, they removed part of the wall and bought three acres of land adjoining it; but this new portion is virtually uninhabited, the graves as before continuing to crowd together near the gate. The watchman, who is also the gravedigger and the church sexton (thus deriving a double profit from the parish corpses) has utilized the vacant land to plant potatoes there. From year to year, however, his little field narrows, and when an epidemic strikes, he doesn't know if he should be happy about the deaths or miserable about the burials.

"You feed on the dead, Lestiboudois!" the parish priest finally said to him one day.

This morbid remark made him ponder; it bothered him for some time. But he still continues to farm his crop and even maintains coolly that his vegetables come up without cultivation.

Since the events about to be recorded here, nothing has changed in Yonville. The tinplate tricolor flag still revolves above the church steeple; the two calico streamers outside the store of the dry-goods man still flap in the wind; the pharmacist's fetuses, like packets of white tinder, grow progressively more rotten in their muddy alcohol; and above the main entrance of the inn, the old golden lion, its gilt worn off by the rains, still displays its poodlelike mane to passersby.

The evening on which the Bovarys were to arrive at Yonville, the Widow Lefrançois, mistress of the inn, was so busy that the perspiration poured off in droplets as she busied herself with her pots. The next day was market day in the town, and meat had to be cut in advance, pullets cleaned, soup and coffee prepared. Besides, she had to feed her boarders, as well as the doctor, his wife, and their maid. The billiard room rang with bursts of laughter. Three millers in the small parlor were calling for brandy. The wood blazed, the coal crackled, and piles of dishes on the long kitchen tables, set down among quarters of raw lamb, trembled at the jolts caused by the spinach chopper. The chickens could be heard squawking as the kitchen maid chased them in order to cut off their heads.

A pockmarked man in green leather slippers, with a gold-tasseled velvet cap on his head, was warming his back against the fireplace. His face expressed nothing but self-satisfaction, and he seemed as much at peace as the goldfinch hanging above his head in a wicker cage; this was the pharmacist.

"Artémise!" shouted the landlady; "chop some firewood! Fill the pitchers! Bring some brandy! Hurry! If I only knew what dessert to serve the people you're waiting for. Good heavens, the moving men are starting their racket in the billiard room again. And their cart is standing right in front of the door! The Hirondelle may smash into it when it gets here! Call 'Polyte to move it away. Just think, they must have played fifteen games since this morning, Monsieur Homais, and drunk eight jugs of cider! They'll tear my cloth," she continued, looking at them from afar with a skimmer in her hand.

"They won't do so much damage," Monsieur Homais answered; "you can buy another."

"Another billiard cloth!" the widow exclaimed.

"This one's falling apart, Madame Lefrançois. I keep telling you, you're making a mistake! A mistake! The players want narrow pockets and heavy cues today. They've stopped playing billiards the way they used to; everything's changed! One must move with the times! Now take Tellier—"

The landlady's face flushed with anger. The pharmacist added: "No matter what you say, his billiard table is nicer than yours. And suppose they thought of sponsoring a match to aid Poland or for the victims of the Lyons flood—"

"Good-for-nothings like him don't frighten me!" the landlady interrupted, shrugging her immense shoulders. "Come on now, Monsieur Homais, as long as the Golden Lion exists, people will come here. My nest is nicely feathered, thank you. You'll see the Café Français closed instead, one of these mornings, and with a pretty sign on the shutters! Change my billiard table," she continued, talking to herself, "that's so convenient for sorting laundry! Why, I've bedded down six travelers at a time on it during hunting season! Where is that slowpoke Hivert!"

"Are you waiting for him to get here before you serve your guests' dinner?" the pharmacist asked.

"Wait for him? What about Monsieur Binet? At six o'clock sharp you'll see him come in. There's no one in the world like him when it comes to being on time. He always has to have his place in the small parlor. Sooner die than eat somewhere else, and he's so fussy! And so choosy about cider! Not at all like Monsieur Léon. Now, he comes sometimes at seven, sometimes even seven-thirty. And he doesn't just stare at his food. Such a nice young man! Never a loud word."

"That's the difference between someone who's received an education and an old cavalryman turned tax collector."

The clock struck six. Binet entered.

He wore a blue frock coat hanging straight down his thin body. His leather cap with the ear flaps tied on top of his head revealed, under the turned-up visor, a bald forehead pressed flat by the helmet worn so many years. He wore a black waistcoat, a horsehair collar, gray trousers, and, in all seasons, carefully polished boots with two parallel swellings where his toes turned up. Not one hair was out of place in the light-colored beard that encircled his jawline like the border of a flower bed, framing his uninteresting face with its small eyes and aquiline nose. He was an able card player, a skilled hunter, and an excellent penman. He kept a lathe at home and made napkin rings with which he littered up his house, with the jealousy of an artist and the selfishness of a bourgeois.

He headed toward the small parlor; but the three millers had to be ejected first; and while they were setting his table, Binet remained silent in his place near the stove. Then as usual, he closed the door and took off his hat.

"His tongue won't wear out from being polite!" said the pharmacist as soon as he was alone with the landlady.

"He never talks much," she answered. "Last week there were two traveling salesmen here, boys full of fun. They told such jokes one evening that I laughed till I cried. And he sat there all clammed up, not saying a word."

"Yes," said the pharmacist, "no imagination, no humor, no social talents."

"But he's supposed to be clever," the landlady objected.

"Clever!" Monsieur Homais retorted. "He clever? Maybe in his own field," he added in a calmer tone.

He continued: "Should an active businessman, a doctor, or a pharmacist be so absorbed in his affairs that he becomes odd and even ill-tempered, I can understand it. Such instances have been recorded. But at least they think about something. Take me, for instance, how many times have I searched for my pen on my desk to write a label, only to end up finding it behind my ear where I had stuck it!"

As he spoke, Madame Lefrançois went out to the doorstep to see if the Hirondelle were in sight. She started as a man dressed in black suddenly came into the kitchen. In the dying glimmers of twilight one could see that he had a ruddy complexion and an athletic body.

"May I help you, Monsieur le Curé?" the landlady asked, reaching for one of the brass candlesticks lined up along the mantelpiece. "Would you like something? A drop of cassis, a glass of wine?"

The priest refused quite politely. He had come for his umbrella: he had forgotten it the other day at the Ernemont convent. After asking Madame Lefrançois to send it to him at the parish house in the evening, he headed back to the church, where the Angelus was ringing.

When the pharmacist could no longer hear the sound of his shoes in the square, he began criticizing the curé's recent conduct. The refusal of a drink seemed to him the most detestable hypocrisy. All priests tippled in secret and were trying to bring back the days of the tithe.

The landlady came to the curé's defense.

"And anyway, he could bend four of you over his knee. Last year he helped our people bring in the hay. He carried six bales at a time, that's how strong he is!"

"Bravo!" said the pharmacist. "So send your daughters to confess to such healthy brutes. Now, if I were the government, I would want the priests bled once a month. Yes, Madame Lefrançois, an extensive bloodletting every month for the sake of law and order."

"Oh, stop talking, Monsieur Homais. You're blaspheming. You have no religion."

The pharmacist answered, "I do have a religion—my religion; and it's even deeper than all of theirs with their mummery and their tricks! On the contrary, I worship God, I believe in a Supreme Being, in a Creator whoever He is, it doesn't matter, who placed us here below to fulfill our duties to family and state, but I don't need to go into a church to

kiss silver plates and fatten up a bunch of fakers who eat
better than we do! You can worship Him just as well in
the woods or in a field or even by studying the heavens,
like the ancients. God, for me, is the God of Socrates,
Franklin, Voltaire, and Béranger! I am for the *Savoyard
Vicar's Profession of Faith* and for the immortal principles of
eighty-nine! So I cannot accept a doddering deity who parades around in his garden with a cane in his hand, sends
his friend up a whale's belly, dies with a shriek, and is
resurrected three days later. These things are obviously absurd, and besides, they're completely opposed to the laws
of physics; which incidentally shows us that the priests have
always wallowed in a shameful ignorance in which they try
to engulf their entire flock!"

He stopped talking and looked around for an audience.
In his fervor the pharmacist had believed himself for a moment in a Town Council plenary session. But the mistress
of the inn had stopped listening to him. She was straining her
ears to hear a distant rumble. The sound of a carriage mingled with a clicking of loose chains hitting the ground, and
the Hirondelle finally stopped at the door.

It had a yellow body supported by two large wheels that,
reaching to the level of the tilt, prevented the passengers
from seeing the road and soiled their shoulders with mud.
The small panes of its narrow transoms rattled in their
frames when the carriage was closed, and there were mud
spots scattered through the old layers of dust that even the
rainstorms did not quite wash off. It was drawn by three
horses, one leading and two in the shafts, and when it went
downhill its bottom portion would bump into the ground.

A group of Yonville residents arrived in the square, all
talking at once, asking for news, information, and food baskets.
Hivert did not know which one to answer first. It was he
who did all the village purchasing in the city. He went to the
shops, brought rolls of leather to the shoemaker, iron to
the blacksmith, a barrel of herring for the inn, bonnets from
the milliner, and wigs from the hairdresser. As he drove back
he distributed his packages along the road, throwing them
over garden walls from his seat and shouting at the top of his
lungs while the horses trotted along by themselves.

He had been delayed by an accident; Madame Bovary's
greyhound had run off across the fields. They whistled for it
a good fifteen minutes. Hivert even retraced his steps for

about a mile, hoping to catch a glimpse of it any minute; but they finally had to move on. Emma burst into tears and lost her temper. She accused Charles of causing the tragedy. Monsieur Lheureux, the dry-goods merchant, who happened to be with her in the carriage, tried to console her with many stories about lost dogs recognizing their masters after many years. There was one such case, he said, of a dog who came back to Paris from Constantinople. Another had done a hundred and twenty miles in a straight line, swimming four rivers. And his own father had owned a poodle that after being lost for twelve years had suddenly jumped on his back in the street one evening as he was going out to dinner.

II

Emma alighted first, followed by Félicité, Monsieur Lheureux, and a nurse. They had to awaken Charles, who had fallen into a deep sleep in his corner as soon as night fell.

Homais introduced himself. He offered his respects to Madame, his compliments to Monsieur, said that he was delighted to have the opportunity to be of some service to them, and added with a cordial air that he had presumed to invite himself along in his wife's absence.

Madame Bovary entered the kitchen and walked over to the fireplace. She took hold of her dress at the knees with the tips of two fingers, and having lifted it in this fashion to the ankles, held out to the flame a foot encased in a black boot, above the leg of lamb turning on a spit. The fire cast a glow over her entire body, its harsh glare penetrating the cloth of her dress, the even pores of her white skin, and the eyelids that she blinked from time to time. The wind coming in through the half-open door intensified the reflection.

On the other side of the fireplace a fair-haired young man looked at her in silence.

Since he was very bored in Yonville, where he was a clerk at Maître Guillaumin's, Monsieur Léon Dupuis (it was

he who was the second of the regular visitors to the Golden
Lion) kept postponing his dinner in the hope that some traveler with whom he could talk would come to the inn. On the
days when he finished his work early, he arrived exactly on
time for want of knowing what else to do and had to endure
Binet's company from soup to cheese. Therefore he accepted
with joy the landlady's suggestion that he dine with the new
arrivals, and they filed into the large room when Madame
Lefrançois had ostentatiously set four places.

Homais asked for permission to keep his skullcap on his
head for fear of catching cold.

Then, turning toward his neighbor: "You are doubtless
a bit tired? We're so frightfully jolted about in our Hirondelle!"

"I am," Emma answered, "but moving around always
amuses me. I love a change of scene."

"It's so dull to live nailed to the same spot," the clerk said,
sighing.

"If you were like me," Charles said, "continually forced
to be on horseback—"

"But," Léon went on, addressing Madame Bovary, "nothing
should be more agreeable, it seems to me. When one has the
choice," he added.

"Besides," the apothecary said, "practicing medicine isn't
too strenuous in these parts because the condition of our
roads permits the use of a trap, and generally, the fees are
pretty good since the farmers are well off. From the medical point of view, we have few serious illnesses apart from
ordinary cases of enteritis, bronchitis, liver ailments, etc.,
and occasionally some intermittent fevers at harvesttime.
Nothing of special note except for many cases of scrofula,
caused no doubt by the deplorable sanitary conditions in the
farmhands' lodgings. Ah! You'll find a lot of prejudices to
combat, Monsieur Bovary, much stubbornness in defense of
traditional methods, with which all your scientific efforts are
going to clash daily. For we still have recourse here to
novenas, relics, and the priest, instead of going naturally
to the doctor or the pharmacist. The climate, however, is not
at all bad, and we even count several ninety-year-olds in
the district. The thermometer (I've made some observations)
goes down in winter to four degrees and in the hot season
touches twenty-five, thirty degrees Centigrade at the most,
which gives us a maximum of twenty-four Réaumur or fifty-

four degrees Fahrenheit, to use the English measure—no more! You see, we are sheltered from the north wind by the Argueil forest on one side and from the west wind by the Saint-Jean Hill on the other. That warmth, however, which arises from the steam given off by the river and the presence of considerable cattle in the meadows, cattle that exhale as you know a great deal of ammonia, that is to say, nitrogen, hydrogen, and oxygen (no, nitrogen and hydrogen only) and which, sucking up the earth's humus and blending all these different emanations, unites them in one bundle, so to speak, and combining with whatever electricity there is in the atmosphere, could in the long run, as in tropical countries, engender unhealthy air; that heat, I say, finds itself tempered in the very place it comes from—from which it should come, I should say, from the south—by the southeastern winds, which, having refreshed themselves passing over the Seine, sometimes reach us all at once, like the winds from Russia!"

"Are there any pleasant places to walk around here?" Madame Bovary continued, speaking to the young man.

"Very few," he answered. "There's one spot called the Pasture on top of the hill, at the edge of the forest. Sometimes on Sunday I go there with a book and watch the sunset."

"I find nothing as inspiring as sunsets," she said, "but especially at the seashore."

"Oh, I adore the sea," Monsieur Léon said.

"And don't you agree," Madame Bovary continued, "that your spirit soars more freely over that limitless expanse? That just looking at it elevates your soul and inspires thoughts about the infinite and the ideal?"

"Mountain landscapes do the same," Léon said. "I have a cousin who traveled through Switzerland last year, and he told me that you can't imagine the poetry of the lakes, the charm of the waterfalls, the gigantic effect of the glaciers. You see evergreens of an unbelievable size spanning the torrents, cabins jutting out over precipices, and there are entire valleys a thousand feet below you, when the clouds part. Sights such as these overwhelm you, dispose you toward prayer and ecstasy! I'm no longer surprised about that famous musician who used to play the piano in front of some imposing sight in order to stimulate his imagination."

"Are you a musician?" she asked.

"No, but I like music very much," he answered.

"Ah, don't listen to him, Madame Bovary," Homais interrupted, leaning over his plate. "It's pure modesty. Why, dear boy, just the other day in your room you were singing *The Guardian Angel* magnificently. I could hear you from my laboratory. You were sending it out like an actor."

Léon happened to lodge at the pharmacist's house, where he had a small room on the second floor facing the square. He blushed at this compliment from his landlord, who had already turned toward the doctor and was enumerating to him the principal inhabitants of Yonville. He was telling stories and supplying information. The notary's exact fortune was not known. As for the Tuvache business firm, they were making a lot of trouble.

Emma went on: "What kind of music do you prefer?"

"German, the sort that sets you dreaming."

"Do you know Italian music?"

"Not yet, but I'll hear some next year when I go to Paris to finish my law studies."

"I've just had the honor," said the pharmacist, "of telling your husband about poor Yanoda, who ran off. Thanks to the idiotic mistakes he made, you will find yourselves enjoying one of the most comfortable houses in Yonville. It's especially convenient for a doctor because it has a door to the lane so that people can enter and leave without being seen. Besides, it's furnished with all sorts of conveniences; it has a laundry, kitchen and pantry, sitting room, storeroom for fruit, etc. He was a bit of a spendthrift. He had an arbor built at the end of the garden beside the river just to have a place to drink beer in summer, and if Madame likes gardening, she'll be able—"

"My wife doesn't care much about it," Charles said. "She prefers to stay in her room all the time and read, even though she's been told to exercise."

"Like myself," Léon said. "What better occupation, really, than to spend the evening at the fireside with a book, with the wind beating on the windows and the lamp burning bright?"

"You're right," she said, fixing her large black eyes on him.

"Nothing disturbs your thoughts," he continued. "The hours pass. Without moving, you walk through the countries you see in your mind's eye; and your thoughts, caught up in

the story, stop at the details or rush through for the plot.
You pretend you're the characters and feel it's your own
heart beating beneath their costumes."

"I know exactly what you mean!" she said.

"Have you ever happened to come across in a book some
vague notion that you've had," Léon went on, "some obscure
idea that returns from afar and that seems to express completely your most subtle feelings?"

"Oh, yes!" she answered.

"That's why I love the poets above all," he said. "I find
verse more tender than prose and much more moving."

"Yet poets are tiring in the long run," Emma said. "Now,
I adore stories that you can read in one gulp, stories that
frighten you. I hate everyday heroes and restrained emotions
like the ones in real life."

"Of course," the clerk said, "those works that don't affect
the emotions miss the real goal of art, I think. With all
the disillusionments of life, it is good to be able to identify
oneself mentally with noble characters, pure affections, and
portrayals of happiness. As for myself, living here far from
the world, it's my one distraction. Yonville has so little to
offer!"

"Like Tostes, no doubt," said Emma. "I always subscribed
to the circulating library there."

"If Madame will do me the honor of using it," said the
pharmacist, who had heard these last words, "I myself place
at your disposal a library composed of the best authors: Voltaire, Rousseau, Delille, Walter Scott, *The Literary Echo*,
etc. Moreover, I receive various periodicals, among them
the daily *Rouen Beacon*, since I have the advantage of being
its correspondent for the area of Buchy, Forges, Neufchâtel,
Yonville, and the surroundings."

They had been at the table for the last two and a half
hours because Artémise, the servant girl, dragging her old slippers over the flagstones with great indifference, had brought
the dishes in separately, forgotten some things, misunderstood
other things, and left open the door to the billiard room so
that the latch banged against the wall.

Without being aware of it, Léon had placed his foot on one
of the crossbars of Madame Bovary's chair as he spoke. She
was wearing a small blue silk scarf that kept her frilled cambric ruff in place, and her chin would gently dip into or

emerge from the material as she moved her head. Sitting
side by side as Charles and the pharmacist chatted, they
entered into one of those vague conversations in which
chance remarks inevitably lead to the discovery of common
tastes. They discussed everything during dinner: Paris plays,
titles of novels, new quadrilles, and the world they didn't
know, Tostes where she had lived, Yonville where they
were.

After coffee was served, Félicité went off to prepare the
bedroom in the new house, and soon after, the diners arose.
Madame Lefrançois was sleeping near the embers, and the
ostler, with a lantern in his hand, was waiting to lead
Monsieur and Madame Bovary to their new home. Wisps of
straw were stuck in his red hair, and he limped with his left
leg. He took the curé's umbrella in his other hand and they
started off.

The town was fast asleep. The marketplace pillars cast
long shadows. The ground was all gray, as on a summer
night.

The doctor's house being but fifty feet from the inn, it
was necessary to say good night almost immediately, and the
company parted.

From the moment she entered the hall, Emma felt the
cold of the plaster falling over her shoulders like a damp
cloth. The walls were freshly painted and the wooden steps
creaked. In the first-floor bedroom a whitish light passed
through the curtainless windows. Through it one could see
treetops, and farther away, the meadow, half drowned in the
mist that wreathed around the river's edge like smoke in the
moonlight. Helter-skelter in the middle of the room there
were chest drawers, bottles, curtain rods, gilt poles, mat-
tresses over the chairs, and basins on the floor—the two men
who had brought the furniture had dumped everything there
without a care.

It was the fourth time she was sleeping in an unknown
place. The first had been the day she entered the convent,
the second her arrival at Tostes, the third at Vaubyessard, the
fourth here; and each of them had turned out to mark a
new phase in her life. She did not believe that things could
turn out the same in different places, and since her life so
far had been bad, maybe that which was to come would be
better.

III

As she got up the next morning, she noticed the clerk in the square. She was in her dressing gown. He glanced up and greeted her. She nodded rapidly and closed the window.

Léon waited all day for six o'clock to come; but when he entered the inn, he found only Monsieur Binet at the table.

The dinner of the previous evening had been a considerable event for him; never until now had he spoken for two consecutive hours with a "lady." How then had he been able to express to her so eloquently so many things he wouldn't have said so well before? He was shy by nature, with the sort of reserve made up of both modesty and dissimulation. In Yonville it was found that he had "very elegant" manners. He listened to older people's opinions and showed no extreme political views, a remarkable thing for a young man. Then too he possessed talents: he painted in watercolors, could read the key of G, and liked to discuss literature after dinner when he wasn't playing cards. Monsieur Homais valued him for his education, and Madame Homais was fond of him for his friendliness since he often took the children to the garden. The Homais brood was a grubby lot, very badly brought up and slightly sluggish, like the mother. Besides the maid, they were looked after by Justin, the pharmacist's apprentice, a distant cousin of Monsieur Homais who had been taken into the house out of charity and who also performed domestic duties.

The apothecary turned out to be the best of neighbors. He gave Madame Bovary information about the tradesmen, had his cider merchant call on her, tasted the brew himself, and supervised the proper installation of the cask in the cellar; furthermore, he showed her how to obtain butter at a cheap price and made an arrangement with Lestiboudois, the sexton, who, in addition to his ecclesiastical and mortuary functions, took care of the principal gardens of Yonville by the hour or the year—as was preferred.

It was not sheer altruism that prompted the pharmacist to so much obsequious cordiality. There was a plan beneath it.

He had violated Article 1 of the law of 19th Ventôse, year XI, which prohibits the practice of medicine to anyone not holding a diploma. On the basis of some obscure denunciations against him, Homais had been summoned to Rouen to the private office of the royal prosecutor. The magistrate, with his ermine robe on his shoulders and wearing the official headpiece, had received him standing up. It was in the morning before the court sat. The policemen's heavy boots could be heard in the corridor, and in the distance the faint noise of huge locks being turned. The pharmacist's ears rang so intensely he thought he was going to have a stroke. He could see himself in the lowest depths of a dungeon, his family in tears, the pharmacy sold, all his display bottles dispersed. He had to go into a café for a glass of rum and seltzer to calm his nerves.

Little by little the memory of the warning grew weaker, and he continued as before to give harmless consultations in his back room. But the mayor had it in for him; some colleagues were jealous. He had to watch his step. By putting Monsieur Bovary in his debt with his favors, he hoped to gain his gratitude and preclude his talking should he notice something later. And so, every morning, Homais would deliver the paper to the doctor and often would leave the pharmacy a minute in the afternoon to visit him and chat.

Charles was despondent. There were no patients. He would sit silently for long hours, fall asleep in his consulting room, or watch his wife sewing. To distract himself he became the handyman in his home and even tried to redo the attic with some paint that the painters had left behind. But money worries preoccupied him. He had spent so much for the repairs in Tostes, for Emma's wardrobe, and for the moving that the entire dowry, more than three thousand crowns, had dwindled away in two years. Then there were so many things damaged or lost in transit from Tostes to Yonville (including the plaster curé, which had fallen from the wagon because of a strong jar and smashed into a thousand pieces on the Quincampoix pavement).

Another, less trying, worry distracted him—his wife's pregnancy. As her term drew to a close, he cherished her more. It was another bond of the flesh between them and seemed to deepen their union and render it more complex. When he watched from afar her lumbering tread and the slow swaying of her uncorseted figure, when he looked at her at his ease as they sat facing each other and she relaxed wearily into her armchair, then his happiness could not contain itself. He would get up, kiss her, caress her face, call her "little mother," try to cajole her into dancing, and half laughing, half crying, utter all sorts of playful endearments that came to his mind. The idea of having begotten a child delighted him. Now he lacked nothing. He knew all there was to know about human existence, and he sat down before its table, as it were, with both elbows planted serenely.

Emma was at first bewildered, then she yearned for the child to be born in order to know how it felt to be a mother. But not being able to spend as freely as she wished— to have a cradle shaped like a boat with pink silk curtains and embroidered baby caps—she abandoned her dreams of a layette in an excess of bitterness and ordered the entire outfit from a village seamstress without choosing or discussing anything. And so she did not enjoy those preparations that stimulate maternal tenderness, and her affection from the beginning was perhaps weakened on that account.

However, since Charles spoke about the child at every meal, she soon thought about it in a more sustained way.

She hoped for a son; he would be strong and dark and she would call him Georges. The thought of having a male child was an anticipatory revenge for all her earlier helplessness. A man, at least, is free. He can explore passions and countries, surmount obstacles, taste the most exotic pleasures. But a woman is continually held back. Inert and flexible at the same time, she has both the susceptibilities of the flesh and legal restrictions against her. Her will, like the veil of her hat that is tied by a ribbon, reacts to every wind; there is always some desire to respond to, some convention that restricts action.

She gave birth one Sunday, at about six A.M., as the sun rose.

"It's a girl!" said Charles.

She turned her head away and fainted.

Madame Homais ran over almost immediately and kissed her, as did old Madame Lefrançois of the Golden Lion.

The pharmacist, as became a man of discretion, merely addressed some provisional congratulations through the half-open door. He asked to see the child and found it well formed.

During her confinement she spent a lot of time seeking a name for her daughter. At first she reviewed all those with Italian endings, such as Clara, Louisa, Amanda, Atala; she was rather partial to Galsuinde and even more to Yseult or Léocadie. Charles wanted the child to be named for his mother; Emma was against it. They went through the calendar of saints' names from one end to the other and consulted strangers.

"Monsieur Léon," said the pharmacist, "with whom I was talking about it the other day, is surprised that you don't choose Madeleine. It's very much in style now."

But Madame Bovary senior protested strongly against this sinner's name. As for Monsieur Homais, he had a predilection for all names that recalled a great man, a famous deed, or a generous conception, and it was in this vein that he had baptized his four children. Thus Napoleon represented glory, and Franklin liberty. Irma perhaps was a concession to romanticism, but Athalie paid homage to the greatest masterpiece of the French theater. Homais's philosophical convictions did not interfere with his artistic tastes; the thinker in him did not stifle the man of sensibility. He knew how to discriminate, where to draw the line between imagination and fanaticism. In Racine's tragedy, for example, he abhorred the idea but admired the style, he cursed the conception but applauded all the details, and although detesting the characters, waxed enthusiastic at their speeches. He was transported when he read the great passages, but when he remembered that the priests were taking advantage of them for their own purpose, he was desolate; and with these confusions of sentiment in which he was thrust, he wanted at the same time to set a laurel wreath on Racine's head with his two hands and to argue with him for a good quarter of an hour.

Finally, Emma remembered that at the Vaubyessard château she had heard the marquise call some young woman Berthe. From that point on the name was decided, and as father Rouault could not come, they asked Monsieur Homais to be godfather. His gifts were all products from his establishment, to wit: six boxes of jujubes, an entire jar of racahout, three tins of marshmallow, and half a dozen sticks of sugar candy that he had found in a cupboard. There was a festive dinner the evening of the ceremony. The curé attended, and excitement ran high. Over the liqueur Monsieur Homais quoted from Béranger's *Le Dieu des bonnes gens,* Monsieur Léon sang a barcarolle, and Madame Bovary senior, who was the godmother, sang a ballad from the days of the Empire. Then Monsieur Bovary senior asked that they bring down the baby and began to baptize her once more with a glass of champagne that he was pouring from above on her head. This mockery of the first sacraments infuriated Abbé Bournisien. Old Bovary countered by citing a passage from the *La Guerre des dieux;* the curé rose to leave. The ladies pleaded; Homais intervened, and they managed to reseat the clergyman, who quietly sipped his half-finished demitasse of coffee.

Monsieur Bovary senior remained one more month in Yonville, where he dazzled the inhabitants by a superb silver-trimmed police cap that he wore in the morning while smoking his pipe in the square. Since he also had a habit of drinking a lot of brandy, he would often send the maid to the Golden Lion to buy him a bottle, which they charged to his son's account; and he used up his daughter-in-law's entire supply of eau-de-cologne to scent his scarves.

Emma was not at all displeased by his company. He had traveled throughout the world; he spoke of Berlin, Vienna, Strasbourg, of his days as an officer, of his old mistresses, of the elegant dinners he had attended. Moreover, he was attentive and would clasp her by the waist occasionally on the staircase or in the garden and shout: "Look out for yourself, Charles!"

Then Madame Bovary senior began to worry about her son's happiness, and fearing that eventually her husband would have an immoral influence on the young woman's notions, she made haste to leave. Her apprehensions may have been more serious. Monsieur Bovary was not a man to respect anything.

One day Emma was suddenly smitten with the desire to see her small daughter, who had been put to nurse with the carpenter's wife. So without checking the almanac to see if the six weeks of the Virgin were over, she set out toward the Rollet dwelling, which was at the end of the village, at the bottom of the hill, between the main road and the meadows.

It was noon. The houses had their shutters closed and the slate roofs that gleamed under the harsh glare of the blue sky seemed to be sending off sparks from the gabletops. A sultry wind was blowing. Emma felt herself weakening as she walked; the pebbles of the sidewalk hurt her; she hesitated, wondering whether to return home or stop in somewhere and sit down.

At that moment, Monsieur Léon came out of a nearby door with a bundle of papers under his arm. He walked over to greet her and placed himself in the shadow in front of Lheureux's store under the gray awning that projected outward.

Madame Bovary said that she was on her way to see her child but that she was beginning to feel tired.

"If—" Léon began, not daring to say more.

"Are you going somewhere?" she asked.

On the clerk's negative reply, she asked him to accompany her. By evening, this was known in Yonville, and Madame Tuvache, the mayor's wife, announced in her maid's hearing that "Madame Bovary was compromising herself."

To arrive at the wet nurse's home, it was necessary to turn left at the end of the street in the direction of the cemetery and follow a narrow path lined with privet that ran between some tumbledown cottages and yard walls. The privets were in bloom, as were the veronica, the dog roses, the nettles, and the slim brambles thrusting forth from the bushes. Through the gaps in the hedges could be seen, outside the huts, pigs on a manure heap and some tethered cows rubbing their horns against the tree trunks. The two of them walked leisurely side by side, she leaning on his arm and he adjusting his pace to hers. A swarm of flies buzzed before them in the warm air.

They recognized the house by an old nut tree that shaded it. Low built and covered with brown tile, it had a string of onions hanging on the outside under the attic window. Some sticks of firewood propped against the thorn hedge surrounded a lettuce patch, a few lavender bushes, and some sweet peas trained on sticks. Dirty water was trickling over the grass, and all around were strewn nondescript garments—knitted stockings, a red calico nightdress, and a large coarse sheet spread out over the hedge. At the sound of the gate, the nurse appeared, holding in one arm an infant she was suckling. With the other hand she was pulling a puny little boy with scabs covering his face, the son of a Rouen hatmaker whose parents, too preoccupied with their business, had left him in the country.

"Come in," she said. "Your little girl is asleep."

The downstairs bedroom, the only one in the house, contained a large, uncurtained bed placed against the back wall, and the kneading trough was set against the side with the window, one pane of which was patched with a blue-paper star. In the corner, behind the door, a row of boots with shiny hobnails was lined up under the drainboard near a bottle of oil with a feather in its neck, and a Mathieu Laensberg almanac lay on the dusty mantelpiece among gunflints, candle ends, and bits of tinder. The final luxury in the room was a picture of Fame blowing her trumpets, no doubt cut out of some perfume advertisement and nailed to the wall with half a dozen shoe nails.

Emma's child was asleep on the floor in a wicker cradle. She picked her up in the cover she was wrapped in and began to sing softly and sway.

Léon was walking about in the room. It seemed strange to him to see this woman in a nankeen dress in the heart of all this misery. Madame Bovary blushed; he turned away, thinking that his eyes perhaps had revealed some impertinence. Then she replaced the child, who had just thrown up on her collar. The nurse came over immediately to wipe it off, insisting that it wouldn't show.

"She gives me plenty more," she said, "and I spend all day washing her! Perhaps you'd be kind enough to tell Camus the grocer to let me have some soap when I need it? It'll be even easier for you if I don't have to keep bothering you."

"Certainly," said Emma. "Good-bye, Madame Rollet!"

And she left, wiping her feet on the doorstep.

The good woman accompanied her through her yard, speaking of the trouble she had of getting up during the night.

"I'm so exhausted from it sometimes that I fall asleep on my chair. Maybe you could give me a pound of ground coffee that I can take in the morning with some milk. It will last me a month."

After acknowledging her thanks, Madame Bovary started off. She had barely moved down the path when the sound of clogs made her turn her head. It was the wet nurse.

"What's the matter?"

The woman, pulling her aside under an elm tree, began to speak of her husband, who, with his job and the six francs a year that the captain—

"Get to the point faster," Emma said.

"Very well!" the wet nurse continued, sighing between each word. "I'm afraid that he'll feel bad seeing me take coffee all by myself. You know how men are—"

"You'll have some," Emma repeated. "I'll give you enough! You're annoying me!"

"Oh dear, my lady, he has terrible pains in his chest from his wounds. He says that even cider weakens him."

"Do hurry up, Madame Rollet."

"So," the latter continued, dropping a curtsy, "if it weren't asking too much of you"—she curtsied one more time—"if you would"—and she implored with a look—"a small jug of brandy," she finally said, "and I'll rub some on your little girl's feet; they're as tender as your tongue."

Rid of the nurse, Emma took Monsieur Léon's arm again. She walked rapidly for a while; then she slowed down and her wandering gaze met the young man's shoulder. His frock coat had a black velvet collar over which fell his chestnut hair, smooth and well combed. She noticed his nails, which were longer than were worn in Yonville. One of the clerk's great occupations was to keep them manicured. He kept a penknife for this very purpose in his writing desk.

They came back to Yonville along the river. During warm weather the riverbank grew wide. They could see the bases of the garden walls, which had short staircases leading toward the water. The river flowed noiselessly, rapid and cold to the eye. Large thin grasses bent together, swaying to the current like abandoned green wigs spread out over the clear water. Here and there, on the tip of a reed or on the leaf of a water lily, a fine-footed insect would alight or crawl. Sun rays pierced through the small blue bubbles the waves made as they broke; the old, branchless willows reflected their gray bark in the water. All around the meadow seemed empty for miles. It was dinnertime on the farms, and the young woman and her companion heard nothing as they walked but the rhythm of their steps on the path, the words they were uttering, and the rustling of Emma's dress.

The garden walls, their copings stuck with pieces of broken bottles, were as warm as greenhouse windows. Wall-

flowers had pushed between the bricks, and with the tip of
her open parasol Madame Bovary, as she walked, scraped
some of their faded petals, which disintegrated into yellow
dust; or some overhanging branch of honeysuckle or clematis
would catch on the fringes for a moment.

They were talking about a Spanish dance company soon
expected in the Rouen theater.

"Will you be going?" she asked.

"If I can," he answered.

Had they nothing else to say to each other? Yet their
eyes were full of more serious statements; and while they
sought for commonplace sentences, they each felt the same
languor. It was like a murmur of the soul, profound and
continuous, dominating that of the voices. Surprised at this
unexpected sweetness, it did not occur to them to discuss
the sensation or discover the cause. Future happiness, like
tropical shores, projects over the vastness that precedes it,
its innate indolence, and wafts a scented breeze that intoxi-
cates and dispels any anxiety about the unseen horizon.

At one point the ground had been trampled by cattle;
they had to step over large mossy rocks evenly spaced
across the mud. She kept stopping to see where to place her
shoe; and faltering on a shifting stone, elbows akimbo, body
bent forward, looking unsure, she laughed out of fear of
falling into the puddle.

When they reached her garden, Madame Bovary pushed
open the small gate, ran up the steps, and disappeared.

Léon went back to his office. His employer was out; he
glanced over the files, trimmed a pen, then picked up his
hat and went off.

He went to the pasture, at the summit of the Argueil
hill, near the forest entrance. He lay down on the ground
under the pine trees and looked at the sky through his
fingers.

"I'm so bored!" he said to himself; "so bored!"

He found it sad that he should have to live in this village, with Homais for a friend and Monsieur Guillaumin
for an employer. The latter, completely occupied with business, with his gold-framed glasses and red sideburns over a
white cravat, understood nothing about the subtleties of the
spirit, although he affected a stiff British manner that had
dazzled the clerk at the beginning. As for the pharmacist's
wife, she was the best wife in Normandy; she was gentle as a

lamb, cherished her children, her father, her mother, her cousins, cried over other people's troubles, made everything run smoothly in her household, and detested corsets; but she was so slow moving, so boring to listen to, so common in looks, and so limited in conversation that he would never have thought, even though she was thirty years old and he twenty, even though they slept next door to each other and he spoke to her each day, that she could be someone's wife, nor that she possessed anything of her sex other than her clothing.

And otherwise, what was there? Binet, a few tradesmen, two or three innkeepers, the curé, and finally, Monsieur Tuvache, the mayor, with his two sons; wealthy people, crude, thick headed, farming their land themselves, keeping their celebrations within the family, sanctimoniously pious, and completely insufferable socially.

But Emma's face detached itself from this background of human faces, isolated yet even further removed; for he sensed undefinable chasms between himself and her.

At the beginning, he had called on her several times in the pharmacist's company. Charles had not appeared very interested in receiving him; and Léon, between the fear of being indiscreet and the desire for an intimacy that he imagined almost impossible, did not know how to proceed.

IV

As soon as the cold weather began, Emma abandoned her bedroom and moved into the parlor, a long, low-ceilinged room with a piece of branched coral spread out on the mantelpiece against the mirror. Sitting in her armchair near the window, she would watch the villagers walking along the sidewalk.

Léon went from his office to the Golden Lion twice a day. Emma heard him coming from afar; she would lean out while she listened, and the young man, always dressed the same way, would glide behind the curtain without turning his head. But at twilight she cupped her chin in her left hand, dropped her unfinished embroidery on her lap, and shuddered at the sudden appearance of this moving shadow. She would get up and order the table to be set.

Monsieur Homais would arrive during dinner. Skullcap in his hand, he entered on tiptoe in order not to disturb anyone and always repeated the same sentence: "Good evening, everyone!" Then, when he had settled in his place at the table, between husband and wife, he asked the doctor for news about his patients, and the latter would consult him about the chance of getting paid. Then they discussed the contents of the newspaper. By that hour Homais knew it almost by heart; and he would report it all, including the editorial comments and the stories of various catastrophes that had occurred in France or elsewhere. And when the subject began to peter out, he threw in some observations about the food he saw. Sometimes he would even half get up and delicately point out the tenderest bit to Madame, or turning to the maid, would offer her advice for the preparation of stews and the hygienic properties of seasonings; he spoke impressively about aroma, osmazome, natural juices, and gelatin. Moreover, his head being more filled with recipes than his pharmacy was with display jars, Homais excelled in making various jams, vinegars, and sweet liqueurs, and he also knew all the latest fuel-saving devices, the art of keeping cheese and of curing ailing wines.

At eight, Justin would come and call him to lock up the pharmacy. Then Monsieur Homais, having noticed that his pupil had a fondness for the doctor's house, looked at him knowingly, especially if Félicité happened to be there.

"My young friend," he would say, "is beginning to have ideas, and devil take me if he isn't in love with your maid!"

But a more serious fault, for which he reproached him, was that of constantly eavesdropping. On Sunday, for instance, one could not make him leave the drawing room into which Madame Homais had called him to take the children, who were falling asleep in the armchairs and disarranging the loose-fitting calico covers.

There were not many people who came to these gatherings at the pharmacist's home, his spiteful tongue and political opinions having alienated various respectable people in succession. The clerk never failed to be there. As soon as he heard the bell, he would run to meet Madame Bovary, take her shawl, and put away under the shop desk the thick list slippers she wore over her shoes when it snowed.

At first they played several games of trente-et-un, then Monsieur Homais would play a game of écarté with Emma; Léon, standing behind her, would offer advice. His hands on the back of her chair, he would look at the teeth of her comb biting into her chignon. Each time she moved to throw down the cards her dress would shift up on the right side. From her pinned-up hair a dark glow reflected down and gradually faded into the shadow. Her dress was draped over both sides of the chair in generous folds, spreading out to the floor. When Léon occasionally felt himself stepping on it, he would jump away as if he were stepping on someone.

When the card games were over, the pharmacist and the doctor would play dominoes, and Emma, changing her seat, would lean her elbows on the table and leaf through *L'Illustration*. She had brought her fashion magazine. Léon would station himself near her; they would look together at the illustrations and would await each other at the bottom of the page. She would often ask him to recite poetry to her; Léon would declaim in a drawling voice that he carefully allowed to expire at the love passages. But the noise of the dominoes irritated him; Monsieur Homais was good at them, he would beat Charles by a full double-six. When their three hundred was finished, they would both stretch before the hearth and lose no time in falling asleep. The fire died out among the embers; the teapot was empty; Léon would still be reading, Emma listening to him, absentmindedly turning the lampshade, on the gauze of which were painted clowns in carriages and tightrope walkers with their balancing poles. Léon would stop, pointing to his sleeping audience; then they spoke in low voices, and their conversation seemed sweeter to them because it was not overheard.

Thus a sort of relationship was established between them, a continual exchange of books and ballads; Monsieur Bovary, not a jealous type, did not wonder about it.

For his birthday he received a handsome phrenological head, marked with numbers as far as the thorax and painted blue. It was a thoughtful gesture from the clerk. He offered many others, even running errands for Charles in Rouen; and when some novelist's book launched a fad for cactus plants, he bought one for Emma, which he brought back on his lap in the Hirondelle, prickling his fingers on its spiky leaves.

She had a small railed window shelf built to hold her flowerpots. The clerk also had his hanging garden. They would see each other when they tended their flowers on the windows.

Among the village windows there was one even more often occupied; on Sunday, from morning until night, and every afternoon if the weather was clear, Monsieur Binet's thin profile could be seen as he leaned over his lathe. Its monotonous hum could be heard as far as the Golden Lion.

One evening when he came home, Léon found in his room a rug worked in velvet and wool, with a leaf design on a pale ground. He called Madame Homais, Monsieur Homais, Justin, the children, and the cook; he spoke about it to his employer. Everyone wanted to see the rug. Why was the doctor's wife making these "generous" gestures to the clerk? It seemed odd, and they thought it definite proof that she was "his good friend."

He spoke so often about her charms and her wit that he seemed to confirm it. In fact, Binet one time answered him rather brusquely: "What difference does it make to me? I'm not one of her friends!"

He tortured himself to discover how he could declare his feelings to her; and always hesitating between the fear of displeasing her and the fear of seeming weak willed, he wept tears of discouragement and desire. Then he made some energetic decisions; he wrote letters that he tore up, set himself deadlines that he would postpone. He would often start out with the intention of daring all; but his resolution would abandon him quickly in Emma's presence, and when Charles would appear and invite him to come along and visit some patient in the area with him, he would accept immediately, bid Madame farewell, and be off. After all, wasn't her husband part of her?

As for Emma, she didn't think she was in love with him. Love, she believed, should arrive all at once with thunder and lightning—a whirlwind from the skies that affects life, turns it every which way, wrests resolutions away like leaves, and plunges the entire heart into an abyss. She did not know that rain forms lakes on house terraces when the gutters are stopped up, and she remained secure in her ignorance until she suddenly discovered a crack in the wall.

V

It was a snowy Sunday afternoon in February.

They had all gone off—Monsieur and Madame Bovary, Homais, and Léon—to see a flax mill that was being built about a mile outside Yonville in the valley. The pharmacist took Napoleon and Athalie with him for the exercise. Justin came along with umbrellas on his shoulder.

Nothing, however, could have been less curious than this curiosity. A great expanse of empty ground in which several already rusted gear wheels could be found scattered among the piles of sand and pebbles surrounded a long, rectangular building, the walls of which were punctured by a number of small windows. The mill was not yet finished, and you could see the sky through the roof beams. Attached to the gable end was a bundle of straw mixed with wheat ears tied with tricolor ribbons flapping in the wind.

Homais was speaking. He was explaining to the group the future importance of this establishment, calculating the strength of the floors, the thickness of the walls, and very much regretting not having a measuring stick like Monsieur Binet's.

Emma, who had taken his arm, was leaning gently on his shoulder, looking at the solar disk gleaming whitely through the mist. Then she turned around. Charles was there, his cap pulled down over his eyebrows and his two thick lips quivering, which gave a rather stupid look to his face; even his back, his placid back, was irritating to see, and she found the flatness of his personality written all over his coat.

While she was looking at him, savoring in her impatience a sort of depraved voluptuousness, Léon moved a step forward. The chilly air that was making him pale seemed to soften his face; between his cravat and his neck the slightly loose collar of his shirt revealed the skin; a bit of ear escaped from under a lock of hair, and his big blue eyes lifted toward the clouds seemed to Emma more limpid and more beautiful than those mountain lakes in which the sky is reflected.

"Idiot!" the pharmacist shouted suddenly.

And he ran over to his son, who had just thrown himself into a heap of lime in order to whiten his shoes. Napoleon began to howl at the reproaches being poured on him while Justin was wiping his shoes with some straw. But a knife was needed; Charles offered his.

"Ah," she said to herself, "he carries a knife in his pocket, just like a peasant!"

The frost was beginning to fall and they headed back toward Yonville.

That evening Madame Bovary did not go to the neighbors', and when Charles had left, when she felt herself alone, the comparison began again with the clarity of an almost immediate sensation and with that lengthening of perspective that memory imparts to things. Looking from her bed at the fire burning brightly, she could still see, as if she were still there, Léon standing up, bending his walking stick in one hand and holding Athalie with the other as she sucked peacefully on a bit of ice. She found him charming; she couldn't get him out of her mind; she remembered his gestures of other days, things he had said, the sound of his voice, his entire person; and she repeated, thrusting her lips forward as for a kiss: "Yes, charming, charming! He must be in love," she told herself. "With whom? ... But it's me!"

The proofs appeared before her all at once; her heart leaped. The flame from the fireplace was flickering merrily on the ceiling; she lay on her back and stretched out her arms.

Then the eternal lamentation began: "If only fate had willed it! Why can't it be? Who prevented it?"

When Charles returned at midnight, she pretended he had just awakened her, and as he made a noise while undressing, she pleaded a headache; then she asked nonchalantly what had happened during the evening.

"Monsieur Léon left early," he said.

She couldn't repress a smile. She fell asleep, her soul filled with a new enchantment.

The next day, at nightfall, she received a visit from Lheureux, the dry-goods merchant. The shopkeeper was a clever man.

Gascon by birth but Norman by adoption, he combined his southern loquaciousness with Cauchois shrewdness. His fat face, smooth and beardless, looked as if it had been colored by watered-down licorice juice, and his white hair heightened even more the hard brilliance of his small black eyes. No one knew what he had been before. Some said a peddler, others a banker. What was certain was that he could do complicated calculations in his head that frightened even Binet. Polite to the point of obsequiousness, he always stood slightly inclined in the posture of someone who is either greeting or inviting.

After leaving his crepebound hat at the door, he set down a green cardboard box on the table and began by lamenting to Madame, with a great show of politeness, that as of that day he had not obtained her confidence. A poor shop like his could never hope to attract "an elegant lady"—he dwelled on the word. She had but to order and he would make it his business to furnish her with whatever she wanted, both in cotton goods and lingerie, hats or novelties, since he went to the city four times a month regularly. He was in contact with the largest firms. One could ask about him at the Three Brothers, at the Golden Beard, or at the Great Savage; all those gentlemen knew him as well as the insides of their pockets! Today he had dropped in to show Madame an assortment of articles that he happened to have, thanks to an unusual opportunity. And he pulled a half dozen embroidered handkerchiefs out of the box.

Madame Bovary examined them.

"I don't need anything," she said.

Then Monsieur Lheureux delicately displayed three Algerian scarves, several packets of English needles, a pair of straw slippers, and finally four eggcups carved from coconut shells by convicts. Both hands on the table, leaning forward with his neck outstretched and his mouth open, he watched Emma as she hovered undecided over this merchandise. Occasionally, as if to brush off the dust, he would flick with his fingernail the silk of the scarves, which were unfolded to their entire length; and they would quiver with a light rustle while the golden threads in their fabric gleamed in the greenish twilight.

"How much are they?"

"A mere nothing," he answered, "a nothing. But there's no hurry. When you're ready. We aren't Jews."

She thought for a few minutes and ended by declining with thanks. Monsieur Lheureux replied without emotion: "Well! We'll come to an understanding later on. I've always worked things out with the ladies. Except with mine!"

Emma smiled.

"That is to say," he continued in jovial fashion after his joke, "it's not the money I worry about. I can give you some if you need it."

She started with surprise.

"Ah!" he said quickly, and in a low voice. "And I wouldn't need to go far to find you some. You can count on that!"

Then he began to ask about the health of old Tellier, the owner of the Café Français, whom Monsieur Bovary was caring for at the time.

"What's wrong with old Tellier? He coughs hard enough to shake the house and I'm afraid he may soon need a wooden overcoat instead of a flannel nightshirt. He carried on enough when he was young! Those people, Madame, did not have the slightest self-control, not the slightest discipline. He burned his insides out with brandy! But it's a sad thing all the same to see an acquaintance go off like that."

And while he was packing up his box, he chatted away in this fashion about the doctor's patients.

"It's the weather, no doubt," he said, looking with irritation out the window, "that causes all those illnesses. I don't feel quite right myself. I'll even have to come see Monsieur one of these days about a pain I have in my back. Well, au revoir, Madame Bovary. At your service. Your humble servant."

And he gently shut the door.

Emma had dinner served to her on a tray in her room, by the fireside. She took a long while to eat. Everything seemed good to her.

"How sensible I was!" she told herself, thinking about the scarves.

She heard steps on the staircase. It was Léon. She stood up and took from the top of the chest of drawers, among the dustcloths to be hemmed, the first one on the pile. She looked quite busy when he appeared.

The conversation languished, Madame Bovary abandoning it every minute while he himself seemed embarrassed. Seated on a low chair near the fireplace, he kept turning the ivory needle case with his fingers; she stitched away, occasionally puckering part of the fabric with her nail. She didn't say a word. He said nothing, as captivated by her silence as he would have been by her words.

"Poor boy," she thought.

"Why do I displease her?" he asked himself.

Léon finally ended by saying that he would have to go to Rouen on business within a few days.

"Your music subscription has run out. Shall I renew it?"

"No," she answered.

"Why?"

"Because—" And compressing her lips, she drew out slowly a long stitch of gray thread.

The embroidering bothered Léon. It seemed to be roughening the tips of her fingers.

He thought of something gallant to say, but didn't dare.

"You're giving it up?" he asked.

"What?" she asked quickly. "Oh, music? My God, yes! Don't I have my house to run, my husband to take care of, a thousand more important duties!"

She looked at the clock. Charles was late. Then she played the worrying wife. Two or three times she repeated: "He's so good."

The clerk liked Monsieur Bovary, but he found this tenderness annoying. Nevertheless he continued the praises he heard everyone sing, especially the pharmacist, he said.

"Ah, he's a good man," Emma said.

"True," said the clerk.

And he began to talk about Madame Homais, whose negligent manner of dressing usually gave them something to laugh about.

"What difference does it make?" Emma interrupted. "A good mother doesn't bother about her appearance."

Then she became silent once more.

She continued in this fashion during the following days; her conversation, her ways, everything changed. She was seen taking her household in hand, going to church regularly, and becoming stricter with her maid.

She took Berthe back from the wet nurse. Félicité would bring her down when visitors came, and Madame Bovary undressed her to show her legs. She asserted that she adored children; they were her consolation, her joy, her madness, and she accompanied her caresses with lyric expansiveness that to people other than the Yonvillites would have evoked memories of Sachette in *Notre-Dame de Paris*.

When Charles came home he would find his slippers warming near the embers. His waistcoats no longer lacked linings, nor his shirts buttons, and he even enjoyed the sight of all his cotton nightcaps arranged in equal piles in the cupboard. She did not look sour, as before, about taking walks in the garden; whatever he suggested was always agreed to, although she did not guess what it was that inspired her to submit without a murmur. And when Léon saw him near the fire after dinner, his two hands folded over his stomach, feet on the fender, flushed from digestion, eyes moist with happiness, while the child crawled on the rug and the slim-waisted woman leaned over the back of his chair to kiss him on the forehead, he told himself, "What madness! How could I ever have won her?"

She appeared so virtuous and inaccessible to him that any hope, even the most lingering, abandoned him.

But this renunciation set her in an extraordinary light. The carnal qualities that he could not obtain seemed extremely remote. She continually rose in his heart, detaching herself from it in the magnificent manner of a goddess soaring to heaven. It was one of those pure sentiments untroubled by the realities of life. One cultivates them because they are rare—and their loss would hurt more than the pleasure of possessing them.

Emma grew thin, her cheeks paled, her face lengthened. With her black hair, large eyes, straight nose, birdlike walk, and her continued silence, she appeared now to be moving through life hardly touching it and to be wearing on her forehead the vague mark of some sublime predestination. She was so sad and so calm, at the same time so sweet and so reserved, that one felt a glacial charm when near her, as one shivers in churches under the scent of flowers blended with the cold of the marble tiles. Even the others felt the power of her personality. The pharmacist said: "She's a woman of great talent who wouldn't be out of place in a sub-prefecture."

The women admired her thrift, the patients her politeness, the poor her charity.

But within she was full of envy, rage, and hatred. That dress with the straight folds hid a heart in turmoil, and those modest lips did not speak of her torment. She was in love with Léon and she longed for solitude in order to dream about him undisturbed. Even the sight of him troubled the voluptuousness of her meditation. Her heart pounded at the sound of his steps; but the emotion subsided in his presence, and only an immense wonder remained, which faded into sadness.

Léon did not know that when he left her home in despair she would watch him walk down the street. His movements made her anxious; she would steal glances at him, invent any story to visit his room. The pharmacist's wife seemed to her very lucky to sleep under the same roof, and her thoughts were constantly alighting on this house, like the pigeons of the Golden Lion that came to wet their pink feet and white wings in the gutters there. But the more Emma grew aware of her love, the more she repressed it, in order to hide and lessen it. She wanted Léon to suspect it, and she envisioned dangers, catastrophes, that would have revealed it. What held her back was no doubt laziness or fright, and also modesty. She thought that she had rejected him too strongly, that there was no more time, that all was lost. Then pride and the joy of telling herself "I am virtuous" and of looking at herself in the mirror while assuming poses of resignation consoled her a little for the sacrifice she believed herself to be making.

And then the fleshly appetites, desire for money, and the melancholy grip of passion combined into one agony. Instead of turning her thoughts from it, she dwelled on it more and more, wallowing in the pain and reaching out for it at all times. She would become irritated at a badly served dish or an unshut door, whimper about the velvet she didn't have, about the happiness she missed, about her unrealistic dreams, her cramped house.

What exasperated her was that Charles did not seem to suspect her suffering. His conviction that he was making her happy seemed an imbecilic insult to her, and his smugness about it sheer ingratitude. For whom then was she being virtuous? Was he not the obstacle to all happiness, the cause of all this misery, the sharp buckle, as it were, of the intricate strap that was binding her on all sides?

Therefore she brought to bear on him alone the intense hatred that resulted from her miseries, and each effort to lessen it served only to increase it; for this useless pain was added to her other motives for despair and contributed even more to the gulf between them. His very kindness to her made her rebel. Domestic mediocrity was pushing her to luxurious fantasies, matrimonial tenderness to adulterous desires. She wanted Charles to beat her so that she could hate him, take revenge. She amazed herself sometimes at the atrocious thoughts that came into her mind; and she had to continue to smile, hear herself repeat that she was happy, pretend to be happy, make others think she was.

But she was disgusted with this hypocrisy. She was filled with temptations to run off with Léon, somewhere, far away, to try a new destiny. But some unknown chasm would immediately open in her soul.

"Besides, he doesn't love me," she would think. "What will become of me? What rescue can I look forward to? What consolation, what lessening of my pain?"

She remained broken, breathless, inert, sobbing in a low voice, with tears flowing.

"Why not tell Monsieur?" the maid asked her when she would come in during these crises.

"It's nerves," Emma would answer. "Don't tell him about it. You'll make him unhappy."

"Ah, yes," Félicité would continue, "you're just like Mademoiselle Guérine, old Guérine's daughter, the Pollet fisherman I knew in Dieppe before coming to you. She was sad, so sad that to see her standing on her doorstep would remind you of a winding sheet hung in front of the door. It seems her trouble was a sort of fog in her head, and the doctors couldn't do anything about it, and the curé couldn't either. When it became too bad for her, she would go off all alone to the seashore, and the customs officer on duty would often find her flat on her belly on the shingles, crying away. It went away after her marriage they say."

"But with me," Emma said, "it began after my marriage."

VI

One evening as she was sitting at the open window and watching Lestiboudois, the sexton, trim the boxwood hedge, she suddenly heard the Angelus ringing.

It was the beginning of April, when the primroses are in bloom; a warm wind blows over the flower beds, and the gardens, like women, seem to be dressing for the summer holidays. Through the arbor lattice and all around beyond it, the river could be seen making its meandering way through the grassy meadow. The evening mist was passing through the leafless poplars, blurring their outlines with a violet haze, paler and more transparent than a fine gauze hung on their branches. Cattle were moving about in the distance; neither their steps nor their lowing was audible; and the bell, still ringing, continued its peaceful lamentation in the air.

At this repeated chiming, the young woman's thoughts strayed to her old memories of youth and school days. She remembered the candelabra, taller than the altar, the vases filled with flowers, and the tabernacle with its little columns. She wished she were still moving in that long line of white veils marked with black by the stiff coifs of the nuns kneeling on their *prie-Dieux*. When she lifted her head during Mass on Sunday, she would see the sweet face of the Virgin in the bluish clouds of incense that were rising. Then a tender emotion would suffuse her; she would feel all limp and abandoned like the down of a bird swirling in the tempest.

Without being aware of what she was doing at that moment, she headed toward the church, prepared for any act of devotion as long as she could give her soul up there and make her entire existence disappear.

In the square she met Lestiboudois, who was returning from church; for in order not to cut his day short, he preferred to interrupt his work and then resume it again. And so he sounded the Angelus at his convenience. Besides, the earlier ringing summoned the youngsters to the catechism class.

Several of them were already there and were playing marbles on the churchyard flagstones. Others, straddling the wall, were swinging their legs, crushing down with their wooden shoes the big nettles growing between the small wall and the most recent graves. It was the only patch of green; everything else was stone and continually covered with a fine powder despite the sexton's broom.

The children, wearing soft shoes, were running around as if on a floor made especially for them. Their voices could be heard across the booming of the bell, which diminished with the oscillations of the thick cord as it fell from the heights of the steeple and was dragged on the ground by

its tip. Swallows were flying by and chirping, cutting through
the air and rapidly returning to their yellow nests under
the tiles of the eaves. A lamp was burning at the back of the
church—that is, a wick of night light in a hanging glass.
From afar its light looked like a whitish spot trembling
over the oil. An elongated ray of sun was crossing the nave
and casting the side aisles and the corners into even greater
darkness.

"Where is the curé?" Madame Bovary asked a young boy
who was jiggling the loosely latched gate.

"He's coming," he answered. And the door of the priest's
residence squeaked open to reveal Abbé Bournisien. The
children flew off into the church.

"Little scamps!" the priest grumbled. "Always the same."
He picked up a tattered catechism that he had just stepped
on. "They have no respect for anything!"

Then he noticed Madame Bovary: "Excuse me," he said,
"I didn't notice you."

He tucked the catechism into his pocket and stood swinging the heavy vestry key with his hand.

The setting sun glowing down on his face bleached his
woolen cassock. It was shiny at the elbows and frayed at
the hem. Grease spots and tobacco followed the line of
small buttons down his broad chest. There was a great
accumulation of them near his clerical bands, on which the
abundant folds of his red skin were resting. His complexion
was dotted with yellow blemishes that disappeared under the
stubble of his graying beard. He had just had his evening
meal and was breathing heavily.

"How are you?" he added.

"Not well," Emma answered, "I am suffering."

"Ah, well, so am I," he answered. "These first hot spells
weaken one terribly, don't they? Well, what do you expect?
We are born to suffer, as Saint Paul says. What does Monsieur
Bovary say?"

"He?" she said with a disdainful gesture.

"But hasn't he prescribed anything for you?" asked the
priest, genuinely surprised.

"Ah," said Emma, "it isn't an earthly remedy that I
need."

The curé kept glancing into the church, where the boys
were squatting and bumping each other's shoulders; they were
falling over like paper dolls.

"I would like to know——," she began.

"Just you wait, Riboudet," shouted the clergyman angrily. "I'm going to box your ears, you rascal!"

Then he turned to Emma: "He's the son of Boudet, the carpenter. His parents are well off and they let him do what he wants. He could learn rapidly if he only wanted, because he's very smart. And I sometimes joke by calling him Riboudet—like the hill you take to go to the Maromme— and I even say: 'Mon Riboudet.' Ha! ha! Mont Riboudet. The other day I told this to Monseigneur, who laughed; he condescended to laugh. . . . And how is Monsieur Bovary?"

She seemed not to hear him. He continued: "He's probably busy all the time. He and I are certainly the two busiest people in the parish. But he is the doctor of the body," he added with a heavy laugh, "and I of the soul."

She looked at the priest with mournful eyes. "Yes," she said, "you comfort all suffering."

"Ah, you don't have to tell me, Madame Bovary. This very morning I had to go to Bas-Diauville to see a cow that had swelled up; they thought it was bewitched. All their cows, I don't understand how— Oh, excuse me. Longuemarre and Boudet! Quiet! Enough of that!" And he leaped into the church.

The boys were crowding around the large lectern, climbing over the precentor's stool, looking into the missal. Others were tiptoeing up to the confessional. But the curé suddenly distributed a volley of slaps right and left. Picking them up by the scruff of the neck, he lifted them off the ground and set them heavily down on their knees in the choir, as if he were going to plant them there.

"Well, now," he said when he returned to Emma, unfolding his large calico handkerchief and putting a corner of it between his teeth, "the farmers have their troubles."

"So have others," she answered.

"Of course! Workers in the city, for example."

"Not them——"

"Please! I've known poor mothers with families, virtuous women, I assure you, truly sainted, who didn't even have bread."

"But," Emma continued (and the corners of her mouth twitched as she spoke), "what about those, Monsieur, who have bread and who don't have——"

"Fire in the winter?" said the priest.

"Oh, what's the difference!"

"What do you mean, what's the difference? It seems to me that when one is properly warmed, well fed— Because, after all—"

"My God, my God," she sighed.

"Do you feel sick?" he asked, coming closer with an anxious air. "Probably something you ate. You ought to go home, Madame Bovary, and drink a little tea. It will strengthen you. Or perhaps a glass of cold water with some brown sugar."

"What for?" She looked like someone who awakes from a dream.

"You were passing your hand over your forehead. I thought you had a dizzy spell." Then, remembering: "But you asked me something. What was it now? I seem to have forgotten."

"Me? Nothing. Nothing," Emma repeated.

Her wandering gaze settled on the old man in the cassock. They stared at each other in silence.

"Madame Bovary," he said finally, "excuse me, but duty calls. You know I must look after my rascals. The first Communions will be here pretty soon. I'm afraid we won't be ready. From Ascension on I'm going to keep them an extra hour every Wednesday without fail. Those poor children! You can't start them too early in the Lord's path, as He Himself ordered through the mouth of His Divine Son. Good day, Madame. My respects to your husband."

And he walked into the church, genuflecting near the door.

Emma watched him disappear between the double line of benches, walking heavily, his head slightly bent toward one shoulder, his hands dangling down.

Then she turned around woodenly, like a statue on a pivot, and headed home. But the curé's gruff voice and the shrill sounds of the boys kept reaching her ear as she walked: "Are you a Christian?"

"Yes, I am Christian."

"What is a Christian?"

"A Christian is one who, being baptized—baptized—baptized—"

She walked up her staircase holding on to the banister and sank into an armchair when she reached her room.

The white light came in gentle undulations through the

windowpane. The pieces of furniture seemed to be even more fixed in their place. They blended into the shadows as into a murky ocean. The fire was out, the clock ticked away, and Emma felt vaguely surprised that there could be such outward calm while there was so much turmoil within her. Little Berthe was standing between the window and the work table, tottering on her knitted booties and trying to get near her mother to pull the ends of her apron.

"Leave me alone!" she said, shoving her away with her hand.

The child soon came back, even closer. She leaned her arms on Emma's lap and lifted her big blue eyes toward her while a rivulet of saliva flowed out of her mouth onto the silk of the apron.

"Will you leave me alone!" she said with fury.

The expression on her face frightened the child, who began to cry.

"Go away!" she said, emphasizing the statement with her elbow.

Berthe fell against the chest of drawers, striking the brass curtain hook; she cut her cheek on it, and it started to bleed. Madame Bovary ran over to pick her up, ripped the bell pull, shouted for the maid at the top of her lungs, and was about to start cursing herself when Charles appeared. He was just coming home for dinner.

"Look, darling," Emma said in a calm voice, "the baby was playing and cut her cheek."

Charles assured her it wasn't serious and went off to find some adhesive plaster.

Madame Bovary did not go down to the parlor; she wanted to remain alone and take care of her child. Her anxiety gradually disappeared as she watched her sleeping, and she thought she had been both foolish and virtuous to worry about so little. Berthe had stopped bleeding. Her breath was now imperceptibly lifting the cotton coverlet. Great big tears were hovering in the corners of her half-closed eyelids. Two pale, deep-set pupils could be seen through the lashes; the sticking plaster on her cheek was pulling the taut skin to one side.

"Strange," Emma thought, "how ugly this child is."

When Charles came back from the pharmacy at eleven (he had gone there after dinner to return the remainder of the plaster), he found his wife standing near the cradle.

"I told you it was nothing," he said, kissing her on the forehead. "Don't worry about it, darling, you'll make yourself sick."

He had remained quite awhile at the pharmacist's. Although he did not seem too frightened, Monsieur Homais nevertheless kept trying to bolster his morale, to "raise his spirits." Then they spoke about the various dangers that threatened childhood and about the stupidity of maids. Madame Homais knew something about it; she still bore on her chest the marks of some hot embers that a cook had once dropped down her smock. And so these devoted parents were extremely cautious. The knives were never sharpened, floors never waxed. There were iron bars on the windows and heavy guards at the fireplace. The Homais children, despite their independent ways, could not budge without someone to keep an eye on them; at the slightest cold their father loaded them down with cough medicine, and until they were four they were tightly bundled up in quilted garments. True, this was an eccentricity of Madame Homais about which her husband worried in silence, fearing the effect on the mind of such compression. He even ventured to ask her: "Do you intend to make Caribs or Botocudos out of them?"

Charles had tried several times to terminate the conversation.

"I'd like to talk to you," he whispered into the clerk's ear. The latter began to lead the way upstairs.

"Does he suspect something?" Léon asked himself. His heart began pounding as he wondered.

Charles shut the door and asked him, finally, to find out in Rouen what a good daguerreotype might cost. It was to be a romantic surprise for his wife, a token of affection —his portrait in his black suit. But he wanted to know what it would cost him beforehand. This errand should not take Monsieur Léon too much out of his way since he went to the city almost every week.

Why did he go? Homais suspected some "youthful carrying-on," some affair. But he was wrong. Léon was not involved in any romantic pursuit. He was unhappier than he had ever been. Madame Lefrançois realized this from the amount of food he left on his plate these days. She questioned the tax collector to get more information. Binet answered, in a knowing tone, that he was "not an informer paid by the police."

His dinner companion seemed quite strange to him, nevertheless. Léon would often lean back in his chair, stretch his arms, and complain vaguely about life.

"You don't have enough distractions," said the tax collector.

"Such as?"

"If I were in your shoes, I'd get a lathe!"

"But I don't know how to use one," the clerk answered.

"I guess that's right," the other said, stroking his chin with an air of smug superiority.

Léon was tired of being in love without results. He began feeling the despondency brought on by the unvarying repetition of the same life, when there is no motivating interest and no sustaining hope. He was so bored with Yonville and the Yonvillites that the sight of certain people and certain houses irritated him beyond endurance, and the pharmacist, as friendly as he was, seemed to have become absolutely unbearable. Yet the prospect of a new situation frightened him as much as it tempted him.

The apprehension soon turned into impatience and then he could hear the distant noises of Paris: the fanfare of its masked balls and the laughter of its grisettes. He was supposed to finish his law studies there. Why not go now? What was holding him back? And inwardly he started making preparations; he arranged his occupations in advance, he furnished his rooms in his imagination. He would lead the life of an artist; take guitar lessons; own a dressing gown, a beret, blue velvet slippers! He visualized already two crossed foils and a skull and the guitar on his Parisian mantelpiece.

The difficulty was in obtaining his mother's consent; yet nothing seemed to him more reasonable. His employer had even been suggesting that he change to another office where he could learn more.

Léon compromised by trying to find a position as second clerk in Rouen but found none. He finally wrote his mother a long, detailed letter in which he outlined his reasons for moving to Paris right away. She gave her consent.

He did not rush off. Every day, for one whole month, Hivert carried his boxes, valises, and packages from Yonville to Rouen, from Rouen to Yonville, and when Léon had replenished his wardrobe, had his three armchairs reupholstered, bought a new supply of scarves, in other words, made more arrangements than for a trip around the world, he kept putting off his move from week to week until his mother sent a second letter suggesting that he go now if he expected to pass his examination before vacation time.

When the moment for farewells came, Madame Homais cried, Justin sobbed, Homais, as befitted a man of dignity, hid his emotion. He wanted to carry his friend's overcoat up to the lawyer's gate. The lawyer was taking Léon to Rouen in his carriage. Léon had only enough time to say good-bye to Monsieur Bovary.

When he reached the top of the staircase, he stopped, out of breath. Madame Bovary started up when he walked in.

"I'm still here!" Léon said.

"I knew you'd come!"

She bit her lip and blushed red from the roots of her hair to the edge of her collar. She remained standing, leaning against the paneling.

"Your husband's not home?" he said.

"He's away." She repeated: "He's away."

Then there was a silence. They looked at each other, and their thoughts, coming together in the same anguish like two pounding hearts, were inextricably united.

"I'd like to kiss Berthe," Léon said.

Emma went down a few steps to call Félicité.

He looked around quickly at the walls, the shelves, the mantelpiece, as if to penetrate into everything, take everything with him.

Then she came back and the maid brought in Berthe, who was dangling a windmill upside down at the end of a string.

Léon kissed her several times on the neck.

"Good-bye, little one, good-bye, sweet child!" And he handed her back to her mother.

"Take her back," the latter said to the servant.

They were alone.

Madame Bovary had her face pressed against a window-pane, her back to him. Léon was holding his cap in his hand and tapping it gently against his thigh.

"It's going to rain," Emma said.

"I have a coat," he answered.

"Oh."

She turned back, chin down and forehead forward. The

light was gleaming on it as if it were marble, as far as the arch of the brows. It was impossible to guess what she was looking at in the distance, nor what she was thinking in her heart of hearts.

"Well, good-bye," he said with a sigh.

She looked up quickly.

They drew closer. He held out his hand. She hesitated.

"English style, then," she said, extending hers and trying to smile.

Léon enclosed her hand in his and the very substance of his entire being seemed to pour into this moist palm.

Then he relaxed his grip. Their eyes met one more time and he disappeared.

When he reached the marketplace, he stopped and hid behind a pillar in order to look at that white house with its four green shutters one last time. He thought he could distinguish a shadow behind the bedroom window, but the curtain, slipping out of its holder by accident, slowly shook out its long slanting folds and fell straight down, as immobile as a plaster wall. Léon began to run.

He noticed his employer's carriage standing on the highway, some distance off. Beside him was a man in a shopapron holding the horse. Homais and Monsieur Guillaumin were talking. They were waiting for him.

"Embrace me," said the pharmacist with tears in his eyes. "Here is your coat, dear boy. Do be careful of the cold! Take good care of yourself. Don't overwork!"

"Come on, Léon, let's go," said the lawyer.

Homais leaned over the mudguard and sobbed out two sad words: *"Bon voyage!"*

"Good-bye to you," answered Monsieur Guillaumin. "We're off!"

They drove away and Homais returned home.

Madame Bovary had opened the window that overlooked the garden and she was looking at the clouds.

They were massing in the west, toward Rouen. Their black wreathlike shapes moved along briskly, pierced by shafts of sunlight that resembled golden arrows stuck into a mounted trophy. The unclouded portion of the sky was as white as porcelain. Then a gust of wind bent the poplars and the rain came suddenly, pattering on the green leaves. The sun soon came out again, and the hens cackled, the sparrows rustled their wings against the wet shrubbery, and the water trickling over the gravel carried away pink acacia blossoms.

"He must be so far away by now," she thought.

As usual Monsieur Homais arrived at six-thirty, during dinner.

"Well," he said as he sat down, "we've sent our young man off!"

"So it seems," answered the doctor. Then he swiveled around in his chair: "What's new with you?"

"Nothing much. My wife was a little upset this afternoon. You know, women can be bothered by trifles. Especially mine. And there's no point complaining about it since their nervous system is much more sensitive than ours."

"Poor Léon!" said Charles. "I wonder how he will manage in Paris. Will he get used to it?"

Madame Bovary sighed.

"Come on, now!" the pharmacist said, clicking his tongue. "Little dinner parties in a restaurant, masked balls, champagne! He'll manage beautifully, I assure you."

"I don't think he'll run wild," Bovary objected.

"Nor do I," Monsieur Homais answered quickly, "even though he will have to go along with his friends or else be taken for a Jesuit. And you don't know the kind of life these young men lead in the Latin Quarter with the actresses! Besides, students are greatly esteemed in Paris. As long as they show a little ability to get along, they're received in the best circles. There are even women of the Faubourg Saint-Germain who fall in love with them, and that kind of an affair helps them make very good marriages later on."

"But, I'm afraid that he may—that he may—" said the doctor.

"You're right," the apothecary interrupted; "it's the other side of the coin! You have to keep your hand on your pocket all the time. Let's say you're in a public garden; a stranger appears, well dressed, even decorated, the type you could mistake for a diplomat. He comes over, you talk, he makes himself friendly, offers you some snuff or picks up your hat for you. Then you get even friendlier; he takes you to a café, invites you to visit his country home, introduces you to all sorts of aquaintances while you're drinking, and three quarters of the time it's only to grab your purse or lead you into evil ways."

"You're right," Charles said, "but I was really thinking
about illnesses—typhoid fever, for instance, which attacks
students from the provinces."

Emma shuddered.

"Because of the change of diet," the pharmacist continued,
"and the disturbance it causes in the general bodily condition. And that Paris water, you know! And restaurant food
—all those spicy dishes end up overheating your blood. No
matter what they say, they're not worth a good stew. I myself have always preferred home cooking. It's much healthier.
When I was studying pharmacy in Rouen, I lived in a board-
inghouse and ate with the teachers."

He continued expatiating on his opinions in general and
his personal preferences until Justin came to fetch him to
prepare an eggnog that had been prescribed.

"Never a moment's rest," he grumbled, "always on call.
I can't go out for a second. Always sweating blood like a
workhorse. I labor under a real yoke of drudgery."

Then, when he was at the door, he said: "By the way,
have you heard the news?"

"No, what?"

"It's very likely," said Homais, raising his eyebrows and
taking on a most solemn look, "that the Seine-Inférieure Agricultural Show will be held in Yonville-l'Abbaye this year.
At least the rumor is making the rounds. The newspaper mentioned it this morning. It would be a real honor for our
community. But we'll talk about that later on. Thank you,
I can see my way; Justin has the lantern."

VII

The next day was a day of mourning for Emma. A
black cloud seemed to hover over everything and envelop
everything, and unhappiness burrowed into her soul like
a winter wind whistling hollowly through an abandoned
château. It was the mood brought on by a permanent rupture,
the lassitude that overcomes you after something is over—the
sadness engendered by the interruption of a customary pat-

tern of action, the abrupt cessation of a long-continuing vibration.

She was suffering the same lifeless melancholy, the same numb despair she had suffered after their return from La Vaubyessard, when the quadrilles were whirling in her head. Léon reappeared, taller, handsomer, more charming—and slightly out of focus. Although he was separated from her, he had not left her; he was still there and the walls seemed to retain his shadow. She could not take her eyes from the rug on which he had walked, from the now empty furniture on which he had sat. The river still flowed and rippled gently along the smooth bank. They had walked along it many times, to this same murmur of the waves, over the moss-covered pebbles. The sun had been so wonderful. And those lovely afternoons alone in the shade at the foot of the garden! With his head bare he would read aloud as he sat on a footstool of dried sticks. The fresh breeze from the meadow would blow on the pages and on the nasturtiums in the arbor. And now he was gone, the one pleasure of her life, the one possible hope for happiness. Why hadn't she seized this happiness when it first appeared? Why hadn't she held him back with her hands or by begging on her knees when he wanted to leave? She cursed herself for not having loved him. She thirsted for his lips. She yearned to run to him, to throw herself into his arms, to tell him: "Take me, I'm yours." But the anticipated difficulties forestalled any action, and her desires, heightened by regret, became even more ardent.

From that point on, the memory of Léon was the focal point of her boredom. It sparkled there more strongly than the fire of travelers abandoned in the snowy Russian steppes. She would rush toward it, revel in it, delicately revive the dying embers. She would seek out anything that could make it glow more brightly, and she utilized everything—the earliest memories and the most recent, her emotions and her thoughts, her craving for luxury and her plans for happiness that were snapping in the wind like dead branches, her sterile virtues and her shattered dreams, the domestic monotony—she seized on everything, to rekindle her misery.

Nevertheless the flames died down, either from an insufficiency of emotion or an excess. Little by little absence caused love to die away and habit smothered regret. The firelight that crimsoned her pale sky became clouded over with shadow and was slowly eclipsed. Her sluggish conscience even mistook the aversion to her husband for yearning toward her lover and the passion of hatred for a renewal of tenderness, but since the storm kept brewing and the passion burning down to its embers with no help in sight, with no sunshine bursting through, there was a total night—and she was overcome by a fearful chill, which permeated her entire body.

Then the bad days of Tostes came back. She felt much more unhappy now because along with the experience of unhappiness, she now had the knowledge that it would never end.

A woman who had sacrificed so much could certainly indulge herself in some whims. She bought a Gothic *prie-Dieu*, purchased fourteen francs' worth of lemons in one month to clean her nails, sent to Rouen for a blue cashmere dress, purchased the most beautiful shawl in Lheureux's store, tied it around her waist over her dressing gown, and dressed thus, would lie on the sofa all day long with the shutters closed and a book in her hand.

She would keep changing her hair style, would arrange it Chinese fashion, in soft waves, in braids, would part it on one side and roll it under, like man.

She decided to learn Italian. She bought dictionaries, a grammar, and a supply of white paper. She tried reading serious books on history and philosophy. Sometimes at night Charles would start up from his sleep, thinking someone had come to fetch him for a patient. "I'm coming," he would say sleepily.

It would be the noise of a match Emma was striking to relight her lamp. But her readings ended like her half-worked tapestries, which were filling up her cupboard; she would start them, drop them, and move on to new ones.

She had moods in which she almost went wild. She announced to her husband one day that she could easily drink a large glass of brandy, and when Charles was foolish enough to challenge her, she swallowed it down to the last drop.

Despite her "flighty" airs (as the Yonvillites called them), Emma did not appear to be happy. She habitually set the corners of her mouth in that pursed look that contracts the faces of old maids and frustrated people. She was extremely pale, as white as a sheet, and the skin on her nose was pulled taut toward the nostrils. Her eyes shifted about. When she discovered three gray hairs on her temples, she spoke about her old age.

She would frequently feel dizzy. One day she even spat blood and when Charles revealed his anxiety by his attention, she said, "Bah! What's the difference?"

Charles went to take refuge in his office. And he cried, sitting in his armchair under the phrenological head with his elbows on the table.

Then he wrote to his mother asking her to come. They spoke about Emma at length.

What would they do? What could be done with her refusal to submit to any treatment?

"You know what your wife needs?" his mother asserted. "To be forced to work. Manual labor. If she had to earn a living, like so many other women, she wouldn't have those spells that come from the ideas she stuffs into her head because she doesn't have enough to do."

"But she keeps busy," said Charles.

"Keeps busy! Doing what? Reading novels, evil books, books against religion where they make fun of priests by quoting Voltaire. But that goes far, my poor child, and a person without religion will always end up bad."

And so it was decided that Emma should be prevented from reading novels. The task did not seem easy. The good lady assumed responsibility: she was to go in person to the lending library when she passed through Rouen and tell them that Emma was canceling her subscription. Wouldn't they have the right to call the police if the bookstore persisted in poisoning her?

The farewells between mother- and daughter-in-law were curt. During the three weeks they had been together they had not exchanged four words outside of household matters or acknowledgments at meals or bedtime.

Old Madame Bovary left on a Wednesday, which was a market day in Yonville.

From morning on, the square was filled with a line of carts that extended along the houses from the church to the inn, with their ends uptilted and shafts in the air. On the opposite side there were canvas booths selling cotton goods, coverlets and wool stockings, halters for horses, and packs of blue ribbon whose tips were streaming into the wind. Heavy hardware goods were spread out over the ground between pyramids of eggs and hampers of cheese

(from which wisps of sticky straw protruded); near the farm
tools, some clucking hens poked their heads through the
bars of their coops. The people were crowding into one spot
and not budging—the pharmacist's window was in imminent
danger of being smashed in. The store never emptied on
Wednesdays People pushed their way in, less for medicine
than for consultations, so great was Homais's reputation
in the neighboring villages. His hearty, reassuring air had
fascinated the country people. They considered him a greater
doctor than all the real ones.

Emma was sitting at the window as she often did, the
window in the provinces substituting for theaters and walking
paths, enjoying the rustic crowd when she noticed a gentleman dressed in a green velvet frock coat. Despite the heavy
gaiters on his legs, he wore elegant yellow gloves. He was
heading toward the doctor's house, followed by a peasant
walking with his head down, a pensive look on his face.

"May I see the doctor?" he asked Justin, who was talking
to Félicité on the doorstep.

Assuming that he was the house servant, he added: "Tell
him that Monsieur Rodolphe Boulanger, of La Huchette, is
here."

The visitor had mentioned his estate, not out of land-own-
ing vanity but rather to introduce himself more fully. La
Huchette was an estate near Yonville whose château he had
just acquired. It contained two farms that he himself was
cultivating in a rather casual way. He lived a bachelor life
and was reputed to have "an income of at least fifteen
hundred pounds."

Charles came into the parlor. Monsieur Boulanger introduced his man, who wanted to be bled because he "felt
as if there were ants crawling up and down his body."

"It will take them away," the peasant maintained against
all arguments.

Bovary therefore began preparing a bandage and a basin,
asking Justin to assist him. Then he said to the villager,
who was already quite pale: "Don't be afraid, my boy."

"Not me," the other answered. "Go ahead." And he held
out his muscular arm with an air of bravado. The blood
spurted out at the prick of the lancet and splattered all
over the mirror.

"Hold the basin closer!" Charles exclaimed.

"Look at that!" said the peasant. "You'd swear it was a

little fountain the way it runs. Look how red my blood is. Must be a good sign, isn't it?"

"Sometimes," said the doctor, "you don't feel anything at first and then you faint away. Especially people as healthy as you."

At these words the man dropped the little box that he had been turning with his fingers. His shoulders jerked so rapidly that they made the back of his chair crack. His hat fell off.

"I thought so," said Bovary, placing his finger over the vein.

The basin began trembling in Justin's hands. His knees shook and he became pale.

"Emma! Emma!" Charles called.

She came running down the stairs.

"Some vinegar," he cried. "Good God, two of them at once!"

He was so upset he could hardly apply the compress.

"It's all right," Monsieur Boulanger said calmly, supporting Justin in his arms. He propped him up on the table with his back against the wall.

Madame Bovary began removing his cravat. There was a knot in his shirt strings, and for a few minutes she moved her fingers lightly over the boy's neck. Then she poured vinegar on her batiste handkerchief and patted his temples gently, blowing on them softly.

The farmhand awoke, but Justin's fainting spell persisted and his pupils were disappearing into their pale eyeballs like blue flowers in milk.

"We'd better hide that from him," Charles said.

Madame Bovary picked the basin up to put it under the table. As she bent down, her dress (a yellow summer frock with four flounces, long-waisted and wide-skirted) billowed around her over the floor. She was slightly unsteady on her legs as she stooped and stretched her arms, and the folds of the fabric collapsed in a few places in response to her gestures. Then she went for a jug of water. She was dissolving some lumps of sugar when the pharmacist arrived. In the general confusion the maid had gone to call him, and when he saw that his apprentice's eyes were open, he took a deep breath. Then he turned him around, looking him over from head to toes.

"Fool!" he said. "Little fool! Fool in four letters! A bleed-

ing is such a big affair? And a strapping lad like you who's
afraid of nothing, who climbs up trees after nuts like a
squirrel! Well, say something! What will you do later on when
you're a pharmacist? What if you're called on to give evidence in court in a serious case—to help the magistrates
make their minds up? You'll have to stay cool and calm then,
remain logical and be a man or else they'll think you're an
idiot!"

Justin said nothing. The apothecary continued: "Who asked
you to come? You're always bothering Monsieur and Madame! Besides, I need you around on Wednesdays. There are
twenty people in the house now. I left everything to see about
you. All right, run along now. Hurry! I'll be back soon. Keep
an eye on the jars."

Justin dressed himself and left, and they spoke for a few
more minutes about fainting spells. Madame Bovary had
never had one.

"That's very strange for a lady," said Monsieur Boulanger.
"Some people are very delicate. I've seen a second pass out
at a duel just from the noise of the pistols being loaded."

"Other people's blood doesn't bother me a bit," said the
apothecary. "But just the thought of mine flowing would
make me feel weak if I thought about it too long."

Monsieur Boulanger dismissed his servant, advising him to
calm down now that his whim was satisfied.

"It did give me a chance to become acquainted with you,"
he added, looking at Emma as he spoke.

Then he placed three francs on the corner of the table,
nodded casually, and went off.

He was soon on the other side of the river (it was the road
back to La Huchette), and Emma could see him in the
meadow, walking under the poplars and slowing down occasionally as if he were thinking.

"She's very pleasing," he told himself. "Very pleasing, that
doctor's wife. Pretty teeth, black eyes, a well-turned foot, and
manners like a Parisienne. Where the devil did she come
from? Where did that coarse fellow find her?"

Monsieur Rodolphe Boulanger was thirty-four years old.
He was hardhearted and extremely intelligent, had spent a
lot of time in female company, and was very knowledgeable
about women. He liked this new one and therefore thought
about her and her husband.

"I find him dull. She must be tired of him. He's got dirty

fingernails and a three-day growth of beard. He trots off to his patients, and she stays home darning his socks. And so bored! Longing to live in town and dance a polka every night. Poor little woman. Gasping for love, like a carp on a kitchen table gasping for water. Three flattering words and she'd adore me, I'm sure. How tender and charming it would be. But how would I get rid of her later?"

At that point the complications connected with pleasure, considered in their true perspective, made him think by contrast, about his mistress. She was an actress in Rouen. The very thought of her made him feel sated. "Madame Bovary is much prettier," he said to himself. "And fresher, especially. Virginie is definitely putting on weight and she's so tiresome with her constant high spirits. Plus that passion for shrimp!"

The countryside was deserted and Rodolphe heard nothing but the steady swish of his feet through the grass and the distant sound of grasshoppers among the oats. He pictured Emma in the room, first dressed as he had seen her and then nude.

"I'll have her!" he exclaimed, grinding his stick into a clump of earth. He began working out the strategy of the enterprise and asked himself: "Where should we meet? How? We'll have the brat on our necks all the time—and the maid and the neighbors and the husband. All kinds of irritations. Damn!" he said. "I'll lose too much time."

Then he started again: "But those eyes of hers go right through to your heart. And that pale skin. I adore pale women."

By the time he reached the summit of Argueil Hill, his mind was made up: "I'll have to look for opportunities. I'll stop by there occasionally, send them some game and poultry. I'll be bled, if I have to. I'll invite them to my place. Ah, of course," he added; "the Agricultural Show is coming! She'll be there and I'll see her. We'll start off boldly—it's the best way!"

VIII

The day of the famous Agricultural Show finally arrived. On that great occasion all the inhabitants stood on their door-

steps from early morning on, discussing the preparations.
They had festooned the front of the Town Hall with ivy; a
tent had been set up in one of the meadows for the banquet;
and in the middle of the square, in front of the church, a
sort of cannon was set up to herald the arrival of the prefect
and salute the names of the winning farmers. The Buchy
National Guard (there was none in Yonville) had come to
join the fire brigade, of which Binet was the captain. He
was wearing a collar even higher than usual and was buttoned so tightly into his tunic that his chest appeared stiff
and motionless. The only parts of him that seemed to be
alive were his two legs, rising and falling with one continuous movement as he marked time. Since a rivalry existed
between the tax collector and the colonel, they were drilling
their men separately in order to demonstrate their individual
talents.

Red epaulets and black starched shirt fronts kept march-
ing forward and facing about in a continuous beginning with
no finish. There had never been such a display of pomp.
Several villagers had washed their houses the night before.
Tricolor flags hung from the open windows. All the inns were
filled with people. In the fine weather the starched bonnets,
gold crosses, and colored neckerchiefs glistened in the glaring
sunshine and relieved with their splashes of color the somber
monotony of the frock coats and the blue smocks. The farmers' wives from the neighboring districts undid the large pins
with which they had draped their dresses tightly around the
body to avoid being splashed, while their husbands, on the
contrary, in order to keep their hats on, had tied handkerchiefs around them and kept the corners in place between
their teeth.

The crowd swarmed onto the main street from both ends of
the village, pouring out from side streets, lanes, and houses.
From time to time you could hear a door knocker banging
behind a village woman in cotton gloves as she stepped out
to watch the goings-on. The main attractions were two long
triangular frames covered with Chinese lanterns, flanking
the platform on which the authorities were to sit.
Against each of the four pillars of the Town Hall stood a
pole bearing a small green canvas standard adorned with in-
scriptions in gold letters. One said "Trade," another "Agriculture," the third "Industry," and the fourth "Fine Arts."

But the glow of delight on everyone's face seemed to make

Madame Lefrançois, the innkeeper, quite gloomy. She was standing on her kitchen steps muttering under her breath: "Foolishness! Foolishness with that tent of theirs. Do they think the prefect will be comfortable eating there like a strolling player? They say such stupidities are for the good of the community! It certainly wasn't worth going to Neufchâtel to fetch that wretched cook. For whom? For cowherds and tramps!"

The pharmacist walked past. He was wearing a black dress coat, nankeen trousers, beaver shoes, and, most surprising for him, a hat—a hat with a low crown.

"Greetings!" he called out. "Excuse me, I'm in a hurry."

The fat widow asked him where he was going.

"Seems strange to see me out, doesn't it? I who always stick closer to my laboratory than a rat does to cheese."

"What cheese?" asked the landlady.

"Nothing, nothing," Homais continued. "I merely meant to explain to you, Madame Lefrançois, that I usually stay home like a hermit. Today, however, in view of the circumstances, I must—"

"Aha! So you're going off there?" she said disdainfully.

"Yes, I'm going," answered the pharmacist with surprise. "Am I not a member of the arrangements committee?"

The Widow Lefrançois stared at him a few minutes, then replied with a smile: "That's another story! But what's your connection with farming? Do you know anything about it?"

"Of course I do, since I'm a pharmacist, that is to say, a chemist. And chemistry, Madame Lefrançois, having as its goal the knowledge of the reciprocal and molecular action of nature's bodies, it follows that agriculture is included in its domain. After all, the composition of manure, fermentation of liquids, analyses of gas, and the influence of miasmas —what is all that, I ask you, if not chemistry pure and simple?"

The innkeeper said nothing. Homais continued: "Do you think that it is necessary to till the soil yourself or feed poultry in order to be an agronomist? One must rather be familiar with the composition of the substances they contain, with geological movements, atmospheric conditions, the quality of the soil, minerals and waters, the densities of different bodies and their capillary attraction. And so on. And one must have a thorough knowledge of all the principles of hygiene in order to direct and criticize the construction of buildings, the feeding of animals and servants. And also, Madame Lefrançois, one must possess a knowledge of botany, be able to distinguish among plants you see. Know which are the beneficial ones, which are harmful, which are unproductive, and which nutritional; if it's a good idea to pull some from one spot and plant them elsewhere; or to cultivate some and destroy others. In short, you must keep up with science by reading scientific papers and government pamphlets, be constantly on the watch to point out improvements—"

The landlady kept staring at the door of the Café Français. The pharmacist continued: "Would to heaven that our farmers were chemists, or at least that they heeded the advice of science more closely. For example, I recently wrote a substantial little paper, a memorandum of more than seventy-two pages entitled 'On Cider: Its Manufacture and Effects with Several New Comments on This Topic,' which I sent to the Agricultural Society of Rouen. It even earned me the honor of being received as a member in the agricultural section, pomology subsection. Ah! If only my work had had a wider publicity—" But the apothecary stopped short since Madame Lefrançois appeared quite preoccupied.

"Just look at them," she said. "I don't understand. To call *that* an eating place."

She shrugged her shoulders so that the stitches in her sweater stretched over her bosom and pointed with both hands to her rival's establishment, from which singing could be heard.

"Anyway, he won't have it much longer," she added. "It'll all be finished in a week."

Homais seemed shocked. She walked down the three steps and whispered into his ear: "Didn't you know? He's going to be taken over this week. Lheureux is foreclosing him. He drove him into bankruptcy."

"What a dreadful catastrophe!" exclaimed the apothecary, who always had the proper expression for any conceivable circumstance.

The landlady began to tell him the story, which she had gotten from Theodore, Monsieur Guillaumin's servant; and even though she loathed Tellier, she blamed Lheureux. He was a wheedling, groveling, loathsome man.

"There he is," she said, "in the market. He's bowing to Madame Bovary, who's wearing that green hat. See, she's holding on to Monsieur Boulanger's arm."

"Madame Bovary!" exclaimed Homais. "I must pay my respects. She might like to have a seat in the enclosure under the colonnade."

And ignoring Madame Lefrançois, who was calling him back in order to continue her story, the pharmacist walked off hurriedly, his mouth fixed in a smile, his bearing erect, distributing a quantity of greetings to the right and to the left, taking up a great deal of space with the large tails of his black frock coat, which floated behind him in the wind.

Rodolphe noticed him from afar and consequently started walking faster. But Madame Bovary was soon out of breath and so he slowed down, smiling at her as he said in a gruff manner, "Let's get away from that terrible man; you know, the pharmacist."

She nudged him with her elbow.

"What's that supposed to mean?" he asked himself, looking at her out of the corner of his eye as they walked.

Her profile was so calm that nothing could be guessed from it. It stood out in the bright sunlight against the oval shape of her bonnet, which was tied with light-colored reed-like ribbons. Her eyes, with their long curving lashes, were directed straight ahead, and even though they were wide open, they seemed slightly narrowed by the cheekbones because of the blood pulsing gently beneath her delicate skin. There was a pinkish tinge across the bridge of her nose. She was leaning her head a bit to one side, and the pearly edges of her white teeth were visible between her lips.

"Is she laughing at me?" Rodolphe wondered.

But Emma's gesture had only been a warning because Monsieur Lheureux was at their side. He kept addressing them every once in a while, trying to engage them in conversation.

"What a magnificent day! Everyone's out. The wind's coming from the east."

Neither Madame Bovary nor Rodolphe made any comment, while he, at their slightest movement, would come closer and say, "I beg your pardon?" and tip his hat with his hand.

When they had reached the blacksmith's, instead of continuing along the road as far as the gate, Rodolphe turned abruptly into a pathway, pulling Madame Bovary along with him. He shouted: "Good-bye, Monsieur Lheureux. See you soon."

"What a way to get rid of him," she said with a laugh.

"Why let people bother you?" he said. "Especially when I have the pleasure of being with you today——"

Emma blushed. He did not complete his sentence. Then he began to speak about the lovely weather and the delight of walking on the grass. A few daisies were up.

"Nice little daisies," he said, "enough to provide prophecies for all the girls around here who are in love."

"What would you say if I picked one?" he added.

"Are you in love?" she asked with a slight cough.

"Who knows?" Rodolphe answered.

The meadow was beginning to fill up, and the people were being jostled by housewives with their huge parasols and baskets and their babies. It was often necessary to move out of the way of a long row of farm girls, blue-stockinged servant girls with flat shoes and silver rings who reeked of milk when you drew near them. They would walk along, holding hands, and were spread out in this fashion all across the meadow, from the line of aspens as far as the banquet tent. Then the time arrived for the judging, and the farmers, one after another, filed into a sort of arena formed by a long rope supported by stakes.

The animals were already there, muzzles facing the rope, rumps of varying sizes more or less aligned. The drowsy pigs were sinking their snouts into the ground; the calves were lowing; the sheep bleating; the cows with their legs folded under were resting their bellies on the ground, and while they slowly chewed their cuds, blinked their heavy eyelids at the flies buzzing around them. Carters with their sleeves rolled up were holding the halters of rearing stallions, which were loudly whinnying in the direction of the mares, who were standing quietly by, stretching their necks, their manes dangling. Their foals rested in their shadows, occasionally approaching to suck. Along the tightly packed line of these undulating bodies could be seen a few white manes flowing in the breeze like waves or a pair of pointed horns jutting forth over the heads of men who were running. Away to one side, about a hundred feet outside the arena, stood a huge black bull, muzzled, with an iron ring through his nostrils, as motionless as a bronze statue of an animal. A child in tatters held him by a rope.

Meanwhile, between the two rows, several gentlemen were walking along with heavy gait, examining each animal and then talking together in low voices. One of them, who seemed more important than the others, was taking notes in a notebook as he walked. He was the president of the jury: Monsieur Derozerays de la Panville. As soon as he noticed Rodolphe, he walked over quickly and said to him with a friendly smile: "Are you deserting us, Monsieur Boulanger?"

Rodolphe assured him that he was going to join them. But when the president had disappeared, he said, "Good grief! I'm not going to go. I prefer your company to his."

Although he poked fun at the show, Rodolphe showed the guard his blue ticket so that they could move about more freely. He even stopped occasionally to admire some interesting exhibit, which Madame Bovary did not find at all to her liking. Realizing this, he began to make jokes about the way the Yonville ladies dressed; then apologized for his own negligence about clothes. His clothes were that hodgepodge blend of ordinary and elegant in which the common man thinks he discerns eccentricity of behavior, lack of disciplined emotions, subservience to the tyranny of art, and a general scorn for social convention. This he finds either very alluring or thoroughly exasperating. Thus, Rodolphe's cambric shirt with its frilled cuffs would puff out through the opening of his gray drill waistcoat when the wind blew, and his broad-striped trousers reached only to his ankles, revealing nankeen boots with patent leather uppers polished so brightly that they reflected the grass. He trampled over the horse dung with them, one hand in his jacket pocket and his straw hat tilted to one side.

"Besides," he said, "when you live in the country—"

"It's all a waste," Emma continued.

"It is," Rodolphe replied. "Just think, not one of these good souls could appreciate the cut of a coat."

And so they spoke about provincial mediocrity, of the lives it stifled, the illusions it killed.

"And I bury myself, in my sadness," Rodolphe said.

"You!" she said with surprise. "I thought you were gay!"

"I am, on the surface, because I wear my jester's mask in public, and yet how many times have I asked myself, seeing a cemetery in the moonlight, if I wouldn't be better off joining those who sleep there."

"What about your friends?" she said. "Don't you think of them?"

"My friends? Which ones? Do I have any? Who cares about me?"

He accompanied these last words with a hissing sound.

Then they had to be separated because of a large scaffolding of chairs being carried by a man behind them. He was so loaded down that only the tips of his wooden shoes and of his outstretched arms were visible. It was Lestiboudois, the gravedigger, transporting the church chairs through the crowd. Always ready with ideas for anything regarding his interests, he had discovered this method of profiting from the show. His notion was succeeding so well he no longer knew which way to turn. The villagers, affected by the heat, were arguing over these straw-filled chairs smelling of incense and leaning against their sturdy backs, soiled by candle wax, with a certain feeling of veneration.

Madame Bovary took Rodolphe's arm again. He kept on speaking, as though to himself: "I've missed so many things! Always alone! If I had only had a goal in my life, if I'd fallen in love, found someone—I would have applied all my energy, overcome everything, surmounted every obstacle!"

"I still think," said Emma, "that you're hardly to be pitied."

"Oh?" said Rodolphe.

"Because—after all," she said, "you're free." She hesitated, "and rich."

"Don't make fun of me," he answered.

She assured him that she wasn't making fun. Just then there was a blast from the cannon. There was an immediate surge of people toward the village.

It was a false alarm. The prefect was not yet there, and the members of the jury found themselves in a very awkward situation, unsure whether they should begin the proceedings or keep on waiting.

Finally, at the far end of the square, a large hired landau appeared, pulled by two scrawny horses that a coachman in a white hat was whipping with all his might. Binet had only enough time to shout "Fall in!" and the colonel to follow suit. The men made a dash for the piled guns, some even forgetting to fasten their collars in their hurry. But the prefect's equipage seemed to be aware of the confusion and the two sorry nags, dawdling at their coupling chain, ambled up to the entrance of the Town Hall just as the

National Guard and the Fire Brigade were deploying to the roll of drums.

"Mark time!" Binet shouted.

"Halt!" shouted the colonel. "Left face!"

And after a "Present Arms!" the clatter of which sounded like a copper kettle bumping down the stairs, all the rifles were lowered again.

Then a gentleman in a short, silver-trimmed jacket was seen alighting from the carriage. He had a bald forehead with a shock of hair behind, a pale complexion, and an appearance of extreme benevolence. His large, heavy-lidded eyes were narrowed as he looked at the assemblage, his pointed nose was high in the air, and there was a smile on his sunken mouth. He recognized the mayor by his sash and informed him that the prefect had not been able to come. He himself was one of the counselors of the prefecture. He added a few words of apology. Tuvache answered with some polite clichés, the other declared himself overwhelmed. And thus they stood, face to face, foreheads almost touching, surrounded by the members of the jury, the municipal council, the notables, the National Guard, and the crowd. The counselor, holding his small black three-cornered hat against his heart, reiterated his greetings while Tuvache, bending like a bow, smiled, stammered, groped for things to say, and declared his devotion to the monarchy and his appreciation of the honor that was being rendered to Yonville.

Hippolyte, the groom from the inn, came limping up on his clubfoot to take the coachman's horses by the bridle and led them through the gates of the Golden Lion, where many of the peasants were gathered to look at the carriage. The drum rolled, the howitzer thundered, and the gentlemen filed onto the platform, seating themselves in the armchairs of red Utrecht velvet that Madame Tuvache had lent them.

They all looked alike. Their pale, flabby faces, slightly bronzed by the sun, had the color of sweet cider, and their bushy whiskers stuck out above their stiff high collars, which were held in place by white cravats tied in generous bows. All the waistcoats had velvet lapels; every watch had an oval cornelian seal at the end of a long ribbon. And they all sat with both hands resting on their thighs, legs carefully spread, the unsponged cloth of their trousers shining more than the leather of their heavy boots.

Their ladies were behind them, between the columns of

the vestibule, while the common horde faced them, standing
or seated on the chairs that Lestiboudois had actually
brought over from the meadow. He kept running every
minute into the church to look for more. He was causing
such a bottleneck with his business that it was very difficult to gain access to the platform steps.

"It seems to me," said Monsieur Lheureux (addressing the
pharmacist, who was walking past to get to his place), "that
they should have put up a couple of Venetian mats with
something rich and a little severe in the way of drapery.
It would have been rather eye-catching."

"You're right," said Homais. "But what do you expect?
The mayor took charge of everything. He has no taste to
speak of, poor Tuvache. Completely lacking in what you
might call artistic sense."

During this time Rodolphe had gone up with Madame
Bovary to the council chamber on the first floor of the
Town Hall. Since it was empty, he said that it would be
quite a comfortable spot from which to watch the proceedings at their ease. He took three stools that were set around
the oval table under the bust of the king and set them near
one of the windows. They sat down side by side.

There was some commotion on the platform, a great deal
of whispering and discussing. The counselor finally arose. His
name, it had been learned, was Lieuvain and people were
repeating it through the crowd. When he had arranged several
sheets of paper and brought them closer to his eyes to
see better, he began: "Gentlemen: May I begin—before addressing you on the subject of this meeting today, and this
sentiment will, I am quite sure, be shared by all of you—may
I begin, I say, by paying my just respects to the national
administration, to the government, to the king, gentlemen,
to our sovereign, to that beloved king to whom no branch of
prosperity, either private or public, is indifferent, and who
steers the ship of state with a hand both firm and wise amid
the ceaseless perils of a stormy sea—who knows, moreover,
how to inculcate respect for peace as well as war, for industry, commerce, agriculture, and the fine arts. . . ."

"I ought to move back a bit," said Rodolphe.

"Why?" Emma asked.

Just then the counselor's voice boomed out in an extraordinary manner. He was declaiming: "The days have passed,
gentlemen, when civil strife spilled blood on our public

places, when the landowner, the tradesman, and even the worker, falling peacefully asleep in the evening, trembled lest they be awakened by the noise of incendiary tocsins, when the most subversive theories were boldly undermining the foundations. . . ."

"I can be seen from here," said Rodolphe, "and it would take me two weeks to clear myself. With my bad reputation—"

"You're too hard on yourself," said Emma.

"No, it's really dreadful, I assure you."

"But gentlemen," the counselor continued, "if I cast those gloomy images from my memory and focus my eyes on the present situation in our fair land, what do I see? Commerce and the arts flourish everywhere, everywhere new systems of communication, like so many new arteries in the body of the State, are establishing new relationships; our great manufacturing centers have regained their activity; religion, more firmly established than heretofore, smiles at every heart; our ports are full, confidence is reborn, and France is finally breathing with ease!"

"Besides," Rodolphe added, "people may be right."

"How so?" she said.

"Well," he said, "don't you know that there are certain souls in perpetual torment? They are constantly in need of either a dream or some occupation, the purest of passions, the most passionate of pleasures, and they throw themselves into all kinds of daydreams and madness."

At that she looked at him as one stares at a traveler who has passed through exotic lands, and said: "We poor women don't even have that distraction."

"A sad distraction in which you don't find any happiness."

"But does one ever find happiness?" she asked.

"Yes, someday," he answered.

"And this is what you have understood," said the councilman. "You farmers and farmhands, you peaceful pioneers in a true task of civilization, you, men of progress and morality. You have understood, I repeat, that political storms remain more to be feared than atmospheric disorders. . . ."

"It appears one fine day," Rodolphe repeated, "suddenly, when you are most despairing. Then the heavens open up and it's as if a voice cried out: 'Here it is!' You feel you must confide your life to that person, confide everything. You don't discuss feelings, you sense them. You've already met in your dreams." And here he looked at her. "Finally there it is, the treasure so long searched for, before you; shining and sparkling. And yet you still doubt, you're afraid to believe. You remain dazzled by it as if you had stepped out of the shadows into the light."

As he finished these words, Rodolphe added pantomime to his speech. He passed his hand over his face in the gesture of a man stunned; then he dropped it onto Emma's. She pulled hers away.

The councilman was still reading: "And who will be surprised at it, gentlemen? Only he who is so blinded, so steeped—I do not fear to say it—so steeped in the prejudices of another age that he cannot comprehend even today the spirit of our farm populations. Where is a more faithful patriotism to be found than in the countryside, more devotion to the public welfare, more intelligence, in a word? And I do not refer, gentlemen, to that superficial intelligence that is the vain adornment of idle minds, but rather that deep and reasoning intelligence that applies itself above all else to the pursuit of necessary goals, contributing in this fashion to the welfare of all, to the public betterment and to the maintenance of the state—the fruit of respect for law and the fulfillment of duty."

"Still at it," Rodolphe said. "Always duty. I'm fed up with those words. They're a bunch of old fogies in flannel waistcoats, bigoted old ladies with foot warmers and beads, who keep singing into our ears, 'Duty! Duty!' Our duty is to discern the great and cherish the beautiful and not to accept all those conventions of society with the ignominies it imposes on us."

"But—but—" Madame Bovary was objecting.

"No! Why argue against the passions? Aren't they the only beautiful things on the earth, the inspiration for heroism, enthusiasm, poetry, music, art, for everything?"

"But you have to go along with society to some extent, and respect its morality," Emma said.

"Ah, but there are two moralities," he answered. "The petty, conventional morality, the morality of men, which is constantly changing and which makes such a loud noise, floundering about on the earth like this collection of imbeciles you see before you. But the other, the eternal morality, is all around and above us like the countryside that surrounds us and the blue sky that sends down its light."

Monsieur Lieuvain had just wiped his mouth with his pocket handkerchief. He went on: "And who am I, gentlemen, to show you here the usefulness of agriculture? After all, who is it who supplies our needs? Who furnishes our food? Is it not the farmer? The farmer, my friends, who, sowing with a weary, hard-working hand the fruitful furrows of the land, brings forth the wheat, which, crushed and ground into powder by means of ingenious machinery, from which it emerges under the name of flour, is transported from there into the cities and soon delivered to the baker, who makes from it a food for poor as well as rich. Is it not the farmer who also fattens his abundant sheep in the pastures for our clothing needs? For how would we dress ourselves and how would we eat without agriculture? And gentlemen, must we go so far to seek examples? Who has not often thought about the importance we derive from that modest animal, the adornment of our farmyards, who furnishes us with soft pillows for our sleep, a succulent meat for our tables, and eggs? But I would never finish if I had to enumerate every single one of the different products that the well-cultivated earth, like a generous mother, lavishes on its children. Here it is the vine; elsewhere, cider apples; in other places, rapeseed; farther on, cheese; and flax—gentlemen, let us not forget flax! Flax, which has made considerable strides these last few years and to which I would particularly like to draw your attention."

He did not have to draw it; every mouth in the crowd was open as if to drink in his words. Tuvache, beside him, was listening with his eyes wide open; Monsieur Derozerays would occasionally close his eyes gently. Farther down, the pharmacist with his son Napoleon between his knees had his hand cupped behind his ear in order not to miss a single syllable. The other members of the jury were nodding their chins slowly into their waistcoats to signify assent. The firemen stood leaning on their bayonets at the foot of the platform, and Binet, motionless and with his elbow sticking out, had his saber pointing into the air. He may have been listening, but he could not have seen anything because the visor of his helmet came down over his nose. His lieutenant, Tuvache's younger son, had his visor at an even more exaggerated angle; he wore an enormous one that wobbled un-

steadily on his head, revealing an edge of his calico kerchief.
Beneath it he was smiling with a childlike meekness, and
his small, pale face, beaded with sweat, revealed an expression of pleasure blended with exhaustion and sleepiness.

The square was crowded as far back as the housefronts.
You could see people leaning out of every window, others
standing on every doorstep, and Justin, in front of the pharmacy window, appeared to be fixedly contemplating some
object. Despite the silence, Monsieur Lieuvain's voice did
not carry through the air. It reached you only in fragments
of sentences, interrupted here and there by the creaking of
chairs in the crowd, or a sudden long lowing of a bull behind you, or of the lambs bleating to each other from the
corners of the streets. The cowherds and shepherds had driv-
en their animals out there where they kept up their lowing
while snatching with their tongues at some bit of foliage hanging above their muzzles.

Rodolphe had drawn closer to Emma and was speaking
rapidly in a low voice: "Doesn't this conspiracy of society
revolt you? Is there one ounce of feeling that it does not condemn? The most noble instincts, the purest emotions, are
persecuted and slandered, and if two poor souls finally meet,
everything is organized so that they cannot unite. But they
will keep trying, beating their wings, calling out to each
other. And, sooner or later, in six months or ten years, they
will reunite and love each other because destiny demands it
and they were born for each other."

He sat with his arms closed on his lap, looking up at Emma and gazing at her closely, steadily. In his eyes she could
distinguish small flecks of gold irradiating all around his black
pupils and could even smell the perfume of the pomade that
made his hair shine. Then a sudden weakness overcame her;
she remembered the viscount who had waltzed with her at
Vaubyessard and from whose beard emanated the same odor
of vanilla and lemon; mechanically, she shut her eyes in
order to smell it better. But as she straightened up in her
chair, she glimpsed in the distance the old diligence, the
Hirondelle, slowly descending Leux Hill and trailing a long
plume of dust behind it. It was in this yellow carriage that
Léon had so often come back to her and by that road that
he had left forever! She had a vision of him across the way,
at his window, then everything seemed to be topsy-turvy,
clouds passed over her; she seemed to be still turning to that

waltz in the viscount's arms—Léon was not far off, he was
going to come—and yet she did not stop being aware of
Rodolphe's head beside her. The sweetness of this sensation
mingled with her old desires, and like grains of sand when the
wind blows, they were tossed about in the subtle gusts of
perfume settling on her soul. She opened her nostrils wide,
wider, to take in the freshness of the ivy winding around the
tops of the columns. She drew off her gloves, dried her hands,
then fanned her face with her handkerchief while through
the throbbing of her temples she could hear the murmurs of
the crowd and the voice of the counselor.

He was saying: "Keep going! Persevere! Heed not the
promptings of routine nor the overhasty advice of rash em-
piricism. Apply yourselves especially to improving the soil,
enriching your fertilizers, to the development of the equine,
bovine, and porcine breeds! May this Show be unto you as a
peaceful arena in which the victor, as he leaves, stretches out
his hand in friendship to the vanquished, wishing him luck
for next time. And you, venerable servitors, humble domestic
help, whose painful labors no government until now has tak-
en into consideration, come take the reward for your silent
virtues and be assured that the state henceforth shall keep
it eyes on you, that it encourages you, protects you, that it
will do justice unto your rightful claims and will lighten,
as much as it is in its power, the burden of your painful
sacrifices."

Monsieur Lieuvain sat down again. Monsieur Derozerays
arose, beginning a new speech. His was not quite as flowery
as the counselor's, but this was compensated for by a more
positive style, that is, by a more specialized knowledge and
more exhalted reflections. Thus, praise of the government was
stressed less and religion and agriculture more. The relation
between the latter two was brought out, and also how they
had always worked together in the interests of civilization.
Rodolphe was talking to Madame Bovary about dreams,
omens, and magnetic attraction. Going back to the cradle of
civilization, the orator was depicting those fierce times when
men lived on acorns deep in the forest. Later they exchanged
the skins of animals for cloth garments, learned to plow the
fields and cultivate the vine. Was this for man's good or was
there not more inconvenience than advantage in this discovery? Monsieur Derozerays asked himself this question.
From magnetic attraction, little by little, Rodolphe had arrived

at the affinities, and while the president was citing Cincinnatus at his plow, Diocletian planting his cabbages, and the emperors of China ushering in the new year by sowing the seed, the young man was explaining to the young woman that the cause of these irresistible attractions derived from some previous existence.

"Take us, for example," he was saying. "Why did we meet? What chance determined it? It is surely because our particular selves inclined us toward each other across the distance, like two rivers that gradually converge toward one another."

He took her hand. She did not take it back.

"Grand prize! To the best all-around farmer!" shouted the president.

"The other day, for example, when I came to your house—"

"To Monsieur Bizet of Quincampoix."

"Did I know that I would be spending today with you?"

"Seventy francs!"

"I've wanted to go off a hundred times, but I've kept by your side, stayed with you."

"Manures."

"As I will remain this evening, tomorrow, all the other days all my life!"

"To Monsieur Caron of Argueil, a gold medal."

"For I have never found anyone's company as charming as yours."

"To Monsieur Bain of Givry-Saint-Martin!"

"And so I will cherish the thought of you."

"For a merino ram—"

"But you'll forget me. I shall pass away like a shadow."

"To Monsieur Belot of Notre-Dame—"

"Oh no. Tell me I will remain in your thoughts, in your life."

"Pig class: a prize of sixty francs divided between Messieurs Lehérissé and Cullembourg."

Rodolphe held her hand tightly; he felt it warm and trembling like a captive dove trying to resume its flight. She moved her fingers either because she was trying to free them or replying to the pressure and he exclaimed: "Thank you. You aren't rejecting me. You're so good. You understand that I am yours. Just let me look at you, gaze at you."

A gust of wind coming in through the window disturbed

the tablecloth. Below, in the square, the large headdresses of all the countrywomen soared upward like the wings of white butterflies.

"Oil-cake," the president continued. He began to go faster: "Flemish fertilizer—flax—drainage—long leases—domestic service—"

Rodolphe was no longer speaking. They were looking at one another. A supreme desire was causing their dry lips to quiver. Gently, without effort, their fingers intertwined.

"Catherine-Nicaise-Elisabeth Leroux, of Sassetot-la-Guerrière, for fifty-four years of service in the same farm: a silver medal—value, twenty-five francs!"

"Catherine Leroux. Where is she?" the counselor repeated.

She did not come forward. People were whispering: "Go on!"

"No."

"To the left." "Don't be afraid." "How silly she is!"

"Well, where is she?" shouted Tuvache.

"Here she is!"

"Come now, come forward."

Then, to the platform came a frightened-looking little old lady who seemed shrunken in her shabby garments. On her feet were heavy wooden clogs and around her hips a large blue apron. Her scrawny face, framed by a borderless cap, was more wrinkled than a shriveled apple, and bony knuckles dangled from the sleeves of her red bodice. They were so encrusted, roughened, and gnarled from barn dust, soapsuds and grease from sheep's wool that they seemed dirty even though they had been washed in clean water. They remained half bent from having worked so long, humble witnesses of so much suffering. The expression on her face was of an almost nunlike inflexibility. Having lived in the company of animals, she had acquired their muteness and placidity. This was the first time that she found herself in the midst of such a numerous group, and inwardly frightened by the flags and drums, by the gentlemen in frock coats, and by the counselor's Cross of Honor, she remained stock-still, not knowing whether to move forward or run off, nor why the people were pushing her and the examiners smiling. There, before these expansive townspeople, stood this half century of servitude.

"Come forth, venerable Catherine-Nicaise-Elisabeth Leroux!" said the counselor, who had taken the list of winners from the president's hands. "Come up, come up," he repeated in a paternal tone, alternately looking at the sheet of paper and the old woman.

"Are you deaf?" said Tuvache, hopping up from his chair.

He began to shout in her ear: "Fifty-four years of service! A silver medal. Twenty-five francs. For you."

When she was finally holding her medal, she looked at it carefully and a blissful smile spread over her face. She could be heard muttering as she walked off: "I'll give it to our curé to say Mass for me."

"What fanaticism!" exclaimed the pharmacist, leaning toward the notary.

The proceedings were over. The crowd dispersed. Now that the speeches had been read, everyone reassumed his station and things reverted to normal. Masters spoke sharply to their servants, and the servants struck the animals, indolent winners returning to the stable with a green wreath set between their horns.

Meanwhile the National Guard had ascended to the first floor of the Town Hall, with rolls impaled on their bayonets, and the battalion drummer was carrying a basketful of bottles. Madame Bovary took Rodolphe's arm. He accompanied her home, and they separated at her door. Then he walked alone through the meadow, awaiting the hour of the banquet.

The meal was long, noisy, and badly served. They were so crowded that there was virtually no elbow room, and the narrow planks that served as benches almost broke under the weight of the guests. They ate huge quantities of food, everyone gorging himself. Perspiration was pouring down every face, and a white vapor, like river mist on an autumn day, was hovering above the table between the hanging lamps. Rodolphe, leaning back against the side of the tent, was concentrating so much on Emma that he heard nothing. Behind him, on the lawn, the servants were stacking the dirty dishes; his neighbors addressed him, but he did not answer. His glass was filled and, despite the increasing volume of the sound, in his mind there was silence. He was dreaming about what she had said and the shape of her lips; her face, as in a magic mirror, was shining on the badges of the military caps. The folds of her dress were draping the walls, and days of love unfurled unto infinity in the perspective of the future.

He saw her again that evening during the fireworks; but she was with her husband, Madame Homais, and the pharmacist, the latter tormenting himself about the danger of stray rockets. He kept leaving his party every minute to give Binet his suggestions.

The fireworks had been sent in care of Monsieur Tuvache, who had locked them in his cellar in an excess of caution, and so the humid powder barely ignited. The principal display, which was to be a dragon biting its tail, failed completely. An occasional lone Roman candle would go off to a clamor from the gaping mass, which included the squeals of women whose waists were being squeezed in the dark. Emma, in silence, was leaning gently against Charles's shoulder, looking up at the luminous track of the rocket in the black sky. Rodolphe looked at her by the light of the Chinese lanterns.

These died down slowly, and the stars appeared. A few drops of rain began to fall. Emma tied her scarf over her unprotected head.

Just then the counselor's carriage came out from the direction of the inn. The coachman, who was drunk, suddenly fell asleep, and from afar, above the hood, between the two lanterns, the hulk of his body could be seen swaying from right to left to the pitching of the vehicle.

"Really," said the pharmacist, "we must deal harshly with intoxication. I would like to see a weekly *ad hoc* list put up on the Town Hall of all those who became drunk on alcohol during the week. Besides, from a statistical point of view we would have a public record, which might do— Oh, excuse me."

And he ran off once more toward the captain, who was going home, to look again at his lathe.

"It might not be a bad idea," Homais said to him, "to send one of your men or go yourself—"

"Leave me alone," the tax collector answered. "There's no danger."

"It's all right," said Homais when he returned to his friends. "Monsieur Binet assured me that all possible measures were taken. No stray spark will fall. The pumps are filled. Let's go home to sleep."

"Lord knows I need it," said Madame Homais, yawning widely. "Never mind, we had a beautiful day for our celebration."

Rodolphe repeated softly, with a tender expression: "Ah, yes, very beautiful."

They bade each other good night and went their separate ways.

Two days later, in the *Rouen Beacon*, there was a lengthy article about the Show. Homais had written it with enthusiasm on the next day:

"Why all these festoons and flowers and garlands? Whither ran this crowd like the waves of an enraged sea, under a tropical sun beating down over our fields?"

He went on to speak about the plight of the peasants. The government was indeed doing a great deal, but not enough! "Be brave!" he advised. "There are a thousand indispensable reforms. Let us accomplish them."

Then, discussing the counselor's arrival, he forgot neither "the martial air of our militia" nor "our sprightly village lasses" nor the bald-headed old men, "those patriarchs who attended, the remnants of our immortal legions, their hearts still beating to the manly roll of the drums." He listed himself among the leading members of the jury, and even mentioned in a note that Monsieur Homais, pharmacist, had sent a memorandum on cider to the Society of Agriculture.

When he reached the distribution of the prizes, he painted the winners' joy in dithyrambic strokes. "Father embraced son, husband wife, brother brother. More than one displayed his humble medal with pride, and doubtless, on his return home, was to hang it in tears upon the modest walls of his humble cottage.

"At six o'clock, a banquet, set out in Monsieur Liégeard's meadow, assembled the principal personalities of the Show. The greatest cordiality reigned throughout. Several toasts were offered; Monsieur Lieuvain proposed the King's health, Monsieur Tuvache that of the prefect; Monsieur Derozerays the farmers' and Monsieur Homais those two sisters industry and the fine arts. Monsieur Leplichey offered his toast to progress. In the evening a brilliant fireworks display suddenly illuminated the heavens. It was a veritable kaleidoscope, a setting for an opera. For a moment our little town believed itself transported to the heart of an Arabian Nights dream.

"Let us note that no untoward event occurred to mar this family reunion."

He added: "However, the absence of the clergy was noted.

Doubtless the gentlemen of the cloth understand progress in a different way. As you will, revered followers of Loyola!"

IX

Six weeks went by. Rodolphe did not return. He finally appeared one evening.

"It would be a mistake to return too soon," he had said to himself. And he went off on a hunting trip the week after the Show.

After the hunt he thought it was too late, and then he reasoned: "If she loved me that first day, her impatience to see me again must be increasing her love. We'll keep this up awhile."

He realized that his reasoning had been sound when he saw Emma turn pale as he entered the room.

She was alone in the fading light. The short muslin curtains along the windowpanes intensified the twilight; the gilt on the barometer, touched by a ray of sunshine, was reflecting sparks onto the mirror hanging between the fretted coral.

Rodolphe remained standing. His opening remarks were conventionally polite; Emma barely answered them.

"I've been busy," he went on, "and ill."

"Nothing serious?" she asked quickly.

"No," he said, sitting down near her on a stool. "I just didn't want to come back."

"Why?"

"You can't guess?"

He looked at her with such intensity that she lowered her head and blushed. He began again: "Emma—"

"Sir!" she said, pulling back a little.

"Ah, you can see," he said in a melancholy tone, "I was right not to come back, since you refuse me that name, that name that courses through my soul and that just escaped from me! 'Madame Bovary!' Everyone calls you that. And it's not even your name, it's someone else's. Someone else's," he repeated, and he hid his face in his hands. "Yes, I

think of you all the time. The memory of you drives me
to despair. Forgive me. I'll leave you. Good-bye. I shall
go far away, so far that you will never hear about me
again. And yet—today—I don't know what power still impelled me toward you. You can't fight fate, or resist the
smile of an angel! You let yourself be lured by what is
beautiful, charming, and adorable!"

This was the first time Emma had heard such things,
and her pride, like someone who lets himself relax in a steam
bath, stretched luxuriously and without reservations in the
warmth of his words.

"But even if I didn't come," he continued, "if I couldn't
see you, at least I studied your surroundings closely. I arose
and came here every night, looked at your house, at the
roof gleaming in the moonlight, at the trees in the garden
swaying near your window, and at that tiny light shining
through the window into the shadows. Ah! Little did you
guess what was there, so near and yet so far, a poor miserable—"

She turned toward him with a sob.

"You are so good!" she said.

"No, I love you, that is all. You don't doubt it? Tell
me, say one word, one single word!"

And Rodolphe let himself slip imperceptibly from the
stool onto the floor. But the sound of clogs was heard from
the kitchen, and he noticed that the door was open.

"It would be so kind of you," he continued, getting up,
"to satisfy a whim of mine."

This was to visit her house. He wanted to know it well.

Madame Bovary saw nothing out of the way in this, and
they were both standing up when Charles came in.

"Good day, doctor," said Rodolphe.

Charles, flattered by the unexpected title, became extrava-
gantly obsequious. The other took advantage of this to regain
his composure. He said, "Your wife was telling me about
her health—"

Charles interrupted him. He had many worries on that
score; his wife's attacks of breathlessness were beginning
again. Rodolphe asked if horseback riding would not be
a good idea.

"Certainly! Excellent! Perfect! A fine idea! You ought to
look into it, dear."

She objected that she did not own a horse. Monsieur

Rodolphe offered one of his. She refused, and he did not insist. Then, to justify his visit, he mentioned that his carter, the man who had been bled, was still suffering from dizzy spells.

"I'll stop by," said Bovary.

"No, I'll send him here. We can come together. It will be more convenient for you."

"Fine. Thank you very much." When they were alone: "Why don't you accept Monsieur Boulanger's suggestion? It was very considerate."

She began to pout, searched about for a quantity of excuses, and finally declared that "it might look strange."

"I don't care if it does!" said Charles, turning on his heel. "Health above all. You're wrong."

"How do you expect me to go horseback riding when I have no riding habit?"

"We'll have to order one for you." The riding habit decided her.

When the outfit was ready, Charles wrote to Monsieur Boulanger that his wife awaited his convenience and that they were counting on his kindness.

At noon the next day Rodolphe arrived at Charles's door with two riding horses. One had pink pompons on its ears and a buckskin sidesaddle.

Rodolphe was wearing high soft-leather boots. He told himself that she had probably never seen their like. Emma was indeed charmed by his appearance when he appeared on the landing in his long velvet coat and his white tricot riding breeches. She was ready and waiting for him.

Justin slipped out of the shop to see her, and the apothecary himself also stopped work. He offered some advice to Monsieur Boulanger: "An accident happens so fast. Take care. Your horses may be spirited."

Emma heard a noise up above. It was Félicité tapping on the panes to amuse little Berthe. The child threw a kiss from afar. Her mother answered with a wave of her riding crop.

"Have a good ride," shouted Monsieur Homais. "Be careful! Be very careful."

He waved his newspaper as he watched them ride off.

Emma's horse broke into a gallop as soon as it felt soft ground. Rodolphe kept alongside. They would exchange an occasional word. With her head slightly lowered, her hand held high, and her right arm outstretched, she abandoned herself to the rhythmic rocking movement on the saddle.

Rodolphe let go the reins at the foot of the hill and they went off together as one. The horses stopped short at the summit, and her large blue veil fell back down.

It was the beginning of October. A mist lay over the countryside, and there were long wisps of vapor along the hills silhouetted against the horizon. Clouds would break apart, float upward, and disappear. Occasionally, when the haze parted, the rooftops of Yonville could be seen in the distance, gleaming in the sun with the gardens along the river's edge, the barnyards, the walls and the church steeple. Emma squinted as she tried to make out her house. This wretched village in which she lived had never appeared so small to her. From the heights on which they were standing, the entire valley seemed to be a pale, immense lake, evaporating in the air. Occasional clumps of trees jutted out like black rocks, and the tall lines of the poplars, extending out of the mist, looked like the windswept shores of the lake.

A brown light hovered in the warm air between the pines. The earth, red-brown like tobacco, muffled the sound of the horses' hooves as they pushed fallen pinecones before them with their iron shoes.

Rodolphe and Emma skirted around the wooded area. She kept turning her head away in order to avoid his gaze, and then she would see nothing but the evenly spaced trunks of the pine trees, the unbroken succession of which made her slightly dizzy.

The sun came out just as they entered the forest. "God is protecting us," Rodolphe said.

"You think so?" she asked.

"Come," he said. He clicked his tongue, and the two horses moved rapidly.

Tall ferns at the side of the road kept catching in Emma's stirrup. Rodolphe would lean over and pull them off as they moved along. At other times, in order to push aside the branches, he came closer, and Emma felt his knee rubbing against her leg. The sky had turned blue and the leaves were still. There were large stretches of heather in bloom. Patches of violets alternated with the tangled undergrowth of the trees, which was gray, fawn colored, or gold, varying according to the tree.

They would often hear a soft flutter of wings beneath

the bushes or the hoarse, soft cry of the rooks as they flew off among the oaks.

They dismounted. Rodolphe tethered the horses. She walked ahead of him over the moss between the car tracks.

But her long riding habit hampered her, even though she was holding it up. Rodolphe, walking behind her, feasted his eyes on the bit of white stocking that showed like naked flesh between the black of the cloth and the boot.

She stopped. "I'm tired," she said.

"Just a little more; keep trying!" he said. "Be brave!"

She stopped again, a few yards farther. The veil slanting down to her hips over her man-styled hat lent a bluish cast to her face, as if she were floating in azure waters. "Where are we going?"

He didn't answer. She was panting slightly. Rodolphe looked about, biting his mustache.

They reached a more spacious clearing in which young trees had been felled and sat down on a log. Rodolphe began telling her of his love.

He avoided frightening her at the beginning by too many compliments. He was calm, serious, and melancholy.

Emma listened to him with her head lowered, pushing at wood shavings on the ground with her toe.

But when he said: "Aren't our destinies united now?" she answered "No!" "You know they aren't. It's impossible." She arose to leave. He grasped her by the wrist. She stopped. Then, after she had looked at him for a while, her eyes moist with love, she said quickly: "Let's not talk about it anymore. Where are the horses? Let's go back."

He reacted with an angry gesture of annoyance. She repeated: "Where are the horses?"

Then he moved toward her with his arms outstretched, smiling strangely. There was a fixed look in his eyes, and his teeth were clenched. She trembled as she retreated from him, stammering: "You're frightening me. You're hurting me. Let's go back."

"If we must," he said, changing his expression. And once more he became respectful, fond, and shy. She took his arm and they turned back. He said: "What's the matter? What is it? I don't understand. You must have mistaken my intentions. In my soul you are a Madonna on a pedestal, exalted, secure, and immaculate. But I need you to survive.

I need your eyes, your voice, your thoughts. Be my friend, my sister, my angel!"

He stretched his arm around her waist. She tried feebly to free herself. He supported her thus as they walked.

They heard the two horses munching leaves.

"Stay awhile," Rodolphe said. "Let's not go back. Stay!"

He led her farther along, around a small pond where the green duckweed covered the water. Wilted water lilies lay motionless among the reeds. At the sound of their steps through the grass, frogs jumped up to find cover.

"I shouldn't, I shouldn't," she said. "I'm mad to listen to you."

"Why? Emma—Emma—"

"Oh, Rodolphe!" the young woman said slowly, leaning on his shoulder.

The cloth of her habit clung to the velvet of his coat. She threw back her head, her white throat swelled in a sigh, and without resisting, tears streaming, with a long shudder and her face hidden, she gave herself to him.

Evening shadows were falling; the horizontal sun, passing through the branches, was blinding her eyes. All around her, in the leaves and on the ground, were luminous shimmering patches, as if hummingbirds had shed their feathers in flight. All was silent; gentleness seemed to emanate from the trees; she could feel her heart beating again, and the blood circulating like a milky river through her body. Then she heard, off in the distance beyond the woods, over the other hills, a vague, prolonged cry, a drawn-out voice to which she listened in silence as it mingled like music with the waning vibrations of her throbbing nerves. Rodolphe, a cigar in his mouth, was fixing one of the two broken bridles with his knife.

They returned to Yonville along the same road. They saw the traces of their horses side by side in the mud; the same bushes, the same stones in the grass. Nothing had changed around them; and yet, for her, something had happened of greater importance than if the mountains had shifted place. Rodolphe would occasionally pick her hand up and kiss it.

She was charming on horseback! Erect, her waist narrow, her knee bent on her horse's mane, and slightly flushed from the fresh air in the glow of evening.

As they entered Yonville, she made her horse prance over the pavement. People looked at her from the windows.

During dinner her husband remarked that she looked very well; but she seemed not to hear him when he asked about her outing; and she remained with her elbow at the edge of her plate, between the two lighted candles.

"Emma!" he said.

"What?"

"You know, I spent this afternoon with Monsieur Alexander; he has an old mare that is still very handsome, only a little broken at the knees. We could have it for a hundred crowns, I'm sure." He added: "I thought you'd be pleased and I said we'd take it. I bought it. Was I right? Tell me."

She moved her head in a sign of assent; then, a quarter of an hour later: "Are you going out tonight?" she asked.

"Yes. Why?"

"No reason, dear."

As soon as she was rid of Charles, she went up to her room and shut herself in.

At first she was in a state of confusion; she saw the trees, the paths, the ditches, Rodolphe, and she could still feel the tightness of his embrace while the leaves rustled and the reeds whistled.

But when she saw her reflection in the mirror, she was astounded at her appearance. Her eyes had never been so large, so black, nor of such a depth. She was transfigured by some subtle change permeating her entire being.

She kept telling herself, "I have a lover! A lover!" relishing the thought like that of some unexpected second puberty. So she was finally going to possess those joys of love, that fever of happiness, of which she had so long despaired. She was entering into something marvelous where all would be passion, ecstasy, delirium; she was enveloped in a vast expanse of blue, the peaks of emotion sparkling in her thoughts. Ordinary existence seemed to be in the distance, down below, in the shadows, between the peaks.

Then she remembered the heroines in the books she had read, and the lyrical legion of these adulterous women began to sing in her memory with sisterly voices enchanting her. She herself became a part of these fantasies. She was realizing the long dream of her adolescence, seeing herself as one of those amorous women she had so long envied. Moreover, Emma was feeling a sensation of revenge. Had she not suffered enough? But now she was triumphing, and love, so long contained, burst forth in its entirety with joyous effervescence. She was savoring it without remorse or anxiety, without feeling troubled.

The next day brought new delight. They made promises to each other. She told him her troubles. Rodolphe interrupted her with his kisses; and she asked him, looking at him through half-closed eyelids, to repeat her name again and to tell her once more that he loved her. Like the preceding day, this took place in the forest, in a clogmaker's hut. The walls were of straw and the roof came down so low that they had to stoop. They sat side by side on a bed of dried leaves.

From that day on they wrote each other regularly every evening. Emma would carry her letter to the back of the garden, near the river, to a crevice in the wall. Rodolphe would come for it and leave another, which she always complained was too short.

One day, when Charles had gone out before dawn, she was seized with the yearning to see Rodolphe right away. She could go quickly to La Huchette, remain an hour, and be back in Yonville while everyone was still asleep. The notion made her pant with desire; she soon found herself walking rapidly through the meadow without a backward glance.

Day was beginning to break. Emma recognized her lover's home in the distance. Its two swallow-tailed weathervanes were silhouetted black in the pale light of dawn.

Beyond the barnyard there was a building that was probably the château. She walked in as if the walls had parted at her approach. A long straight staircase led up to a corridor. Emma lifted a door latch and suddenly, at the back of the room, she saw a man sleeping. It was Rodolphe. She uttered a cry.

"You!" he said. "You! How did you get here? Your dress is all wet!"

"I love you," she answered, twining her arms around his neck.

This first risk having succeeded, each time from then on that Charles left early, Emma would dress rapidly and walk stealthily down the flight of steps leading to the water's edge.

But when the plank for the cows was taken away, she had to walk along the walls beside the water; the bank was slippery; to keep from falling, she would grasp the tufts of faded wallflowers. Farther on, she would turn into the plowed fields, where she would stumble as her thin boots sank deep and filled with mud. Her kerchief, tied around her head, would flutter in the wind of the meadows; she was afraid of the oxen and would begin to run; she would arrive out of breath, her cheeks flushed, and her body exuding a fresh fragrance of sap, verdure, and open air. Rodolphe would be still sleeping at that hour, and it was as if a spring morning had come into his bedroom.

Through the yellow curtains along the windows a heavy light softly penetrated. Emma blinked, groping her way, while the drops of dew on her hair resembled a topaz halo around her face. Rodolphe would laughingly pull her to him and hold her close to his chest.

Later she would look around the room, open the furniture drawers, comb her hair with his comb, and stare at herself in the shaving mirror. Often she placed between her teeth the stem of a large pipe that was on the night table, along with the lemons and the sugar lumps, near a water pitcher.

They needed a good fifteen minutes for their good-byes. Emma would cry; she didn't want to leave him ever again. Something stronger than herself was pushing her toward him, so that one day, seeing her appear unexpectedly, he frowned as if he were annoyed.

"What's the matter?" she asked. "Are you ill? Tell me!"

He declared, very gravely, that her visits were becoming imprudent and that she was compromising herself.

X

Gradually Rodolphe's fears began to affect her. At first she had been so drunk with love that she thought of nothing beyond it. But now that it was so indispensable to her life, she was terrified that it might be disturbed or even destroyed. She would look around anxiously when returning from his house, stare at every shadow on the horizon and each attic window in the village from which she might be seen. She strained her ears for the sound of footsteps, shouts, the noise of plows; and she would stop short, more pale and quivering than the poplar leaves swaying above her.

As she was returning home in this state of mind one morning, she suddenly thought she saw the long barrel of a gun pointing directly at her. It was sticking out at an angle from a small barrel half hidden in the grass at the edge of a ditch. Although she was frightened almost to the point of fainting, Emma kept on walking. A man came out of the barrel like a jack-in-the-box. He had leggings buckled at his knees and a cap pulled down over his eyes. His teeth were chattering and his nose red. It was Captain Binet, hunting for wild duck.

"You should have called out before you came so close," he shouted. "When you see a gun, you should always give warning."

The tax collector was trying to cover up the fright he had just received. A decree from the prefect had outlawed duck hunting except from boats, and Monsieur Binet, despite his respect for the law, was acting illegally. He expected to hear the game warden arrive at any moment. But the danger added spice to his enjoyment, and all alone in his barrel he congratulated himself on his luck and his cunning.

When Emma appeared he looked greatly relieved and began to chat: "It's certainly not warm; there's a definite chill in the air."

Emma said nothing. He continued: "You're up so early?"

"Yes," she said with a stammer, "I've been to see my daughter at her nurse's."

"Ah, I see, I see. I've been here since daybreak; but the weather's so foul that unless you have your bird right at the end of your gun—"

"Good day, Monsieur Binet," she interrupted, turning away from him.

"Your servant, Madame," he answered curtly, and climbed back into his barrel.

Emma regretted having left the tax collector so abruptly. He would surely become suspicious. The story about the nurse was the worst possible excuse, since everyone in Yonville knew that the Bovary child had been home with her parents for a year. Besides, no one lived in this direction; the road led only to La Huchette. Binet had therefore guessed where she was coming from, and he would not keep quiet.

He would certainly talk! She spent the entire day torturing herself, thinking up all kinds of plausible lies, continually haunted by the face of this fool with his game bag.

Charles noticed her worried air and wanted to distract her after dinner by taking her to the pharmacist's. The first person she met in the pharmacy was the tax collector himself! He was standing at the counter in the light of the red jar and saying: "Give me half an ounce of vitriol, please."

"Justin!" shouted the apothecary. "Bring some sulfuric acid." Then to Emma, who was about to go upstairs to Madame Homais: "No, don't bother. Stay here, she's coming down. Warm up at the stove while you're waiting. Excuse me. Good evening, doctor (the pharmacist loved pronouncing the word *doctor*, as if in addressing another person, some of the glory in it reflected back on himself). Don't upset those mortars, boy! Go get some chairs from the sun parlor! You know you're not supposed to move the living-room furniture!"

And Homais was halfway out from behind the counter to put his armchair back where it belonged when Binet asked him for half an ounce of sugar acid.

"Sugar acid?" the pharmacist repeated with contempt. "I don't know what that is. Perhaps you mean oxalic acid? It is oxalic, isn't it?"

Binet explained that he needed an abrasive to make a solution of copper with which he could remove the rust from his hunting gear. Emma shuddered. The pharmacist said: "I guess the weather's been bad, what with all this humidity."

"Well," said the tax collector with a sly look, "some people don't seem to mind it."

She was stifling.

"And I also want—"

"He'll never go!" she thought.

"Half an ounce of resin and some turpentine, four ounces of beeswax, and an ounce and a half of animal black, please, to polish the patent leather on my gear."

The apothecary was beginning to cut the wax when Madame Homais appeared with Irma in her arms, Napoleon at her side, and Athalie following behind. She sat down on the plush-covered bench beneath the window. The boy squatted on a footstool while his older sister hovered around the jujube box near her darling papa, who was filling containers, corking them, pasting labels, and tying parcels. No one spoke to him, and the only sound was the occasional clink of the weights on the scale and a few whispered words from the pharmacist instructing his pupil.

"How's your little girl?" Madame Homais suddenly asked.

"Quiet!" said her husband, who was entering figures in the notebook.

"Why didn't you bring her?" she continued in softer tones.

"Ssh!" Emma said, pointing to the pharmacist.

But Binet, completely involved in checking the bill, had probably heard nothing. He finally left, and Emma heaved a deep sigh of relief.

"You're breathing so heavily," Madame Homais said.

"It's so warm," she answered.

The next day they decided, because of the incident, to arrange their meetings better. Emma wanted to bribe his maid by a gift, but he felt it would be still better to find some discreet house in Yonville. Rodolphe promised to look for one.

All through the winter, three or four times a week, he came to the garden in the dead of night. Emma had purposely removed the key from the garden gate. Charles thought it was lost.

Rodolphe would announce his presence by throwing a handful of gravel against the shutters. She would jump up. Sometimes she had to wait because Charles had a habit of sitting by the fireside and chattering interminably.

She would rage with impatience. If looks could have done it, she would have pushed him out the window. Finally she would begin undressing, then pick up a book and start quietly reading with obvious pleasure. Charles, already in bed, would call to her.

"Emma, come to bed, it's late," he would say.

"I'm coming," she would answer.

But as the candles were too bright for his eyes, he would turn toward the wall and fall asleep. Then, holding her breath, she would sneak out of the room, a smile on her face and her heart pounding, half undressed.

Rodolphe had a voluminous cloak that he would wrap around her. He would wind his arms around her waist and lead her silently to the back of the garden.

They would stay in the arbor on the same bench of rotting wood where in the old days Léon had looked at her so lovingly in the summer nights. She rarely thought of him now.

The stars shone through the leafless jasmine branches. They could hear the river flowing behind them and an occasional crackling of dry reeds on the bank. Great masses of shadow loomed up against the obscurity and sometimes, rising as if with a shudder, they would advance like huge black waves ready to engulf them. The cold of the night made them hold each other even more tightly; the sighs emerging from their lips seemed louder; their eyes, which they could discern only with difficulty, seemed even larger; and in the midst of the silence, their whispered words fell crystal clear on their souls and echoed and reechoed with continuing vibrations.

When it rained, they took shelter in the consulting room, between the shed and the stable. She would light one of the kitchen candles, which she had hidden behind the books. Rodolphe would make himself as comfortable as if he were at home. The sight of the bookcase and the desk, of the entire room, intensified his gaiety; he could not refrain from making various jokes at Charles's expense, which Emma found embarrassing. She wanted him to be more serious and even more dramatic on occasion. Once, for example, she thought she heard approaching footsteps in the lane.

"Someone's coming!" she said.

He blew out the light.

"Do you have your pistols?"

"What for?"

"To—to defend yourself," Emma said.

"Against your husband? That poor fellow!" And Rodolphe finished his sentence with a gesture signifying: "I could crush him with a flick of the finger."

She was amazed at his courage, although she sensed in it an indelicacy and blatant vulgarity that she thought shocking.

Rodolphe thought a long while about this talk of pistols. If she had meant it seriously, it would be the height of idiocy, even odious, for he personally had no reason to hate good old Charles. Rodolphe was not a man "devoured with jealousy." Besides, in this connection Emma had made a solemn promise to him that, moreover, he did not find in the best of taste.

She was also becoming quite sentimental. They had had to exchange miniatures and locks of hair and now she wanted a ring, an actual marriage band as a sign of eternal union.

She would often speak to him of the bells of evening or of the "voices of nature." She would talk to him about her mother and his. Rodolphe had lost his mother twenty years before. Emma, nevertheless, consoled him with the gushing language one uses to a bereaved child. She even said to him, sometimes, looking up at the moon: "I'm sure that they're together up there, smiling down on our love!"

But she was so pretty! He had had few mistresses as unspoiled as she was. This love without guile was something new to him. It had taken him out of his free-and-easy ways, flattered his pride, and quickened his sensuality. Emma's emotional raptures, which his middle-class common sense disdained, seemed charming to him, deep down, since he was the recipient. Then, when he was sure of being loved, he stopped trying to please her, and his ways changed imperceptibly.

He no longer used words so sweet that they made her cry, as he had in the old days; nor were his caresses so ardent that they drove her mad. So the great love affair in which she had plunged seemed to diminish under her like the water of a river being absorbed into its own bed, and she began to see slime at the bottom. She didn't want to believe it and redoubled her tenderness. Rodolphe hid his indifference less and less.

She did not know if she regretted having given in to him or if she wished, on the contrary, to love him even more. The humiliation of feeling how weak she was where he was concerned turned into a resentment tempered only by sensual pleasure. It was not an attachment, but a permanent seduction. He was subjugating her. She was almost afraid of him.

The surface, however, was calmer than ever, Rodolphe having succeeded in conducting the affair to suit his whims, and when half a year had gone by and springtime came, they were like a married couple peacefully tending the domestic fires.

It was the time of year when old Rouault sent his turkey in memory of Charles's setting his leg. The gift always arrived with a letter. Emma cut the cord tying it to the basket and read the following lines:

My dear children,
    I hope that this letter will find you in good health and that the bird is as good as the others. It looks a bit more

tender, if I may say so, and larger. Next time I'll send you a cock for a change, unless you would rather stick to the gobblers, and send back the basket please with the two from before. I had trouble with the cart shed. The roof flew off into the trees one night when it was very windy. And the harvest hasn't been very good. Anyhow, I don't know when I'll be coming to see you. It's so hard for me to leave the house now that I'm all alone, Emma dear!

There was a space after these lines, as if the old man had dropped his pen to dream for a while.

As for me, I'm fine except for a cold I caught the other day at the Yvetot Fair, where I went to hire a shepherd. I sent mine off because he was too fussy about food. What trouble these rascals cause us! And he wasn't honest either.

I heard from a peddler who traveled through your district this winter and had a tooth pulled that Bovary is still working hard. I'm not surprised. He showed me his tooth, and we had a cup of coffee together. I asked him if he saw you and he said no, but that he'd seen two horses in the stable, so I imagine that business is good. Welcome news, dear children. May God send you all possible happiness.

I'm very unhappy that I don't know my beloved granddaughter, Berthe Bovary, as yet. I've planted a plum tree for her in the garden under your window, and I won't let anyone near it except to make jam for her, which I can put aside in my cupboard for her visit.

Good-bye, my dear children. I kiss you, daughter, and you, dear son-in-law, and the little one, on both cheeks.

With much love,

> Your devoted father,
> Theodore Rouault

She sat for a few minutes holding the coarse paper in her hands. There were many spelling errors, and Emma followed the loving thoughts that cackled through them like a hen half hidden in a thorn hedge. He had blotted the writing with ashes from the fireplace, because some gray dust fell off the letter onto her dress. She could almost see her father bending over the hearth to pick up the tongs. How long it was since she had sat with him on the bench near the fireplace, burning a stick in the blazing furze fire as it crackled! She remembered summer evenings filled with sunshine. The foals would whinny as you passed, and run and run. Under her window there was a beehive, and sometimes the bees flying around in the sunlight would strike against her windowpanes like golden balls. She had been so happy in those days! Days of freedom and hope, filled with illusions! There were no illusions left now. She had gradually spent them in all the adventures of her soul, in all her successive conditions, in her virginity, in her marriage, and in love; losing them continually as she grew older, like a traveler who leaves part of his money in every inn along the highway.

But what was making her so unhappy? Where was the extraordinary calamity that had overwhelmed her? She lifted her head and looked around as if to seek the cause of her suffering.

An April sunbeam was glowing over the china figures on the cabinet; the fire was blazing. She felt the softness of the rug through her slippers. The day was clear and warm and she could hear her child laughing.

The little girl was rolling on the lawn while the grass was being cut. She was face down on top of a haystack while her nursemaid held onto her skirt. Lestiboudois was raking on one side, and each time he came near she leaned forward, flailing her arms through the air.

"Bring her here," said her mother, rushing out to kiss her. "I love you so much, my darling child, so much!"

Then she noticed that the tips of her ears were slightly dirty. She rang for warm water at once and washed her, changing her underwear, stockings, and shoes and asking a thousand questions about her health, as if she had returned from a trip. Finally, still kissing her and crying a little, she handed her back to the maid, who was quite amazed at this excess of affection.

Rodolphe found her more serious than usual that evening. "It will pass," he told himself. "It's a mood."

And he missed three meetings in a row. When he returned, she was cold and almost disdainful.

"You're wasting your time, my pet!" And he pretended to notice neither her melancholy sighs nor the handkerchief she pulled out.

And then Emma repented.

She even asked herself why she loathed Charles so, and

if it would not be better to be able to love him. But there
was very little he could offer for the return of her affection,
and she remained quite bewildered about her impulse to
sacrifice until the pharmacist showed up at the right moment
to provide her with an opportunity.

XI

Homais had recently read an article praising a new
method for curing clubfoot; and since he was an enthusiast for
progress, he thought up the patriotic notion that Yonville, "to
put itself on the map," should have some operations for talipes,
as he called it.

"After all, what's the risk?" he asked Emma. "Let's see"—
he ticked off on his fingers the advantages of such an
attempt—"an almost certain success, relief and improved
appearance of the patient, and a rapid rise to fame for the
surgeon. Why, for example, wouldn't your husband want
to help poor Hippolyte from the Golden Lion? He wouldn't
fail to tell all the travelers about his cure, you know, and
besides," here Homais lowered his voice and looked around,
"what's to stop me from sending a short article about it
to the paper? And, by God, an article gets around; people talk
about it; it begins to snowball! And then, who knows? Who
knows?"

It was true: Bovary might well succeed. Emma had no
reason to think he wasn't a capable doctor, and what a
satisfaction for her were she to get him to take a step that
would increase his reputation and his fortune. She wanted
desperately something more substantial than love to lean on.

Urged on by her and by the apothecary, Charles let himself be convinced. He ordered Doctor Duval's book on
clubfoot from Rouen and would bury himself in it every evening, holding his head in his hands.

While he was studying the various forms of talipes—
equinus, varus, and valgus—scientifically called *strephocato-
podia, strephendopodia, and strephexopodia* (or, in more
simple terms, the different ways the foot deviates—down-

wards, inwards, or outwards), as well as *strephypopody* and
strephanopody (in other words, torsion downward or upward),
Monsieur Homais was urging the stableboy, with all kinds of
reasons, to let himself be operated.

"You'll probably feel almost nothing, just a little pain.
It's just an injection, like being bled, less than removing
certain kinds of corns."

Hippolyte rolled his eyes stupidly and tried to think.

"Besides," the pharmacist continued, "it's not for me. It's
for you, purely out of goodwill. I'd like to see you rid of
your ugly deformity, my friend, and that lumbar region of
yours straightened out. No matter how much you say, I'm
sure it hurts you terribly in your work."

Then Homais pointed out to him how much more cheerful
and agile he would feel later on, and even hinted that
he would find himself more likely to please women. The
stableboy began to grin sheepishly. Then he played on his
vanity: "Aren't you a man, damn it! Suppose you had to
join the army and fight to defend our flag? Ah, Hippolyte!"

And Homais walked away, asserting that he could not
understand this stubbornness, this blindness in refusing to
benefit from science.

The poor soul finally gave in, yielding to what became a
veritable conspiracy against him. Binet, who never meddled
in other people's affairs, Madame Lefrançois, Artémise, the
neighbors, and even Monsieur Tuvache, the mayor—everyone
approached him, lectured him, shamed him; but what finally
convinced him was that "it wouldn't cost a cent." Bovary
took it upon himself to provide the apparatus for the operation.

Emma had thought of this generous gesture, and Charles
consented, thinking to himself that his wife was an angel.

With the pharmacist's advice, and after two false starts,
he had the carpenter, aided by the locksmith, construct a
boxlike contraption, weighing about eight pounds, in which
neither iron, wood, sheet metal, leather, screws, nor nuts
were spared.

Then, in order to decide which of Hippolyte's tendons
to cut, it was necessary to figure out first which sort of
clubfoot he had.

His foot was in an almost completely straight line with
his leg; nevertheless, this did not stop it from being turned
inward. So it was an equinus with slight varus characteristics,

or, alternatively, a slight varus with pronounced equinus characteristics. But with this equinus, as large as a horse's hoof, with rough skin, brittle tendons, thick toes, and blackened toenails resembling the nails of a horseshoe—on that foot the taliped raced about from day to night like a deer. He was constantly to be seen in the square, hopping around the carts, putting his bad foot forward. He actually seemed stronger on that foot than on the other. By dint of having been used, it had in a sense acquired the moral qualities of patience and energy, and when he was given some heavy work, he actually preferred to shift his weight onto it.

Now, since it was an equinus, the Achilles tendon had to be cut first, and later the anterior tibial muscle, to take care of the varus; for the doctor did not dare to risk two operations at once, and he was even trembling already, afraid of interfering with some important area of the foot that he did not know.

Neither Ambrose Paré, applying an immediate ligature to an artery for the first time since Celsus, after an interval of fifteen hundred years; nor Dupuytren, opening an abscess through a thick layer of brain; nor Gensoul, performing the first removal of an upper maxillary, could have suffered such palpitations of the heart, such trembling hands, such mental strain as did Monsieur Bovary when he approached Hippolyte, with his tenotomy knife in his hands. And, as in a hospital, on a table at his side were a pile of lint, waxed thread, a quantity of bandages—a pyramid of bandages, all the bandages there were in the pharmacist's shop. It was Monsieur Homais who had been organizing all these preparations since early morning, as much to bedazzle the crowd as to inflate his own ego. Charles pierced the skin; a brittle snap was heard. The tendon was cut, the operation finished. Hippolyte could not get over his surprise; he leaned over Bovary's hands to cover them with kisses.

"Calm down," said the pharmacist. "You'll show your gratitude to your benefactor later!"

And he went down to announce the results to five or six curious souls lingering in the yard who imagined that Hippolyte would appear walking properly. Charles, having strapped his patient into the mechanical motor, went home, where Emma was anxiously awaiting him on the doorstep. She threw herself at him; they went in to eat. Charles ate with gusto and even asked for a cup of coffee with dessert, an extravagance he permitted himself only on Sundays when they had company.

The evening passed beautifully, filled with talk, with day-dreams in common. They spoke about their future fortune, about improvements they would make in the house; he fore-saw his reputation increasing, his prosperity growing, his wife loving him always; and she felt happy to revive herself with a healthier emotion, a better and different one, to feel, finally, some affection for this poor boy who adored her. The thought of Rodolphe passed through her head at one moment, but she looked at Charles and even noticed with surprise that his teeth were not at all bad.

They were in bed when Monsieur Homais, despite the cook's protests, walked right into the bedroom holding a newly written sheet of paper in his hand. It was the pub-licity article he was going to send to the *Rouen Beacon*. He had brought it to read to them.

"Read it to us," said Bovary.

He read: " 'Despite the network of prejudices that still covers part of the map of Europe, light is nevertheless be-ginning to penetrate our countrysides. And so, last Tuesday, our small city of Yonville was the scene of a surgical ex-periment that is, at the same time, an act of great philan-thropy. Monsieur Bovary, one of our most distinguished doctors——' "

"That's too much, too much," said Charles, choking with emotion.

"Not at all! Please! '... operated on a clubfoot....' I didn't use the scientific term because in a newspaper, you know, not everyone would understand; the masses need——"

"Exactly," said Bovary. "Continue."

"I'll start over," said the pharmacist. " 'Monsieur Bovary, one of our most distinguished doctors, operated on the club-foot of one Hippolyte Tautain, stableboy for the past twenty-five years at the Golden Lion Hotel, overlooking the Place d'Armes, run by the Widow Lefrançois. The novelty of the attempt and the interest inherent in the subject had attracted so many people that there was a veritable crush at the door of the building. The operation, moreover, was carried out beautifully and there were only a few drops of blood on the skin, as if to bear witness that the rebellious tendon had finally yielded to the surgeon's art. The patient, strange to say (we can report this as eyewitnesses), seemed

to feel no pain. Everything leads us to think that the convalescence will be of short duration. Who knows, perhaps
at the next village festival we shall see our brave Hippolyte
taking part in the Bacchic dances in a ring of jolly com-
panions, and thus proving to all eyes his complete recovery
by his liveliness and his capers.

"'All honor to our generous men of science! All honor to
those untiring souls who deprive themselves of sleep for the
improvement or the healing of their fellow men! All honor
to them! Should we not cry aloud that the blind will see,
the deaf hear, and the crippled walk? But what fanaticism
once promised to its elect, science shall now accomplish for all
mankind! We shall keep our readers informed of the further
stages of this remarkable cure.'"

None of this prevented Madame Lefrançois, five days later,
from arriving in fright and screaming: "Help! He's dying!
I'm going out of my mind."

Charles rushed over to the Golden Lion. The pharmacist,
seeing him hasten through the square without his hat, left
his store and appeared, out of breath, red in the face, and
anxious, asking everyone going up the stairs: "What's wrong
with our interesting taliped?"

The taliped was twisting about in dreadful convulsions;
the apparatus in which his foot was encased was hitting the
wall hard enough to smash it.

Taking many precautions so as not to disturb the position
of the limb, they pulled off the box. A hideous sight was
revealed. The foot was swollen to an unrecognizable shape,
the skin seemed about to burst open. It was covered with
black and blue marks caused by the famous machine. Hippolyte had already complained that it hurt him, but no one
had heeded him. They had to admit that he wasn't entirely
wrong and left him alone for a few hours. But hardly had
the swelling subsided when the two scientists decided it was
time to put the foot back in the apparatus. They even tightened
it to obtain quicker results. Finally, three days later, when
Hippolyte could not endure it any longer, they removed the
mechanism once more. They were greatly surprised at the
result which greeted them. A livid tumescence was spread all
over the leg, dotted with blisters oozing a dark liquid. Things
were taking a serious turn. Hippolyte was beginning to fret
and Madame Lefrançois settled him into the small parlor,

near the kitchen, so that he would at least have some distraction.

But the tax collector, who dined there daily, complained bitterly about such a neighbor. And so they moved Hippolyte into the billiard room.

There he lay, moaning under his heavy blankets, pale, unshaven, eyes sunken, from time to time turning his perspiring face over the filthy pillow, on which the flies were settling. Madame Bovary came to visit him. She brought him linen for his poultices; she comforted him, tried to encourage him. He did not lack for other company either, especially on market days, when the farmers pushed their billiard cues all around him or fenced with them while smoking, drinking, singing, and shouting.

"How are you?" they would ask, clapping him on the shoulder. "You don't look very good. But it's your fault. You should have—"

And they would tell him stories of people who had all been cured by remedies other than his; then, as a consolation, they would add: "You're coddling yourself. Come on, get up! You're treating yourself like a king. Ah, never mind, old boy. You don't smell very good."

The gangrene was actually moving higher and higher. Bovary himself was sick of it. He came every hour, every minute. Hippolyte would look at him with fear-filled eyes and sob and stammer: "When will I be cured? Save me, please! I feel awful! I feel awful!"

And the doctor would go off, always telling him to eat lightly.

"Don't listen to him, my poor boy," said Madame Lefrançois. "They've made enough of a martyr out of you. You'll get even weaker. Here, swallow this."

And so she would offer him some tasty bouillon, a slice of lamb, a rasher of bacon, and occasionally tiny glasses of brandy which he lacked the strength to bring to his lips.

Abbé Bournisien, hearing that he was growing worse, asked to see him. He began by offering his regrets for the illness, all the while declaring that he ought to rejoice over it since it was the Lord's will and take quick advantage of the opportunity to reconcile himself with heaven.

"Because," said the clergyman in a fatherly tone, "you were neglecting your religious duties a bit; you were rarely seen at Mass; how many years has it been since you came to Communion? I realize that your occupations, amid the distractions of the world, lured you away from thinking about your salvation. Now is the time to think about it. Don't despair. I've known really great sinners who, when they were about to appear before God—you aren't anywhere near that point, I know—begged for mercy and who certainly died in a state of grace. Let us hope that like them you will set us a good example! And so, as a precaution, what's to prevent you from reciting 'Hail Mary, full of grace' morning and evening and an 'Our Father, who art in heaven'? Yes, do it. For me. To make me happy. What will it cost you? Will you promise me?"

The poor devil promised. The curé came back the following days. He chatted with the landlady and even told humorous anecdotes and puns that Hippolyte did not understand. Then, when the opportunity presented itself, he reverted to religion, his face taking on an appropriate expression.

His zeal seemed to be succeeding because the taliped soon expressed his desire to go on a pilgrimage to Bon-Secours if he recovered—to which Abbé Bournisien answered that he saw no objection; two precautions were worth more than one. "You wouldn't lose anything by it."

The apothecary grew angry at what he called the "priest's maneuvers." They were harming Hippolyte's convalescence, he claimed. "Leave him alone," Homais told Madame Lefrançois. "You damage his morale with that mysticism of yours."

But the good lady refused to heed the apothecary any longer. He was "to blame for the whole thing." Out of contrariness she even hung a basin filled with holy water and a sprig of boxwood at the invalid's bedside.

But religion seemed to be helping him no more than surgery, and the gangrene kept spreading relentlessly from the extremities toward the trunk. In vain did they vary the medicines and change poultices; the muscles grew more lax each day, and finally, with a nod of his head, Charles assented when Madame Lefrançois, out of desperation, asked if she could send for Monsieur Canivet, who was quite a famous surgeon in Neufchâtel.

An M D., fifty years old, of fine standing and great self-assurance, Charles's colleague did not bother to conceal a contemptuous laugh when he uncovered the gangrenous leg, infected all the way to the knee. Then, having flatly stated that he would have to amputate, he crossed over to the pharmacist's shop to rail against the idiots who could have reduced an unfortunate man to such a state. Taking hold of Monsieur Homais by the button of his coat, he boomed out all over the pharmacy: "Those are your Paris inventions for you! Now you see the ideas of the gentlemen from the capital! It's like strabismus, chloroform, and lithotripsy—a bunch of nonsense the government ought to forbid! But they care only about being clever, and they load you down with remedies without worrying about the consequences. We aren't as clever as all that here in the country; we aren't specialists, and we don't dress up like dandies! We practice medicine, we cure, and we never think of operating on someone who's perfectly healthy! Straighten a clubfoot indeed! Is it possible to straighten a clubfoot? It's like wanting to make a hunchback straight!"

Homais suffered as he listened to this speech, hiding his discomfort under an obsequious smile. It was necessary to curry favor with Monsieur Canivet, whose prescriptions were sometimes brought into Yonville to be filled; and so he did not defend Bovary, nor even comment, and abandoning his principles, sacrificed his dignity to the weightier interests of his business.

This amputation at the thigh by Doctor Canivet was an event of considerable importance in the village. All the villagers arose early that day, and the main street, despite being filled with people, had a certain gloomy air about it, as if an execution were to take place. At the grocer's, people talked about Hippolyte's condition; the stores made no sales, and Madame Tuvache, the mayor's wife, did not budge from the window in her impatience to see the surgeon.

He arrived in his gig, which he drove himself. The spring on the right side had given way to his corpulence over the years and the carriage tilted slightly to one side as it moved, revealing, on the cushion at his side, a large red leather case, its three brass clasps gleaming with authority.

After he had entered the yard of the Golden Lion like a whirlwind, the doctor, shouting loudly, ordered his horse unhitched, then went into the stable to see if the animal was being well fed. He took care of his mare and his gig first when he arrived at his patients' homes. People commented about this: "Ah, that Canivet is a character!" And they respected him all the more for this imperturbable coolness. The population of the entire world could expire to the last man before he would change a single one of his habits.

Homais came in.

"I'm counting on you," said the doctor. "Are we ready? Let's go."

But the apothecary turned red and announced that he was too sensitive to be present at such an operation.

"When you're just a spectator," he said, "your imagination takes hold of you, you know. And I have such a sensitive nervous system that——"

"Nonsense!" interrupted Canivet. "You look to me more inclined to apoplexy. Although it doesn't surprise me. You pharmacists are always cooped up in your kitchens, which probably affects your constitution in the long run. Now take me. I get up at four every morning, shave with cold water, never feel chilly. Never wear flannel, never have a sniffle. Body sound as can be! I manage any old way, like a philosopher; eat whatever comes along. That's why I'm not so delicate like you, and it's all the same to me if I carve up a Christian or any old chicken that's available. And you'll probably say it's habit, just habit."

Then, with no consideration whatever for Hippolyte, who was perspiring with terror under the bedclothes, the gentlemen began a conversation in the course of which the apothecary compared a surgeon's coolheadedness to that of a general. The comparison pleased Canivet, who launched into a discussion of the demands of his profession. He looked upon it as a sacred calling, even though the health officers were dishonoring it. Finally, getting back to the present patient, he examined the bandages Homais had brought (the same ones that had appeared at the operation) and asked for someone to hold the leg for him.

They sent for Lestiboudois, and Monsieur Canivet, having rolled up his sleeves, went into the billiard room, while the pharmacist remained with Artémise and the landlady, both whiter than their aprons, and all three with their ears glued to the door.

During this time Bovary did not dare budge from his house. He remained downstairs, in the parlor, seated near the empty fireplace, his chin sunk on his chest, hands clasped, his eyes staring. "What a misfortune!" he thought. "What a disappointment!" And yet he had taken every conceivable precaution. Fate intervened. But what difference did it make? If Hippolyte were to die later on, he would be the assassin. And what answer would he give in his visits later on when people asked him questions? Perhaps he *had* nevertheless made a mistake somewhere? He sought to find one, but could not. But the greatest surgeons made mistakes. No one would believe that now. They would laugh at him, gossip about him. The story would spread all the way to Forges, to Neufchâtel, Rouen, everywhere! Some of his colleagues might attack him. There would be a controversy; he'd have to reply in the newspapers. Hippolyte might even sue him. He saw himself dishonored, ruined, lost. And his imagination, assailed by so many fears, was tossed about among them like an empty barrel washed out to sea, rolling over the waves.

Emma sat opposite, looking at him. She was not sharing his humiliation, but enduring a private one, that of having imagined that such a man could be worth something. As if she had not already clearly perceived his mediocrity twenty times over.

Charles was pacing back and forth in the room; his boots creaked on the floor.

"Sit down," she said. "You're making me nervous."

He sat down again.

How could she—she who was so intelligent!—have fooled herself one more time? Moreover, what deplorable mania had made her ruin her life by these constant sacrifices? She recalled all her yearnings for luxury, all the privations to which she had subjected her soul, the sordidness of her marriage, of the household, her dreams falling into the mud like wounded swallows, everything she had wanted and denied herself, everything she could have had! Why? Why?

In the midst of the silence that filled the village, a piercing cry shattered the air. Bovary turned pale and seemed about to faint. She frowned, with a nervous twitch, then went on: yet it was for him, for this creature, for this man who understood nothing, who felt nothing! There he was, quite calm, not even suspecting that the ridicule henceforth attaching itself to his name would now smear her as well. She had tried to love him and had even repented in tears her affair with another man.

"Maybe it was a valgus!" Bovary, who had been lost in thought, suddenly exclaimed.

Emma started at the unexpected shock of this statement

crashing into her thoughts like a lead bullet into a silver dish. She looked up to see what he meant; and they stared at each other in silence, almost astonished to see each other, so far apart were they in their respective meditations.

Charles looked at her with the troubled gaze of a drunken man. At the same time, he was numbly listening to the last cries of the amputee, which followed each other in drawn-out waves interspersed by sharp screams, like the far-off howling of some animal being slaughtered. Emma bit her pale lip, rolled between her fingers some bits of the coral she had broken off, and fixed the blazing centers of her eyes, like two fiery arrows about to be released, on Charles. Everything about him irritated her now, his face, his clothes, the things he didn't say, his entire person, his very existence. She lamented her virtuous past as if it had been a crime, and whatever virtue still remained collapsed beneath the fury of her pride. She reveled in all the evil ironies of adultery triumphant. The memory of her lover returned to her with dizzying attraction; she threw her soul into her longing, surging toward it with a new enthusiasm. Charles seemed detached from her life, forever gone, as impossible and annihilated as if he were dying and passing away before her eyes.

There was a noise of steps on the sidewalk. Charles looked out; across the lowered blinds he could see, at the edge of the square, in the sunlight, Doctor Canivet wiping his forehead with his scarf, and Homais behind him, carrying a large red box. They were both heading toward the pharmacy.

Then, out of a sudden impulse of tenderness and discouragement, Charles turned toward his wife and said: "Kiss me, darling."

"Leave me alone!" she exclaimed, scarlet with anger.

"What's wrong? What's wrong?" he repeated, dumbfounded. "Calm down, pull yourself together. You know how I love you. Come here."

"Enough!" she cried with a terrible look. And she ran from the room, closing the door so violently that the barometer fell from the wall and crashed into pieces on the floor.

Charles sank into his armchair, overwhelmed, trying to puzzle out what was wrong with her, imagining some nervous ailment, crying, and vaguely sensing something dire and incomprehensible hovering around him.

When Rodolphe reached the garden that night, he found

his mistress awaiting him at the foot of the stairs. They embraced, and all their bitterness melted away like snow in the warmth of their kiss.

XII

They fell in love all over again. Often Emma would write to him suddenly even in the middle of the day. Then she would signal through the window to Justin, who would untie his apron quickly and fly off toward La Huchette. Rodolphe would come; she wanted to tell him that she was bored, that her husband was hateful and life unbearable.

"What can I do about it?" he asked impatiently one day.

"If you only wanted to—"

She was seated on the ground leaning against his knees, her hair ribbons undone, staring into a void.

"Wanted to what?" Rodolphe asked.

She sighed: "We could go and live elsewhere—somewhere—"

"You're really mad!" he said, laughing. "How could we?"

She repeated her thought. He seemed not to understand and changed the subject. What he didn't understand was all this fuss over something as simple as love. She had a motive, a reason, a kind of impetus to her affection.

This love increased each day in proportion to the revulsion she felt for her husband. The more she gave herself to the one man, the more she loathed the other. Never did Charles appear so repulsive to her, to have such coarse fingers, such a dull mind, such common manners, as when they happened to be together after her meetings with Rodolphe. At such moments, while she was outwardly playing the part of a virtuous wife, she would be burning within at thoughts of that head of black hair curling over a suntanned forehead, of that body that was both robust and elegant at the same time, of this man who was so mature in judgment and so passionate in love. Because of him she filed her fingernails with the precision of an engraver, because of him there was never enough cold cream on her skin, nor enough scent of patchouli in her handkerchiefs. She loaded herself down with bracelets, rings, and necklaces. When he was expected, she filled her two big blue glass vases with roses and arranged her room and her person like a courtesan awaiting a prince. The maid had to keep washing her underthings. Félicité did not budge from the kitchen all day long. Little Justin, who often kept her company, would watch her work.

His elbow on the long board on which she was ironing, he would look avidly at all the female garments strewn around him: dimity petticoats, fichus, muslin collars, and pantaloons with drawstrings, voluminous around the hips and tapering near the bottom.

"What's this for?" the boy would ask, stroking a crinoline or fingering some hooks.

"Haven't you ever seen anything?" Félicité replied with a laugh. "As if your mistress, Madame Homais, didn't wear these same things."

"Oh, Madame Homais—" And he added, thinking out loud: "As if she were a lady like Madame!"

But Félicité was getting impatient at the sight of him hovering around her. She was six years older than he, and Theodore, Monsieur Guillaumin's manservant, was beginning to court her.

"Leave me alone!" she said, picking up her starch pot. "Why don't you go grind some almonds? You're always snooping around women's affairs. Wait till you have a beard on your chin before you mix into such matters, you nasty little boy."

"Don't get angry; I'm going to do *her* boots for you."

And he immediately reached up to the doorsill for Emma's shoes, encrusted with dried mud—mud from their meetings—that crumbled away at his touch and the particles of which he watched float upward into a sunbeam.

"How frightened you are of spoiling them!" said Félicité, who didn't go to so much trouble when she herself cleaned them, because Emma would hand them on to her as soon as the fabric lost its freshness.

Emma had a supply of them in her wardrobe that she was recklessly using up, pair by pair, without Charles's allowing himself the slightest comment.

He also had to spend three hundred francs for a wooden leg that she felt should be given as a gift to Hippolyte. Its top was trimmed with cork; it had joints and levers set on springs, a complicated mechanism covered with a black trouser leg ending in a patent-leather boot. But Hippolyte, not daring to use such a beautiful leg every day, begged Madame Bovary to get him another, more simple one. The doctor of course bore the expense of this new one as well.

The stableboy gradually resumed his work. He could be seen as before wandering around the village. When Charles heard from afar the sharp tap of his cane on the pavement, he would quickly change his route.

Monsieur Lheureux, the merchant, had taken care of the order; this gave him the opportunity to associate with Emma. He chatted with her about the new goods from Paris, about a thousand feminine trifles, made himself extremely obliging, and never asked for money. Emma abandoned herself to this easy way of satisfying all her whims. She wanted, for example, a very handsome hunting crop that was in an umbrella store in Rouen—as a gift for Rodolphe. Lheureux placed it on her table the following week.

But the very next day he turned up at her home with a bill for 270 francs, not counting the centimes. Emma was very embarrassed: all the drawers of the writing desk were empty, they owed more than two weeks' wages to Lestiboudois, six months' wages to the maid, and many other items as well. Bovary was impatiently awaiting a remittance from Monsieur Derozerays, who was in the habit of paying him once a year around the end of June.

She managed to put Lheureux off for a while. Finally he lost patience: he was being pressed, he had no ready funds, and if he didn't collect some of his debts, he'd be forced to take back all the things he had brought her.

"Then take them back!" Emma said.

"Oh, I was only joking," he answered. "I'm only sorry about the hunting crop. I think I'll ask Monsieur if I may have it back."

"No!" she cried.

"Aha! I've got you!" thought Lheureux.

And sure that he had discovered her secret, he left, saying to himself under his breath, with his usual slight wheeze: "All right. We'll see. We'll see."

She was dreaming up ways to extricate herself from the situation when the cook came in and placed on the mantelpiece a small roll of blue paper. "From Monsieur Derozerays," she said. Emma pounced on it and opened it. It contained fifteen napoleons, payment in full. She heard Charles on the stairs; she threw the gold pieces into her drawer and took the key.

Lheureux reappeared three days later.

"I have a suggestion for you," he said. "If, instead of the amount agreed on, you would be willing to take—"

"Here it is!" she said, handing him fourteen napoleons.

The merchant was dumbfounded. To mask his disappointment, he multiplied apologies and offers of service, all of which Emma declined. Afterward she stood for a few moments fingering in the pocket of her apron the two five-franc pieces he had given her in change. She resolved to economize so that she would be able to restore the money later.

"Never mind!" she thought. "He won't think about it again."

Besides the hunting crop with a silver-gilt handle, Rodolphe had received a seal with the motto *Amor nel cor,* a scarf to be used as a muffler, and finally a cigar case identical to the viscount's, the one Charles had picked up on the road and which Emma had been saving. However, the gifts humiliated him. He refused several others. She insisted and he finally gave in, finding her high-handed and too demanding.

She was also filled with strange notions: "At the stroke of midnight," she would say, "you must think of me."

If he confessed that he hadn't thought of her, there were countless reproaches, which always ended in the eternal question: "Do you love me?"

"Of course I love you," he would answer.

"Very much?"

"Certainly!"

"You've never loved any other women?"

"Do you think I came to you a virgin?" he would exclaim with a laugh.

Emma would cry and he would try to console her, enlivening his protestations with little jokes.

"Oh, how I love you!" she would continue. "I love you so much I couldn't live without you, do you realize? I sometimes want to see you so badly that I feel torn apart. I ask myself: 'Where is he? Perhaps he's talking to other women? They're smiling at him. He's going up to them—' Oh no!

Tell me it isn't so. No one else pleases you. There are women who are prettier than I am, but I know how to love better. I'm your servant and your mistress. You're my king, my idol. You're so good, so handsome, so intelligent, so strong!"

He had heard these things so many times that they no longer held any interest for him. Emma resembled all his old mistresses, and the charm of novelty, falling away little by little like articles of clothing, revealed in all its nakedness the eternal monotony of passion, which always assumes the same forms and speaks the same language. This man, who was so experienced in love, could not distinguish the dissimilarity in the emotions behind the similarity of expressions. He couldn't really accept Emma's lack of guile, having heard similar sentences from the mouths of venal and immoral women. One should be able to tone down, he thought, those exaggerated speeches that mask lack of feeling—as if the fullness of the soul did not sometimes overflow into the emptiest of metaphors. No one can ever express the exact measure of his needs, or conceptions, or sorrows. The human language is like a cracked kettle on which we beat out a tune for a dancing bear, when we hope with our music to move the stars.

But with that superior critical ability of those who hold themselves back from any and all involvements, Rodolphe found other pleasures to exploit in this love. He discarded the last shreds of modesty and treated her without consideration, making her into something compliant and corrupt. It was an idiotic, one-sided attachment, filled with admiration for him, and sensual satisfaction for herself. She was in a blissful state of numbness. Her soul sank deeper into this inebriation and was drowned in it, shriveled up like the Duke of Clarence in his butt of malmsey.

Madame Bovary's manner changed as a result of her constant indulgence in love. Her gaze became bolder, her talk freer. She even had the audacity to parade with Monsieur Rodolphe, a cigarette in her mouth, "as if to defy everyone." Finally, those who were still in doubt doubted no more when she was seen one day, stepping down from the Hirondelle, wearing a masculine-styled, tight-fitting waistcoat. Madame Bovary senior, who had come to seek refuge with her son after a frightful scene with her husband, was as scandalized as the other women in town. Many other things displeased her. First of all, Charles had not taken her advice about banning novels from the house. Also, the "way the house was run" did not suit her. She offered unasked-for advice and they quarreled, once in particular about Félicité.

While crossing the hallway the night before, Madame Bovary senior had surprised the maid in the company of a man—a man with dark chin whiskers, about forty years of age, who escaped through the kitchen at the sound of her steps. Emma began to laugh about it, but the good woman lost her temper and declared that unless one scoffed at morals, one should keep an eye on those of one's servants.

"What sort of world do you live in?" asked her daughter-in-law, so impertinently that Madame Bovary inquired if she were not really defending her own behavior.

"Get out!" said the young woman, jumping up.

"Emma! Mama!" Charles exclaimed, trying to reconcile them.

But each fled in exasperation. Emma trembled with rage and kept repeating: "What a lack of manners! What a peasant!"

He ran to his mother; she was seething. She stammered: "She's an insolent, irresponsible woman! And maybe worse!"

She threatened to leave immediately if Emma did not apologize. Charles returned to his wife and begged her to give in. He went down on his knees. She finally said: "All right, I'll go."

She offered her hand to her mother-in-law with the dignity of a marquise, saying: "Excuse me, Madame."

Then, back in her own room, she threw herself onto the bed and cried like a child, her head buried in her pillow.

She and Rodolphe had agreed that in case anything unusual happened, she would attach a small piece of white paper to the shutter so that if he should by chance happen to be in Yonville he would hurry to the lane behind the house. Emma hung out the signal; she had been waiting for three quarters of an hour when she suddenly noticed Rodolphe at the corner of the market. She was tempted to open the window and call to him, but he had already disappeared. She sank back in despair.

Soon, however, she sensed that someone was walking along the sidewalk. It was surely he. She went downstairs, crossed the yard. He was there, outside. She threw herself into his arms.

"Be careful," he said.

"If you only knew!" she answered.

She began to tell him everything, in haste, without sequence, exaggerating some facts, inventing others, and introducing so many parenthetical remarks that he did not understand her story.

"There, there, my poor angel, be brave! Cheer up, be patient."

"I've been patient for four years now and look how I'm suffering! We should be able to declare a love like ours to the world! They're torturing me. I can't stand it anymore. Save me!"

She clung to him tightly. Her eyes, filled with tears, sparkled like flames under water, her throat rose and fell rapidly as she gasped for air; he had never loved her so much, so much that he lost his head and said: "What should we do? What do you want?"

"Take me away," she sobbed. "Take me away. Please!"

She kissed him passionately, as if to draw the unexpected consent from his mouth.

"But—" he said.

"But what?"

"Your daughter?"

She thought for a while, then answered: "We'll take her. It can't be helped."

"What a woman!" he thought, watching her go off. For she had just run off into the garden. Someone was calling her.

Mother Bovary was amazed at the change in her daughter-in-law in the days that followed. Emma really appeared to be more amenable and even extended her deference to the point of consulting her about a recipe for pickling gherkins.

Was it in order to dupe the two of them more easily? Or rather did she want, by a kind of voluptuous stoicism, to taste more profoundly the bitterness of the things she was about to leave? It could not be the latter, for she was paying no attention to them; she lived as if lost in the anticipated enjoyment of her approaching happiness. It was a constant subject for discussion with Rodolphe. She would lean on his shoulder and murmur: "Just think! When we're in the mail coach! Do you think about it? Is it possible? It seems to me that the moment I feel the carriage start off, it will feel as if we're going up in a balloon, soaring toward the clouds. Do you know that I'm counting the days? Are you?"

Never had Madame Bovary been so beautiful as now. She had that indefinable beauty that comes from joy, enthusiasm, and success, a beauty that is but the blending of temperament with circumstances. Her desires, her regrets, her experience of sensual pleasure, and her continually youthful illusions had nurtured her gradually, as fertilizer, rain, wind, and sunshine nurture a flower, and she finally blossomed forth in all the fullness of her being. Her eyelids seemed purposely shaped for her long amorous gazes, in which the pupils disappeared, while her heavy breathing caused her delicately chiseled nostrils to flare and raised the fleshy corners of her upper lip (which was lightly shaded by a slight black down). One would have said that some artist skilled in depravity had arranged the coil of hair on the nape of her neck. It was wound carelessly, in a heavy mass, and loosened every day by the chance meetings with her lover. The inflections of her voice became more languid, and also her body. A certain penetrating subtlety detached itself even from the folds of her dress and the instep of her foot. As he had during the first days of their marriage, Charles now found her delicious and completely irresistible.

When he would come home in the middle of the night, he was afraid to wake her. The porcelain night lamp threw a flickering circle of light on the ceiling, and the drawn curtains of the small cradle were like a white tent billowing out in the dark at the edge of the bed. Charles would look at them. He thought he could hear his daughter's gentle breathing. She was going to grow up now; each season would bring quick progress. He already saw her coming back from school in the late afternoon, laughing gaily, her blouse ink-stained, her basket dangling from her arm. Then he would have to send her to boarding school, which would be expensive. How would he do it? He pondered. He thought about renting a small farm in the area that he himself could supervise every morning as he went out to see his patients. He would save the profits and deposit them in the bank. Later he would purchase stock somewhere, it didn't matter where. Besides, his clientele would increase. He was counting on it because he wanted Berthe to be well brought up, to be talented, to learn to play the pi-

ano. Ah! How pretty she would be later on, at fifteen,
when, resembling her mother, she would wear great big
straw hats like hers in the summertime. From afar they
would be taken for two sisters. He pictured her to himself
working near them in the evening under the lamplight. She
would embroider slippers for him, busy herself with household chores, fill the whole house with her engaging ways
and her gaiety. Eventually they would think about getting
her settled. They would find her some fine young man with
a solid business who would make her happy. It would last
forever.

Emma was merely pretending to be asleep. While he
dozed off at her side, she awoke to other dreams.

For the last week she had galloped off with the speed of
four horses toward a new land from which she and Rodolphe would never return. Farther, farther, they went, arms
entwined, without saying a word. Often, from atop a mountain, they would suddenly see some splendid city with domes,
bridges, ships, forests of lemon trees, and white marble ca-
thedrals whose pointed steeples sheltered stork nests. They
would stroll leisurely because of the large flagstones, and
there would be bouquets of flowers on the ground offered
by women in red bodices. They could hear the bells ringing and mules braying, the murmur of guitars and fountains.
The mist from the fountains would spray the pyramids of
fruit arranged at the feet of the pale statues that seemed
to smile under the streams of water. Then they would arrive in a fishing village one evening where brown fishnets
were drying in the wind along the cliff and in front of the
huts. There they would settle. They would live in a low,
flat-roofed house in the shade of a palm tree, bordering on
a bay near the sea. They would float off in a gondola,
swing in a hammock; and their existence would be as relaxed and easy as their silk clothes, as warm and starry
as the gentle nights they would contemplate. Nevertheless, in
the vastness of this future she was creating for herself, nothing in particular stood out. The days, all magnificent, resembled each other like waves. They seemed to sway against
the horizon, infinite, harmonious, tinted with blue, awash
with sunshine. But the baby in her cradle began to cough
or Bovary would snore harder and Emma would not fall
asleep until morning, when the dawn was bringing light in

through the windows and little Justin was already in the square opening the shutters of the pharmacy.

She sent for Monsieur Lheureux and told him: "I'm going to need a cloak, a large lined one with a deep collar."

"You're taking a trip?" he asked.

"Not at all! Only— Never mind. I can rely on you for it, can't I? And quickly?"

He bowed.

"I'll also need a trunk," she continued, "not too heavy— roomy."

"Yes, I understand. About three feet by a foot and a half, they're made now."

"And an overnight bag."

"There's definitely something fishy going on," thought Lheureux.

"And here," said Madame Bovary, unfastening her watch from her belt, "take this, you can pay for the things you get me out of it."

But the merchant protested that she was mistaken. They knew each other. Didn't he trust her? What childishness! She insisted however that he at least take the chain, and Lheureux had already put it into his pocket and was walking off when she called him back.

"You will leave everything at your place. As for the cloak," she seemed to reflect for a moment, "don't bring that either. Just give me the address of the tailor and tell him to hold it for me."

They were to go off the following month. She would leave Yonville as if she were going shopping in Rouen. Rodolphe would have booked passage, obtained passports, and even written to Paris so as to have the entire coach to themselves as far as Marseille. There they would buy a carriage and continue without a stop along the road to Genoa. She would send her baggage to Lheureux, to be taken directly to the Hirondelle, in such a way that no one would be suspicious. In all of this, there was never any mention of her daughter. Rodolphe avoided discussing her; perhaps Emma wasn't thinking about her any longer.

He needed two more weeks to wind up some business. Then, after one week had passed, he asked for two more. Then he said he felt ill. Then he took a trip. The month of August passed. After all these delays, they decided that it would be, without fail, Monday, September 4.

The Saturday preceding the fatal day arrived.

Rodolphe came in the evening, earlier than usual.

"Is everything ready?" he asked.

"Yes."

They walked around a flower bed and sat down on the edge of the wall near the terrace.

"You're sad," Emma said.

"No. Why?" Yet he was looking at her in an unusually tender way.

"Is it because you're going away?" she continued, "leaving things you're attached to, your life here? Oh, I understand. But I have nothing in the world. You're everything for me. And I'll be everything for you. I'll be your whole family, your country. I'll take care of you. I'll love you."

"What a darling you are," he said, taking her into his arms.

"Really?" she asked with a sensuous laugh. "Do you love me? Swear it."

"Do I love you? Do I love you! I adore you, my dearest!"

The full orange moon rose out of the earth on the other side of the meadow. It quickly climbed between the branches of the poplar trees that obscured it here and there, as if it were shining through a torn black curtain. Then it burst forth into the empty sky, lit it with a blaze of white, and then, becoming more subdued, dropped a great patch of light onto the river. The patch splintered into an infinity of stars and their silvery light seemed to slither all the way down like a headless snake covered with luminous scales. It resembled, too, a monstrous candelabrum dripping with molten diamonds running together. The lovely night was all around them, patches of shadow hovering over the foliage. Emma, her eyes half closed, was breathing the cool breeze with great gulps. They were so lost in their dreams that they didn't say a word. The tenderness of the old days came back to them, abundant and silent as the flowing river, as soft as the perfume of the syringa. It projected shadows into their memories, shadows more distorted and melancholy than those of the motionless willows on the grass. Occasionally some night animal, a hedgehog or weasel, would begin to run and make the leaves rustle. From time to time they would hear a ripe peach falling from a tree.

"What a lovely night," said Rodolphe.

"We'll have many more," she answered, and as if she were speaking to herself: "Yes, it will be good to travel. Then why am I so sad? Is it the fear of the unknown? Because I'm leaving behind this life I'm used to? Or what? No! It's from too much happiness! How weak I am. Forgive me."

"There's still time," he said. "Think carefully; you may regret it."

"Never," she said impetuously. And she drew closer to him: "What harm can come to me? There is no desert, no precipice, no ocean that I wouldn't cross with you. Each day that we live together will be like a tighter, more complete embrace. We'll have nothing to bother us, no worries, nothing in our way. We'll be alone, all to ourselves, forever. Say something, answer me."

He kept saying "Yes, yes," at regular intervals. She ran her fingers through his hair and repeated in a childlike voice through large tears that were flowing from her eyes: "Rodolphe! Rodolphe! Oh Rodolphe, my dearest Rodolphe!"

Midnight struck.

"It's midnight!" she said. "It's already tomorrow. One more day!"

He arose to go. Emma suddenly came alive, as if this movement were the signal for their flight. "You have the passports?"

"Yes."

"You won't forget anything?"

"No."

"You're sure?"

"Positive."

"You'll be waiting for me at the Hotel de Provence? At noon?"

He nodded.

"Until tomorrow then!" said Emma with one last caress. And she watched him walk away.

He didn't turn back. She ran after him, leaned over the water between the bushes and cried: "Until tomorrow!"

He was already on the other side of the river, striding quickly through the meadow.

Rodolphe stopped after a few minutes. When he saw her in her white dress gradually fading into the dark like a ghost, his heart began to beat so wildly that he had to lean against a tree to keep from falling.

"What a fool I am," he said, cursing furiously. "Ah well! She was a pretty mistress."

Emma's beauty suddenly reappeared in front of his eyes and he thought of all the pleasures of their love. At first he softened, then he became angry at her.

"After all," he exclaimed with a gesture, "I can't become an expatriate, and be saddled with a child."

He talked aloud, looking for more reasons to reassure himself.

"And besides, the bother, the expense— No, no, absolutely not! It would be too stupid!"

XIII

As soon as Rodolphe arrived home, he sat down abruptly at his desk, under the stag's head hanging on the wall. But when he had the pen in his hand he could find nothing to write, and so he leaned on his two elbows and began to think. Emma seemed remote to him, in the distant past, as if the decision he had taken had suddenly placed an immense time gulf between them.

In order to recapture something of her, he went to get an old Rheims biscuit box in the wardrobe at the head of his bed. In it he always saved the letters he received from women. It exuded an odor of damp dust and withered roses. The first thing he saw was a handkerchief covered with faint stains. It was one of hers. She once had had a nosebleed while they were out walking—he no longer remembered when. Nearby, knocking against the corners of the box, was the miniature Emma had given him: her clothes seemed pretentious to him and the ogling look in her eyes in the most lamentable taste. Emma's features slowly blurred in his memory as he stared at the picture and at the same time evoked the memory of Emma herself. It was as if the living face and the painted one, rubbing against each other, had erased each other. Finally he read some of her letters. They were short, factual, and as urgent as business letters, full of details about their trip. He wanted to see the longer ones again, those written in the old days. In order to find them at the bottom of the box, Rodolphe shuffled together all the others and began to search mechanically through the pile of papers and objects, finding a varied assortment of bouquets, a garter, a black mask, pins, locks of hair—so many locks! Brunette ones, blonde ones: some were even stuck to the hinges of the box and broke off when it was opened.

Browsing in this fashion among his souvenirs, he studied the handwriting and styles of the letters, as varied as the spelling. Some letters were tender, some gay, others humorous or sad. Some asked for love and some for money. One word would bring back a face, a gesture, the sound of a voice; sometimes, however, he could remember nothing.

Actually, these women rushing into his thoughts at the same time tended to get in one another's way. They faded into the background, as if equalized on the same level of love.

Rodolphe took up a random handful of letters and amused himself for a few minutes by letting them cascade from his right hand to his left. Finally, bored and tired, he put the box back into the cupboard, saying to himself: "What a collection of nonsense!"

This summed up his opinion, because pleasures, like children in a schoolyard, had so trampled on his heart that nothing green could grow there. What did pass through was more thoughtless than schoolchildren: it did not even leave, like them, a name scribbled on the wall.

"All right," he said to himself, "let's begin."

He wrote: "Courage, Emma, courage! I don't want to ruin your life."

"It's really true," he thought. "I'm acting in her interest. I'm being honest."

"Have you seriously considered your decision? Do you know what an abyss I was dragging you into, my poor angel? No, you don't, do you? You were going off, rashly confident, believing in happiness, in the future. Ah! What wretched, insane creatures we are!"

Rodolphe paused here in order to think up some good excuse.

"Suppose I tell her my entire fortune is lost? No, that

wouldn't stop anything. It would start all over again later on. Is there any way to make such women listen to reason?"

He pondered, then added: "You must believe me when I say I shall never forget you. I shall continue to feel a deep affection for you. But one day sooner or later, our passion would doubtless have lessened—that is the way things are in life. We would have grown weary. I might even have had the terrible pain of witnessing your remorse and even of sharing it since I caused it. The mere thought of the unhappiness you are undergoing tortures me, Emma. Forget me. Why did I have to know you? Why were you so beautiful? Is it my fault? Oh my God! No, no, fate alone is to blame!"

"A word that is always effective," he said to himself.

"Ah! Had you been one of those frivolous women, I would certainly have been able, by sheer egotism, to try an experiment. And it would have been without danger for you. But your wonderful exaltation, which is both your charm and your undoing, has prevented you, adorable creature that you are, from understanding the falsity of our future position. Nor did I think about it clearly at first. I was relaxing in the shade of our ideal happiness as if it were some poisonous tree of the tropics, without giving a thought to the consequences."

"She may think I'm giving her up out of stinginess. Well, what can I do? It's too bad but I've got to end it."

"The world is cruel, Emma. It would have pursued us everywhere we went. You would have had to endure indiscreet questions, slander, disdain, actual insults perhaps. Insults to you! And I who wanted to seat you on a throne, who will carry away the memory of you like a talisman. For I am punishing myself for all the evil I have done to you by going into exile. I am leaving. Where? I have no idea. I feel I am losing my mind. Farewell! Always remain as good as you are. Do not forget the unhappy man who has lost you. Teach my name to your child so that she will repeat it in her prayers."

The candles flickered. Rodolphe arose to shut the window. When he sat down again, he said to himself: "I think that's all. No, let's add this so she won't come back for me":

"I shall be far away when you read these sad lines. I wanted to flee as quickly as possible in order to avoid seeing you again. I won't weaken! I shall return later on and perhaps after that we will chat together, without passion, about our former love. Farewell!"

And there was one last farewell separated into two words: "Fare well!" which he deemed to be in excellent taste.

"How shall I sign?" he wondered. "Your devoted— No. Your friend? Yes, that will do."

"Your friend."

He reread the letter and found it good.

"Poor little woman," he thought, feeling tender. "She's going to think me harder than a rock. It needs a few tears on it, but unfortunately I just can't cry." He poured some water into a glass, dipped his finger into it, and let a big drop fall on the letter. It made a pale splotch on the ink. Then, looking for a seal for the letter, he came upon the one: *Amor nel cor.*

"It hardly suits the occasion. Oh, well, what's the difference?"

After which he smoked three pipes and went to bed.

The next day, after he was up (toward two in the afternoon—he had slept late), Rodolphe had some apricots picked and placed in a basket. He placed the letter at the bottom, under the vine leaves, and immediately ordered his plowboy, Girard, to bring it to Madame Bovary. This was his usual way of corresponding with her, sending her fruit or game according to the season.

"If she asks about me," he said, "tell her that I've left on a trip. You must put the basket into her hands. Go along now. Be careful!"

Girard put on his new shirt, tied his kerchief around the apricots, and set off tranquilly along the road to Yonville, taking long heavy strides in his hobnailed clogs.

When he reached the house, he found Madame Bovary and Félicité sorting a bundle of laundry on the kitchen table.

A feeling of dread seized her. While she groped in her pocket for some small change, she kept looking at the peasant with a frightened stare. He in turn gazed at her with astonishment, unable to comprehend why such a gift should move someone so much. At last he left. Félicité remained. Emma couldn't bear it any longer. She ran into the living room as if to bring the apricots there, turned the basket upside down, ripped away the leaves, and found the letter, opened it, and fled toward her bedroom, terror-stricken, as if there were some terrible fire behind her.

Charles was there; she saw him. He spoke to her; she heard nothing and continued to climb the stairs rapidly; she was breathless, lost, and drunk, still clutching in her fingers that horrible sheet of paper that rattled in her fingers like a sheet of tin. On the second floor, she stopped in front of the attic door, which was closed.

She tried to calm down, then thought about the letter. It had to be finished. But she didn't dare. Besides, where? How? She would be seen.

"No," she thought, "I'll be safe here."

Emma pushed open the door and walked in.

The oppressive heat, rising from the roof slates, closed in around her temples and stifled her. She dragged herself to the closed shutters of the dormer and pulled the bolt; the dazzling sunlight rushed in.

Beyond the rooftops the countryside spread out as far as the eye could see. Down below, the village square was empty, the cobblestones of the pavement sparkled, the weather-vanes of the houses were lifeless. At the corner of the street, some sort of strident whirring noise came from a lower floor. It was Binet, turning his lathe.

She leaned against the window frame, rereading the letter with sneers of anger. But the more she tried to concentrate on it, the more confused she became. She could see him in front of her, hear him; she was wrapping her arms around him. Her heart was pounding like a sledgehammer, furiously, irregularly, constantly accelerating. She looked all around her, hoping that the earth would crumble. Why not end it all? Who was keeping her back? She was free. She moved forward, concentrating on the pavement, and said: "Now! Now!"

The beam of sunlight reflecting directly up at her from below was pulling the weight of her body into an abyss. She felt as if the square were swinging to and fro, its ground climbing the walls. The floor was tilting at one end like a vessel in a storm. She was right at the edge, almost hanging out, surrounded by a great vastness. The blue of the sky flooded over her; the air rushed through her hollow brain. All she had to do was give in, let herself go. The whirr of the lathe kept on unceasingly, like a furious voice summoning her.

"Emma! Emma!" Charles shouted.

She stopped.

"Where are you? Come down!"

The thought that she had just escaped death almost made her faint from terror. She closed her eyes. Then she shivered as a hand touched her sleeve. It was Félicité.

"Monsieur is waiting for you, Madame. The soup is ready."

And she had to go down—had to seat herself at the table.

She tried to eat, but the food choked her. Then she unfolded her napkin as if to examine the darns. She began to concentrate on this, to count the threads in the fabric. Suddenly she thought about the letter again. Had she lost it? Where was it? But she felt such a weariness of the spirit that she could not bring herself to invent an excuse to leave the table. Then she became frightened, afraid of Charles. He knew everything. She was sure of it. And he did utter these strange words: "It seems we aren't likely to see Monsieur Rodolphe again soon."

"Who told you?" she asked with a start.

"Who told me?" he repeated, slightly surprised at her sharp tone. "Girard. I met him a few minutes ago at the door of the Café Français. He's gone off on a trip, or he's about to leave."

She caught her breath with a sob.

"What's so surprising about it? He occasionally goes off like this for some distraction. I must say, I approve. When you're rich and a bachelor! Besides, he has himself a good time, our friend. He's a bit of a rake. Monsieur Langlois told me—"

He stopped talking because the maid had just come in. She put the apricots, which had been scattered on the sideboard, back into the basket. Charles did not notice his wife's redness. He had the fruit brought to him, took one, and bit into it.

"Perfect," he said. "Here, taste one." And he held out the basket, which she pushed away gently.

"Smell that fragrance," he said, moving it back and forth under her nose.

"I'm choking," she cried, jumping up. But she managed to gain control of the spasm. "It's nothing," she said, "nothing. Just nerves. Sit down and eat."

She was afraid he might question her, pay attention to her, not leave her alone.

Charles sat down again in order to please her. He was spitting the apricot pits into his hand and then placing them on his plate.

Suddenly a blue tilbury passed rapidly through the square. Emma moaned once, then fell back on the floor and lay there rigidly.

Rodolphe, after much thought, had decided to leave for Rouen. But since there was no other road from La Huchette to Buchy except the one through Yonville, it was necessary for him to cross the village. Emma had recognized him by the light of the lanterns that cut through the twilight like a streak of lightning.

The pharmacist, hearing the commotion, rushed to the house. The table and all the plates were overturned. Sauce, meat, knives, salt shaker, and oil cruet littered the room. Charles was shouting for help. Berthe was frightened and crying. Félicité, with trembling hands, was unlacing her mistress, whose entire body shuddered convulsively.

"I'll run back to my laboratory and get some aromatic vinegar," said the apothecary.

When she opened her eyes after inhaling from the bottle, he said: "I was sure of it. This stuff would awaken the dead."

"Speak to me," said Charles; "talk to me. Pull yourself together. It's I, Charles—I love you. Don't you know me? Look, here's our little girl. Kiss her."

The child tried to place her arms around her mother's neck, but Emma turned her head away and said in a quivering voice: "No, no—no one!" Then she fainted again and they carried her to bed.

There she remained, stretched out, mouth agape, eyes shut, hands open and motionless. She was as white as a waxen image. Two rivulets of tears flowed slowly out of her eyes over the pillow.

Charles was standing at the back of the alcove. The pharmacist stood near him, maintaining that thoughtful silence that is appropriate to life's serious moments.

"Don't worry," he said, nudging Charles with his elbow. "I think the crisis is over."

"Yes, she's resting a little now," answered Charles, who

was watching her as she slept. "Poor thing! Poor thing! Look how weak she is."

Homais asked how the incident had happened. Charles answered that it had seized her suddenly while she was eating apricots.

"Extraordinary!" said the pharmacist. "But it is possible that the apricots caused the fainting spell. Some natures are so sensitive to certain smells. It would even be a rather interesting phenomenon to study, from the pathological as well as the physiological aspects. The priests know how important it is. They've always introduced aromatic spices into their ceremonies. They do so in order to stupefy the senses and induce a state of ecstasy—a condition, moreover, that is easier to obtain in women, who are more delicate than men. I've heard cases of people fainting at the smell of burnt hartshorn, or fresh bread."

"Be careful, don't wake her!" said Bovary in a low voice.

"And not only are humans susceptible to these anomalies," continued the pharmacist, "but animals are also. You are of course aware of the powerful aphrodisiac effect produced by *Nepeta cataria*, commonly known as catnip, on the feline race? Furthermore, to cite an example that I will vouch for as authentic, Bridoux—an old friend of mine who's currently in business on the Rue Malpalu—owns a dog that falls into convulsions as soon as he's offered a snuffbox. Bridoux even performs the experiment quite often for his friends at his summer home in Bois-Guillaume. Would you believe that a simple sneezing powder could cause such havoc in a quadruped's body? Extremely curious, isn't it?"

"Yes," said Charles, who wasn't listening.

"Which proves to us," continued the other, smiling with an air of benign self-satisfaction, "the innumerable irregularities of the nervous system. Insofar as Madame is concerned, she has always seemed to me, I must admit, genuinely sensitive. Nor will I suggest to you at all, my friend, any of those so-called remedies that, under the guise of attacking symptoms, attack one's constitution. No, no useless medication! Diet alone. Sedatives, emollients, dulcifiers. And don't you think perhaps that we should stir up her imagination?"

"In what way? How?" asked Bovary.

"Ah, that's it! That's just it. 'That is the question,'" he

quoted in English, "as I was reading in the newspaper the other day."

But Emma, awakening, cried out: "The letter! The letter!"

They thought she was delirious, and she was, from midnight on. Brain fever had broken out.

Charles did not leave her side for forty-three days. He neglected all his patients. He no longer slept, was constantly feeling her pulse, applying mustard plasters, cold compresses. He would send Justin as far as Neufchâtel to fetch ice. The ice would melt on the way. He would send the boy back. He called Monsieur Canivet into consultation, had Dr. Larivière, his old teacher, come from Rouen. He was in despair. What frightened him most was Emma's state of prostration; she didn't speak, appeared not to hear, and even seemed not to suffer—as if body and soul were now resting together after all their exertions.

Toward the middle of October she could sit up in bed propped up by pillows. Charles cried the first time he saw her eating bread and jam. Her strength returned. She would get up for a few hours in the afternoon. One day when she was feeling better, he tried to take her for a walk in the garden, supporting her on his arm. The sand of the paths was disappearing from sight under the dead leaves. She took one step at a time, dragging her slippers, and continued to smile as she leaned on Charles's shoulder.

They walked in this manner to the back of the garden, near the terrace. She straightened up slowly and shielded her eyes with her hand in order to look about. She stared as far as possible into the distance, but against the horizon there were only huge grass fires smoking on the hillsides.

"You'll get tired, darling," said Bovary. He pushed her gently into the arbor. "Sit down on this bench. You'll be comfortable."

"No, not there, not there," she said in a faltering voice.

She had a dizzy spell. That very evening her illness began again, in a much less clearly defined way, it is true, and with more complex symptoms. Sometimes it was her heart that pained her, then her chest, head, or limbs; she had vomiting spells in which Charles thought he saw the first signs of cancer.

And besides all this, the poor young man was worried about money!

XIV

In the first place, he didn't know how he could reimburse Homais for all the medicines he had supplied; and although as a doctor he didn't have to pay, he still felt embarrassed. Then too, now that the cook was mistress, the household expenses were becoming frightening; bills poured into the house, the tradespeople grumbled. Lheureux in particular was dunning him. He had even, when Emma was at the critical point in her illness, taken advantage of the circumstance to increase his bill; he had quickly delivered the cloak, traveling bag, two trunks instead of one, and a number of other things as well. Charles protested vainly that he didn't need them. The shopkeeper answered with arrogance that all the items had been ordered from him and he wouldn't take them back. Besides, if he did, it might be detrimental to Madame in her convalescence. Monsieur ought to think about it. In brief, he was determined to bring him into court rather than give up his rights and take the merchandise back. Charles then ordered the goods to be returned to the store; Félicité forgot, Charles had other worries, and they thought no further about it. Monsieur Lheureux resumed the attack and managed, by alternating whines and threats, to maneuver Bovary into signing a promissory note to be paid within six months. The ink was barely dry on the note when Charles had a daring thought. This was to borrow a thousand francs from Lheureux. And so he asked with embarrassment if he could borrow them, adding that the loan would be for one year and at the stipulated rate of interest. Lheureux ran to his store, brought back the money, and dictated another note, on which Bovary declared that he had to pay to his order, on September 1 following, the sum of thousand seventy francs, which, with the 180 already stipulated, made an even 1,250. Thus, lending at six percent, plus twenty-five percent commission, and with the goods bringing in another third at least, he would have 130 francs' profit in a year. He was hoping that the matter wouldn't

stop there, that Charles wouldn't be able to pay the notes
and that they would be renewed, and that his meager funds,
having nourished themselves at the doctor's expense like a
patient in a rest home, would return to him one day consid-
erably plumper, and fat enough to burst his moneybag.

Besides, everything was going his way. He had the con-
tract for supplying cider to the Neufchâtel poorhouse; Monsieur Guillaumin had promised him shares in the Grumesnil
peat bogs; and he was thinking about establishing a new
coach line between Argueil and Rouen, which would certainly put a quick end to the rickety old Golden Lion carriage
and which with its greater speed, lowered prices, and greater baggage capacity would concentrate all the business of
Yonville in his hands.

Charles kept wondering how he would be able to pay
back so much money the following year; he tried to think
up various schemes—such as turning to his father or selling
something. But his father would turn a deaf ear, and he personally had nothing to sell. Then the difficulties began to
loom so large that he thrust the unpleasant thoughts from
his mind. He reproached himself for forgetting Emma as if
he owed her all of his thoughts and were robbing her by
thinking of other matters.

It was a severe winter. Emma's convalescence made
slow progress. When the weather was good, they would push
her chair over to the window, the one overlooking the square,
because she hated the garden now and the shutter on that
side was always closed. She wanted the horse sold; everything
she had once loved now displeased her. She seemed able to
think only of her own state of health. She remained in bed
eating little meals, then would ring for the maid to inquire
about her medicinal tea or to chat. Meanwhile the snow would
cast a still, white light into the room. Then the rains came.
And Emma would await, almost anxiously, the inevitable re-
currence of some trifling daily event, even when it did not
concern her. The most important was the arrival of the Hirondelle each evening. Then the landlady would cry out and
other voices would answer, while Hippolyte's lantern would
glow like a star as he hunted among the boxes in the baggage
compartment. Charles would come in at noon. Afterwards
he would leave and she would have her broth, and then at
sunset, around five o'clock, the children returning from class

would drag their wooden shoes over the sidewalks and
take turns running their rulers along the shutters.

Abbé Bournisien came to see her at that hour. He would
ask about her health, bring her the news, and try to nudge
her toward religion with some unctuous gossip that was not
without charm. The very sight of his cassock comforted her.

One day, at the height of her illness, she believed herself
dying and asked for Communion; and as the preparations for
the sacrament went on in her room, as they arranged the
dresser with its clutter of medicine bottles into an altar and
Félicité scattered dahlia petals over the floor, Emma sensed
something powerful passing over her, freeing her from all
her pains, from all perception and feeling. Her body, freed
of its burden, no longer thought; another life was beginning;
it seemed to her that her being, ascending toward God, was
going to be destroyed in that love like a burning incense
that is dissolved in smoke. They sprinkled holy water over
the sheets; the priest took the white wafer from the holy
pyx; and she nearly fainted with a celestial joy as she offered
her lips to receive the body of the Saviour. The curtains of
her alcove swelled out gently, like clouds, and the rays of the
two candles burning on the chest of drawers seemed to her
to be two dazzling haloes. Then she dropped her head,
thinking she could hear the far-off song of heavenly harps
and see God the Father on a golden throne in an azure sky, in
the midst of saints bearing green palms, a God radiant with
majesty, signaling to angels with flaming wings to descend
to earth and take her off in their arms.

This splendid vision remained in her memory as the most
beautiful dream imaginable, so much so that she kept trying to recapture the sensation, which continued with the
same sweetness, albeit less intensely. Her soul, aching with
pride, was at last reposing in Christian humility; she relished
the pleasure of having succumbed and studied the destruction
of her will within herself, which was to allow free entry
of heavenly grace. And so there existed greater joys than
mere happiness, another love above all other loves, with neither interruption nor end, which would grow eternally! In
her illusions born of hope she envisaged a state of purity
floating above the earth, blending with the heavens, into
which she longed to be absorbed. She wanted to become a
saint. She bought rosaries and wore amulets; she wanted an

emerald-studded reliquary at her bedside so that she could
kiss it every night.

The curé was delighted at this condition, although he felt
that Emma's religious leanings, because of their very fervor,
might end in heresy, even extravagance. But since he was not
very well versed in these matters once they passed a certain
limit, he wrote to Monsieur Boulard, bookseller to the bishop, to send him "something really worthwhile for a lady
with a fine mind." The bookseller, as casually as if he were
sending hardware off to some ignorant savages, sent a random collection of his current accumulation of religious tracts.
There were little manuals of questions and answers, arrogant-
sounding pamphlets in the style of Monsieur de Maistre, and
a certain type of cloying novel with pink binding, turned out
by sentimental seminarists or penitent blue-stockings, like
Think It Over; The Man of the World at Mary's Feet, by
*Monsieur de——, Holder of Several Decorations; Some Er-
rors of Voltaire; For the Benefit of the Young*; etc.

Madame Bovary was not yet mentally well enough to apply herself seriously to anything at all; besides, she plunged
into the books with too much haste. She grew annoyed at
the rules of ritual; the arrogance of the written polemics displeased her by their pitiless attacks on people she didn't
know; and the secular tales, with their religious touches,
seemed to have been written out of such ignorance of the
world that imperceptibly they drove her away from the truths
she was seeking. She persisted, however, and when the book
would fall from her hands, she believed herself permeated
with the most refined Catholic melancholy that could enter
an ethereal soul.

As for the memory of Rodolphe, she had buried it in the
very bottom of her heart and it remained there, more solemn
and motionless than a royal mummy in a subterranean tomb.
A fragrance was emanating from this great embalmed love
that suffused with tenderness the atmosphere of immaculate
purity in which she wanted to live. When she knelt at her
Gothic *prie-Dieu*, she addressed to the Lord the same
fond words she had formerly murmured to her lover in the
ecstasies of adultery. She was trying to entice faith. But no
joy descended from the heavens, and she would stand up with
her legs aching and the vague feeling that it was all a huge
fraud. She told herself that this search would earn her even
more credit, and in the pride of her devotion, she com-

pared herself to those great women of yesteryear whose glory she had dreamed of over a portrait of La Vallière, and who had retired into solitude (trailing their lace-edged trains with so much majesty) to pour out at the feet of Christ all the tears of a heart wounded by life.

Then she became excessively charitable. She would sew clothes for the poor, she sent wood to women in labor, and one day on his return home Charles found three tramps sitting at the kitchen table and drinking soup. She had her little daughter, whom Charles had sent back to the nurse during her illness, brought home. She wanted to teach her to read. Berthe could cry and cry, she did not let it upset her. She had made up her mind to be resigned, and was indulgent toward everyone. Her language was continually filled with lofty phrases. She would ask the child: "Is your stomachache better, my angel?"

Madame Bovary senior found nothing to criticize in Emma except perhaps her zealousness in knitting undershirts for orphans instead of mending her own dishcloths. The good woman, beset by constant quarrels at home, felt comfortable in this peaceful house. She even remained until after Easter in order to avoid the sarcastic comments of old Bovary, who invariably ordered pork sausages on Good Friday.

Apart from the company of her mother-in-law, whose correctness of judgment and dignified ways lent her moral support, Emma received different guests almost every day. Mesdames Langlois, Caron, Dubreuil, and Tuvache came, and the goodhearted Madame Homais would come every afternoon from two to five. She had never wanted to believe any of the gossip about her neighbor. The Homais children also visited, Justin accompanying them. He would go up to the room with them and remain standing near the door, motionless and silent. Often Madame Bovary would start dressing without paying any attention to him. She would begin by taking out her comb and shaking her head rapidly. The first time the poor boy saw the mass of black ringlets fall to her knees, it meant to him a sudden entry into some extraordinary new country, the splendors of which terrified him.

His silent ardor and his shyness were lost on Emma. She never dreamed that the love that had disappeared from her life was throbbing so close to her, under that homespun shirt, in that adolescent heart so receptive to the emanations of her beauty. Besides, everything seemed indifferent to her now.

She would speak with affection but look with disdain. Her conduct was so contradictory that it was impossible to distinguish selfishness from charity, corruption from virtue. One evening, for example, when the maid was asking permission to go out and stammering out an excuse, she grew angry. Then she suddenly asked, "So you love him?" And without awaiting an answer from the blushing Félicité, she added sadly, "Well, run along. Have a good time."

She had the garden completely rearranged at the beginning of spring, despite Bovary's objections; but he was happy to see her finally showing some signs of will. She showed more as she grew stronger. First she managed to get rid of Madame Rollet, the nurse, who had fallen into the habit, during Emma's convalescence, of going into the kitchen too often with her two foster-children and her little boarder, who had a more voracious appetite than a cannibal. Then she saw less and less of the Homais family, dismissed the other visitors one by one, and even attended church less regularly, which earned her the warm approval of the apothecary. He commented, in a rather friendly fashion, "You were taken in a bit by all that rigmarole!"

Abbé Bournisien, as before, showed up every day after the catechism class. He preferred to stay outside in the fresh air "in the grove," as he called the arbor.

Charles came home at that hour, and the men (who felt warm) would be served sweet cider. They drank to Emma's complete recovery.

Binet was present, a bit further down, that is, leaning against the terrace wall fishing for crayfish. Bovary would invite him over for some refreshment. He was an expert at uncorking wine bottles.

He would look around smugly at the countryside and say: "The bottle should be placed this way, straight up on the table, and when the wires are cut, the cork should be removed a little at a time, gently, gently, the way they handle seltzer in restaurants."

But the cider often spurted forth right in their faces during his demonstration. The priest never missed his chance to make the same joke with a heavy laugh: "Its goodness just jumps right out at you."

The abbé was really a good sort and was not even scandalized one day when the pharmacist advised Charles to distract Emma a bit by taking her to the theater in Rouen to hear Lagardy, the famous tenor. Homais, surprised at his silence, asked what he thought, and the priest asserted that he considered music less dangerous to morals than literature. Then the pharmacist began to defend the latter. The theater, he claimed, served to expose prejudice and taught virtue under the guise of pleasure.

"*Castigat ridendo mores,* Monsieur Bournisien! Consider the majority of Voltaire's tragedies, for example. They are cleverly larded with philosophical reflections that provide the people with a veritable education in morality and diplomacy."

Binet said: "I once saw a play. It was called *The Urchin from Paris,* and it portrayed an old general to a T. He slaps down a young man of society who seduces a working girl, who ends by—"

"Of course," Homais continued, "there is bad literature as there is bad pharmaceutical practice, but to condemn *in toto* the most important of the fine arts seems to me a stupid error, a Gothic notion worthy of those awful days when they imprisoned Galileo."

"I'm sure," the curé protested, "that there are good works and good authors, but the mere fact of people of both sexes being brought together in seductive surroundings decorated with worldly pomp, with pagan disguises and cosmetics, flaming lights and effeminate voices—all of that must in the long run give rise to a certain mental abandon and inspire dishonest thoughts and impure temptations. At least this is the opinion of all the Fathers. Finally," he added, suddenly assuming an unctuous tone while he rolled a pinch of snuff between his fingers, "if the Church has condemned theatrical performances, she has her reasons; we must submit to her decrees."

"Why does she excommunicate actors?" asked the pharmacist. "At one time they openly took part in religious ceremonies. In fact they acted out right in the middle of the choir certain types of farcical plays called mysteries in which the laws of decency were often offended."

The clergyman contented himself with a low moan, and the pharmacist continued: "It's like it is in the Bible. There is —you know—more than one spicy detail of really—lively— things."

And in reply to a gesture of irritation from Abbé Bournisien: "Ah! You'll agree that it's not a book to put into the hands of the young and I would be angry if my daughter, Athalie——"

"But it's the Protestants, not us, who recommend the Bible," the other exclaimed with impatience.

"It doesn't matter," Homais said. "I'm surprised that in our time, in an enlightened century, we still persist in forbidding an intellectual relaxation that is inoffensive, edifying, and even sometimes therapeutic, isn't it, doctor?"

"I suppose so," the doctor answered casually, either because, sharing the same ideas, he didn't want to offend anyone or else because he didn't have any ideas.

The conversation seemed over when the pharmacist saw fit to make one last jab.

"I've known priests who dressed in street clothes to go see dancing girls wriggling around."

"That's ridiculous!" said the curé.

"Yes, I've known some." And, drawing out his sentence, Homais repeated: "I—have—known—some."

"Well, then, they were wrong," said Bournisien, resigned to hearing anything.

"Believe me, they do more than that!" exclaimed the apothecary.

"Monsieur!" the clergyman retorted, looking so fierce that the pharmacist was finally intimidated.

"I only mean," the other answered in a less antagonistic tone, "that toleration is the surest way to attract people to religion."

"True, true," the curé conceded, sitting down again in his chair. But he only stayed two more minutes.

Then, as soon as he was gone, Homais said to the doctor: "That's what I call a real argument! Did you see how I won! Anyway, take my advice and take Madame to the theater, if only to irritate one of those old crows for once in your life! If someone could take my place I'd go with you myself. But hurry! Lagardy is giving only one performance; he's been engaged for England at a very impressive fee. From what I hear, he's quite a fellow—he's rolling in money and travels with three mistresses and a cook. All those great artists burn the candle at both ends. They need a wild life to stimulate their imagination. But they die in the poorhouse because they didn't have the foresight to save their money in their youth. Well, hearty appetite! See you tomorrow."

The idea of the theater grew quickly in Bovary's mind; he mentioned it to his wife right away. She at first refused, pleading the fatigue, discomfort, and expense. But for once Charles did not give in, so much did he think the relaxation would do her good. He foresaw no difficulties; his mother had sent them three hundred francs that he had not counted on, the current debts were not very large, and the due date of Lheureux's notes was so far off that he didn't have to worry about them. Besides, thinking that she was refusing out of consideration for him, he insisted all the more and she finally gave in to his arguments. So the next day, at eight o'clock, they set off in the Hirondelle.

The apothecary, who had nothing to keep him in Yonville, but felt himself unable to budge from there, sighed as he saw them off.

"Bon voyage!" he called out to them. "You're lucky people!"

Then he said to Emma, who wore a blue silk dress with four flounces: "You're as lovely as a goddess. You'll make quite an impression in Rouen."

The stagecoach stopped at the Red Cross Hotel, on the Place Beauvoisine. It was one of those inns that are found in all provincial towns, with huge stables and tiny bedrooms, where the yard is filled with chickens pecking oats under the mud-spattered gigs of the traveling salesmen—a solid old house with a worm-eaten wooden balcony that creaked in the wind on winter nights; always filled with people, noise, and eating; with black tables sticky from spilled brandy-laced coffee; thick windows yellowed by the flies; and damp towels stained by wine. Always smelling of the village, like farmhands dressed in city clothes, such hotels have a café on the street side and a vegetable garden on the country side. Charles went out immediately. He mixed up the stalls with the gallery, the pit with the boxes, asked for explanations that he didn't understand, was sent from the box office to the manager, came back to the inn, returned to the box office, and thus several times covered the entire length of the town from the theater to the boulevard.

Madame Bovary bought a hat, gloves, and a bouquet. Charles was very frightened of missing the opening, and without stopping for even a bit of soup, they walked to the theater and found the doors still closed.

XV

The crowd outside was gathered against the wall, which was symmetrically enclosed between the railings. At the corner of the neighboring streets huge posters announced in ornate letters: *"Lucia de Lammermoor—Lagardy—Opéra—* etc."* It was lovely outside but warm, and perspiration dampened hairdos. Handkerchiefs were removed from pockets, mopping red foreheads. An occasional warm breeze coming from the river would gently flutter the border of the canvas awnings hanging over the doors of the bars. A bit farther along, people were cooled by an icy draft of air smelling of tallow, leather, and oil. This was the smell from the Rue des Charrettes, filled with large black buildings in which barrels were stored.

Afraid of looking ridiculous, Emma suggested taking a walk along the promenade before they went in. Bovary kept the tickets cautiously in his hand, and the hand in his trousers pocket, pressing it against his stomach.

Emma's heart began to beat as soon as they neared the foyer. She involuntarily smiled with self-satisfaction at seeing the crowd rushing toward the right, through the other corridor, while she ascended the staircase to the reserved seats. She was as thrilled as a child when she pushed the large tapestried doors with her finger; she took in the dusty odor of the corridors with a deep breath, and when she was seated in her box, she leaned forward with the ease of a duchess.

The hall was beginning to fill up, opera glasses were being removed from their cases, and the subscribers, glimpsing each other, bowed across the distance. They came to relax in the theater from the anxieties of business; but not forgetting work entirely, they were still talking of cottons, brandy alcohol, or indigo. There were faces of old people, impassive and peaceful, which resembled, with their white hair and coloring, silver medals tarnished by leaden fumes. The handsome young men were strutting about in the pit,

showing off pink or apple-green cravats above their waistcoats. Madame Bovary admired them from above as they
rested the open palms of their yellow gloves on their golden-
knobbed canes.

Then the orchestra lights were lit, the chandelier, let down
from the ceiling, cast a sudden gaiety over the room with
the sparkles from its crystals; the musicians filed in one at
a time. At first there was a lengthy din of rumbling basses, squeaking violins, blaring cornets, piping flutes and flag-
eolets. Then came three knocks on the stage; there was a
roll of drums, the brass section played some chords, and the
curtain rose to reveal a country setting.

It was a crossroads in a wood with a fountain on the left,
shaded by an oak tree. Peasants and lords with plaids on
their shoulders were singing a hunting song together. Then
a captain appeared, lifting his two arms to heaven and calling down the angel of evil. Then another character appeared,
they went off together, and the hunters took over.

She felt transported to the readings of her childhood—
to the books of Walter Scott. She felt as if she could hear,
across the fog, the sound of Scottish bagpipes echoing through
the heather. Moreover, her recollection of the novel made
it easier for her to understand the libretto, and she kept
pace with the action phrase by phrase, while elusive thoughts
crossing her mind were quickly dispelled by the gusts of music. She gave herself up to the lulling melodies, felt herself
vibrating with all her being, as if violin bows were being
drawn over her nerves. Her eyes were not large enough
to take in the costumes, the sets, the actors, the painted trees
trembling at the slightest footsteps, the velvet hats, cloaks,
swords—all these fantasies floating together in harmony as
if in another world. But a young woman stepped forth,
throwing a purse to a squire in green. She was left alone
and then a flute was heard, like the murmur of a fountain
or the warbling of birds. Lucia, looking solemn, launched into
her cavatina in G major. She bemoaned love, and yearned
to have wings. Emma, too, would have wanted to escape
from life and fly off in an embrace. Suddenly, Edgar Lagardy
appeared.

He had that splendid pallor that lends something of the
majesty of marble to the passionate races of the south. His
vigorous body was encased in a brown doublet; a small
carved dagger hung against his left thigh. He was posing

languorously and displaying his white teeth. It was said that a Polish princess, hearing him sing one night on the beach at Biarritz, where he mended boats, had fallen in love with him. She had ruined herself for him. Then he left her for other women, and this romantic fame had but served to enhance his reputation as an artist. The publicity men always took care to slip into his advertisements some poetic phrase about his fascinating personality and the sensitivity of his soul. A beautiful voice, complete self-possession, more temperament than intelligence and more bombast than true lyricism—thus was constituted this admirable charlatan, in whose nature there was a blend of hairdresser and toreador.

He had the audience with him from the very first scene. He pressed Lucia to his chest, left her, came back, appeared to be desperate; he burst out in anger, then sang throaty elegies of infinite sweetness. Notes filled with sobs and kisses escaped from his bare throat. Emma leaned over to see him, digging her nails into the plush of the box. Her heart filled with the melodious lamentations that were drawn out to the accompaniment of the double basses, like the cries of the drowning amid the tumult of a storm. She recognized all the intoxication and anguish of which she had nearly died. The voice of the soprano seemed but the echo of her own conscience, and this illusion enchanting her as something of her own life. But no one on earth had loved her with such a love. *He* did not cry like Edgar that last night in the moonlight when they told each other: "Until tomorrow! Until tomorrow!" The theater rang with bravos; they repeated the entire passage; the lovers spoke about the flowers on their grave, of oaths, exile, fate, hope, and when they uttered the final adieu, Emma let out a sharp cry that blended into the sound of the last chords.

"Why is that lord persecuting her?" Bovary asked.

"No, no," she answered. "He's her lover."

"But he's swearing to revenge himself on her family while the other one, the one who came only a few minutes ago, said 'I love Lucia and I think she loves me.' And besides, he went off with her father arm in arm. He is her father, isn't he, the ugly little man with a cock feather in his hat?"

Despite Emma's explanations, as soon as the recitative duet began in which Gilbert reveals to his master, Ashton, his detestable machinations, Charles, seeing the false engagement

ring that is to trick Lucia, thought that it was a token of
love sent by Edgar. Indeed, he confessed he couldn't understand the story—because the music drowned out much of the
words.

"What's the difference?" Emma said. "Be quiet!"

"But I like to understand what's going on; you know that,"
he said, leaning on her shoulder.

"Do be quiet!" she said with impatience.

Lucia came forward, half supported by her ladies, an
orange wreath in her hair and paler than the white satin
of her dress. Emma dreamed of her wedding day; she could
see herself down there, in the middle of the cornfields, on
the tiny path, as they walked toward the church. Why had
she not resisted, implored, like Lucia? On the contrary, she
had been happy, without perceiving the abyss into which
she was rushing. Ah! If, in the freshness of her beauty,
before the defilements of marriage and the disillusionments
of adultery, she had been able to offer her life to some
generous, solid heart. Then virtue, tenderness, sensual delights, and duty would have mingled. Never would she have
fallen from such high happiness. But such happiness, no
doubt, was a lie invented to cause the despair of all desire.
Now she knew the petty quality of the passions that art
exaggerated. Making an effort to turn away from such
thoughts, Emma saw this reconstruction of her sorrows as
nothing but a colorful fantasy, an entertaining spectacle for
the eyes. And she even smiled to herself with disdainful
pity when a man in a black cloak appeared under the velvet curtains at the back of the stage.

His large Spanish hat fell at a single gesture. Immediately
the instruments and singers began the sextet. Edgar, flashing
rage, dominated all the others with his clear voice; Ashton
flung the homicidal provocations at him in deep tones; Lucia
emitted her shrill lament; Arthur sung his asides in middle-
register notes; and the chaplain's baritone boomed out like
an organ, while the voices of the women, repeating his
words, sang in a delightful chorus. Now they were all lined
up and gesticulating; anger, vengeance, jealousy, terror, mercy, and amazement issued forth at the same time from
their open mouths. The outraged lover brandished his un-
sheathed sword; his lace ruffle rose and fell with the heaving of his chest; and he walked from right to left across the
stage, taking large steps, clicking on the floor the silver-

gilt spurs of his soft boots that widened out at the ankles. He must, she thought, have an inexhaustible love to pour so much out over the crowd, and so effusively. All her critical objections faded away under the poetry of the role that was absorbing her, and attracted to the man by the fictional character he was portraying, she tried to imagine his life, that glamorous life, out of the ordinary and splendid and yet one that she could have led if fate had so willed it. They might have met and loved! With him she would have traveled from capital to capital through all the kingdoms of Europe, sharing his weariness and his pride, picking up the flowers thrown at him, she herself embroidering his costumes. Then, each evening, at the back of a box, sitting open-mouthed behind the golden trellis work, she would have breathed in the outpourings of this soul who would sing only for her; he would look for her from the stage, even while acting. Then a mad notion struck her; he was looking at her, she was sure of it! She wanted to run into his arms, to take refuge in his strength as in the incarnation of love itself, and to say to him, to cry out: "Take me away, take me with you, let us go! I am yours, yours; all my passion and all my dreams are yours!"

The curtain fell.

The smell of gas mingled with that of human breathing; the stir of the fans made the atmosphere seem even more stifling. Emma wanted to go out; people were crowding the corridors and she fell back into her chair with stifling palpitations. Charles, afraid that she was going to faint, ran to the bar to get her a glass of barley water. He had a difficult time getting back to the box; his elbows were jostled at every step because of the glass he was carrying in both hands. He even spilled three fourths of it on the shoulders of a Rouen lady in short sleeves, who, feeling the cold liquid trickling down her back, screamed like a peacock, as if she were being assassinated. Her husband, a mill owner, began to shout at the clumsy oaf. While she was dabbing at the spots on her lovely cherry-colored taffeta dress with her handkerchief, he muttered with anger about damages, coats, and reimbursement. Charles finally reached his wife and gasped: "I thought I'd never get back! Such a crowd!" He added: "Guess who I saw over there? Monsieur Léon."

"Léon?"

"Yes, Léon. He's coming over to say hello." Just as he finished these words, the one-time Yonville clerk entered the box.

He extended his hand with aristocratic nonchalance; and Madame Bovary mechanically offered hers, no doubt obeying the attraction of a stronger will. She had not felt that hand since the spring evening when the rain was dropping on the green leaves and they had bade each other farewell standing near the window. But she quickly reminded herself of the propriety of the situation and with an effort shook off the old memories. She began chattering rapidly.

"Why, hello! What a surprise! What are you doing here?"

"Quiet!" cried a voice from the pit, for the third act was beginning.

"You're in Rouen?"

"Yes."

"Since when?"

"Put them out!" People were staring at them. They stopped talking.

But from that moment on, she listened no longer to the music; and the chorus of the guests, the scene between Ashton and his attendant, the great duet in D major—for her everything took place in the distance, as if the instruments had been muffled and the characters moved farther off. She remembered the card games at the pharmacist's house, the walk to the wet nurse's, the readings in the arbor, the tête-à-têtes by the fireside, all of that pathetically calm and long-enduring love, so discreet and tender, which she had nevertheless forgotten. Why had he come back? What combination of events was bringing him back into her life? He stood behind her, leaning his shoulder against the wall of the box, and she quivered occasionally at the warm breath from his nostrils blowing into her hair.

"Are you enjoying this?" he said, leaning so close to her that the tip of his mustache brushed against her cheek.

She answered casually: "Lord no, not very much!"

Then he suggested that they leave the theater and stop somewhere for an ice.

"Oh, not yet," said Bovary. "Let's stay. Her hair's come undone; it looks as if it's going to be tragic."

But the mad scene did not interest Emma at all, and the soprano's acting seemed overdone.

"She's shouting too loud," she said, turning toward Charles, who was listening.

"Yes, maybe—a bit," he answered, undecided between his own genuine pleasure and his respect for his wife's opinions.

Then Léon said with a sigh: "It's so warm—"

"Unbearable, isn't it?"

"Are you uncomfortable?" asked Bovary.

"Yes, stifling. Let's go."

Carefully, Monsieur Léon placed her long lace shawl around her shoulders, and the three of them went off to sit near the waterfront, in the open air, on a café terrace. At first they talked about her illness, even though Emma kept interrupting Charles for fear, she said, that they were boring Monsieur Léon; and then the latter told them that he had come to Rouen to spend two years in a large office in order to gain experience in Normandy, where business methods were different from those in Paris. Then he asked about Berthe, about the Homais family, about the Widow Lefrançois; and since they had nothing more to say to each other in the husband's presence, the conversation soon died.

People coming out of the theater passed by on the sidewalk, humming or yelling as loud as possible: *"O bel ange, ma Lucie!"* Then Léon, playing the dilettante, began to talk of music. He had seen Tamburini, Rubini, Persiani, and Grisi. Compared to them, Lagardy, despite his powerful outbursts, was nothing.

"But," said Charles, who was taking small licks of his rum sherbet, "they say he was just wonderful in the last act. I'm sorry we left before it was over. It was just beginning to amuse me."

"Anyway," said the clerk, "there will be another performance."

But Charles answered that they were leaving the next day.

"Unless you want to stay alone, my kitten," he added, turning to his wife.

Changing his tactics in the face of this unexpected opportunity, the young man began praising Lagardy in the final number. It was something superb, sublime. Then Charles insisted: "You can come back Sunday. Go on, make up your mind. You'll make a mistake by leaving if you feel this will do you the least good."

The tables around them were beginning to empty; a waiter approached discreetly, taking up a position near them. Charles, who understood, pulled out his purse; the clerk held back his arm and did not even forget to leave a couple of silver coins for the waiter, which he noisily tossed on the table.

"I'm really sorry," Bovary murmured, "about the money that you're—"

The other made a nonchalant, extremely cordial gesture and picked up his hat, saying, "It's agreed, then, isn't it, tomorrow at six?"

Charles explained once more that he couldn't stay away any longer but that nothing prevented Emma . . .

"But—" she stammered, with a peculiar smile, "I really don't know—"

"Well, think about it. We'll see. The night will bring counsel." Then to Léon, who was walking along with them: "Now that you're back in our part of the world, you'll drop in for dinner once in a while, I hope?"

The clerk said that he certainly would, especially since he had to go to Yonville on some office business. And they said good night at the Passage Saint-Herbland, just as the cathedral clock struck half past eleven.

PART III

I

While studying law, Monsieur Léon had also been a fairly frequent visitor to the Chaumière cabaret, where he even did rather well with the grisettes, who thought him "distinguished." He was the most personable of the students: he wore his hair neither too short nor too long, did not spend his whole quarter's allowance on the first day of the month, and managed to stay on good terms with his professors. And he always avoided going to excesses in his behavior, as much from timidity as from fastidiousness.

Often when reading in his room or when sitting in the evening under the linden trees of the Luxembourg Gardens, he would let his law book fall to the ground, and he would think of Emma. But the feeling gradually lessened in intensity, and other sensual desires replaced it. Nevertheless the old sentiment still persisted, for Léon had not lost all hope. The idea remained for him like some vague promise dangling in the future, a golden fruit hanging on some imaginary tree.

Then, seeing her after three years' separation, his passion revived. This time, he thought, he must finally make up his mind to possess her. Moreover, his shyness had worn off in the gay company he had kept, and he returned to the provinces despising everyone who had not trod the Paris boulevards with a polished boot. In the presence of an elegant Parisienne in the drawing room of some decorated doctor who owned a carriage, the poor clerk would doubtless have trembled like a child; but here in Rouen, on the river front with this wife of a country doctor, he felt at ease, sure in advance that he would dazzle her. Self-possession depends on one's environment; one doesn't speak in a drawing room as one does in an attic, and a rich woman's virtue seems to be protected by the thought of all her bank notes that she wears, like so much armor, in the lining of her corset.

When he had taken leave of Monsieur and Madame Bovary that evening, Léon followed them at a distance in the street until he saw them stop at the Red Cross Hotel. Then he turned around and spent the whole night working out a plan.

The next day, at about five o'clock, his throat constricted, his cheeks pale, and with that cowardly determination that stops at nothing, he entered the inn's kitchen.

"Monsieur is not in," answered a maid.

That seemed to him a good omen. He went upstairs.

Emma was not disturbed by his coming; on the contrary, she apologized for having forgotten to tell him where they were staying.

"I guessed," said Leon.

"How?"

He pretended that he had been guided to her by chance, by instinct. She began to smile, and Léon in order to make up for his foolishness quickly told her that he had devoted the morning to looking for her in all the hotels of the city, one by one.

"So you decided to stay?" he added.

"Yes," she said, "and I made a mistake. I shouldn't get used to impractical pleasures, I who have a thousand responsibilities."

"Oh! I can imagine."

"No, you can't! You're not a woman." But men also have their troubles, and the conversation began with a few philosophical reflections. Emma commented at length about the futility of earthly affections and the eternal isolation in which every heart remains.

Either to sound impressive or in a naïve imitation of her melancholy mood, the young man declared that he had been dreadfully bored with his studies. Legal procedure irritated him, other professions attracted him, and his mother kept tormenting him anew in each letter. They became more specific about the causes of their unhappiness as they spoke, and freer with their confidences. Sometimes they stopped short before the completion of their thought and then groped for some phrase that could translate it. She omitted any mention of her passion for another; nor did he say that he had forgotten her.

Perhaps he no longer recalled his suppers after fancy-dress balls with costumed girls; and she no doubt no longer remembered the meetings of earlier days, when in the morning she ran through the grass to her lover's château. The sounds of the town barely reached them. The room seemed tiny, as if to emphasize their solitude. Emma, dressed in a dimity dressing gown, was leaning her head against the back of the old armchair. The yellow wallpaper lent her a golden background; and her bare head was reflected in the mirror, with the white center part in the middle and the tips of her ears showing from under her hair.

"You must forgive me for talking like this," she said. "I'm boring you with my continual complaints."

"Not in the least!"

"If you only knew," she continued, lifting to the ceiling her beautiful eyes, in which tears were forming, "all the things I've dreamed of."

"And I too! Oh, I've suffered so! I would often go out, walk off, and dawdle along the waterfront trying to lose myself in the noise of the crowd, unable to drive out the obsession pursuing me. There's a print seller on the boulevard who has an Italian engraving that shows a Muse. She is draped in a tunic and looking at the moon, with forget-me-nots in her flowing hair. Something drove me there time and again; I spent hours on end there." Then, in a trembling voice: "She resembled you a little."

Madame Bovary turned her head away so that he would not notice the irrepressible smile she felt on her lips.

"Often," he went on, "I wrote you letters and then tore them up."

She was silent. He went on: "I sometimes imagined that we would meet by some chance. I thought I saw you on street corners. I would run after all the carriages from which a shawl or veil like yours fluttered from the window...."

She seemed determined to let him talk without interruption. Crossing her arms and lowering her head, she studied the rosettes on her slippers and wiggled her toes occasionally under the satin.

Then she sighed: "The saddest thing of all, it seems to me, is to drag out, as I do, a useless existence. If our misfortunes were of use to someone, we could console ourselves with the thought of sacrifice."

He began to praise virtue, duty, and silent sacrifices. He himself had an incredible need for self-sacrifice that he couldn't satisfy.

"I would dearly love," she said, "to be a nursing sister in a poorhouse."

"Unfortunately," he replied, "men don't have such sacred missions, and I see no occupation anywhere—unless perhaps that of a doctor."

With a slight shrug of her shoulders, Emma interrupted to regret that she had not died of her illness. A pity she hadn't died; she wouldn't be suffering now. Léon immediately envied "the peace of the grave." He had even written his will one evening, asking that he be buried in that handsome velvet-striped coverlet she had given him. This was how they wanted to be, each of them imagining an ideal toward which they would now readjust their past lives. Besides, the spoken word is like a rolling machine that draws feelings out.

At his made-up story of the coverlet, she asked, "But why?"

"Why?" He hesitated. "Because I loved you so."

And congratulating himself on having overcome that hurdle, Léon studied her face out of the corner of his eye.

It resembled the sky when a gust of wind chases away the clouds. The mass of sad thoughts that had darkened her blue eyes seemed to go away: her entire face was radiant.

He waited. Finally she answered: "I always thought so. . . ."

Then they talked over the trivial events of that far-off time, the pleasures and the sorrows which they had just evoked in a single word. He remembered the clematis arbor, the dresses she had worn, the furniture in her room, her house.

"And our poor cactuses? What's happened to them?"

"They died of frost last winter."

"Ah! You don't know how often I've thought of them. I've imagined them as they used to be on summer mornings when the sun was beating down on the shutters—and I saw your two bare arms among the flowers."

"Poor boy," she said, holding out her hand.

Léon quickly pressed his lips to it. Then, when he had taken a deep breath: "In those days you were, to me, some mysterious force captivating my life. Once, for example, I came to your home; but you don't remember, do you?"

"Of course I do," she said. "Go on."

"You were downstairs in the hall, about to go out, standing on the bottom step. You even had on a hat with little blue flowers; and without being invited, in spite of myself, I accompanied you. And each minute I grew more and more aware of my foolishness, yet I kept walking near you, not daring to follow you completely and yet not wanting to leave you. When you went into a shop, I stayed in the street and watched you through the windowpane as you took off your gloves and counted your change on the counter. Then you rang Madame Tuvache's bell and went in, and I remained like an idiot in front of the big heavy door that had just slammed behind you."

Madame Bovary, listening to him, was surprised at feeling so old. All these things reappearing seemed to enlarge her life. They offered her, in a sense, vast sentimental areas to wallow in; and she kept repeating in a low voice, with her eyelids half shut: "Yes, you're right, that's how it was—you're right."

They heard eight o'clock strike from the various clocks around the Place Beauvoisine, which is filled with boarding schools, churches, and large deserted mansions. They no longer spoke, but as they looked at each other they felt a throbbing in their heads as if some vibrating impulse were in their mutual glances. They had just joined hands; and past and future, memory and dreams—everything mingled in the sweetness of this ecstasy. Night was darkening the walls on which there still gleamed, half lost in the shadow, the loud colors of four prints representing four scenes from the *Tour de Nesle*, with captions on the bottom in Spanish and French. A patch of black sky between gabled rooftops showed through the window.

She rose to light two candles on the chest of drawers, then sat down again.

"Well?" asked Léon.

"Well?" she answered.

He was groping for a way to renew the interrupted conversation when she said: "Why has no one ever spoken to me like this before?"

The clerk warmly explained that ideal natures were difficult to understand. He had loved her at first sight and he

was in despair when he realized the happiness he would have
had if, by the grace of fate, they had met earlier and been
indissolubly bound to each other.

"I thought about it sometimes," she said.

"What a dream!" Léon murmured. And delicately fingering the blue binding of her long white belt, he added:

"What's stopping us from starting all over again?"

"No, my friend," she answered. "I am too old—you are
too young—forget me! Others will love you—you will love
them."

"Not as I love you," he cried.

"What a child you are! Come now, let's be sensible. I
want us to be."

She pointed out the impossibility of their love and said
that they could still remain, as before, on terms of fraternal
friendship.

Was she serious when she said this? No doubt herself did
not know, involved as she was with the charm of the seduction and the need to defend herself; and giving the young
man a tender look, she gently repulsed the timid caresses
his trembling hands were attempting.

"Ah! Forgive me," he said, pulling back.

Emma was seized by a vague fear at this timidity, more
dangerous for her than Rodolphe's boldness when he advanced with his arms outstretched. Never had any man appeared so handsome to her. She sensed an exquisite candor
emanating from him. He lowered his long, fine, curling lashes.
His smooth-skinned cheek was blushing—with desire for her
body, she thought—and Emma felt an unquenchable longing to place her lips on it. Then, leaning toward the clock
as if to see the time, she said, "My goodness, how late it is.
We've been such chatterboxes."

He understood the hint and looked around for his hat.

"I've even forgotten about the opera. And poor Bovary
left me here especially for it. Monsieur Lormeaux, who lives
on Rue Grand-Pont, was to take me with his wife."

And the opportunity was lost, since she was leaving the
next day.

"Definitely?" asked Léon.

"Yes."

"But I must see you again," he said. "I have something to
tell you."

"What?"

"Something important, serious. Well, no, anyway you can't leave, it's impossible. If you only knew— Listen—haven't you understood me? Haven't you guessed?"

"But speak plainly enough," she said.

"Oh! Please don't joke! Please, pity me, let me see you once more—only once."

"Very well," she said, and then stopped as if changing her mind, "but not here!"

"Anywhere you want."

"Would you—" She seemed to reflect, then said briefly, "Tomorrow, at eleven, in the cathedral."

"I'll be there!" he exclaimed, grasping her hands. She pulled them away.

As they were both standing, he behind her and she with her head lowered, he leaned toward her neck and kissed her lingeringly on the nape.

"You're mad, absolutely mad!" she said with little bursts of laughter, while the kisses multiplied.

Then he leaned over her shoulder and seemed to be seeking her consent in her eyes. But she gazed back at him with icy majesty.

Léon stepped backward to go out. He stopped on the threshold and then whispered in a trembling voice: "Until tomorrow!"

She replied with a nod and disappeared like a bird into the next room.

That evening Emma wrote the clerk an endless letter in which she canceled their meeting; everything was now at an end and they were not to meet anymore, for the sake of their happiness. But when the letter was sealed, she found herself in quite a predicament. She didn't know Léon's address.

"I'll give it to him myself," she thought. "He'll be there."

The next day, humming on his balcony with his window open, Léon applied several layers of polish to his pumps. He donned white trousers, fine socks, a green coat, poured all the scent he had over his handkerchief, and then, having curled his hair, uncurled it in order to give it a more natural elegance.

"It's still too early," he thought, looking at the cuckoo clock, which was striking nine.

He read an old fashion magazine, went out, smoked a

cigar, walked up three streets, thought that it was time, and
headed slowly toward Notre Dame.

It was a lovely summer day. Silverware gleamed in jewel-
ers' windows, and the light slanting down on the cathedral
made the gray stones glitter. A flock of birds was whirling
around in the blue sky around the trefoiled bell turrets. The
square, echoing with cries, was fragrant with the flowers that
lined its pavement—roses, jasmine, carnations, narcissus,
and tuberoses, irregularly laid out between watered greenery,
catmint, and chickweed for the birds. The fountain gurgled;
and in the center, beneath large umbrellas, among the can-
taloupes piled up in pyramids, bareheaded flower women
were wrapping bunches of violets in paper.

The young man took one. It was the first time he had
bought flowers for a woman, and as he sniffed them his chest
swelled with pride, as if the homage intended for her were
reflecting back on him.

However, he was afraid of being seen; so he resolutely entered the church.

The verger was just then standing on the doorstep, in the
middle of the left doorway beneath the figure of the Dancing
Marianne, with plumed hat on his head, rapier at his side,
and cane in his hand, more majestic than a cardinal and
shining like a pyx.

He walked over toward Léon and asked, with that benevo-
lent wheedling smile that priests use when they question children, "You are a stranger to these parts, I believe? Would
you care to see the curiosities of the church, sir?"

"No," said Léon.

At first he went around a side aisle. Then he went back
to look at the square. Emma was not in sight. He went up
into the choir.

The filled holy-water fonts reflected the nave, the beginning of the arches, and some sections of the stained-glass
windows. The reflection of the painted windows broke off
at the edge of the marble and continued over the flagstones
like a many-colored carpet. The daylight streamed into the
church in three enormous rays through the three open
portals. A sacristan would pass through the far end occasionally, genuflecting before the altar in the half-turned fashion of worshipers in a hurry. The crystal chandelier hung
motionless. A silver lamp was burning in the choir, and
from the side chapels and dark places in the church there

would sometimes be heard sounds like the heaving of a sigh and a clanging noise as a grating was shut, its echo reverberating beneath the vaulted roof.

Léon was walking near the walls with measured steps. Life had never appeared so good to him. She would soon be there—charming, high spirited, glancing behind her to see if she were being followed—and with her flowered dress, her golden lorgnette, and narrow boots, with all sorts of elegant touches that he had never enjoyed, and with the ineffable allure of virtue succumbing. The church, like an immense boudoir, spread out around her; the arches bent over to receive in the shadows the confession of her love; the windows shone resplendent to illuminate her face and the censers were going to burn so that she would appear like an angel amid clouds of perfume.

But she did not appear. He sat down on a chair and his eyes fell upon a blue window depicting boatmen carrying baskets. He looked at it for a long time, attentively, counted the scales of the fish and the buttonholes in the doublets, while his thoughts wandered off in search of Emma.

The verger, standing off to one side, was secretly angry at this man who allowed himself to admire the cathedral alone. It seemed to him a monstrous sort of conduct, as if he were robbing him in some way and almost committing sacrilege.

But there was a rustle of silk over the flagstones, the brim of a hat, a black cape. . . . It was she! Léon arose and ran toward her.

Emma was pale. She walked rapidly. "Read it," she said holding a paper out to him. "Oh, no!" And she abruptly pulled her hand back, entered the chapel of the Virgin, where, kneeling down against a chair, she began to pray.

The young man was irritated by this whim of piety, but then he found a certain charm in seeing her in the midst of their rendezvous as lost in prayer as an Andalusian *marquesa*. But he soon grew bored, for she seemed to be going on endlessly.

Emma was praying, or rather forcing herself to pray, hoping that some sudden strength of will would descend from heaven; and in order to win divine help, she filled her eyes with the splendors of the tabernacle, inhaled the perfume of the white blossoms in the huge vases, and intently heeded the silence in the church, which only intensified the tumult in her heart.

She stood up, and they were about to leave when the verger approached them rapidly, saying: "Madame is probably not from around here? Madame would like to see the curiosities of the church?"

"Absolutely not!" exclaimed the clerk.

"Why not?" she said. For in her wavering virtue she was clutching at the Virgin, the sculptures, the tombs, at anything.

Then, in order to proceed "in proper order," the verger led them as far as the entrance near the square, where, indicating with his cane a large circle of black paving blocks, with neither inscription nor engravings: "There," he declared majestically, "is the circumference of the beautiful bell of Amboise. It weighed forty thousand pounds. Its like does not exist in all of Europe! The worker who cast it died of joy. . . ."

"Let's leave," said Léon.

The old man moved on; when he came back to the chapel of the Virgin, he extended his arms in an all-embracing gesture and said, prouder than a country squire showing off his fruit trees: "This simple stone marks the grave of Pierre de Brézé, lord of Varenne and Brissac, grand marshal of Poitou, and governor of Normandy, killed in the battle of Monthéry, July 16, 1465."

Léon bit his lips and fumed.

"And to the right, that gentleman all encased in iron, on the prancing horse, is his grandson, Louis de Brézé, lord of Breval and Montchauvet, count of Maulevrier, baron of Mauny, king's chamberlain, knight of the order, and also governor of Normandy, died July 23, 1531, on a Sunday, as the inscription notes; and below, that man about to descend into the tomb, is the same one. It is not possible, is it, to see a more perfect representation of man's mortality."

Madame Bovary took up her lorgnette. Léon, motionless, stared at her, no longer trying to speak or make any gesture, so discouraged did he feel at this deliberate combination of chatter and indifference.

The never-ending guide continued: "Near him, that kneeling woman in tears is his wife, Diane de Poitiers, countess of Brézé, duchess of Valentinois, born 1499, died 1566; and to the left, the woman carrying the child is the Holy Virgin. Now, turn this way; here are the graves of the Amboises. They were both cardinals and archbishops of Rouen. That one was a minister of King Louis XII. He was a great benefactor of the cathedral. In his will he left thirty thousand gold crowns for the poor."

And without stopping, talking all the while, he ushered them into a chapel filled with railings, pushed a few of them aside, and uncovered a sort of block that might have been a badly carved statue.

"It once decorated," he said with a profound sigh, "the tomb of Richard the Lion-Hearted, king of England and duke of Normandy. The Calvinists, sir, reduced it to this condition. They buried it for spite in the ground under the episcopal seat of Monseigneur. See, this is the door through which Monseigneur goes home. Let us move on to the gargoyle windows."

But Léon quickly pulled some silver from his pocket and grasped Emma's arm. The verger was struck dumb, not understanding this premature generosity, when the stranger still had so much to see. Then calling him back: "But Monsieur, the steeple! The steeple!"

"No, thank you," said Léon.

"You are mistaken, sir! It is four hundred forty feet high, nine less than the Great Pyramid of Egypt. It is all cast, it—"

Léon fled. It seemed to him that his love, which for the past two hours had been kept as stationary in the church as the stones themselves, was now going to evaporate like smoke through that truncated funnel, that oblong cage, that open chimney, that rises so grotesquely from the cathedral like the fantastic invention of some imaginative metal worker.

"But where are we going?" she asked.

He continued to walk rapidly without replying. Madame Bovary was already dipping her finger into the holy water when they heard behind them a panting breath punctuated at regular intervals by the tapping of a cane. Léon turned around.

"Monsieur!"

"Yes?" He recognized the verger, carrying under his arms and balancing against his stomach about twenty heavy paperbound books. These were works "about the cathedral."

"Imbecile!" Léon growled, dashing out of the church.

A street urchin was playing on the pavement. "Get me a cab!" The child flew off like a shot, through the Rue des Quatre-Vents. They remained alone for several minutes, facing each other and slightly embarrassed.

"Ah! Léon, really—I don't know—if I ought—" she simpered. Then, with a more serious expression: "It's very improper, you know."

"How so?" answered the clerk. "It's done in Paris!" And that statement convinced her. It was an irresistible argument.

The cab was slow to appear. Léon feared she might go back into the church. Finally the cab came.

"At least go out through the north portal!" shouted the verger, who had remained on the threshold, "to see the *Resurrection,* the *Last Judgment,* Paradise, King David, and the *Damned in the Flames of Hell.*"

"Where to, sir?" asked the coachman.

"Anywhere!" Léon said, pushing Emma into the carriage. And the lumbering vehicle started off.

It went down the Rue Grand-Pont, crossed the Place des Arts, the Quai Napoléon, the Pont Neuf, and stopped short before the statue of Pierre Corneille.

"Keep going," cried a voice from within.

The carriage started off again, and as soon as it reached the Carrefour La Fayette, headed downhill, galloping toward the railroad station.

"No, straight ahead!" cried the same voice.

The cab emerged through the gate, and when it reached the boulevard, trotted gently beneath the large elms. The driver mopped his forehead, put his leather cap between his legs, and drove the vehicle beyond the sidelines near the meadow to the water's edge.

It traveled along the length of the river, moving over the cobbled towing path and went for a long time in the direction of Oyssel, beyond the islands.

But suddenly it made a leap across Quatre-Mares, Sotteville, the Grande-Chaussée, the Rue d'Elbeuf, and made its third stop before the botanical gardens.

"Will you keep going?" shouted the voice with greater anger.

And immediately resuming its course, it passed by Saint-Sever, along the Quai des Curandiers, the Quai aux Meules, once more over the bridge, through the Place Champ-de-Mars, and behind the poorhouse gardens, where the old men in black coats were walking in the sun along a terrace green with ivy. It went up the Boulevard Bouvreuil, along the Boulevard Cauchoise, then crossed the whole of Mont-Riboudet as far as the Deville hills.

Then it came back, and with neither fixed plan nor direction, wandered about at random. It was seen at Saint-Paul, at Lescure, Mont Gargan, at Rouge-Mare, and at the Place du Gaillardbois; in the Rue Maladrerie, the Rue Dinanderie, in front of various churches—Saint-Romain, Saint-Vivien, Saint-Maclou, Saint-Nicaise—in front of the customs house—at the Basse-Vieille-Tour, at the Trois-Pipes, and the Cimetière Monumental. Occasionally the coachman on his box would cast looks of despair at the cafés. He did not understand what kind of a rage for locomotion inspired these people, who did not want to stop. He attempted to a few times and immediately heard angry outbursts at him from behind. Then he lashed his two sweating nags even more furiously, without paying attention to the jolts, bumping into things here and there, not caring, demoralized, and almost weeping from thirst, fatigue, and unhappiness.

And at the harbor, amid the wagons and the barrels in the streets, the inhabitants at the corners were wide-eyed with astonishment at this most extraordinary spectacle in a provincial town—a constantly reappearing cab with closed blinds, shut up more tightly than a tomb and tossing about like a boat.

Once, in the middle of the day, in the open country, at a moment when the sun beat strongest against the old silver-plated lanterns, a bare hand reached out under the little yellow homespun curtains and threw out some scraps of paper that scattered in the wind, to alight farther along like white butterflies on a field of red clover in bloom.

Then, about six o'clock, the carriage stopped in a side street of the Beauvoisine section and a woman stepped down, walking away with her veil pulled down and without looking back.

II

Madame Bovary was surprised at not seeing the stage-coach when she reached the inn. Hivert had waited for her for fifty-three minutes and finally gone off.

Yet nothing forced her to leave except that she had promised she would come back that evening. Besides, Charles was expecting her; and she already felt in her heart that cowardly submissiveness that is, for many women, both the punishment and the atonement of their adultery.

She packed quickly, paid the bill, took a cab in the yard, and hurrying the driver, urging him on, asked the time and elapsed distance every minute. They managed to catch up with the Hirondelle as it neared the outskirts of Quincampoix.

She was barely seated in it when she closed her eyes and did not open them until they arrived at the foot of the hill, where she recognized Félicité from afar. The girl was stationed outside the blacksmith's, on the watch for her. Hivert pulled up the horses, and the maid, standing on tiptoe to talk to her through the window, said mysteriously, "Madame, you must go to Monsieur Homais's right away. It's very important."

The village was silent as usual. There were small pink mounds smoking in the gutters, for it was jelly-making time and everyone in Yonville made his year's supply the same day. But in front of the pharmacist's shop there was a much larger mound, which surpassed all the others: a laboratory must always be superior to ordinary home ovens; a general demand must take precedence over private tastes.

She walked in. The large armchair was overturned and even the *Rouen Beacon* lay scattered over the floor between the two pestles. She pushed open the hall door, and in the middle of the kitchen, amid the brown jars filled with stemmed currants, powdered sugar, and lump sugar, amid the scales on the table and pots on the fire, she saw the entire Homais family, big and little, with aprons reaching to their chins and forks in their hands. Justin stood with his head lowered, and the pharmacist was shouting: "Who told you to look for it in the capharnaum?"

"What's the matter? What happened?"

"What happened?" answered the apothecary. "We're making jelly; it's simmering but the supply was just about to overflow because it was boiling too much. I asked for another pan. So this blockhead, out of sheer laziness, went to my laboratory and took from the hook the key to the capharnaum!"

This was what the druggist called a room under the roof filled with tools and supplies. Often he spent long hours

there all by himself, labeling, decanting, repacking; and he
considered it not a simple storeroom but a true sanctuary
from which would emerge later on, made by his own hands,
all sorts of pills, boluses, infusions, lotions, and potions, des-
tined to spread his fame far and wide. No one else in the
world set foot in there, and he respected it so much that
he even swept it himself. If the pharmacy, open to all
visitors, was the place where he displayed his pride, the
capharnaum was the refuge where, selfishly secluding himself, Homais delighted in the exercise of his professional talents. So Justin's stupidity appeared to him a monstrous bit
of irreverence; and redder than the currants, he repeated:
"Yes, the capharnaum! The key that locks up the acids and
caustic alkalies! To go in there and take a spare pan! A
pan with a lid! One I may not ever use! Everything has its
importance in the delicate operations of our art! But devil
take it, one must make distinctions and not employ for
near-domestic uses what is meant for prescriptions! It's as
if one were to behead a fowl with a scalpel; as if a judge
were to—"

"Don't get excited," said Madame Homais.

And Athalie, tugging at his coat, cried: "Papa! Papa!"

"No! Leave me alone," he shouted, "leave me alone.
Damn it! Might as well set myself up as a grocer, I swear!
Go on! Don't respect a thing! Break everything! Let the
leeches go! Burn the marshmallow! Pickle cucumbers in my
medicine jars! Tear the bandages!"

"You did want to—" said Emma.

"Just a minute! Do you know the risk you were running?
Didn't you see something in the corner to the left on the
third shelf? Answer me, say something!"

"I—don't—know," the boy stammered.

"Ah! You don't know. But I do. You saw a blue bottle sealed with yellow wax that contains a white powder.
And on it, I myself wrote 'Dangerous!' And do you know
what was inside it? Arsenic! And you touch it! You take a
pan standing beside it!"

"Beside it," cried Madame Homais, clasping her hands.
"Arsenic? You could have poisoned us all!"

And the children began to cry as if they already felt
atrocious pains in their insides.

"Or poisoned one of the patients!" continued the apothecary. "Did you want me to be brought to court and put in

the prisoner's dock? Did you want to see me dragged to the scaffold? Have you never noticed the care I take in handling things, even though I've done it time and again? Sometimes I get frightened at myself when I think of my responsibility! The government hounds us, and the absurd laws restricting us are a veritable sword of Damocles hanging over our heads!"

Emma had given up asking what they wanted of her, as the pharmacist went on breathlessly: "See how you pay back all the kindness we have shown you. See how you reward me for the fatherly care I've lavished on you. Where would you be without me? What would you do? Who would give you food and education and clothing and every opportunity to become one day a respectable member of society? But you have to pull hard on the oar for that—and get, as they say, callouses on your hands. *Fabricando fit faber, age quod agis.*"

He was so furious that he was quoting Latin. He would have quoted Chinese or Icelandic had he known those two languages, for he found himself in one of those crises in which the entire soul reveals everything that is in it, like the ocean, which, in storms, opens wide to reveal the seaweed on its shores as well as the sands of its greatest depths.

And he continued: "I'm beginning to be terribly sorry that I ever promised to take care of you! I would have been much better off if I had left you to rot in your misery and in the filth you were born in! You'll never be good for anything except taking care of the cows! You have no talent for science! You hardly know how to paste on a label! And you live here in my home, snug as a parson, like a pig in clover!"

But Emma, turning toward Madame Homais: "They told me to come here—"

"Oh, dear Lord!" the good lady interrupted sadly. "How can I possibly tell you? It's a tragedy!"

She did not finish. The apothecary thundered: "Empty it! Scour it! Take it back! And hurry up!" And as he shook Justin by the collar of his blouse, a book dropped out of his pocket.

The boy stooped down, but Homais was faster, and when he picked up the book he stared at it, his eyes wide open and mouth agape.

"*Conjugal—Love!*" he said, pronouncing the two words slowly. "Ah, very good, very good, a pretty state of affairs! And illustrations! Oh, this is just too much!"

Madame Homais drew nearer.

"No! Don't touch it!"

The children wanted to see the pictures.

"Out of here!" he said imperiously. And they filed out.

First he paced back and forth, taking big steps, holding the open book between his fingers, rolling his eyes, choking, puffing, apoplectic. Then he walked up to his apprentice and planted himself before him with folded arms: "So you have all the vices, eh, you little monster? Take care, you're going downhill fast. Did it ever occur to you that this wicked book might fall into the hands of my children, inflame their thoughts, sully Athalie's purity, corrupt Napoleon? Physically, he's already built like a man. Are you at least sure that they have never read it? Can you swear to me?"

"Monsieur Homais, once and for all," Emma said, "do you have something to tell me?"

"Ah, yes, Madame! Your father-in-law is dead."

Actually, Charles's father had suddenly died two nights before, of an attack of apoplexy as he was finishing his dinner: and Charles had asked Monsieur Homais to reveal the terrible news to Emma gently, being worried about how she might take it.

He had pondered the announcement he would make, rounded it out, polished it, made it rhythmic; it was to be a masterpiece of discretion and transition, of subtle and delicate phrasing. But anger had swept rhetoric away.

Emma, giving up any hope of hearing details, left the pharmacy because Homais had resumed his vituperations. He was calming down, however, and now grumbled in a fatherly way, all the while fanning himself with his skullcap.

"It's not that I disapprove entirely of the book! The author was a doctor. There are certain scientific aspects in it that are not bad for a man to know—which, I dare say, a man should know. But later, later! At least wait until you're a man and your character's formed."

At Emma's knock, Charles, who had been awaiting her, advanced with his arms outstretched, and said to her with tears in his voice: "Oh, my dearest darling—" And he leaned forward gently to kiss her. But at the touch of his

lips, the memory of Léon took hold of her and she passed
her hand over her face, shuddering. But she did manage to
say: "Yes, I know, I know."

He showed her the letter in which his mother told what
had happened, without any sentimental hypocrisy. She only
regretted that her husband had not received the consolations of religion, since he had died at Doudeville in the
street at the door of a café after a patriotic banquet with
old army-officer friends.

Emma handed the letter back to him; then, at dinner,
out of politeness she pretended she had lost her appetite.
But as he insisted, she began to eat heartily while Charles,
sitting opposite her, remained motionless, looking stunned
with grief.

He would occasionally lift his head and look at her
mournfully, lingeringly. Once he sighed: "If only I had
seen him once again!"

"How old was your father?"

"Fifty-eight."

"Ah!"

And that was all.

Fifteen minutes later he added: "My poor mother. What's
to become of her now?"

She shrugged her shoulders in a gesture of ignorance.

Seeing her so taciturn, Charles assumed she was upset and
restrained himself from talking in order not to revive her
sorrow, which he found moving. Then, shaking off his own
grief, he asked: "Did you have a good time yesterday?"

"Yes."

Bovary did not budge after the table had been cleared.
Nor did Emma; and as she looked at him, the monotony
of the sight banished little by little all the pity in her heart.

He seemed so weak and puny to her, a nonentity—in
short, a contemptible man in every respect. How could she
rid herself of him? What an interminable evening! Something stultifying, like opium fumes, engulfed her.

From the hall they heard the dry tap of a stick on the
floor. Hippolyte was bringing in Emma's luggage. In order
to set it down, he painfully described a ninety-degree angle
with his stump.

"Charles doesn't even think of him anymore," she told
herself, looking at the poor devil whose mop of red hair
was dripping with perspiration.

Bovary was looking for a coin at the bottom of his purse. He seemed unaware of all the humiliation there was for him in the mere presence of this man who stood there like a living reproach to his incurable ineptness.

"That's a pretty bouquet you have," he said, noticing Léon's violets on the mantelpiece.

"Yes," she said casually, "I bought it as I was leaving—from a beggar woman."

Charles picked up the violets and refreshed his tear-reddened eyes against them, sniffing them delicately.

She pulled them quickly from his hand and went to put them into a glass of water.

The next day Madame Bovary senior arrived. She and her son wept copiously. Emma left them to themselves, claiming she had household chores.

The following day they all had to consult about the mourning. They sat down—the women with their workbaskets—at the water's edge under the arbor.

Charles was thinking about his father and was amazed to feel so much affection for the man. Until now, he had thought he cared only slightly about him. His mother thought of her husband. The worst days of the past seemed enviable to her now. Everything was softened by a kind of instinctive regret after such a long-time relationship; and occasionally as she plied her needle, a big tear would slide down her nose and hang there from its tip for a moment.

Emma was thinking that barely forty-eight hours ago they had been together, far from the world, intoxicated and unable to gaze enough at each other. She tried to recapture the slightest details of that vanished day. But the presence of her mother-in-law and her husband interfered. She wanted to hear nothing and see nothing: she wanted to be alone to enjoy the memory of her love, which was dwindling away under the impact of external impressions no matter what she did to recapture it.

She was ripping out the lining of a dress, and the pieces of material were scattered around her. Mother Bovary was using the scissors without once looking up, and Charles, in his cloth slippers and the old brown frock coat that he used as a dressing gown, kept his hands in his pockets and also said nothing. Near them, Berthe, in a tiny white apron, was shoveling the gravel in the walk with her spade.

Suddenly they heard Monsieur Lheureux, the dry-goods merchant, enter through the gate.

He had come to offer his services "in view of the sad circumstances." Emma replied that she thought they could do without them. The merchant refused to take no for an answer.

"I beg your pardon," he said. "I was hoping to have a private talk with you." Then, in a lowered voice: "It's about that matter—you know which one?"

Charles blushed to the tips of his ears. "Oh, yes—of course." And in his agitation he turned to Emma and said: "Darling, could you—?"

She seemed to understand him, for she arose. "It's nothing," Charles said to his mother. "Some household detail, I suspect."

He did not want her to know the story of the note, since he feared her comments.

The moment they were alone, Monsieur Lheureux began congratulating Emma quite openly on the inheritance. Then he chatted about unimportant matters, about fruit trees, the harvest, his own health, which was "merely so-so, with continual ups and downs." As a matter of fact he was working like a slave and still didn't earn even enough to butter his bread, despite what people said about him.

Emma let him talk on. She had been so bored these last two days!

"And you're all better again?" he continued. "I tell you, your poor husband was in a very unhappy state! He's a fine fellow, even though we've had our difficulties."

"What difficulties?" she asked, for Charles had concealed from her the dispute over the goods she had ordered.

"But you must know!" said Lheureux. "Over those notions of yours—the luggage for the trip."

He had pulled his hat down over his eyes, and his hands were behind his back as he smiled and softly whistled. He was staring into her face in an intolerable manner. Did he suspect something? She was lost in all sorts of apprehensions. Finally, however, he said: "We managed to get together, and I came to suggest another arrangement to him."

This was to renew the note signed by Bovary. Of course the doctor would do as he thought best; he mustn't be upset, especially now that he was going to have all kinds of bothersome things on his mind.

"He might do best by turning them all over to someone like you, for example; with a power of attorney it would be easily arranged, and then you and I would manage our little affairs together. . . ."

She didn't understand. He stopped talking. Then, returning to his dry-goods business, Lheureux announced that Madame must certainly need something from him. He would send her a dozen meters of black barège for a dress.

"The one you're wearing is good enough for the house. But you need another one for going out. I noticed that as soon as I came in. I have as sharp an eye as an American."

Instead of sending the fabric, he brought it. Then he came for the measurements; then again on different pretexts, each time trying to show how amiable and helpful he was, "ingratiating himself," as Homais would have said, and always slipping some hint to Emma about the power of attorney. He didn't mention the note and she forgot about it. Charles, at the beginning of her convalescence, had told her something about it, but so much had passed through her head since then that she no longer remembered. Besides, she was careful not to mention money; her mother-in-law was surprised at this and attributed her changed attitude to the religious feelings she had acquired during her illness.

But as soon as her mother-in-law left, Emma lost no time in amazing Bovary by her solid good sense. They were going to have to obtain information, verify mortgages, see if they should consider an auction or a liquidation.

Technical terms rolled off her tongue. She pronounced impressive words—"order," "future," and "foresight"—and continually exaggerated the troubles attendant on settling wills; and she did so thorough a job that one day she even showed him the form of a general authorization to "manage and administer his business matters, effect all loans, sign and endorse all notes, pay all sums, etc." She had profited by Lheureux's lessons.

Charles naïvely asked her where the document came from.

"From Monsieur Guillaumin." And with the utmost coolness, she added: "I don't trust him too much. Notaries have such bad reputations. We might perhaps consult— We know no one who—no one, really."

"Léon might—" Charles replied, thinking out loud.

But it was hard to make things clear by letter. So she offered to take the trip. Charles was grateful but reluctant to let her go. She insisted. It was a duel of mutual politeness. Finally, she exclaimed in a tone of mock rebellion: "No, I insist, I'll go!"

"How good you are!" he said, kissing her on the forehead.

The next day she set out in the Hirondelle to go to Rouen and consult Monsieur Léon; and there she remained three days.

III

They were three exquisitely full days, glorious days, a real honeymoon.

They stayed at the Hotel de Boulogne on the riverfront. And they lived there, with shutters closed and doors locked, with flowers on the floor and iced fruit drinks brought up from morning on.

In the evening they took a covered boat and went to dine on one of the islands.

It was the time of day when caulking hammers could be heard ringing against hulls in every shipyard. The tar fumes rose up between the trees and on the river there were large oily patches undulating unevenly in the scarlet light of the setting sun, like floating plaques of Florentine bronze.

They rowed among the moored boats, whose long, slanting cables grazed the top of their boat.

Imperceptibly the city noises faded away: the rattle of the wagons, the tumult of voices, the yapping of dogs on the boat decks. She untied the ribbon of her hat and they landed on their island.

They sat in the low-ceilinged room of a tavern, on whose door hung black fishnets. There they ate fried smelts and cream and cherries. Later they lay down on the grass and embraced in the shade of the poplar trees. They wanted to live forever in this tiny spot, like a couple of Robinson Cru-

soes. In their joy it seemed to them the most magnificent
place on earth. It was not the first time that they had seen
trees and blue sky and grass, that they had heard water
flowing and the wind rustling through the leaves, but they
had certainly never before admired all these things so much.
It was as if nature had not existed before or had only
begun to be beautiful since the gratification of their desires.

They returned at nightfall. The boat skirted the edge of the
islands. They sat in the stern, hidden in the shadow without talking. The square-tipped oars grated in the iron oar-
locks and punctuated the silence like a metronome, while
the rope trailing behind them rippled gently in the water.

One night the moon appeared and so they proceeded to
invent beautiful phrases about the melancholy, poetical orb.
She even began to sing:

Do you remember the evening we drifted . . .

Her weak but musical voice died away on the water;
and the wind carried off the trills that Léon heard flutter all
around him like wings.

She sat facing him, leaning against the bulkhead, the moon
coming down on her through one of the open shutters. Her
black dress, fanning out around her, made her appear thinner and taller. Her head was raised and her hands clasped.
She was staring at the sky. Occasionally the shadows of
the willows hid her completely, then she reappeared suddenly like a vision in the moonlight.

Léon, sitting beside her on the bottom of the boat, came
upon a bright red silk ribbon.

The boatman looked at it awhile and then said: "Ah, it
must belong to a group I took out the other day. A lively
bunch of jokers, gentlemen and ladies, came on board with
cakes and champagne and musical instruments and Lord
knows what else! There was one handsome man, specially,
a tall man with a tiny mustache. He was very funny. They
kept saying to him, 'Come on, tell us a story, Adolphe'—
Dodolphe, I think."

She shuddered.

"Are you uncomfortable?" Léon said, coming closer.

"It's nothing. Probably the chill of the night."

"And that gentleman doesn't have to worry about not

having ladies either," the old boatman added softly, thinking he was complimenting the stranger.

Then he spat into his hands and picked up his oars.

But finally they had to part! The farewells were sad. He was to send his letters in care of Madame Rollet, the wet nurse. She was so precise in her details about using a double envelope that he greatly admired her shrewdness in love matters.

"So, you're sure that everything is all right?" she said during the last kiss.

"Yes, of course!"

"But why is she so insistent about that power of attorney?" he asked himself later as he walked back alone through the streets.

IV

Léon soon assumed an air of superiority in front of his friends, kept aloof from their company, and completely neglected his work.

He awaited her letters, read them over and over again. He wrote her, evoking all the power of his passion and his memories. Instead of diminishing with absence, the desire to see her grew so strong that finally one Saturday morning he had to get away from his office.

When from the top of the hill he saw down in the valley the Yonville church steeple with its tin flag turning in the wind, he felt that combination of delight, vanity triumphant, and condescending sentimentality that must be the emotion of a millionaire returning to visit his native village.

He wandered around her house. A light was shining in the kitchen. He sought her shadow behind the curtains. No one appeared.

The Widow Lefrançois exclaimed loudly when she saw him that he was "taller and thinner," whereas Artémise, on the contrary, thought him "stouter and darker."

He dined in the small dining room, as in the old days, but alone, without the tax collector, because Binet, tired of

waiting for the Hirondelle, had permanently advanced his meal
by an hour and now ate at five o'clock sharp. He still complained that the "broken-down old clock was slow."

Léon finally made up his mind; he knocked on the doctor's
door. Emma was in her room and only emerged a quarter of
an hour later. The doctor appeared delighted to see him but
did not leave the house that whole evening or all the next day.

He saw her alone late at night in the lane behind the
garden—the same lane where she had been with Rodolphe!
A storm was raging and they spoke under an umbrella, catching glimpses of each other by the flashes of lightning.

The thought of separation was becoming unbearable.

"I'd rather die," Emma said. She was writhing in his arms,
in tears.

"Good-bye, good-bye! When will I see you again?"

They turned back to kiss once more; and it was then
that she promised him to find some permanent way, and
quickly, by whatever means necessary, to see him freely at
least once a week. Emma was sure she could. Moreover, she
was full of high spirits. She was going to have some money.

And so she bought a pair of yellow curtains with wide
stripes for her room that Monsieur Lheureux had proclaimed
a bargain; she yearned for a rug, and Lheureux, commenting
that, "it won't be *that* hard a job," politely took it on himself to find her one. She could no longer do without his services. Twenty times a day she sent for him and he would
immediately drop what he was doing without a murmur of
protest. Nor did anyone understand why Madame Rollet
lunched at her house every day and even paid her private
visits.

Toward this period—at the approach of winter—she
seemed smitten by a passion for music.

One evening as Charles was listening to her, she started
the same piece four times in a row and always with great
irritation, while he, without noticing the difference, exclaimed:
"Bravo! Very good. You're wrong to stop. Keep going."

"I can't. It's terrible. I'm all thumbs."

The next day he asked her to "play something for him
again."

"All right, if it makes you happy."

And Charles had to admit that she had lost some of her
ability. She played the wrong notes, stumbled, and then

stopped short: "That's enough! I really should take lessons, but—" She bit her lips and added: "Twenty francs a session is much too expensive."

"Yes, it is—a bit—" said Charles, snickering a bit. "But you might be able to get someone for less. There are artists who aren't famous who are sometimes better than celebrities."

"Find them!" said Emma.

When he came home the next day he looked at her slyly and finally couldn't resist saying: "You can be so stubborn sometimes! I went to Barfeuchères today and Madame Liégeard assured me that her three girls, at the Miséricorde school, take lessons for fifty sous an hour, and from a well-known teacher too!"

She shrugged her shoulders and did not open the piano again. But when she passed near it (if Bovary were in the room) she would sigh: "Ah, my poor piano!"

And when visitors came, she made sure to inform them that she had given up music and could no longer take it up again, for very good reasons. Everyone pitied her. What a shame! She had such a fine talent! They even spoke about it to Bovary, and embarrassed him, especially the pharmacist: "You're making a mistake. One should never neglect nature's gifts. Besides, think of it, my friend, by letting your wife study, you'll save later on when it comes to your daughter's musical education. I think that the mothers should teach their children themselves. It's one of Rousseau's theories, perhaps still a bit new, but it will win out in the end, I'm sure, like mothers' breast-feeding and vaccination."

And so Charles brought up the question of the piano once more. Emma answered caustically that it was better to sell it. But Charles felt that if that poor old piano, which had pleased her vanity so much, were taken away, it would be like a partial suicide of his wife.

"If you really wanted—" he said. "A lesson now and then wouldn't be that ruinous."

"Lessons are worthwhile only when they're taken regularly," she answered.

And that was how Emma managed to obtain her husband's permission to go to the city once a week to see her lover. People even commented, at the end of a month, that she had made considerable progress.

V

Her day was Thursday. She got up and dressed silently to avoid waking Charles, who would have commented that she was getting ready too early. Then she paced back and forth, stationed herself at the windows, and looked at the square. Dawn would be breaking through the pillars of the marketplace, and in the early morning light you could read the block letters of the pharmacist's sign standing out against the closed shutters.

When the clock pointed to seven-fifteen, she walked over to the Golden Lion, where a yawning Artémise opened the door for her, and then raked out the embers for her. Emma remained alone in the kitchen, occasionally stepping outside. Hivert harnessed the horse leisurely, while listening at the same time to Madame Lefrançois. The widow, with her nightcap still on, stuck her head out through a window and was giving him instructions on what to buy and elaborate explanations that would have tried the patience of any other man. Emma tapped her feet against the cobblestones in the yard.

Finally, when he had swallowed his soup, pulled on his driving coat, lit his pipe, and picked up his whip, he would calmly get up on the seat.

The Hirondelle started off at a slow trot and stopped frequently for the first mile to pick up the passengers watching for it along the road outside their gates. Those who had reserved seats the night before kept it waiting; some were even still at home in bed. Hivert would call out, shout, and swear. Then he would step down from his seat and knock furiously on the doors while the wind blew through the cracked blinds.

Finally the four benches filled up and the carriage rolled along, row after row of apple trees appearing to file past; and the road, running between two long ditches filled with yellow water, seemed endless, dwindling off toward the horizon.

Emma knew it from one end to the other; she knew that after a certain meadow there was a signpost, then an elm, a barn, or a road repairer's hut; she would sometimes shut her eyes to try to surprise herself, but she never lost her true sense of the remaining distance.

Finally the brick houses grew more frequent, the ground rang out beneath the wheels, the Hirondelle glided between the gardens where an opening would reveal statues, arbors, clipped yew trees, and a swing. Then, suddenly, the city appeared.

Sloping down like an amphitheater, drowned in the fog, it sprawled amorphously beyond the bridges. Then the open country climbed monotonously upward until it seemed in the distance to touch the faint edge of the pale sky. From this height, the entire landscape looked as still as a painting; the boats at anchor were crowded into a corner; the river curved around the foot of the green hills and the oblong-shaped islands looked like large, motionless black fish on the water. The factory chimneys belched forth huge brown plumes of smoke that drifted away in the breeze. The roar of foundries mingled with the clear ringing of chimes from churches that loomed in the mist; leafless trees on the boulevard formed violet patches in the midst of the houses, and the rooftops, glistening with rain, gave off reflections that varied according to the height of the different parts of town. An occasional gust of wind would carry the clouds off toward Sainte-Catherine's Hill, like airborne waves breaking in silence against a cliff.

The thought of the people huddled below gave her a feeling of dizziness. Her heart swelled as if the 120,000 souls who pulsated there had sent forth, all at once, the breath of the passions she attributed to them. Her love expanded before this vastness and filled with the tumult of the vague hum rising from the valley. She poured it back again, over the squares, the walking paths, and the streets, and the old Norman city spread out before her eyes like an immense metropolis, a Babylon into which she was entering. She leaned out the window, holding on with both hands, and breathed in the air. The three horses galloped, the stones were heard grinding in the mud, the coach swayed, and Hivert hailed the wagons along the way from afar, while townfolk who had spent the night in Bois-Guillaume descended the hill slowly in their small family traps.

They stopped at the city gate. Emma unbuckled her over-shoes, pulled on a fresh pair of gloves, adjusted her shawl, and stepped down from the Hirondelle twenty steps farther on.

The city was waking up. Clerks in caps were dusting showcase windows, and women with baskets on their hips were periodically shouting loud cries from the street corners. She walked along, looking down, keeping close to the house walls, and smiling with pleasure beneath her lowered black veil.

For fear of being seen, she usually did not take the short-est road. She plunged into dark alleys and would arrive cov-ered with perspiration at the lower end of the Rue Nationale near the fountain. This is the theater section, with its cafés and prostitutes. Often a wagon would pass near her, carrying shaky pieces of stage scenery. Waiters in aprons were scat-tering sand over the flagstones between the tubs of green bushes. There was a mingled smell of absinthe, cigars, and oysters.

She turned a corner and recognized his curly hair escaping from under his hat.

Léon would keep walking along the sidewalk. She would follow him to his hotel. He would go up, open the door, and go in; and then, what a passionate embrace!

After the kisses came an outpouring of words. They told each other all the woes of the past week, their misgivings, their anxieties about letters; but now all that was forgotten and they looked at each other laughing with sensual delight and uttering terms of endearment.

The bed was a large mahogany one shaped like a boat. The red silk curtains that hung from the ceiling were bunched very low near the bell-shaped headboard—and nothing in the world was as beautiful as her dark hair and white skin stand-ing out against the deep red when she covered her face with her two hands in a gesture of modesty and revealed her nude arms.

The warm room with its noise-muffling rug, its gay orna-ments, and soft light, seemed exactly right for the intimacies of passion. The arrow-shaped curtain rods, brass hooks, and large oak bowls gleamed when the sun suddenly entered. Between the candlesticks on the mantelpiece there were two of those large pink shells that echo the sound of the sea when held next to the ear.

How they loved that dear room filled with gaiety, despite its slightly faded splendor. They always found the furniture as they had left it, and sometimes even found hairpins beneath the base of the clock that she had forgotten the previous Thursday. They would sit and eat by the fire on a small table inlaid with rosewood. Emma would carve the food and put the pieces into his plate, chattering all the while, and she would laugh loudly and dissolutely when the champagne froth spilled over the fragile glass onto the rings on her fingers. They were so completely lost in each other that they actually believed they were living in their own house and would remain there until death like a couple eternally young. They said *our room, our rug, our armchairs;* she even said *our slippers.* They were a gift from Léon, in response to a whim of hers—pink satin slippers trimmed with swansdown. Her leg dangled in midair when she sat on his lap, since she was too short for it to reach the floor; and the charming backless little slipper was held on solely by the toes of her bare foot.

For the first time in his life he was tasting the inexpressible subtlety of feminine grace. He had never before encountered this refinement of speech, this quiet elegance of dress, these poses of a soothed dove. He admired the raptures of her spirit and the laces of her petticoat. Moreover, wasn't she "a woman of the world"—and a married woman? In other words, a real mistress.

She awoke a thousand desires in him, evoked instincts or reminiscences by her changing moods. She was in turn mystic or gay, chattering or taciturn, wildly passionate or casual. She was the *amoureuse* in every novel, the heroine of every drama, the vague "she" of every book of poetry. He found her shoulders glowing with amber, like "Odalisque at Her Bath"; she was long waisted like the feudal châtelaines, and she resembled "The Pale Lady of Barcelona"—but above all she was an angel!

Often, as he looked at her, it seemed to him that his soul, reaching out toward her, was spreading like a wave over the outline of her head and was being drawn down into the whiteness of her bosom.

He would sit on the floor at her feet with his elbows on his knees and look up at her with a smile.

She would lean over toward him murmuring, as if suffocating with passion: "Don't move! Don't say a word! Just look at me! There's a sweetness in your eyes that I adore!"

She called him "child": "Child, do you love me?" And she barely heard his answer in the rush of his lips to meet her mouth.

On the clock there was a small bronze Cupid with a simpering smile, who curved his arms beneath a gilded garland. They laughed at it many times. But when they had to part, everything became serious.

Motionless they faced each other, saying: "Until Thursday! Until Thursday!" Suddenly she would take his head in her hands, kiss him quickly on the forehead while sobbing "Adieu!" and rush off into the hall.

She headed toward a hairdresser's on the Rue de la Comédie, to have her hair done. Night would be falling, and they would light the gas in the shop.

She could hear the theater bell calling the performers to their rehearsal; and she could see, across the street, men with whitened faces and ladies in faded finery entering the stage door.

It was always stuffy in this little low-ceilinged room, where the stove hummed amid the wigs and the hair cream. The odor of the curling irons and the oily hands working over her head never failed to soothe her into somnolence, and she would doze off awhile in her wrapper. The hairdresser, while combing her hair, would often ask her to buy tickets for a masked ball.

Afterwards she would start for home. She would go up the streets toward the Croix-Rouge, pick up the overshoes she had hidden in the morning beneath one of the benches, and settle into her seat among the impatient passengers. A few of them got off at the other side of the hill. She would be left alone in the carriage.

Each turn in the road revealed more of the lights of the city. They glowed like a broad luminous mist above the blurred-looking houses. Emma would kneel on the cushions and gaze at the dazzling sight. She would sob, call out to Léon, and send him tender words and kisses that would be lost in the wind.

On the hill a poor wandering beggar with a cane appeared right in the middle of all the carriages. He wore a mass of rags, and a battered old beaver hat, shaped like a basin, hid his face; but when he pulled it off, he revealed two gaping bloody orbits where the eyelids should have been. His skin was peeling away in red strips; liquid matter flowed from it, hardening into green scabs as far as his nose, the black nostrils of which sniffed convulsively. When he wanted to speak he would throw back his head with an idiot's laugh, and then his blue pupils would roll continuously toward the temples, close to the live wound.

He would sing a little song while trailing after the coaches:

> Often the warmth of a lovely day
> Makes a girl dream of love.

The rest of it was about birds, sunshine, and leaves.

Sometimes he would suddenly appear bareheaded behind Emma. She would start back with a cry, but Hivert would joke with him, tell him to take a boat to the Saint-Romain Fair, or sometimes ask him with a laugh how his girl friend was.

Often while they were moving, his hat would suddenly enter the coach through the window while he clung with one arm to the footboard between the mud-spattering wheels. His voice, at first low and moaning, would become shrill. It would echo into the night like an indistinct wail of distress; and through the ringing of the bells, the murmur of the trees, and the rumble of the empty coach, it had a kind of far-off quality that terrified Emma. It plunged deep into her soul like a whirlwind in a chasm and swept her away into an expanse of limitless melancholy. But Hivert, who noticed the weight behind, would lash out at the blind man with his whip. The thong would cut into his wounds and he would fall into the mud shrieking.

Afterwards the remaining occupants of the Hirondelle would fall asleep, some of them with their mouths open, others with their chins sunk down, leaning on a neighbor's shoulder or with an arm passed through the strap, all the while swaying rhythmically with each jolt; and the reflection of the lantern swinging outside above the rumps of the horses penetrated into the interior through the chocolate-colored calico curtains, sending a blood-red light over all these motionless people. Emma, numb with sadness, would shiver under her clothes and grow continually colder down to her feet, with death in her soul.

Charles would be waiting for her at home; the Hirondelle was always late on Thursday. Emma would finally arrive, then give her child a cursory kiss. Dinner was not ready. It did not matter! She forgave the maid. Now the girl was allowed to do anything.

Her husband would often notice her pallor and ask her if she felt ill.

"No," Emma would say.

"You seem so strange this evening," he would comment.

"Oh, it's nothing! Nothing!"

There were even days when she went straight to her room as soon as she came in; Justin would be there and would walk on tiptoes. He was better at serving her than the best of maids. He would set down the matches, candlestick and book, then prepare her nightdress and turn down the bed.

"All right," she would say, "that will do. You may go now." For he would remain standing there, arms dangling and eyes wide open as if enmeshed in countless threads of a sudden dream.

The next day was always terrible and the following ones even more unbearable because of Emma's impatience to be happy again—hers was a burning desire, inflamed by all her memories, and it exploded on the seventh day at Léon's caresses. His own raptures were shown by his expressions of wonder and gratitude.

Emma savored this love in a discreet and intense way, cultivating it with all the artifices of her sentiment and trembling all the while that later on it might end.

She would often say to him, with a sweet, melancholy voice: "Ah! You'll leave me, you will. You'll marry. You'll be like the others."

"Which others?" he asked.

"Men, all of them," she said. Then she added, pushing him away with a languid gesture: "You're all heartless!"

One day as they were talking philosophically about earthly disillusionments, she happened to say (to test his jealousy, or perhaps giving in to some inordinate need for confession) that once before him she had loved someone. "Not like you!" she immediately went on, swearing on her daughter's head that "nothing ever happened."

The young man believed her but nevertheless asked her who the man was.

"He was a ship's captain, darling."

Wasn't this done to prevent any inquiries, and at the same time gain impressive status by a pretended involvement with a man who by nature must have been strong willed and accustomed to being worshiped?

The clerk then felt the lowliness of his own position; he envied epaulets, crosses, titles, things that were probably pleasing to her, he suspected, knowing her expensive tastes.

And yet Emma suppressed many of her extravagant notions, such as the yearning for a blue tilbury drawn by an English horse and driven by a groom in top boots to take her to Rouen. Justin had inspired this fancy in her by begging her to take him on as a footman; and while the privation did not lessen the pleasure of arriving at each rendezvous, it definitely increased the bitterness of the return trip.

Often when they were talking about Paris, she would murmur: "Ah! We'd be so happy living there!"

"Aren't we happy?" the young man would say softly, caressing her hair.

"Yes, of course," she would say; "I'm being silly. Kiss me."

She was more charming than ever to her husband, prepared pistachio creams for him, and played waltzes after dinner. He considered himself the most fortunate of mortals, and Emma lived in tranquillity until suddenly one evening: "It's Mademoiselle Lempereur you're taking lessons from, isn't it?"

"Yes."

"Well I saw her today at Madame Liégeard's," Charles said, "and mentioned you to her. She doesn't know you."

It was like a thunderbolt. Yet she answered in a natural tone: "She's probably forgotten my name."

"There may be several ladies named Lempereur in Rouen who teach piano," the doctor said.

"It's possible." Then quickly: "But I have her receipts. Wait a minute! Here." And she went to the secretary, looked through all the drawers, and finally became so agitated that Charles begged her not to trouble herself so much about those silly receipts.

"Oh, I'll find them," she said.

And actually on the following Friday as he was pulling on one of his boots in the dark little room where his clothes were kept, he felt a piece of paper between the leather and his sock, pulled it out, and read: "Received, for three months of lessons and various supplies, the sum of sixty-five francs. Félicie Lempereur, music teacher."

"How the devil did this get into my boot?"

"It probably fell from the old bill box on the edge of the shelf." From that moment on, her existence was a continuous string of lies, in which she wrapped her love as if in layers of veiling in order to hide it.

Lying became a need, a mania, a pleasure, so much so that if she said she had walked along the right side of the street yesterday, one had to assume it had been the left.

One morning, just after she left, dressed lightly as usual, a sudden snow started falling; and as Charles stood at the window watching it fall he noticed Monsieur Bournisien sitting in Monsieur Tuvache's cart, which was to take him to Rouen. And so he went down to give the priest a heavy shawl to be transmitted to Emma at the Croix-Rouge. As soon as Bournisien arrived at the inn, he asked for the wife of the Yonville doctor. The landlady replied that she spent very little time there. In the evening, when the curé met Madame Bovary in the Hirondelle, he mentioned his difficulty, without appearing to attach any great importance to it; for he began praising a preacher who was causing a sensation in the cathedral and whom all the women were running to hear.

But even if he had not asked for explanations, others, later on, might be less discreet. And so she deemed it advisable to stop at the Croix-Rouge each time so that the good people from her village, seeing her on the staircase, would suspect nothing.

One day, however, Monsieur Lheureux met her leaving the Hotel de Boulogne on Léon's arm. She was afraid, thinking he would talk. He was not so stupid.

Three days later, he came into her room, shut the door and said: "I want some money."

She declared she had none to give him. Lheureux burst into complaints and reminded her of all his past favors.

In fact, of the two notes signed by Charles, Emma had paid only one as of this moment. As for the second, the merchant had consented, on her plea, to replace it by two others, which had also been renewed for a very long term. Now he pulled from his pocket a list of unpaid goods, to wit: curtains, the rug, fabric for the armchairs, several dresses, and various toilet articles, the total value of which came to about two thousand francs.

She lowered her eyes. He went on: "But if you don't have cash, you do have property."

And he mentioned a miserable little shack in Barneville, near Aumale, which brought in almost nothing. It had once been part of a little farm sold by old Bovary: Lheureux knew all about it, even the number of acres and the names of the neighbors. "If I were you," he said, "I'd get rid of it and even have some money left over."

She protested that it would be difficult to find a buyer. He offered to find one for her. Then she asked how she would be able to sell it.

"Don't you have the power of attorney?" he asked. The phrase seemed to her a breath of fresh air.

"Leave me the bill," Emma said.

"Oh, don't bother about it," said Lheureux.

He came back the following week and boasted that he had found, after several false starts, a man named Langlois who had been eying the property for some time without offering a price.

"The price doesn't matter," she exclaimed.

On the contrary, he said: they should wait to smoke out the gentleman in question. It was worth the trouble of a trip, and since she couldn't make it, he offered to go and discuss the matter with Langlois. When he returned, he announced that the buyer was offering four thousand francs.

Emma was overjoyed at this news.

"Frankly," he added, "it's a good price."

Half the money was paid immediately, and when she offered to settle her bills the merchant said: "It hurts me, honestly, to see you part with such a large sum as that all at once."

Then she stared at the bank notes and dreamed of the countless number of meetings these two thousand francs represented. "But what—" she stammered. "What do you mean?"

"Oh," he said, laughing amiably, "you can put any sum you want on the sales receipts. Don't you think I know about household finances!" And he stared hard at her as he ran his fingers up and down over two long documents. Finally, opening his pocketbook, he spread out on the table four promissory notes, each one for one thousand francs.

"Sign these for me," he said, "and keep everything."

She uttered a shocked cry.

"But if I give you the balance," Lheureux answered with brazen effrontery, "am I not doing you a favor?"

And taking a pen, he wrote at the bottom of the account: "Received of Madame Bovary, four thousand francs."

"What are you worrying about? In six months you'll receive the balance due on the shack, and I've placed the due date of the last note after that payment."

Emma was a bit confused by his calculations, and her ears rang as if pieces of gold, bursting forth from their sacks, had clanked all around her on the floor. Finally Lheureux explained that he had a friend named Vinçart, a Rouen banker, who was going to discount these four notes and then he himself would remit to her the payment of the real debt.

But instead of two thousand francs, he brought back only eighteen hundred, for friend Vinçart (as was "only fair") had taken two hundred as his commission and expenses.

Then he casually asked for a receipt. "In business, you understand—sometimes—And please date it."

A horizon opened up before Emma—a horizon of dreams she could now realize. She was careful enough to put aside three thousand francs with which the first three notes were paid, when they fell due, but the fourth one by chance came to the house on a Thursday, and a stunned Charles patiently awaited his wife's return for some explanation.

She hadn't told him about the note because she wanted to spare him domestic worries; she sat down on his knees, caressed him, cooed, enumerated at length all the indispensable items she had bought on credit: "And you must admit that the amount isn't so high when you consider the number of items."

Charles, at his wits' end, soon had recourse to the indispensable Lheureux, who promised to straighten matters out if Monsieur would sign two notes for him, one for seven hundred francs, payable in three months. In order to be able to meet it, he wrote a pathetic letter to his mother. Instead of sending an answer, she herself came, and when Emma asked if he had managed to get something from her, he said, "Yes, but she wants to see the bill."

At daybreak the next morning Emma ran to Monsieur Lheureux to ask him to make up another note not to exceed a thousand francs; for if she showed the one for four thousand, she would have to explain that she had paid two thirds, and consequently reveal the sale of the property, which had been so well handled by the merchant that it was not discovered until later.

Despite the low price for each article, Madame Bovary senior quickly found that she had spent too much. "Couldn't you do without a rug? Why did you have the armchairs re-upholstered? In my day, you had one armchair in a house, for older people—at least that's how it was in my mother's home, and she was a proper woman, I assure you. Everyone can't be rich! There's no fortune will last if you fritter it away. I would blush to pamper myself the way you do, and yet I'm old and need care. Look at this! Repairs, frills! What nonsense! Silk for lining at two francs a yard! When you can find perfectly suitable cotton for ten sous, and even eight!"

Emma lay on the lounge and answered in the calmest manner possible: "All right, Madame, that's enough!"

The other woman continued to lecture, predicting that they would end up in the poorhouse. But it was Bovary's fault. Fortunately he had promised to cancel the power of attorney.

"What?"

"He swore he'd do it," the woman answered.

Emma opened the window and called out to Charles. The poor fellow was forced to admit the promise his mother had wrested from him.

Emma disappeared and then returned quickly, holding out a large sheet of paper with an imperious manner.

"Thank you," said the old woman, and she threw the document into the fire.

Emma began to laugh—a strident, shrieking, hysterical laugh; she was suffering an attack of nerves.

"Dear Lord," cried Charles, "you're wrong too. You shouldn't have come to make scenes."

His mother, shrugging her shoulders, claimed that "it was all play-acting."

But Charles, rebelling for the first time in his life, took his wife's part—and so well that his mother decided to leave. She left the next day, and as he was trying to get her to stay, she said on the doorstep, "No, you love her more than you love me and you're right. That's how it should be. Besides, so much the worse for you. You'll see. Stay well.

It'll be a long time before I come back here to 'make scenes,' as you call it."

Yet Charles felt no less guilty toward Emma. She made no effort to hide the bitterness she felt for his lack of confidence in her. He had to plead at great length before she would consent to take back the power of attorney, and he even accompanied her to Monsieur Guillaumin's to have him prepare a second one, just like the first.

"I understand," said the notary, "a man of science cannot be bothered with the practical details of life."

Charles felt comforted by this smug comment, which flattered his weakness, and made it look like a lofty virtue.

What a scene there was the following Thursday in the hotel, in the room with Léon! She laughed, cried, sang, danced, ordered sherbets sent up, wanted to smoke cigarettes—she seemed wild to him, but adorable and superb.

He did not know what there was within her that drove her recklessly toward the pleasures of life. She was becoming irritable, greedy, and voluptuous. She would walk with him in the streets, her head held high, without fear of being compromised, she said. Occasionally, however, Emma would shudder at the sudden thought of meeting Rodolphe; for it seemed to her that even though they were separated forever, she was not completely liberated from his power over her.

One evening she did not go back to Yonville. Charles was out of his mind with worry, and little Berthe, who did not want to go to bed without seeing her mama, sobbed as if her heart were breaking. Justin had gone off along the road to look her her. Even Homais left his pharmacy.

Finally, at eleven, not being able to stand it any longer, Charles harnessed his cart, jumped into it, whipped the horse, and arrived at the Croix-Rouge at about two in the morning. No sign of her. He thought that Léon might have seen her; but where did he live? Happily, Charles remembered his employer's address. He hurried there.

Day was beginning to break and he could make out the signs above a door. He knocked. Someone shouted out the information he wanted, without opening the door, meanwhile loudly cursing those who disturbed people during the night.

The house in which the clerk lived had neither bell, knocker, nor porter. Charles banged against the shutters with all his strength. A policeman passed by; he became frightened and went off.

"I'm mad," he told himself, "she probably stayed with the Lormeaux family after dinner." But the Lormeaux family no longer lived in Rouen.

"She must have stayed to take care of Madame Dubreuil. But Madame Dubreuil died ten months ago! So where can she be?"

A thought came to him. He asked for the directory in a café and quickly looked up the name of Mademoiselle Lempereur, who lived at 74 Rue de la Renelle-des-Maroquiniers.

Just as he turned into that street, Emma herself appeared at the other end. He threw himself at her, more in a lunge than an embrace, exclaiming: "What kept you yesterday?"

"I didn't feel well."

"What was it? Where? How?"

She passed her hand over her forehead and answered: "At Mademoiselle Lempereur's."

"That's what I thought! I was going there."

"Well, don't bother," said Emma. "She just went out. But in the future, don't worry. I won't feel free, you know, if I have to remember that the slightest delay worries you so much."

This was a sort of permission she was giving herself in order not to be hampered in her future escapades. And she took free and full advantage of this. When she had a sudden desire to see Léon, she would leave at the slightest excuse, and since he would not be expecting her that day, she would call for him at his office.

At first it made him very happy. But soon he told her that his employer was very displeased by these intrusions.

"So what!" she would say. "Come along." And he would slip out.

She wanted him to dress all in black and grow a pointed beard on his chin to resemble the portraits of Louis XIII. She wanted to see his rooms, found them mediocre. He blushed at the remark. She didn't notice and advised him to buy curtains like hers. And when he objected to the expense: "You do pinch your pennies!" she laughed.

Each time Léon had to tell her everything that had happened during the week. She asked for poetry, poetry written just for her, "a love poem" in her honor. He could never find a rhyme for the second line and would end up copying a sonnet from a keepsake.

This was less out of vanity than from a desire to please

her. He did not argue about any of her notions; he accepted all her tastes, becoming her mistress rather than she being his. She offered tender words and kisses that drove him mad. Where, where had she learned this corruption, so deep and yet so disguised that it appeared almost disembodied?

VI

When he traveled to Yonville to see her, Léon often dined at the pharmacist's home, and he felt obliged out of politeness to reciprocate an invitation.

"Gladly!" Homais had replied. "I really should take a bit of a plunge. I'm getting fossilized here. We'll go to a show and eat in a restaurant. We'll carry on a bit!"

"Oh dear!" Madame Homais murmured affectionately, frightened by the vague perils to which he was exposing himself.

"Why, what's the matter? You think I don't ruin my health enough living with those constant fumes from the pharmacy? That's the female character for you—they're jealous of science, yet they're opposed to one's enjoying the most legitimate distractions. Never mind, you can definitely expect me. One of these days I'll turn up in Rouen and we'll throw our money around!"

In the old days the apothecary would not have used such an expression; but nowadays he was using a colloquial and Parisian way of speech that he considered to be in the best of taste; and like his neighbor Madame Bovary, he questioned the clerk curiously about the life in the capital, even using slang to dazzle the "bourgeois," saying such things as *turne, bazar, chicard, chicandard, Breda-Street* and "I'll cut along now" for "I'm leaving."

And so Emma was surprised one Thursday to see Monsieur Homais in the Golden Lion kitchen. He was dressed in his traveling clothes, that is, enveloped in an old cloak that no one had seen before, carrying a valise in one hand and the foot warmer from his shop in the other. He had told no one of his plan, fearing that the public would become uneasy in his absence.

The thought of revisiting the places in which he had spent his youth probably excited him because he did not stop talking during the entire trip. The moment they arrived, he jumped from the carriage to go off in search of Léon. The clerk protested in vain. Homais dragged him toward the Café de Normandie, where he entered with great self-importance, not removing his hat since he felt it was very provincial to be bareheaded in a public place.

Emma waited for Léon for three quarters of an hour. Finally she ran to his office. Then, lost in all sorts of conjectures, accusing him of indifference and reproaching herself for her weakness, she spent the afternoon with her forehead glued to the windowpanes.

At two o'clock they were still at the table. The large dining room was emptying. The stovepipe shaped like a palm tree spread its gilt leaves on the white ceiling; near them, inside the café window, in the bright sunlight, a small fountain was gurgling in a marble basin where, among the watercress and the asparagus, three torpid lobsters stretched their claws toward a heap of quail.

Homais was in seventh heaven. Even though he was drunk more on the luxury than the good fare, the Pommard did go to his head a little. And when the rum-flavored omelet appeared he put forth some immoral theories about women.

What attracted him above all was chic. He adored an elegant manner of dress in a well-furnished apartment, and in the matter of physical attributes he didn't dislike a "pleasingly plump little morsel."

Léon looked at the clock—in despair. The apothecary went on drinking, eating, talking.

"You must be rather hard up here in Rouen," he suddenly said. "But then, your love's not far from here."

And as the other blushed: "Come now, admit it. Will you deny that in Yonville—"

The young man stammered something.

"At Madame Bovary's, weren't you courting—"

"Whom?"

"The maid!" He wasn't joking. But vanity conquering caution, Léon denied it vehemently, despite himself. Besides, he liked only dark women.

"You're right," said the pharmacist. "They have more temperament." And leaning over toward his companion's ear, he listed the signs by which a woman with temperament can be recognized. He even launched into an ethnic digression. German women were moody, French women wanton, and Italians passionate.

"And Negro women?" asked the clerk.

"They're preferred by artists," said Homais. "Waiter! Two demitasses!"

"Shall we go?" Léon finally asked with impatience.

"Yes," said Homais in English.

But before they left he wanted to see the owner of the place and offer his congratulations.

Then the young man pleaded, in order to get rid of him, that he had a business appointment.

"I'll go with you!" Homais announced. And as they walked down the streets together, he spoke about his wife, his children and their future, and the pharmacy, talking about the state of disrepair he had found it in—and the height of perfection to which he had brought it.

When they reached the Hotel de Boulogne, Léon abruptly left him and ran up the stairs, where he found his mistress in a highly excited state.

She grew furious at the mention of the pharmacist's name. But he sought to justify himself. Had it been his fault? Didn't she know Homais? Could she believe that he would prefer his company to hers? She turned away. He took hold of her, and falling to his knees, put his arms around her waist in a languorous pose full of desire and pleading.

She stood with her large flashing eyes looking at him seriously, almost fiercely. Then they were clouded by tears, her reddened eyelids lowered, she let her hands fall, and Léon brought them to his lips. Just then a servant appeared to tell Léon that someone was asking for him.

"You'll come back?" she said.

"Yes."

"When?"

"Right away."

"It's a trick," the pharmacist said, seeing Léon. "I wanted to get you away from that appointment. I thought you weren't very happy about it. Let's go to Bridoux's and have a glass of cordial."

Léon insisted he had to go back to his office. The apothecary became facetious about legal paperwork and legal procedure.

"Forget about your Cujas and Barthole for a while! Devil take it! Who's stopping you? Buck up, man! Come along to Bridoux's. You'll see his dog—it's very odd." And when the clerk proved stubborn: "Then I'll go with you. I'll read a newspaper while waiting, or I'll leaf through a law journal."

Léon, bewildered by Emma's anger and Homais's incessant talk, and perhaps affected by the heavy lunch, stood undecided and as if under the spell of the pharmacist, who kept repeating: "Let's go to Bridoux's! It's only two steps from here—on Rue Malpalu."

Then, out of cowardice or foolishness or that elusive feeling that commits us to the actions we dislike most, he let himself be taken to Bridoux's. They found him in his small yard, keeping an eye on three workers who were painting as they tugged at the big wheel of a seltzer-making machine. Homais gave them a few suggestions and embraced Bridoux, and they had their drinks. Twenty times Léon was on the point of leaving, but Homais would tug at his arm and say, "I'm leaving too; wait a minute! We'll go to the *Rouen Beacon* and see the people there. I'll introduce you to Thomassin."

He did manage to get rid of him, however, and rushed to the hotel. Emma was no longer there.

She had just left in exasperation. Now she detested him. His failure to keep his promise about their rendezvous seemed an outrage to her. She kept looking for other reasons to break with him: he was incapable of heroism, weak, commonplace, banal, softer than a woman, stingy, and what is more, cowardly.

Then, calming down, she finally realized that she had probably unjustly condemned him. But the disparagement of those we love always erodes a bit of the affection. One must not touch idols; the gilt rubs off on one's hands.

From now on, matters apart from their love entered into their correspondence. Emma's letters to him talked of flowers, poetry, the moon and the stars, naïve expedients of a weakening passion trying to revive itself by external devices. She kept promising herself a profound joy for their next meeting; then she would admit to herself that she had felt nothing extraordinary. This disappointment soon gave way to a renewed hope, and Emma would return to him more impassioned and avid. She would undress savagely, tearing at the thin lacing of her corset, which fell down around her hips like a gliding snake. She would tiptoe on her bare feet to see once more if the door were locked, then she would drop all her clothes in one movement—and pale, without speaking, solemn, she would fall against his chest with one long shudder.

Yet there was something wild, something strange and tragic in this forehead covered with cold sweat, in those stammering lips and wildly staring eyes, in the embrace of those arms—something that seemed to Léon to be coming between them subtly as if to tear them apart.

He did not dare question her, but seeing how experienced she was, he told himself that she must have known all the extremes of suffering and pleasure. What had once charmed him now frightened him a little. He was also rebelling against the increasing encroachment upon his personality. He resented Emma for this permanent victory over him, even tried not to want her; and then at the sound of her footsteps he felt himself grow weak like an alcoholic at the sight of strong liquor.

She did not fail, it is true, to lavish all sorts of attentions on him, from choice foods to tricks of dress and languishing looks. She brought roses from Yonville in her bosom, and tossed them at him. She became anxious about his health, advised him on his conduct, and in order to bring him closer to her, hoping perhaps that heaven would help, she slipped a medal of the Blessed Virgin around his neck. Like a virtuous mother, she would ask about his friends. She told him: "Don't see them, don't go out, think only of us. Love me!"

She wanted to be able to keep track of his life, and it occurred to her to have him followed in the streets. There was always some sort of vagabond near the hotel who accosted travelers and who would not refuse. But her pride asserted itself. "Too bad, then! Let him deceive me, what of it? Do I really care?"

One day when they had parted early, she was walking alone along the boulevard. She noticed the walls of her convent and sat down on a bench in the shade of the elm trees. How calm those days had been! How wistful she was about the indescribable ideas of love she had tried to imagine for herself from books.

The first months of her marriage, her horseback rides in the forest, the viscount waltzing, and Lagardy singing—all of this passed before her eyes. And Léon suddenly appeared to be as far from her as the others. "But I love him!" she told herself. Nonetheless she was not happy, had never been happy. Why then was life so inadequate? Why did she feel this instantaneous decay of the things she relied on? If there existed somewhere a strong and handsome being, a valiant nature imbued with both exaltation and refinement, the heart of a poet in the shape of an angel, a lyre with strings of bronze, sounding elegiac nuptial songs toward the heavens—why, why could she not find him? How impossible it seemed! And anyway, nothing was worth looking for; everything was a lie. Each smile hid a yawn of boredom, each joy a curse, each pleasure its aftermath of disgust, and the best of kisses left on your lips only the unattainable desire for a higher delight.

A metallic clang rang through the air and there were four strokes from the convent clock. Four o'clock! And it seemed to her that she had been there on that bench for eternity. But an infinity of passions can be contained in a minute, like a crowd in a tiny space.

Emma lived only for her passions, no more concerned about money than an archduchess.

One day, though, a puny little man, red-faced and bald, came to her house and declared that he had been sent by Monsieur Vinçart of Rouen. He removed the pins that closed the side pocket of his long green frock coat, stuck them into his sleeve, and politely held out a paper.

It was a note for seven hundred francs, signed by her, that Lheureux, despite all her protests, had endorsed over to Vinçart.

She sent her maid to fetch him. He couldn't come.

Then the stranger, who had remained standing and glancing about left and right (his curiosity concealed by his heavy blond lashes), asked with a naïve air: "Is there any message for Monsieur Vinçart?"

"Well, tell him—" said Emma, "tell him—that I don't have the money! It will be paid next week. Ask him to wait. Yes, next week." And the man went off without a word.

But at noon on the next day she received a summons; and the sight of the stamped paper, over which was written in several places in large letters "Maître Hareng, Bailiff at Buchy," frightened her so that she quickly ran to the dry-goods merchant.

She found him in his shop, tying up a package. "At your service, Madame," he said, but did not stop his work. He was assisted by a girl of about thirteen, slightly hunchbacked, who worked as both salesgirl and cook.

Then, his clogs clattering over the shop's floor, he preceded Emma one flight up the stairs and escorted her into a narrow room. Here there was a large fir desk on which were several ledgers secured by locked metal bars. Against the wall beneath some calico samples was a safe so large that it probably contained something besides notes and money. Monsieur Lheureux, as a matter of fact, also acted as a pawnbroker, and it was there that he had put Madame Bovary's golden chain, along with Tellier's golden earrings. The poor old man had been finally forced to sell out, and had bought a little grocery store in Quincampoix, where he was dying of catarrh among tallow candles less yellow than his face.

Lheureux sat down in his large rattan armchair, saying: "What's new?"

"Look!" And she showed him the paper.

"Hmm, well. What can I do?" Then she became angry, remembering the promise he had given her not to endorse her notes. He acknowledged it. "But I myself was forced to. The knife was at my throat."

"And what's going to happen now?" she asked.

"Oh, it's simple enough; a court judgment and then a seizure—and that's it!"

She had to restrain herself from hitting him. Then she asked quietly if there were no way to placate Monsieur Vinçart.

"What! Placate Vinçart! You don't know him. He's fiercer than an Arab."

But Monsieur Lheureux simply had to do something!

"Listen to me," he said, "I think I've been nice enough to you until now." And he opened one of his ledgers: "Look," working up the page with his finger: "Let's see— August 3, 200 francs—June 17, 150, March 23, 46—April —" He stopped as if afraid of committing a blunder. "And I'm not even mentioning the notes signed by your husband, one for seven hundred francs and another for three hundred! As for your little payments on account and the interest, we'll never get through with them, they're so tangled up. I'm not going to involve myself anymore!"

She cried, she even called him "my good Monsieur Lheureux." But he kept referring to that "scoundrel Vinçart." Besides, he didn't have a centime, no one was paying him right now, they were taking the shirt off his back; a poor shopkeeper like him couldn't lend money.

Emma stopped talking, and Lheureux, who was nibbling on the feathers of a quill, seemed worried by her silence because he said: "At least, if one of these days some money came in—I could—"

"Anyhow," she said, "as soon as the balance on Barneville—"

"What?" He seemed very surprised to learn that Langlois had not yet paid. Then, in honeyed tones: "And we can agree, you say—"

"On anything you want!"

Then he closed his eyes to think, jotted down some figures, and asserting that it would be a lot of trouble to him, that it was a tricky business, and that he was "bleeding himself," he wrote out four notes for 250 francs each, one payable every month.

"If Vinçart will only listen to me. Anyway, we're all agreed. I don't play around. I'm as straight as a die!"

Then he casually showed her some new merchandise, though none of it was good enough for her in his opinion.

"When I think that this is dress goods at seven sous a meter, and guaranteed color fast! And they believe it! Of course, you realize I don't tell them what it really is," he said, hoping by this confession of skullduggery toward others to convince her of his honesty toward her.

Then he called her back to show her three lengths of lace he had recently come upon "in a sale."

"So handsome!" said Lheureux. "They use a lot of it now for antimacassars; it's the style." And more rapidly than a juggler he wrapped the lace in blue paper and placed it in Emma's hands.

"At least tell me how much—"

"Oh, later!" he said, turning quickly away from her.

She began pressing Bovary that very evening to write his mother to send them the entire balance of his inheritance immediately. The mother-in-law answered that she had nothing more; the estate was settled, and except for Barneville, there remained for them an annual income of six hundred francs, which she would forward regularly.

Then Emma sent off bills to two or three patients and before long had frequent recourse to this method, which worked well for her. She was always careful to write as a postscript: "Don't mention this to my husband; you know how proud he is. . . . Please forgive me. . . . Your humble servant." There were a few complaints. She intercepted them.

To make some money she began selling her old gloves, hats, household utensils; and she drove hard bargains, her blood inciting her to gain. Then, during her trips to the city she would pick up trifles that Lheureux would certainly buy from her if no one else did. She bought ostrich feathers, Chinese porcelain, and old chests; she borrowed from Félicité, from Madame Lefrançois, from the landlady of the Croix-Rouge, from everyone, no matter who. With the money she finally received from Barneville, she paid off two notes; the other fifteen hundred francs were frittered away. She signed new notes, and so it went on.

Sometimes she did try to add some figures, but she uncovered such exorbitant sums that she couldn't believe it. So she began again, became quickly confused, stopped working at it, and thought no more about it.

The house was very sad now. The tradesmen left with furious faces. Handkerchiefs were left lying on the stoves; and little Berthe, to Madame Homais's great horror, had holes in her stockings. If Charles timidly made some comment, Emma answered harshly that it wasn't her fault.

Why these fits of rage? He attributed it all to her old nervous ailment and reproached himself for having considered her infirmities as faults. He accused himself of selfishness, felt like running over to her and kissing her.

"I mustn't," he told himself; "I'll irritate her." And so he held back.

After dinner, he would walk alone through the garden, take Berthe on his knees, and unfolding his medical journal, would try to teach her to read. The child, who had never had any schooling, soon opened two large sad eyes and cried. Then he would console her by going off to find water in the sprinkling can to make rivers in the sand; or he would break off branches from the privet hedge to plant trees in the flower beds. They didn't really harm the garden, as it was all clogged up with weeds. They owed Lestiboudois for so many days' work! Later the child would feel cold and ask for her mother.

"Call the maid," Charles would say. "You know, child, that Mama doesn't want to be bothered."

Autumn was already beginning and the leaves were falling, just like two years ago when she was sick! When would all of this end? And he would keep on walking, his hands behind his back.

Emma would stay in her room. No one went up. She would remain there all day long, in a torpor, only half dressed, burning incense that she had bought in Rouen in an Algerian shop. She managed by enough fussing to relegate Charles to the second floor, so that she wouldn't have to sleep next to him. All night long she would read sensational books in which there were orgies and gory situations. Often she would be terrified by a sudden thought and scream. Charles would come running.

"Oh, go away," she would say.

At other times, burning violently from her adulterous passion, panting and shaking, throbbing with desire, she would open her window, breathe in the cold air, let down her heavy mass of hair, and stare at the stars, yearning for the love of a prince. She would think of *him*, of Léon. At that moment she would have given anything for one of those meetings that sated her desires.

Those were her festive days—when they met. She wanted them to be splendid, and when he alone could not pay for them, she freely paid the difference. This happened nearly every time. He tried to make her understand that they would be just as comfortable elsewhere, in a more modest hotel, but she always objected.

One day she pulled from her bag six little silver-gilt spoons (the wedding gift from her father, old Rouault), asking him to go immediately to the pawnbroker's for her. Léon obeyed, even though this business displeased him. He was afraid of compromising himself.

Thinking about it later, he found that his mistress was taking on strange ways. Perhaps the people who wanted him to leave her weren't so wrong.

As a matter of fact, someone had sent his mother a long anonymous letter, warning her that he "was ruining himself with a married woman," and immediately the good lady —visualizing that eternal threat to families, the insidious pernicious creature, the siren, lurking like a fantastic monster in the depths of love—wrote to Monsieur Dubocage, his employer, who behaved splendidly in the circumstances. He talked to Léon for three quarters of an hour, trying to open his eyes for him, to warn him away from the chasm. Such an intrigue would later be harmful to his career. He begged Léon to break it up, and if he wouldn't make this sacrifice for his own sake, at least to do it for him, for Dubocage!

Léon finally swore not to see Emma again, and he reproached himself for not having kept his word when he considered all the trouble and blame this woman could still bring upon him, not to mention the jokes of his fellow clerks as they sat around the stove. Besides, he was going to be head clerk and this was the moment of decision. And so he gave up his flute, his elevated sentiments, and his dreams. Every bourgeois in the heat of his youth has believed himself capable—if only for a single day, a single moment —of tremendous passions and noble exploits. The most mediocre rake has dreamed of sultanas; every notary carries within himself the remains of a poet.

Now he was bored when Emma would suddenly sob on his chest; and his heart, like people who can stand only a certain amount of music, languished with indifference amid the stridency of a love whose subtleties left him cold.

They knew each other too well to feel those mutual revelations of possession that multiply its joys a hundredfold. She was as sated with him as he was tired of her. Emma was finding in adultery all the banalities of marriage.

But how could she break free? Though she felt humiliated by the base quality of such happiness, she clung to it out of habit or depravity. Each day she clung more desperately to it, thus destroying all happiness by demanding too much of it. She blamed Léon for her disappointed hopes as if he had betrayed her, and she even wished for some catastrophe that would cause their separation since she lacked the courage to bring it about herself.

Nevertheless, this did not stop her from continuing to write him loving letters, in line with the idea that a woman should always be writing to her lover.

But even as she wrote she perceived another man, a phantom fabricated from her most ardent memories, her most beautiful literary memories, her strongest desires; and he finally became so real and accessible that she trembled with amazement, yet without being able to visualize him clearly, since he was so hidden, like a god, under his many attributes. He inhabited that enchanted country where silken ladders swing from balconies among flowers, by the light of the moon.

She felt him near her; he would come and sweep her away in one kiss. Then she fell back to earth, broken, for her surges of imaginary love tired her more than wild debauches.

She was now living in a state of chronic and complete wretchedness. She would often receive summonses, official documents she barely glanced at. She wished she were dead, or continually asleep.

The day of Mid-Lent she did not return to Yonville, but went to a masked ball in the evening. She wore velvet trousers and red stockings, a wig and a cocked hat over one ear. She danced all night to the wild sound of the trombones. People formed a circle around her, and she found herself in the morning in front of the theater entrance with five or six masked figures dressed like longshoremen and sailors— friends of Léon who were talking about getting something to eat.

The neighboring cafés were full. They found a second-rate restaurant down by the river where the proprietor showed them to a little room on the fifth floor.

The men whispered in one corner, probably discussing the expenses. There were a clerk, two medical students, and a shop assistant. What company for her! As for the women, Emma quickly realized from their voices that almost all of them were from the dregs of society. Then she grew frightened, pushed back her chair, and lowered her eyes.

The others began to eat. She couldn't. Her forehead was on fire, her eyes smarted and she felt an icy coldness on her skin. She could still feel the floor of the ballroom in her head, resounding under the rhythmic beat of a thousand dancing feet. Then the odor of punch mingled with cigar smoke made her dizzy. She fainted, and they carried her to the window.

It was growing light and a large reddish patch showed against the pale sky toward Sainte-Catherine hill. The blue river quivered in the wind. There was no one on the bridges. The streetlights were going out.

Eventually she came to and began thinking of Berthe, who was sleeping somewhere out there, in the maid's room. Then a wagon loaded with long strips of iron passed by, causing a deafening metallic clang against the walls of the houses.

She slipped away abruptly, removed her costume, told Léon that she had to go back, and finally remained alone

at the Hotel de Boulogne. She found everything, herself included, unbearable. She yearned to escape like a bird, to go
somewhere and recapture her youth, somewhere far off, in
the immaculate expanse of space.

She went out, crossed the boulevard, the Place Cauchoise,
and the outskirts of the city, and came to an open street
overlooking some gardens. She was walking rapidly, the fresh
air soothing her; and gradually the faces of the crowd, the
masks, the quadrilles, the chandeliers, the supper, and those
women she had been with—all disappeared like mist floating off. Then, having returned to the Croix-Rouge, she
threw herself on her bed in the little third-floor room where
the Tour de Nesle prints hung. Hivert woke her at four in
the afternoon.

When she returned home Félicité showed her a gray sheet
of paper behind the clock. She read: "By virtue of the seizure, in due and legal execution of the judgment—"

What judgment? As a matter of fact, the day before, they
had brought another document, which she had not seen,
and so she was stunned by these words: "Ordered on behalf
of the King, the law, and the courts to Madame Bovary—"

Then, skipping several lines, she read: "Within twenty-
four hours, without fail—"

What?

"To pay the total sum of eight thousand francs."

And lower down, it even said: "She will be constrained
thereto by the full power of the law and notably by the
seizure of her furniture and effects."

What could she do? In twenty-four hours. That meant
tomorrow! Lheureux, she thought, probably wanted to frighten
her still more. Now suddenly she understood all his maneuvers,
the end goal of all his favors. What reassured her, however,
was the very enormity of the sum.

However, by dint of all her buying, and not paying,
borrowing, signing promissory notes, then renewing the notes,
which swelled each time they fell due, she had finally built
up a capital for Monsieur Lheureux, who was impatiently
awaiting it to use in his speculations.

She walked into his house as casually as she could. "Do
you know what has happened to me? It must be a joke."

"No."

"What do you mean?"

He turned away slowly and said to her, crossing his

arms: "Did you think, dear lady, that I was going to be your source of supply and your banker until the end of time, just out of sheer affection? I really have to get my money back; let's be fair!"

She protested the amount.

"That's too bad! The court acknowledged it. There's been a judgment. They've summoned you. Anyway, it's not me, it's Vinçart."

"Can't you do—"

"Nothing at all."

"But—still—let's talk—" And she began stammering: she hadn't known anything—it was a complete surprise—

"Whose fault is it?" Lheureux said, bowing low with irony. "While I work like a slave, you have yourself a good time."

"Don't you preach morality to me!"

"It never hurts," he retorted.

She lost all shame, she implored him; she even placed her lovely long white hand on the merchant's knee.

"Leave me alone! One would think you were trying to seduce me."

"You're a monster!" she cried.

"Oh! How you do go on," he said with a laugh.

"I'll let people know what you are. I'll tell my husband—"

"Is that so? Then I'll show your husband something!" And Lheureux took from the safe a receipt for eighteen hundred francs that she had given him after Vinçart discounted the note.

"Do you think he won't see through your little theft," he said, "that poor, dear man?"

She sank back, more stunned than if she had been hit by a club. He was pacing up and down between the window and the desk, saying: "Ah! I'll show him good and proper —good and proper."

Then he walked over to her and said in a less harsh tone: "It's not pleasant, I know. But after all, no one ever died from it, and since it's the only way left for you to repay me my money—"

"But where will I find the money?" Emma said, wringing her hands.

"Bah! With the friends you have?" And he looked at her in such a knowing and terrible way that her whole being shuddered.

"I promise you," she said. "I'll sign—"

"I've had enough of your signatures!"

"I'll sell—"

"Come now!" he said, shrugging his shoulders. "You have nothing left." And he shouted through the peephole that opened onto the store: "Annette! Don't forget the three remnants of Number 14."

The servant appeared. Emma understood and asked, "How much money would it take to stop the legal action?"

"It's too late!"

"But if I brought you several thousand francs, a fourth of the sum, a third, nearly all?"

"No! It's a waste of time." He pushed her gently toward the staircase.

"I beg of you, Monsieur Lheureux, a few days more." She was sobbing.

"So! Now we have tears!"

"You're making me desperate!"

"As if I care!" he said, slamming the door.

VII

She appeared stoical the next day when Maître Hareng, the bailiff, appeared with two witnesses to draw up the inventory for the seizure.

They began with Bovary's consulting room but omitted the phrenological head, which was considered "a professional instrument"; however, in the kitchen, they counted the plates, pots, chairs, and lamps, and in her room all the articles on the whatnot. They examined her dresses, linen, and dressing room; and her entire existence, even in its most intimate details, was laid out at full length like a corpse being autopsied before the eyes of these three men.

Maître Hareng, buttoned up in a narrow black coat, with a white tie, and wearing tightly fastened bootstraps, kept repeating: "With your permission, Madame? With your permission?"

Often he would exclaim: "Charming! So pretty!" Then he would begin writing again, dipping his pen into the inkwell he held with his left hand.

When they finished with the various rooms they went up to the attic.

She kept a desk there in which Rodolphe's letters were locked. She had to open it.

"Ah! Personal correspondence!" said Maître Hareng with a discreet smile. "May I, please? I must make sure that the box doesn't contain anything else." He tilted the papers slightly, as if to shake out gold pieces. Then she grew indignant, seeing this coarse hand, with fingers reddened and as soft as slugs, touching the pages that had caused her heart to pound.

Finally they left! Félicité came back in. She had sent her to be on the lookout for Bovary, to keep him away; and they quickly installed the bailiff's watchman in the attic, where he promised to stay.

Charles, she thought, looked worried during the evening. Emma kept stealing anguished glances at him, thinking she could see accusations written in the lines on his face. Then, when her eyes fell on the mantelpiece adorned with Chinese screens, on the full curtains, on the armchairs, over all these things that had sweetened the bitterness of her life, she was overcome by remorse, or rather by an immense regret that stimulated passion, instead of suppressing it. Charles kept quietly poking the fire, his two feet on the fender.

At one moment the watchman, probably bored in his hiding place, made a bit of noise.

"Is somebody walking around upstairs?" Charles asked.

"No," she said. "It's an open window rattling in the wind."

The next day, Sunday, she left for Rouen in order to go to all the bankers whose names she knew. Most of them were in the country or away on trips. She was not discouraged, and asked those whom she did meet for money, insisting that she needed it and would repay it. A few laughed in her face; all refused.

At two o'clock she ran to Léon's and knocked on his door. No one came to open. Finally he appeared.

"What brings you here?"

"Am I disturbing you?"

"No—but—" And he said that the landlord did not like him to receive "women."

"I must speak to you," she said. Then he reached for his key but she stopped him. "No, let's go to our place."

And they went to their room at the Hotel de Boulogne.

When they got there she gulped down a large glass of water. She was very pale. "Léon, you'll have to do me a favor," she told him. Then shaking him by his hands, which she squeezed tightly, she added: "Listen, I need eight thousand francs."

"You must be mad!"

"Not yet." Quickly she told him the story of the seizure, revealing her distress to him. Charles was ignorant of the entire matter; her mother-in-law detested her; old Rouault could do nothing; but he, Léon, would have to go out and begin looking for that indispensable sum.

"How do you expect me to—?"

"What a coward you are!" she cried.

Then he said stupidly: "You're exaggerating the trouble. Maybe three thousand francs would calm him down."

All the more reason for trying to do something. It wasn't possible that they couldn't find three thousand francs. Besides, Léon could sign the notes for her. "Go ahead and try! You must! Run! Oh, try, please try! I'll love you so much."

He went out, came back after an hour, and said solemnly: "I went to three people—no use." Then they sat facing each other at the two sides of the fireplace, not moving, not speaking. Emma shrugged her shoulders, tapping her foot. He heard her murmur: "If I were in your place, I'd find the money."

"Where?"

"In your office." She looked intently at him. A criminal boldness was in her flaming eyes and her eyelids narrowed with voluptuous suggestiveness—so much so that the young man felt himself weakening before the mute will of this woman who was suggesting a crime to him. Then he grew afraid, and in order to avoid any explanations, struck his forehead and said: "Morel is due back tonight! He won't refuse me, I hope! (This was one of his friends, the son of a very wealthy businessman.) I'll bring it to you tomorrow," he added.

Emma did not appear to accept this hope of a solution with as much joy as he had thought. Did she suspect his lie? He continued, blushing: "But if you don't see me at three o'clock, don't wait for me anymore, darling. I must go. Forgive me. Good-bye!"

He pressed her hand but it felt completely lifeless. Emma no longer had the strength for any emotion.

Four o'clock struck and she arose to return to Yonville, obeying her habit pattern like an automaton.

It was a lovely day, one of those clear, sharp March days when the sun gleams in an all-white sky. Dressed in their Sunday best, the people of Rouen were walking along happily. She reached the Place du Parvis. Vespers had just ended; the crowd poured through the three portals like a river through the three arches of a bridge, and in the middle, motionless as a rock, stood the verger.

Then she remembered that day when, tremulous and filled with hope, she had entered under that tall nave that stretched out before her—yet not as lofty as her love; and she continued to walk, sobbing under her veil, dazed, stumbling, almost fainting.

"Look out!" shouted a voice as a carriage gate opened. She stopped to let pass a black horse, prancing in the shafts of a tilbury being driven by a gentleman in a sable coat. Who was it? She knew him. The carriage rushed forward and disappeared.

It was he—the viscount! She turned around but the street was deserted. And she felt so overwhelmed and sad that she leaned against a wall in order not to fall.

Then she thought that she might have been mistaken. Besides, she wasn't sure of anything anymore. Everything, within her and without, was abandoning her. She felt herself lost, rolling beyond control in bottomless abysses; and it was almost with joy that she caught sight of good old Homais when she reached the Croix-Rouge. He was watching a large box filled with pharmaceuticals being loaded on the Hirondelle; in a handkerchief in his hand he carried six *cheminots* for his wife.

Madame Homais loved these heavy little rolls, shaped like turbans, which are eaten during Lent with salted butter—last remnants of medieval food, dating back to the century of the Crusades, on which the robust Normans of old gorged themselves, imagining they saw Saracen heads waiting to be devoured, by the light of the yellow torches between tankards of mead and huge joints of meat.

The apothecary's wife crunched them as they had done, heroically, despite the terrible condition of her teeth; and so every time that Homais went into the city he did not fail to bring some back for her. He always bought them from the large bakery on the Rue Massacre.

"Delighted to see you," he said, offering Emma his arm to help her into the Hirondelle. Then he hung the *cheminots* on the netting of the baggage rack and sat with his head uncovered and arms crossed in a pensive, Napoleonic pose.

But when the blind man, as usual, appeared at the foot of the hill, he exclaimed: "I don't understand why the authorities tolerate such goings-on! They ought to shut these unfortunates up and force them to work. My word, progress moves at a snail's pace. We are wallowing in sheer barbarism."

The blind man held out his hat, which flopped about at the window like a loose piece of upholstery.

"There, you see," said the pharmacist, "a scrofulous infection." And despite the fact that he knew the poor devil, he pretended to be seeing him for the first time, murmuring the terms, "cornea," "opaque cornea," "sclerotic," "facies," and then asking him in a paternal tone: "Have you had this dreadful infirmity a long time, my friend? Instead of getting drunk in the tavern, you'd be better off on a special diet." He advised him to take good wine, good beer, good roasts. The blind man continued to sing. In fact, he seemed to be almost an idiot. Finally Homais opened his purse.

"Here's a sou for you; take half and give me back my change. And don't forget my advice, you'll be better for it."

Hivert allowed himself to express some doubt about Homais's advice. But the apothecary was absolutely certain that he could cure the blind fellow with an antiphlogistic salve of his own making, and he gave his address: "Monsieur Homais, near the marketplace, known by all."

"Now then," said Hivert, "for all this trouble, you show us your act."

The blind man squatted down on his haunches, threw back his head, rolling his glaucoma-affected eyes, stuck out his tongue, and rubbed his stomach with both hands as he emitted a kind of low howl, like a starving dog.

Emma, filled with disgust, threw him a five-franc piece over her shoulder. It represented her entire fortune. She thought it a beautiful gesture to squander it like this.

The carriage had started off again when Homais suddenly leaned out the window and shouted: "No farinaceous foods or dairy products! Wear wool against the skin and expose the diseased portions to the fumes of juniper berries."

The familiar objects unfurling before her eyes distracted Emma gradually from her present misery. She was overcome by a heavy fatigue and arrived home numbed, discouraged, almost asleep.

"What will come will come!" she told herself. After all, who could tell? Why shouldn't some extraordinary event occur at any moment? Lheureux might even die.

At nine in the morning she was awakened by a noise of voices in the square. There was a crowd gathered in the marketplace to read a large notice attached to one of the posts, and she saw Justin climbing onto a stone and ripping it down. Just then the village policeman grabbed him by the collar. Monsieur Homais left the pharmacy and Madame Lefrançois seemed to be making a speech in the midst of the crowd.

"Madame! Madame!" Félicité cried as she rushed in. "It's terrible!" And in her distress the poor girl held out to her a yellow piece of paper that she had just torn from the door. Emma read at a glance that all her household furnishings were to be sold.

Then they looked at each other in silence. Servant and mistress had no secrets from each other. Finally Félicité sighed: "If I were you, Madame, I'd go see Monsieur Guillaumin."

"You think so?"

And this question meant: "You who know the Guillaumins via their manservant; do you know if the master has occasionally mentioned me?"

"Yes, do go. You'll be doing the right thing."

She dressed, put on her black dress and the bonnet with jet beads; and in order not to be seen (there was still a crowd of people in the square), she took the back road near the river, beyond the village.

She reached the notary's gate quite out of breath. The sky was dark and there was a light snow falling.

At the sound of the bell, Theodore, in a red vest, appeared on the porch; he let her in almost familiarly, as if he knew her well, and showed her into the dining room.

A large porcelain stove was humming beneath a cactus plant that filled the alcove. Framed in black wood, against the oak-grained wallpaper, were Steuben's "Esmeralda" and Schopin's "Potiphar." Everything glistened with spotless English cleanliness, the table already set, the silver dishwarmers, the crystal doorknobs, the floor, and the furniture. The windows were decorated in each corner with colored glass.

"This is the kind of dining room I would like," Emma thought.

The notary entered, pressing his left arm tightly to his chest against his dressing gown embroidered with palm designs, while with the other hand he lifted and quickly replaced his chestnut-colored velvet skullcap. He kept it jauntily tilted to the right side. The ends of three blond tufts of hair, combed up from the back around his bald pate, dangled down.

He offered her a seat and sat down to his breakfast, apologizing profusely for his impoliteness.

"Monsieur," she said, "I would ask of you——"

"What, Madame? I'm listening."

She began to relate her predicament.

Maître Guillaumin knew all about it. He was secretly in league with the dry-goods merchant, from whom he always got capital for the loans on mortgages that he was asked to arrange. Therefore he knew (and better than she) the long history of these notes, small at first, which had had various endorsers, had been spaced out over long periods, and had been continually renewed until the day when, gathering together all the protests for nonpayment, the merchant had asked his friend Vinçart to institute the necessary proceedings in his own name since he did not want to appear a bloodsucker before his fellow townspeople.

She kept interrupting her tale with recriminations against Lheureux, recriminations to which the notary replied from time to time with some perfunctory remark. Eating his chop and drinking his tea, he buried his chin in his sky-blue cravat, secured by two diamond pins linked by a gold chain, and smiled strangely—a smile in which there were elements of unction and ambiguity. But noticing that her feet were damp, he said: "Come closer to the stove. Put your feet up higher, against the porcelain."

But she was afraid she would dirty it. The notary replied gallantly: "Beautiful things never do harm."

Then she tried to arouse his emotions, and became aroused herself. She told him of the lack of funds in her home, her difficulties, her needs. He could understand that: such an elegant lady! He had managed to turn toward her completely without ceasing to eat, and his knee rubbed against her shoe, the sole of which was curling up a little from the smoke of the stove.

But when she asked him for three thousand francs, he pursed his lips. Then he declared that he regretted very much not having been able to take charge of her fortune earlier, for there were a hundred easy ways, even for a lady, to earn a profit on her money. They could have made some excellent speculations, with almost no risk, either in the Grumesnil peatbogs or Le Havre building sites. And he let her eat her heart out with rage at the thought of the fantastic sums she would certainly have made.

"Why didn't you come to me?" he said.

"I just don't know."

"But why? Did I frighten you? It's I, on the contrary, who ought to pity myself. We hardly know each other! And yet I'm very devoted to you. You no longer doubt it, I hope?"

He stretched out his hand, took hold of hers, and covered it with a greedy kiss, then kept it on his knee. He played gently with her fingers, while paying her all sorts of compliments.

His monotonous voice droned on like a flowing brook. His eyes gleamed through his glasses and his hands were moving up into Emma's sleeves, caressing her arm. She felt a panting breath against her cheek. This man was repulsive to her.

She leaped up and said: "Monsieur, I am waiting!"

"For what?" asked the notary, who suddenly became very pale.

"The money."

"But—"

Then he gave in to the explosion of an irresistible desire: "Very well, yes!"

He was crawling on his knees to her, with no concern for his dressing gown: "Stay, please. I love you!" He grasped her around the waist.

Madame Bovary's face immediately flushed red. She recoiled with a terrible look on her face, exclaiming: "You're brazenly taking advantage of my distress, Monsieur! I am to be pitied, but I'm not for sale!"

And she went out.

The notary remained there, stunned, his eyes fixed on his handsome embroidered slippers. They were a gift from a mistress, and the sight of them finally consoled him. Besides, he felt that such an adventure might have involved him too deeply.

"What a monster! What an unspeakable cad!" she said to herself, running nervously beneath the aspens that lined the road. Disappointment at her lack of success intensified her indignation about her outraged honor. She felt that Providence was determined to hound her, and the thought strengthened her pride. Never had she had so much respect for herself or so much scorn for others. A kind of warlike emotion was transporting her. She wanted to fight all men, spit in their faces, crush them all; and she continued to walk rapidly, pale, trembling, and furious, scanning the empty horizon with tear-filled eyes and almost relishing the hatred that was stifling her.

At the sight of her house she suddenly felt paralyzed. She could not go forward, but she had to. Besides, where could she flee?

Félicité was waiting for her at the door.

"Well?"

"No!" Emma said. And for a quarter of an hour they went over the different people in Yonville who might be able to help her. But each time Félicité mentioned someone, Emma would reply: "Impossible! They wouldn't want to."

"But the doctor will be home soon."

"I know. Leave me alone now."

She had tried everything. Now there was nothing more to do. So when Charles appeared she was going to tell him: "Don't come in. That rug you're walking on is no longer ours. You don't have one piece of furniture left in your house, not a pin or a piece of straw—and I'm the one who's ruined you, poor man."

Then she would give one great sob, he would cry profusely, and finally, when he recovered from the shock, he would forgive her.

"Yes," she muttered, grinding her teeth. "He'll forgive me. Even if he offered me a million, I wouldn't forgive him for having known me. Never! Never!"

The thought of Bovary's having something over her enraged her. For whether she confessed or not, in a little while, today or tomorrow, he would get to know all about the catastrophe, and she had to look forward to that horrible scene and endure the weight of his magnanimity. A sudden impulse urged her to return to Lheureux. What for? Write to her father? It was too late. Perhaps she was sorry now for not having yielded to the notary—when she heard the sound of a horse trotting up the lane. It was he. He opened the gate. His face was whiter than the plaster on the wall. Running down the staircase, she quickly escaped across the square; and the mayor's wife, talking with Lestiboudois in front of the church, saw her enter the tax collector's house.

She ran to tell Madame Caron. The two ladies climbed up to the attic, and hidden by the laundry stretched out over the line, they posted themselves in a convenient spot from which they could see everything going on in Binet's house.

He was alone in his garret, making a wooden replica of one of those indescribable ivories that consist of crescents and spheres carved one inside the other, the whole straight as an obelisk and quite useless. He was just beginning to work on the last piece. The end was in sight!

In the dim light of the studio the white dust flew off from his tool like a shower of sparks beneath the hooves of a galloping horse. The two wheels turned and whirred. Binet was smiling, chin down, nostrils dilated; he seemed absorbed in one of those states of total happiness that come only with humble occupations—amusing the intelligence by easy difficulties and satisfying it with a complete sense of ultimate achievement.

"Ah! There she is!" said Madame Tuvache. But it was barely possible to hear what she was saying because of the lathe.

Finally the ladies thought they could make out the word "francs," and Madame Tuvache whispered quite low: "She's begging for more time to pay her taxes."

"Apparently!" said the other.

They saw her walking back and forth, examining the napkin rings on the wall, the candlesticks, the bannister knobs, while Binet stroked his chin with satisfaction.

"Do you suppose she's gone there to order something from him?" asked Madame Tuvache.

"But his things aren't for sale!" her neighbor objected.

The tax collector seemed to be listening. He was opening his eyes wide as if he didn't understand. She kept on in a gentle, pleading manner. She drew closer. Her breast was heaving. They stopped talking.

"Is she making advances to him?" said Madame Tuvache.

Binet was blushing to the tips of his ears. She took his hands.

"Oh, this is just too much!" She was probably making some outrageous proposal to him, for the tax collector—he was a brave man, had fought at Bautzen and Lutzen and the campaigns of France and had even been recommended for the Legion of Honor—suddenly drew back quite far as if he had caught sight of a snake and shouted: "Madame, what's got into you?"

"They ought to whip women like that!" said Madame Tuvache.

"Where is she?" said Madame Caron. For she had disappeared during his words. Then they saw her flying along the Grand Rue and turning to the right as if heading for the cemetery, and they lost themselves in all sorts of conjectures.

"Madame Rollet," she said, arriving at the wet nurse's home, "I'm choking! Unlace me!"

She fell on the bed and sobbed. Madame Rollet covered her with a petticoat and stood near her. Then, since Emma didn't speak the other woman moved away, sat down at her wheel, and began to spin flax.

"Stop it, please!" she murmured, thinking she was hearing Binet's lathe.

"What's the matter with her?" wondered the nurse. "Why did she come here?"

She had run there impelled by a sort of terror that drove her from home.

Lying motionless on her back, her eyes in a fixed stare, she could only vaguely discern the objects, even though she was trying to concentrate with a kind of idiot persistence. She focused her eyes on the peeling plaster on the wall, on two sticks smoking in the fire end to end, and on a large spider climbing above her head in a crack of the rafter. She finally collected her thoughts. She remembered— One day, with Léon— Oh, how far off it was! The sun was shining over the water and the clematis scenting the air. Then, carried off by her memories as if by a raging torrent, she soon remembered the previous day.

"What time is it?" she asked.

Madame Rollet walked outside, lifted the fingers of her

right hand toward the brightest part of the sky, and walked back in slowly, saying: "Almost three o'clock."

"Oh, thank you! Thank you!"

He was going to come. She was sure of it! He would find the money. But he might go down there, to her house, not knowing that she was here; so she asked the nurse to run to her home and bring him back.

"Hurry!"

"I'm going, dear lady, I'm going!"

She was amazed now that she had not thought of him immediately. He had given his word yesterday, and he would not fail. She saw herself at Lheureux's already, spreading out on his desk the three bank notes. Then she would have to invent a story to explain things to Bovary. But what?

It seemed to be taking the nurse a very long while to return. But since there was no clock in the cottage Emma feared she might be exaggerating the time elapsed. She began to walk in the garden with measured steps, went down the path along the hedge, and came back quickly, hoping that the nurse would have come back by another road. Finally, tired of waiting, tortured by suspicions that she kept trying to repress, not knowing any longer whether she had been there for a century or a moment, she sat down in a corner, closed her eyes, and covered her ears with her hands. The gate squeaked. She leaped up. Before she spoke, Madame Rollet said to her: "There's no one in your house!"

"What?"

"No one! And your husband's crying. He's calling you. They're looking for you."

Emma did not answer. She was panting heavily and rolling her eyes around, while the peasant woman, frightened at the expression on her face, drew back instinctively, thinking her mad. Suddenly she struck her forehead and uttered a cry, for the thought of Rodolphe, like a great lightning flash in a dark night, had just passed through her soul. He was so good, so sensitive, so generous! And besides, if he hesitated to render her this service, she knew very well how to force him to do it, by reminding him with one flick of an eyelash of their lost love. And so she went off toward La Huchette, without realizing that she was running to offer herself—the very thing that had so outraged her a little while ago—and quite unaware that she was prostituting herself.

VIII

As she walked along, she asked herself: "What am I going to say? Where shall I begin?" And as she came closer, she recognized the bushes, the trees, the furze on the hill, and the château below. She was reliving the sensations of her first tenderness, and her poor constricted heart was expanding with the memory of love. A warm breeze played over her face. The melting snow was falling drop by drop from the young buds onto the grass.

As in the old days she walked in through the little park gate, then reached the courtyard that was lined by a double row of thickset linden trees. Their long branches rustled as they swayed. The dogs in the kennel barked, and though the sounds of their yapping echoed, no one appeared in sight.

She climbed the straight, wide staircase with its wooden banisters. It led to the corridor paved with dusty flagstones onto which several rooms in a row opened, as in a monastery or an inn. His was at the far end, on the left. When she finally placed her fingers on the latch, her strength suddenly left her. She was afraid he wouldn't be there, almost hoped he wouldn't be—and yet he was her only hope, her last chance for salvation. She held back a minute; then, mustering up her courage at the thought of the present necessity, she went in.

He was seated before the fire, his feet on the fender, smoking a pipe.

"You!" he said, jumping up.

"Yes, it's me. I came—to ask your advice, Rodolphe."

Despite her efforts to talk, it was impossible for her to go on.

"You haven't changed. You're as charming as ever."

"Oh," she replied with bitterness, "they must be dreary charms, my friend, since you were able to spurn them."

Then he launched into an explanation of his conduct, apologizing in vague terms, for lack of any better excuses.

She allowed herself to be taken in by his words, even

more by his voice and his physical presence, so much so that she pretended to believe, or perhaps even did believe, in the excuse he gave for their rupture. He claimed it was a secret on which depended the honor and perhaps even the life of a third person.

"It doesn't really matter," she said, looking at him sadly. "I suffered enough."

He answered philosophically: "That's the way life is."

"Has it at least been good to you since our separation?" Emma asked.

"Neither good nor bad."

"It might have been better had we never separated."

"Yes—maybe."

"Do you really think so?" she said, drawing closer. And she sighed: "Oh, Rodolphe, if you only knew! I loved you so!"

Then she took his hand and they remained for a while with their fingers intertwined, like that first day at the Agricultural Show. Out of pride, he fought against any display of tenderness. But nestling against his chest, she said: "How did you expect me to live without you? One can't learn to do without happiness. I was desperate. I thought I would die. I'll tell you all about it. And you—you kept avoiding me."

It was true. For three years he had carefully avoided her, out of that natural cowardice that characterizes the stronger sex. Emma went on speaking, with coquettish movements of her head, as coaxing as an amorous kitten: "You love other women, admit it. Oh, I can understand them. I can. I forgive them. You seduced them as you seduced me. You're a man. You have all you need to make yourself loved. But we'll begin all over again, won't we? We'll love each other. See, I'm laughing. I'm happy! Say something!"

She was adorable to watch, with that expression in which a tear trembled, like a raindrop in a blue flower cup.

He pulled her onto his lap. With the back of his hand he caressed her smooth hair on which, in the twilight glow, there shimmered one last ray of sunlight like a golden arrow. She bent her head. He finally kissed her gently on her eyelids, with the tips of his lips: "But you've been crying?" he said. "Why?"

She burst into sobs. Rodolphe thought that it was the explosive violence of her love. As she said nothing, he took her silence to be a last show of modesty. Then he exclaimed:

"Forgive me! You're the only one I care for. I was a fool and a monster! I love you, I'll always love you. What's wrong? Tell me."

He knelt down.

"All right, then— I'm ruined, Rodolphe. You've got to lend me three thousand francs."

"But—but—" he said, rising slowly, while his face took on a somber expression.

"You know," she went on quickly, "that my husband placed his entire fortune with a notary. Well, he's run off. We had to borrow money. The patients haven't paid. And the estate isn't settled yet. We'll have money later. But today, just for three thousand francs, we're going to be dispossessed. Right now, at this very moment. And I came here counting on your friendship."

"Ah," thought Rodolphe, who suddenly became very pale, "so that's why she came!"

Finally he said, very calmly: "Dear lady, I don't have it."

He was not lying. Had he had the money, he probably would have given it to her, even though as a rule he disliked doing such bighearted things. A demand for money, of all the winds blowing down on love, was the coldest and the most uprooting.

She stared at him for a few minutes.

"You don't have it!" She repeated several times: "You don't have it! I should have spared myself this last humiliation. You never loved me! You're no better than the others!" She was betraying herself, losing control over her words.

Rodolphe interrupted her, insisting that he himself was "hard up for cash."

"How I pity you!" Emma said. "Yes, I pity you very much!" She happened to glance at a damascened rifle gleaming in the gun rack, and said: "But when you're so poor, you don't put silver on the stocks of your guns. You don't buy clocks inlaid with tortoiseshell"—she continued, pointing to the Boulle clock—"or silver-gilt whistles for your whips" —she touched them—"or charms for your watch chains. Oh, you have everything, even a liquor stand in your room. How you love yourself. You live well. You have a château, farms, a forest. You ride to hounds, travel to Paris — Why, these alone," she cried, taking his cuff links from the mantelpiece, "the smallest of these knickknacks you could turn into money. But you can keep them, I don't want them!"

She threw the cuff links away so violently that their golden chain broke when it hit the wall.

"But I, I would have given you everything, sold everything; I would have worked with my hands, begged along the highways, for one smile, one look, just to hear you say 'Thank you.' And you sit there relaxed in your armchair, as if you haven't made me suffer enough already! Without you, do you know, I would have been able to live happily. What made you do it? Was it a bet? But you did love me. You said so—and again just now— You'd have done better to drive me away. My hands are still warm from your kisses. And here on the rug is the spot where you swore on your knees you would love me forever. You made me believe it. For two years you led me through the most magnificent, the sweetest dream. And our plans for a trip—do you remember them? And your letter, that letter! It broke my heart. And when I come back to him, to this man who is rich, happy, free—when I beg him for help that any stranger would give, pleading and reminding him of all my love, he refuses me, because it would cost him three thousand francs!"

"I don't have it," Rodolphe replied with that perfect calm that masks anger as if with a shield.

She left. The walls were trembling, the ceiling seemed to be crushing her. She walked down the long path, stumbling against the piles of dead leaves scattering in the wind. Finally she reached the ditch near the gate. She broke her nails against the latch, so eager was she to open it. A hundred yards beyond, she stopped, out of breath and nearly falling. And then, turning around, she took one last look at the impassive château, with its park and gardens, its three courtyards, and all the windows of its facade.

She stood there in a daze, conscious of herself only because of the beating of her pulse. She thought she could hear it escaping and merging with a deafening music filling the countryside. The ground beneath her feet was more yielding than water, and the furrows looked to her like immense dark waves breaking. All the memories and thoughts in her head rushed out in a single motion like the thousand bits of a fireworks display. She saw her father, Lheureux's office, their room in the Rouen hotel, a different landscape. Madness seized her. She took fright and managed to take hold of herself, but still in a state of confusion. She no longer remembered the cause of her dreadful state—the matter of money. She was suffering only from love, and felt that her soul was draining away at the thought of it—like the mortally wounded, who in their agony feel their lives ebbing away through the bleeding wound.

Night was falling. The crows were overhead.

Suddenly she felt as if the air were filled with balls of fire, bursting like bullets through the air, spinning around and around and flattening out as they melted in the snow among the tree branches. In the center of each one of them, Rodolphe's face appeared. They multiplied, crowded together, seemed to penetrate her. Then everything disappeared. She recognized the lights of houses, shining from afar through the mist.

Her troubles loomed before her like an abyss. She was panting as if her lungs would burst. Then, in a transport of heroism that made her almost joyful, she ran down the hill, crossed the cow plank, went past the path and the lane, reached the marketplace, and finally, came to the pharmacist's shop.

No one was there. She was about to enter but feared they might come at the sound of the bell. So she slipped through the gate, holding her breath and groping at the walls. She got as far as the entrance to the kitchen, where there was a candle burning on the stove. Justin, in shirt sleeves, was carrying out a platter.

"Ah, they're eating. I'll have to wait."

He came back. She rapped on the window. He came out.

"The key! The key for upstairs, where the—"

"What?" He looked at her, aghast at the pallor of her face, which stood out white against the blackness of the night. She seemed extraordinarily beautiful to him, with a ghostly majesty. Without understanding what she wanted, he had a premonition of something terrible.

But she quickly continued in a low voice, gentle and melting, "I want it. Give it to me!" Through the thin wall they could hear the rattle of forks on the plates in the dining room.

She pretended she had to kill some rats that were keeping her from falling asleep.

"I'll have to ask Monsieur."

"No! Stay here." Then, very casually, "Oh, don't bother. I'll tell him later. Come along. You can light the way for me."

She walked into the hall that led to the door of the

laboratory. Hanging on the wall was a key marked "Capharn-aum."

"Justin!" shouted the apothecary, who was becoming impatient.

"Let's go up!"

He followed her.

The key turned in the lock and she went straight to the third shelf—so well did her memory guide her—seized the blue jar, pulled out the stopper, plunged her hand in, and pulled it out filled with a white powder that she began to stuff into her mouth.

"Stop!" he shouted, hurling himself at her.

"Quiet! They'll hear us."

He was in despair and wanted to call for help.

"Don't say a word; your master will be blamed!"

Then she went back home, suddenly relieved and almost as serene as if she had done her duty.

When Charles, shocked by the news of the dispossession, came home, Emma had just left. He shouted, wept, fainted, but she did not come back. Where could she be? He sent Félicité to Homais, to Tuvache, Lheureux, to the Golden Lion, everywhere. In the calmer moments of his anguish he saw his reputation ruined, their fortune lost, Berthe's future shattered. Why? Not a word! He waited until six in the evening. Finally, unable to stand it any longer and imagining that she had left for Rouen, he went off on the highway for about a mile, found no one, waited a bit longer, then came back.

She had returned.

"What happened? Why? Tell me."

She sat down at her desk and wrote a letter that she slowly sealed, adding the date and the hour. Then she said solemnly: "You will read this tomorrow; from now until then, I beg you not to ask me a single question. No, not even one."

"But—"

"Oh, leave me alone!" And she stretched out on her bed.

A bitter taste in her mouth awoke her. She caught sight of Charles and closed her eyes again.

She was studying herself attentively to see if she was suffering. No, nothing yet. She heard the clock ticking, the flames crackling, and Charles breathing as he stood near her bed.

"It's really quite simple to die," she thought. "I'll fall asleep and it will all be over."

She drank some water and turned toward the wall. The loathsome taste of ink continued.

"I'm thirsty, so thirsty!" she sighed.

"What's the matter with you?" asked Charles, holding out a glass.

"Nothing! Open the window, I'm stifling." And she was seized by such a sudden attack of nausea that she barely had time to pull her handkerchief from under the pillow.

"Take it away!" she said quickly. "Throw it out!"

He questioned her. She didn't answer. She kept herself from moving, fearing that the slightest emotion would make her vomit. Then she felt a glacial chill creep up from her feet to her heart

"Ah, it's beginning now," she murmured.

"What did you say?"

She twisted her head slowly, with anguish, continually opening her mouth as if she had something very heavy on her tongue. The vomiting started again at eight o'clock.

Charles noticed some sort of gritty white sediment clinging to the bottom of the basin.

"How strange," he said, "how very odd."

But she said in a loud voice: "No, you're wrong."

Then gently, almost caressingly, he passed his hand over her stomach. She let out a piercing cry. He drew back in terror.

Then she began to moan, at first feebly. Her shoulders heaved in a mighty shudder and she became paler than the sheet into which her taut fingers were digging. Her irregular pulse was almost imperceptible now.

Drops of sweat stood out on her face. It was bluish now and rigid, as if from the exhalation of some metallic vapor. Her teeth were chattering, her enlarged eyes roamed around vaguely, and she replied to all questions only by nodding her head. She even smiled two or three times. Then the groans grew louder. A muffled scream broke from her. She insisted she was feeling better and would soon get up. But convulsions seized her. She shouted out: "Oh, my God, it's horrible!"

He threw himself on his knees beside the bed.

"Tell me! What did you eat? Answer me for the love of God!" And he looked at her with a tenderness in his eyes such as she had never known.

"All right—there—over there," she said in a faltering voice.

He ran to the desk, broke the seal, and read out loud: "No one is guilty—" He stopped, passed his hands across his eyes, and read it again.

"What! Help! Help!" He was only able to repeat the word "Poisoned! Poisoned!" Félicité ran to Homais, who shouted it out as he crossed the square; Madame Lefrançois heard it at the Golden Lion; a few people rose from bed to tell it to their neighbors. No one in the village slept that night.

Dazed and mumbling, barely able to stand, Charles wandered around the room. He stumbled against the furniture and tore at his hair. The pharmacist had never thought he would see such a pathetic sight.

He went back home to write to Monsieur Canivet and Doctor Larivière. He couldn't concentrate and made more than fifteen drafts. Hippolyte left for Neufchâtel, and Justin spurred Bovary's horse so hard he was forced to leave it, foundered and all but dead, on the Bois-Guillaume hill.

Charles tried to leaf through his medical dictionary, but the lines danced so that he couldn't read them.

"Stay calm," said the apothecary. "We have only to administer a powerful antidote. What was the poison?"

Charles showed him the letter. It was arsenic.

"Well then," said Homais, "we'll have to make an analysis."

He knew that analyses were always necessary in cases of poisoning; and Charles, who did not understand, answered: "Do it, do it. Save her!"

He returned to her side, sank down on the rug, and remained sobbing with his head against the edge of the bed.

"Don't cry," she said. "Soon I won't torment you any longer."

"Why? What made you do it?"

"I had to, my dear," she answered.

"Weren't you happy? Is it my fault? But I did everything I could."

"Yes, I know. You're very good." And she caressed his hair slowly. The sweetness of this sensation was the last straw: he felt his whole being crumble in despair at the thought that he was going to lose her just now when she was showing more love for him than ever before. He could think of nothing to do. He did not know, did not dare—the urgent need for an immediate solution left him in utter confusion.

Now she was through, she thought, with treachery, baseness, and the endless desires that had ravaged her. She hated no one now; a twilight confusion was descending over her thoughts, and of all the sounds on earth, Emma could hear only the intermittent lament of this poor soul at her side, gentle and indistinct, like the last echo of a symphony dying away in the distance.

"Bring me the child," she said, raising herself on her elbow.

"You aren't feeling worse, are you?" asked Charles.

"No, no!"

The child was carried in by the maid. She wore a long nightdress from which her bare feet peeped out. She was solemn and still partially asleep. She stared with surprise at the sight of the disordered room and blinked her eyes, dazzled by the candles burning on the furniture. They probably reminded her of the mornings of New Year's Day or of Mid-Lent, when she was thus awakened early by the light of candles to come to her mother's bed to receive her presents, for she began to ask: "Where is it, Mama?" And when no one spoke: "But I don't see my little stocking."

Félicité held her over the bed while she continued to look toward the fireplace. "Did Nanny Rollet take it?" she asked.

At the mention of this name, which brought back to her the memory of her adulteries and miseries, Madame Bovary turned her head away as if in disgust at a poison even stronger than the one mounting into her mouth. Berthe remained on the bed. "Oh, Mama, your eyes are so big! And you're so pale. You're sweating."

Her mother looked at her.

"I'm afraid!" said the child, pulling back.

Emma took her hand to kiss it, but she struggled.

"Enough! Take her away!" said Charles, who was sobbing in the alcove.

The symptoms stopped for a moment. She seemed less agitated and at each insignificant word, at each more relaxed breath she took, he regained hope. When Canivet finally came in, he threw himself into his arms, crying: "Ah, it's you! Thank you. You're so kind. But she's getting better. See, look at her."

His colleague did not share his opinion at all, and without as he put it, beating around the bush, he prescribed an emetic in order to empty her stomach completely.

She soon began vomiting blood. Her lips pressed tighter together. Her limbs were tensed, her body was covered with brown patches, and her pulse quivered under the fingers like a taut thread, like a harpstring about to break.

Then she began to scream horribly. She cursed the poison, damned it, begged it to work faster, and pushed away with her stiffened arms everything that Charles, in greater agony than she, kept trying to get her to drink. He stood with his handkerchief to his lips and a hoarse rattle in his throat, crying, choked by sobs that shook his entire body. Félicité was running all over the room; Homais stood still, heaving great sighs, and Monsieur Canivet, although still maintaining his composure, was beginning to be worried.

"Damn it all! Yet she's been purged, and from the moment that the cause ceases—"

"The effect should cease," said Homais. "It's obvious."

"Save her!" cried Bovary.

Paying no attention to the pharmacist, who was venturing the hypothesis that "It might be a salutary paroxysm," Canivet was about to administer an antidote of theriaca when they heard the crack of a whip. All the windows rattled and a stagecoach drawn at full speed by three horses, mud spattered to the ears, came hurtling around the corner of the marketplace. It was Doctor Larivière.

The sudden appearance of a god would not have caused more excitement. Bovary lifted up both his hands, Canivet stopped short, and Homais pulled off his cap well in advance of the doctor's entrance.

He belonged to the great surgical school founded by Bichat, to that generation, now gone, of philosopher-practitioners who cherished their art with a fanatic love and exercised it with zeal and wisdom. When his anger was roused everyone in his hospital trembled, and his students revered him so deeply that they tried to imitate him as much as possible as soon as they began their own practice. So in every town for miles around there were replicas of his long

merino overcoat and his full black frock coat, whose
unbuttoned cuffs slightly covered his fleshy hands, handsome
hands that were never gloved, as if to be the readier to
plunge into misery. Disdaining honors, titles, and academies,
hospitable and generous, like a father to the poor, practicing virtue without believing in it, he would almost have
been taken for a saint had not the keen quality of his mind
made him feared as a devil. His glance, more piercing than
a scalpel, penetrated straight into your soul, cutting through
every excuse and prudery to the underlying lie. And so he
went his way, filled with that quiet majesty that comes
of the consciousness of a great talent, of a fortune, and of
forty years of hard work and irreproachable private life.

He frowned the moment he entered the room and saw
Emma's cadaverous face as she lay stretched out on her
back with her mouth open. While appearing to listen to Canivet, he passed his forefinger under his nose and kept saying: "Yes, yes."

But he shrugged his shoulders slowly. Bovary noticed it.
They stared at each other, and this man, accustomed as he
was to the sight of unhappiness, could not restrain a tear
that dropped onto his shirtfront.

He tried to lead Canivet into the next room. Charles followed.

"She's very bad, isn't she? What about a mustard plaster? Anything! Just find something. You've saved so many
others!"

Charles placed his two arms around him. There was a
look of terrified supplication in his eyes, as he almost collapsed on his chest.

"Be brave, my poor boy! There's nothing more to be
done." And Doctor Larivière turned away.

"Are you leaving?"

"I'll be back." He went out as if to give an order to
the coachman. Doctor Canivet followed. He too did not
care to see Emma die under his care.

The pharmacist joined them in the square. He was tem-
peramentally unable to keep away from famous people. So
he invited Doctor Larivière to do him the signal honor of
having lunch with him.

They immediately sent to the Golden Lion for pigeons,
to the butcher for all the chops he had, to Tuvache for
cream, and to Lestiboudois for eggs. The apothecary him-

self helped in the preparations, while Madame Homais, pulling at the strings of her bodice, said: "You'll excuse us, sir, in our poor village, without a day's warning—"

"The wineglasses!" whispered Homais.

"At least in the city we could have served stuffed pigs' feet."

"Be quiet! Shall we sit down, doctor?"

After the first few mouthfuls, he deemed it appropriate to furnish some details about the catastrophe: "We had a dryness of the pharynx at first, then unbearable pains in the epigastrium, excessive vomiting, and coma."

"How did she poison herself?"

"I have no idea, doctor. I don't even know where she could have obtained the arsenious acid."

At that moment Justin, who was carrying in a pile of dishes, began trembling.

"What's the matter with you?" asked the pharmacist.

At this question the boy dropped everything to the floor, making a loud crash.

"Imbecile!" shouted Homais. "Clumsy fool! Blockhead! Jackass!"

But he quickly regained control of himself and said: "I wanted to do an analysis, doctor, and *primo,* I carefully introduced into a tube—"

"It would have been better," said the surgeon, "had you introduced your fingers into her throat."

Doctor Canivet said nothing. He had just received a severe scolding in private about his emetic; consequently poor Canivet, who had been so arrogant and talkative about Hippolyte's clubfoot, sat very quietly today, a fixed smile of approval on his lips.

Homais was blossoming out with pride at being a host. The painful thought of Bovary somehow added to his pleasure by a selfish contrast with his own lot. Moreover, the presence of the doctor enraptured him. He displayed his erudition, making all sorts of random remarks about cantharides, the upas, the manchineel, and the adder.

"I've even read that various people have been poisoned, doctor, really struck down suddenly by black puddings that had been smoked too much. At least so I read in a very impressive report drawn up by one of our leading pharmacists, one of our masters, the famous Cadet de Gassicourt!"

Madame Homais reappeared carrying one of those unsteady contraptions that have to be heated with a spirit lamp;

for Homais believed in making his coffee at the table, having first roasted and ground the beans himself and then blended them.

"*Saccharum*, doctor?" he asked, passing the sugar.

Then he sent for all his children, curious to have the surgeon's opinion on their constitutions.

When Doctor Larivière was about to leave, Madame Homais consulted him about her husband. He was "thickening his blood" by falling asleep every night after dinner.

"Oh, it's not his *blood* that's thick." And smiling a bit at his undetected joke at Homais, the doctor opened the door. But the pharmacy was crowded with people, and he had a great deal of trouble getting rid of Tuvache, who feared his wife had an inflammation of the lungs since she was always spitting into the fire; then of Binet, who sometimes had hunger pangs; of Madame Caron, who suffered from a prickling sensation; of Lheureux, who had dizzy spells; of Lestiboudois, who had rheumatism; and of Madame Lefrançois, who had heartburn. After the three horses finally went off, the consensus was that he had not been very gracious.

Public attention was distracted by the appearance of Monsieur Bournisien walking through the marketplace with the holy oils.

Homais, out of obligation to his principles, compared priests to crows attracted by the smell of death. The sight of a priest was personally distasteful to him: the cassock reminded him of a shroud and he cursed the one partly out of fear of the other.

Nevertheless, not flinching before what he called "his mission," he returned to the Bovary house with Canivet, whom Monsieur Larivière, before leaving, had strongly urged to remain; and had his wife not objected, he would have taken his two sons with him in order to accustom them to painful situations and to give them an object lesson, a solemn spectacle that they would remember later on.

When they entered the bedroom, they found it filled with a mournful solemnity. On the worktable, covered with a white napkin, were five or six small balls of cotton in a silver dish near a large crucifix between two lighted candles. Emma lay with her chin sunk on her breast; her eyes were unusually wide open, and her poor hands were grasping at the sheets in that terribly moving gesture of the dying that suggests that they already want to cover themselves with a winding sheet. Pale as a statue, his eyes red as coals, Charles, no longer crying, stood at the foot of the bed looking at her, while the priest, on one knee, was murmuring in a low voice.

She turned her head slowly and seemed suffused with joy at the sudden sight of the purple stole—probably rediscovering in this instant of extraordinary peace the lost ecstasy of her first flights of mysticism and beginning to have visions of eternal bliss.

The priest stood up to take hold of the crucifix. She stretched out her neck like one who is thirsty, and pressing her lips to the body of the Man-God, she placed on it, with all her fading strength, the most passionate kiss of love she had ever given. Then he recited the *Misereatur* and the *Indulgentiam,* dipped his right thumb into the oil, and began the unctions; first on the eyes, which had been so covetous of earthly splendors; then on the nostrils, avid for warm breezes and scents of love; then on the mouth, which had opened to emit lies, had groaned with pride, and had cried out in lust; then over the hands, which had reveled in sensual contacts; and finally on the soles of the feet, which had once moved so rapidly when she was hurrying to quench her desires and which now would walk no longer.

The priest wiped his fingers, threw the oil-soaked bits of cotton into the fire, and came back to sit near the dying woman, to tell her that now she must unite her sufferings to those of Jesus Christ and give herself up to Divine mercy.

As he ended his exhortations, he tried to place a consecrated candle in her hands, symbol of the celestial glories with which she would shortly be surrounded. Emma was too weak to close her fingers, and had it not been for Monsieur Bournisien, the candle would have fallen to the floor.

But she was no longer so pale, and her face wore an expression of serenity, as though the sacrament had cured her.

The priest did not fail to point this out. He even explained to Bovary that the Lord sometimes prolonged people's lives when He thought it necessary for their salvation; and Charles remembered the day when, as now, she was about to die and had received Holy Communion.

"Maybe we shouldn't give up hope," he thought.

Indeed, she was looking all around her, slowly, like someone waking from a dream. Then, in a clear voice she asked for her mirror, and she leaned over it awhile, big tears trickling from her eyes. Then she threw her head back with a sigh and fell back on the pillow.

Her breast began heaving rapidly. Her whole tongue protruded from her mouth; her rolling eyes grew pale, like two lamps about to die out. She might have been thought dead already except for the frightful pounding of her ribs, shaken by a furious breathing as though the soul were leaping to get free. Félicité knelt down before the crucifix, and even the pharmacist flexed his knees a bit, while Monsieur Canivet looked vaguely out into the square. Bournisien had begun to pray again, his face bowed over the edge of the bed, his long black cassock trailing behind him in the room. Charles was on his knees on the other side, his arms stretched out toward Emma. He had taken her hands and was holding them tightly, shuddering at each beat of her heart, as at the reverberation of a falling ruin. As the death rattle grew louder, the priest hurried his prayers. They mingled with Bovary's muffled sobs, and at times everything seemed to merge with the monotonous murmur of the Latin syllables that sounded like the tolling of a bell.

Suddenly there was a clatter of heavy clogs on the sidewalk and the tapping of a stick. Then a voice arose, singing raucously:

> Often the warmth of a lovely day
> Makes a girl dream of love.

Emma lifted herself up like a galvanized corpse, her hair undone, her eyes fixed and staring.

> To gather up the corn
> That the scythe has reaped,
> My Nanette bends to the furrow
> In which it was born.

"The blind man!" she cried. And she began to laugh —a horrible, frenzied, despairing laugh—imagining that she could see the hideous face of the beggar standing out against the eternal darkness like a nightmare.

> There was a strong breeze that day

And her short petticoat flew away!

A convulsion pulled her back down on the mattress. They all drew near the bed. She was no more.

IX

There is always a kind of numbness after a person's death, so difficult is it to understand this new state of non-existence and to accept the fact that it has occurred. But when he saw that she no longer moved, Charles threw himself on her and cried: "Good-bye! Good-bye!"

Homais and Canivet led him from the room. "Control yourself."

"All right," he said, trying to break free, "I'll be reasonable. I won't do anything wrong. But leave me alone. I want to see her. She's my wife." He began crying.

"Yes, cry," said the pharmacist, "let nature take its course. You'll feel better."

Weaker than a child, Charles let himself be led downstairs into the dining room. Monsieur Homais soon went home.

In the square he was accosted by the blind man who had dragged himself as far as Yonville, hoping to obtain the antiphlogistic salve, and now asked each passerby where the apothecary lived.

"Well! That's all I need! No, I can't do a thing right now. Come back later." And he hurried into his pharmacy.

He had to write two letters, prepare a sedative for Bovary, and think up a lie to conceal the poisoning for the *Rouen Beacon* obituary, as well as for the people waiting to hear the news from him. When all the people of Yonville had heard his story about Emma's mistaking arsenic for sugar while making a vanilla cream, Homais returned once more to the Bovary house.

He found Bovary alone (Monsieur Canivet had just left), seated in the armchair near the window and staring vacantly at the flagstones on the floor.

"Now you'll have to decide on the hour for the ceremony," said the pharmacist.

"Why? What ceremony?" Then, in a frightened voice, he stammered, "No, no, do I have to? I want to keep her here."

Homais, to maintain his composure, took a pitcher from the whatnot and watered the geraniums.

"Thank you," said Charles, "you are so kind." He suddenly stopped talking, overwhelmed by a flood of memories evoked by the pharmacist's gesture.

Homais thought he might distract him by talking about horticulture. "Plants need moisture," he said. Charles nodded his head in a sign of agreement. "Anyway, we'll soon have good weather."

"Ah!" said Bovary.

The apothecary, at a loss for subjects of conversation, began quietly to draw back the small curtains.

"Look, there's Monsieur Tuvache."

Charles repeated mechanically: "There's Monsieur Tuvache."

Homais did not dare mention the funeral plans again. It was the priest who finally persuaded Charles to make the arrangements.

He shut himself up in his consulting room, took a pen, sobbed for quite a while, then wrote: "I want her to be buried in her wedding dress, with white shoes and a wreath. Her hair is to be spread out over her shoulders. Three coffins—one of oak, one of majogany, and one of lead. No one has to talk to me, I'll be strong enough. Let her be covered with a large piece of green velvet. These are my wishes. Carry them out."

The two men were greatly surprised at Bovary's romantic notions, and the pharmacist immediately said to him: "The velvet seems superfluous to me. Besides, the expense—"

"Is it any of your business?" shouted Charles. "Leave me alone! You didn't love her! Go away!"

The clergyman took him by the arm for a walk in the garden. He talked about the vanity of earthly things. God was great and good; we should submit to His decrees without complaining; we should even rejoice.

Charles burst out blaspheming: "I detest that God of yours!"

"The spirit of rebellion is still in you," sighed the cleric.

Bovary had walked away from him and was striding alongside the wall of trained fruit trees, grinding his teeth. He looked up to the heavens with curses in his eyes, but not a leaf stirred.

It was raining lightly. Charles, whose chest was uncovered, finally began to shiver. He went in the house and sat down in the kitchen.

At six o'clock a clanking of metal was heard in the square: The Hirondelle was arriving; and he glued his forehead to the windowpanes to watch the passengers get out of the carriage, one after the other. Félicité laid a mattress out for him in the parlor. He threw himself on it and fell asleep.

Philosopher that he was, Monsieur Homais still respected the dead. And so, without feeling bitter toward poor Charles, he came back in the evening to watch by the body, carrying with him three volumes and a writing pad for taking notes.

Monsieur Bournisien was already there. Two large candles were blazing at the head of the bed, which had been pulled out of the alcove.

The apothecary, oppressed by the silence, soon uttered a few sad remarks about "that unfortunate young woman." The priest answered that all one could do for her now was to pray.

"Yet," said Homais, "it can't be both ways. Either she died in a state of grace (as the Church puts it), in which case she doesn't need prayers; or she died unrepentant (I believe that's the ecclesiastical term), and in that case—".

Bournisien interrupted, replying in an irritable tone that one needed to pray, no matter what.

"But," the pharmacist objected, "since God knows all our needs, what's the use of prayer?"

"What do you mean?" asked the priest. "Prayer! Aren't you a Christian?"

"I beg your pardon," said Homais. "I admire Christianity. In the first place, it freed the slaves, introduced into the world a morality—"

"Never mind about that! All the texts—"

"Texts, bah! Open up the history books. We know they were falsified by the Jesuits."

Charles came in and walked toward the bed. He drew the curtains back slowly.

Emma's head was turned toward her right shoulder. The corner of her mouth (which was open) seemed like a black

hole in the lower part of her face. Her two thumbs were
flexed inwards toward her palms; a kind of white powder was
scattered over her lashes and her eyes were beginning to disappear under a viscous pallor, as if spiders had spun a web
over them. The sheet sagged between her breasts and her
knees and then rose again over her toes, and it seemed to
Charles that an infinite mass, an enormous weight, was
pressing down on her.

The church clock struck two. They could hear the deep
murmur of the river flowing past the terrace through the
shadows. Monsieur Bournisien would occasionally blow his
nose noisily, and Homais's pen kept scratching the paper.

"I think you should go back to bed, my good friend," he
said. "The sight of her is tearing you apart."

After Charles left, the pharmacist and the curé resumed
their discussion.

"Read Voltaire!" said the one. "Read D'Holbach!" said the
other. "Read the encyclopedia!"

"Read the *Letters of Some Portuguese Jews*! Read *The
Proof of Christianity* by Nicolas, a former judge!"

They grew heated, became red in the face, spoke simul-
taneously, neither listening to the other. Bournisien was
shocked by such audacity, Homais amazed at such stupidity,
and they were on the verge of insulting each other when
Charles suddenly reappeared. He was drawn there by a re-
lentless fascination and kept coming up the stairs.

He stationed himself opposite her to see her more clearly,
and he lost himself in a contemplation so deep that it
ceased to be painful.

He remembered stories he had heard about catalepsy and
miracles of magnetism. He told himself that by wanting it
very much he could perhaps succeed in bringing her back to
life. Once he even leaned over her and cried in a very low
voice: "Emma! Emma!" The force of his breath made the
candleflames flicker against the wall.

His mother arrived at dawn the next day. Charles burst
into fresh tears when he kissed her. She tried, as had the
pharmacist, to say something to him about the funeral expenses. He became so furious that she stopped talking. He
even told her to go into the city immediately to buy what
was needed.

Charles remained alone all afternoon. Berthe had been

taken to Madame Homais's. Félicité was upstairs in the bedroom with Madame Lefrançois.

Some visitors came in the evening. He would get up and shake hands without being able to speak, then the newcomer would sit down with the others, who had formed a large semicircle around the fireplace. They sat with their heads lowered and would dangle their crossed legs, sighing deeply now and then. They were all extremely bored, but no one wanted to be the first to go.

When Homais returned at nine (for the past two days he had been seen constantly in the square), he brought with him a supply of camphor, benzoin, and aromatic herbs. He also carried a vase filled with chlorine to purify the air.

Just then Madame Lefrançois, Félicité, and Madame Bovary senior were busy with the final stages of dressing Emma; they lowered the long stiff veil that covered her down to her satin slippers.

"Félicité sobbed: "Oh! My poor mistress! My poor mistress!"

"Just look at her," sighed the landlady. "How pretty she still is. You'd swear she'd be getting up in a little while."

They leaned over to place the wreath on her head. It was necessary to lift the head slightly, and as they did this a stream of black liquid poured out of her mouth as if she were vomiting.

"Dear Lord! The dress! Take care!" shouted Madame Lefrançois. "Help us," she said to the pharmacist. "You're not afraid, are you?"

"Me afraid?" he answered, shrugging his shoulders. "Not me! I saw lots of them at the hospital when I was studying pharmacy. We would make punch in the dissecting room. Death doesn't frighten a philosopher. I even say quite often that I intend to bequeath my body to a hospital in order eventually to serve the cause of science."

When the curé arrived, he asked how Charles was and commented after the apothecary's reply: "The shock is still too fresh, you know."

Then Homais congratulated him at not being exposed, like everyone else, to the danger of losing a beloved mate. This gave rise to a discussion about celibacy of the clergy.

"It's not natural," said the pharmacist, "that a man should do without women. There have been crimes—"

"Bless me!" cried the clergyman. "How would you expect

a man who was married to keep the secrets of the confessional?"

Homais attacked the confessional. Bournisien defended it; he dwelled on the acts of restitution it inspired. He cited several different instances of thieves suddenly becoming honest men. Soldiers, approaching the tribunal of penitence, had felt the scales falling from their eyes. There was a minister in Fribourg—

His companion was asleep. He himself felt a bit warm in the heavy atmosphere of the room and opened the window. This awakened the pharmacist.

"Have a pinch of snuff," he said. "Take it. It'll clear your head."

There was an incessant howling somewhere in the distance.

"Do you hear a dog barking?" asked the pharmacist.

"People say that they sense death," answered the priest. "It's the same with bees. They leave the hive when someone dies." Homais did not criticize these superstitions since he had fallen asleep again.

Monsieur Bournisien, more robust, continued to move his lips awhile longer. Then his chin dropped gradually; his thick black book slipped from his hand and he began to snore.

So they remained facing each other, paunches protruding, faces puffy and scowling, finally united in the same human frailty after so much disagreement. They budged no more than the corpse beside them, which appeared to be sleeping.

Charles did not wake them when he came in. It was the last time. He had come to say farewell to her.

The aromatic herbs were still smoking and wisps of blue vapor mingled at the window with the incoming fog. There were a few stars out. The night was mild.

The wax from the candles fell in large drops onto the bedsheets. Charles watched them burn, straining his eyes at the yellow flames.

On Emma's satin dress, as white as a ray of moonlight, the watered texture shimmered. She seemed to disappear beneath it; and it seemed to him that she was escaping from herself and had blended in a confused way with the surroundings and the silence, with the night and the passing breeze, with the damp odors that were rising.

He suddenly saw her in the garden at Tostes on the bench

against the thorn hedge; or in the street in Rouen; on the doorstep of their house; in the yard at Les Bertaux. He could still hear the laughter of the boys dancing gaily beneath the apple trees. The room was filled with the scent of her hair, and her dress rustled in his arms, making a noise of crackling sparks. It was this same dress!

He stood a long time remembering his lost happiness, the way she carried herself, her gestures, the tone of her voice. After one wave of despair came another and still another, unceasingly, like the waters of an overflowing tide.

He was smitten by a terrible curiosity; slowly, with the tips of his fingers, his heart pounding, he lifted her veil. His cry of horror woke the other two men. They led him downstairs into the dining room. Then Félicité came up to say that he wanted a lock of her hair.

"Cut some off," said the apothecary. But she didn't dare, so he himself approached, the scissors in his hand. He was trembling so violently that he nicked the skin near the temples in several places. Finally, steeling himself against emotion, Homais made two or three random cuts which left white patches in the beautiful black hair.

The pharmacist and the curé resumed their occupations, not without occasional naps, of which they accused each other in turn each time they awoke. Then Monsieur Bournisien sprinkled the room with holy water and Homais threw some chlorine on the floor.

Félicité had set out for them, on the chest of drawers, a bottle of brandy, some cheese, and a large brioche. At about four in the morning the apothecary could stand it no longer.

"Lord," he sighed, "I'm really hungry."

The priest did not wait to be asked twice. He went out to say Mass and came back. Then they ate and drank, chuckling slightly without knowing why, enlivened by that vague feeling of gaiety that takes hold of us after gloomy vigils. As he drained his glass, the priest said to the pharmacist, throwing an arm over his shoulder: "We'll end up being friends!"

Downstairs in the hall they met the workers who were just arriving. For two hours Charles had to endure the torture of the hammer resounding on the wood. Then they brought her down in her oak coffin and enclosed it in the other two; but as the outer one was too large, they had to stuff the space between with the wool from a mattress. Finally, when the three lids were planed, nailed down, and soldered, they placed

it in front of the door. The house was thrown open and the
people of Yonville began to crowd in.

Old Rouault arrived and fainted away in the square at the
sight of the black cloth.

X

He had not received the pharmacist's letter until thirty-
six hours after the event; and out of consideration for his
feelings, Monsieur Homais had written it in such a fashion
that it was impossible for him to know what it was all about.

At first the old man collapsed as if struck down by apoplexy. Then he interpreted it to mean she *wasn't* dead. But
she might be. . . . Finally he put on his smock, picked up
his hat, strapped on his spurs, and went off at a gallop. All
along the road he was breathless and torn by anguish. Once
he even had to dismount. He could no longer see, began
hearing voices around him, and felt he was going mad.

Day broke. He saw three black hens roosting in a tree
and shuddered in terror at the omen. Then he promised
the Blessed Virgin three chasubles for the church and vowed
he would walk barefoot from the cemetery of Les Bertaux
to the chapel at Vassonville.

He rode into Maromme, shouting for the innkeeper, el-
bowed his way through the stable door, headed for the oat
sack, poured a bottle of sweet cider into the manger, and
remounted his nag, whose feet struck fire as it flew off.

He told himself that they would surely save her. The doctors would certainly find a cure. He was sure of it. He reminded himself of all the miraculous cures he had heard of.

Then he had a vision of her dead—there she was before
him, stretched out on her back in the middle of the road. He
drew rein and the hallucination vanished.

At Quincampoix he drank three cups of coffee in a row
to muster up his courage.

He thought that they might have made a mistake in the
name. He felt for the letter in his pocket but did not dare
open it.

Then he began to wonder if it were a practical joke on the part of someone who had a grudge against him. Besides, if she were dead, wouldn't he know it? But the countryside showed no unusual signs: the sky was blue, the trees swaying, a flock of sheep passed by. He caught sight of the village. They saw him rushing up on his horse, whipping it so furiously that its flanks dripped blood.

When he came to, he fell into Bovary's arms, crying: "My daughter! Emma! My child! Tell me—"

"I don't know, I don't know. It's a curse!" Charles replied, sobbing.

The apothecary separated them: "These dreadful details are useless. I'll explain things later. People are coming. Come now, be dignified! Be philosophical!"

The poor young man wanted to appear strong and he repeated several times: "Yes—courage!"

"All right then, me too," cried the old man. "I'll be brave, damn it all! I'll stay with her to the very end!"

The bell began tolling. Everything was ready. It was time to start out.

Sitting beside each other in a choir stall, they watched the three choristers constantly pass back and forth, chanting. The serpent player blew as hard as he could. Monsieur Bournisien, in full vestments, was singing in a shrill voice. He bowed before the tabernacle, lifted his hands, spread his arms. Lestiboudois moved about the church with his whale-bone staff. The coffin had been placed near the lectern between four rows of candles. Charles felt like getting up and blowing them out.

He tried, however, to kindle a religious feeling in himself, to lose himself in the hope of a future life in which he would see her. He pretended that she had gone off long ago on a trip to a far-distant place. But when he remembered that she lay in that coffin there, that it was all over, that they were going to carry her off and place her in the earth, he was seized by a black, despairing, furious rage. At times he would think he no longer felt anything; and he welcomed this lessening of his misery, although reproaching himself for being heartless.

They heard a sharp, regular noise—like the tapping of a metal-tipped cane—on the flagstones. It came from the far end of the church and stopped short in the side aisle. A man in a coarse brown jacket kneeled with difficulty. It was Hippolyte, the stableboy of the Golden Lion. He had put on his new leg.

One of the choristers went around the nave to take up the collection. The heavy copper coins rang in the collection plate one after the other.

"Hurry up, please! I can't stand it!" cried Bovary, angrily throwing a five-franc piece at him.

The churchman thanked him with a low bow.

They sang, kneeled, arose. It seemed to go on and on! He remembered how, once, a long time ago, in the early days, they were seated side by side during Mass. They had been on the other side, on the right, against the wall. The bell began to toll again. There was a great scraping of chairs. The pallbearers slipped their three poles under the bier and left the church.

Just then Justin appeared on the threshold of the pharmacy. He suddenly went back in, pale and unsteady on his feet.

People were stationed at windows to watch the procession pass. Charles walked in front, holding himself erect. He tried to look brave and nodded to those who poured out of lanes and doorways to join with the crowd. The six men, three on each side, walked slowly, slightly out of breath. The priest, choristers, and the two choirboys were reciting the *De profundis*, and their voices rose and fell rhythmically over the countryside. Occasionally they would disappear as the path curved, but the great silver cross was always visible between the trees.

The women followed, wrapped in black mantles with the hoods lowered; they carried large lighted candles in their hands. Charles felt himself weakening at this constant succession of prayers and tapers beneath the cloying smell of wax and cassocks. A fresh breeze was blowing. The rye and the colza were turning green. Droplets of dew glistened on the thorn hedge by the side of the road. All sorts of joyous sounds filled the air: the clatter of a distant cart rolling over the ruts, the echoing cry of a cock, the sound of a foal scampering off beneath the apple trees. Pink clouds dotted the clear sky and a bluish haze hung over the iris-covered thatched cottages. Charles recognized the yards as he passed by. He remembered other mornings like this one when after visiting some of his patients he would return home to her.

The black pall, strewn with white teardrops like beads,

would blow off at times and reveal the bier. The tired pall-bearers were slowing down, and the bier advanced in a series of jerks like a boat tossing at every wave.

They arrived at the cemetery.

The men continued all the way to the far end to a place in the grass where the grave had been dug.

They gathered around it, and as the priest spoke, the red earth piled up at the edges slipped back into the corners—noiselessly and unceasingly.

Then, when the four ropes were in place, they pushed the coffin over them. He watched it go down. It went down, down. . . .

Finally a thud was heard. The ropes creaked as they came back up. Then Bournisien took the spade that Lestiboudois held out to him; with his left hand, all the while sprinkling holy water with the right, he vigorously pushed in a large spadeful of earth; and the wood of the coffin, hit by the stones, made that terrible noise that sounds like the echo of eternity.

The priest passed the sprinkler to his neighbor. This was Monsieur Homais. He shook it solemnly, then held it out to Charles, who fell to his knees on the ground, and threw handfuls of earth, crying: "Farewell!" He blew her kisses and crawled toward the grave to be swallowed up with her.

They led him away, and he soon grew calmer, sensing perhaps, like the rest of them, a vague feeling of relief that it was over.

On the way back old Rouault began quietly smoking his pipe, which Homais privately thought quite out of place. He also noticed that Binet had not shown up, that Tuvache "had slipped away" after the Mass, and that Theodore, the notary's manservant, wore a blue coat "as if he couldn't find a black one, since it's the custom, devil take it!" He went from one group to another, giving vent to his observations. They were all deploring Emma's death, especially Lheureux, who had not failed to come to the burial.

"Poor little woman! Such a tragedy for her husband!"

The apothecary said: "If it hadn't been for me, you know, he might have done something fatal to himself."

"Such a dear lady. And to think that I saw her in my shop only last Saturday."

"I didn't have the time to prepare a short speech to make over the grave,'" said Homais.

Charles changed his clothes when they returned home and Rouault put on his smock again. It was a new one, and as he had kept wiping his eyes with his sleeves on the road, some dye had come off on his face. Now there were traces of tears that still showed through the layer of dust covering it.

Madame Bovary senior was with them. All three were silent. Finally the old man sighed: "Do you remember, my friend, that time I came to Tostes when you lost your first wife? And I consoled you? Then I was able to find things to say; but now—" He heaved a deep sigh and groaned: "It's the end for me, you know. I saw my wife die, then my son, and today my daughter." He wanted to go right back to Les Bertaux, saying that he wouldn't be able to sleep in this house. He even refused to see his grand-daughter.

"No, no, it would be too painful. But kiss her for me. Good-bye! You are a good lad. And you know, I'll never forget this," he said, smacking his thigh, "don't worry. You'll always have your turkey."

But when he reached the summit of the hill he turned back, as once before in parting from her he had turned around on the Saint-Victor road. The village windows were lit up by the oblique rays of the sun setting beyond the meadow. He shielded his eyes with his hand and looked in the distance, where he saw a walled enclosure in which the treetops showed black between white stones. Then he continued along the road at a slow trot, for his mare was limping.

Despite their weariness, Charles and his mother stayed up very late to talk. They discussed the old days and the future. She would come to live in Yonville and take care of the house. They would never part again. She was tactful and comforting, secretly rejoicing at having regained the affection that had eluded her so many years. Midnight sounded. The village, as usual, was silent. Charles, wide awake, lay thinking of her.

Rodolphe, who had been trapping in the woods all day to distract himself, slept peacefully in his château. Léon was sleeping too, in Rouen.

There was someone else who was not asleep at this hour. Between the firs, a kneeling boy was crying on her grave. His chest was shaking with sobs beneath the burden of great sorrow that was more tender than the moon and more unfathomable than the night. Suddenly the gate creaked. It was Lestiboudois, who had come to look for his spade, which he had forgotten earlier. He recognized Justin climbing the wall and then knew who the culprit was who had been stealing his potatoes.

The next day Charles sent for his daughter. She asked for Mamma and was told she was away on a trip and would bring her back some toys. Berthe mentioned her mother several times again; then she gradually forgot her. Bovary felt sick at heart at the child's cheerfulness. The pharmacist's words of consolation also were hard to bear.

Money troubles soon started again, Lheureux again urging his friend Vinçart on. Charles signed notes for some exorbitant sums since he was determined not to let the least bit of furniture that had belonged to "her" be sold. His mother was furious with him. He grew angrier than she. He had changed completely. She left the house for good.

Then everyone began taking advantage of him. Mademoiselle Lempereur sent a bill for six months' worth of piano lessons, even though Emma had never taken a single one, despite the receipt she had shown him—that had been an arrangement between the two women. The lending library sent in a bill for three years of subscription. Madame Rollet, the wet nurse, asked to be paid for delivering twenty letters, and when Charles asked for an explanation, had the tact to answer: "Oh, I've no idea. Personal matters, I think."

Each time he settled a debt, Charles thought it was the last, but others continually cropped up.

He sent out bills for outstanding accounts. He was shown letters his wife had sent, and so he had to apologize.

Félicité now wore Emma's dresses; not all of them, for he had kept some and would shut himself up in her dressing room to look at them. The maid was about her height, and often, seeing her from behind, Charles would be seized by an illusion and cry out: "Oh! Stay! Please stay!"

But at Whitsuntide she ran away from Yonville with Theodore, stealing all that remained of the wardrobe.

About this time the Widow Dupuis had the honor to announce to him the "marriage of her son, Monsieur Léon Dupuis, notary in Yvetot, to Mademoiselle Léocadie Leboeuf, of Bondeville." In the congratulatory letter he sent her,

Charles wrote this phrase: "How happy my poor wife would have been!"

One day as he was roaming aimlessly through the house, he climbed up to the attic. He felt a ball of thin paper beneath his slipper. He opened it and read: "Be brave, Emma. Be brave. I don't want to ruin your life." It was Rodolphe's letter. It had fallen to the floor between the trunks and had remained there until the wind coming in through the window pushed it toward the door. Charles stood there without moving, gaping at it—in the same spot where a desperate Emma, paler than he, had once wanted to die. Finally he made out a small *R* at the bottom of the second page. Who was it? He remembered Rodolphe's assiduous attentions, his sudden disappearance, and his air of constraint the two or three times they had met since. But the respectful tone of the letter fooled him.

"Maybe they loved each other platonically," he told himself.

Anyhow, Charles was not the sort of man who went right to the heart of things. He shut his eyes to the evidence, and his vague jealousy was lost in the immensity of his sorrow.

They all must have adored her, he thought. Certainly every man must have desired her. She appeared even more beautiful to him because of this; and he conceived for her a permanent, maddening desire that intensified his despair and that was limitless since it could never be satisfied.

To please her, as if she were still alive, he adopted her preferences and ideas. He bought himself patent-leather boots, began wearing white cravats. He waxed his moustache, signed promissory notes as she had done. She was corrupting him from beyond the grave.

He was obliged to sell the silverware, piece by piece, then the parlor furniture. All the rooms were stripped; but the bedroom, *her* bedroom, remained as it always had been. Charles would go up there after dinner. He would push the round table to the fire, pull up *her* armchair, and sit down facing it. A candle would burn in the gilded candlesticks. Berthe would sit near him, coloring pictures.

The poor man suffered to see her so badly dressed, her shoes without laces and the armholes of her smocks torn to the hips, for the housekeeper paid no attention to her. But she was so sweet and gentle, and her tiny head bent forward

so graciously, dropping her blond hair over pink cheeks,
that he was filled with infinite delight, with a pleasure laced
with bitterness like badly made wines tasting of resin. He
mended her toys, made cardboard puppets for her, or sewed
up the torn bodies of her dolls. If his eyes happened to light
on the workbox, a dangling ribbon, or even a pin stuck in
a crack of the table, he would begin to dream; and then he
looked so sad that she would feel sad too.

No one came to see them now, for Justin had run off to
Rouen, where he became a grocer's assistant, and the apothecary's children mingled less and less with Berthe. Monsieur
Homais did not care to prolong the intimacy in view of their
different social stations.

The blind man, who had not been helped at all by his
salve, had returned to the Bois-Guillaume hill, where he told
travelers of the pharmacist's vain attempt. It got so bad that
Homais, when he went into the city, cringed behind the curtains of the Hirondelle to avoid meeting him. He hated
him. For the sake of his own reputation, he sought to get
rid of him by any means; so he launched a secret campaign
against him, which revealed both the depth of his cunning
and the viciousness of his vanity. For six months in a row
paragraphs like this could be read in the *Rouen Beacon:*

Travelers to the fertile fields of Picardy have probably
noticed, on the Bois-Guillaume hill, a wretched creature
afflicted with a horrible facial wound. He annoys travelers,
persecutes them, imposes a veritable tax on them. Are we
still in those monstrous days of the Middle Ages when
vagabonds were permitted to display in our public places
the leprosy and scrofula they had brought back from the
Crusades?

Or:

Despite the laws against vagrancy, the approaches to our
large cities continue to be infested by bands of the poor.
Among them are some who move about alone and who
perhaps are not the least dangerous. What is the municipal
government going to do about it?

Then Homais invented anecdotes:

Yesterday, on the Bois-Guillaume hill, a skittish horse—

And then followed the story of an accident caused by the presence of the blind man.

He did such a good job that they jailed the blind man. But he was let out and began again. So did Homais. It was a battle. Homais was the victor, for his enemy was permanently committed to an asylum.

This success emboldened him. From then on there wasn't a dog run over in the district, a barn burned down, a wife beaten up that Homais did not immediately relate to the public, always guided by his love of progress and hatred of priests. He drew comparisons between public and parochial schools, to the detriment of the latter; he mentioned the Saint Bartholomew Massacre in connection with a one-hundred-franc grant to the Church; he denounced abuses and launched, to use his word, fireworks.

Homais was "undermining foundations"; he was becoming dangerous.

But he felt stifled in the narrow lines of journalism. He wanted to write a book, a "work"! So he composed his *General Statistical Survey of the Canton of Yonville,* Followed by *Climatological Observations.* Statistics led him toward philosophy. He began to concentrate on major issues: social problems, morals of the poor classes, fish breeding, rubber, railroads, etc. He began to feel ashamed about being a bourgeois. He affected "the artistic approach," took up smoking, bought two chic Pompadour statuettes to decorate his parlor.

He did not give up the pharmacy. On the contrary, he kept abreast of all discoveries. He followed every stage in the development of chocolates; he was the first to introduce the chocolate foods, *Cho-ca* and *Revalentia* into the Seine-Inférieure district. He was smitten with enthusiasm for the Pulvermacher hydroelectric belts and wore one himself. In the evening, when he removed his flannel undershirt, Madame Homais was dazzled by the golden spiral under which he almost disappeared. She felt her passion redoubled for this man more swathed than a Scythian and as splendid as a Magian priest.

He had some elaborate notions for Emma's tombstone. First he suggested a broken column with drapery, then a pyramid, then a Vestal temple, a sort of rotunda—or even a "pile of ruins." And in all his plans he included a weeping willow, which he considered the obligatory symbol of sorrow.

Charles and he traveled to Rouen together to see some tombstones at a monument works. They were accompanied by an artist named Vaufrilard, a friend of Bridoux, who kept making puns. Finally, after examining a hundred designs, asking for an estimate, and making a second trip to Rouen, Charles decided on a mausoleum that was to bear on its two main sides "a spirit carrying an extinguished torch."

For the inscription, Homais found nothing as impressive as *Sta viator* and that was as far as he could get. He racked his brain, constantly repeating *Sta viator*. Finally he discovered *amabilem conjugem calcas*—and this was adopted.

It was strange how Bovary was forgetting Emma, even while thinking continually about her. He was in despair when he found her image fading from his memory despite all his efforts to retain it. And yet he dreamed of her each night, always the same dream: he approached her, but she would crumble into dust before he could embrace her.

For one whole week he was seen entering the church every night. Monsieur Bournisien even visited him two or three times, then gave him up. Anyhow, the old man was becoming intolerant and fanatic, said Homais; he was thundering against the spirit of the times and never failed to preach every second week about the agony of Voltaire—who died eating his own excrement, as everyone knows.

Despite the frugal way Bovary lived, he was quite unable to pay off his old debts. Lheureux refused to renew a single note. Dispossession was imminent. Then he had recourse to his mother, who consented to let him take a mortgage on her property—but not without indulging in a good many recriminations against Emma. In return for her sacrifice, she asked for a shawl that had escaped Félicité's clutches. Charles refused to give it to her. They quarreled.

She made the first overtures toward reconciliation by suggesting that she take in the child, who would be a comfort to her in the house. Charles consented. But his courage failed him at the moment of parting. This time it was a permanent and complete break.

As his other ties weakened, he devoted himself more and more to his daughter. But he was worried about her. She coughed sometimes and she had red splotches on her cheeks.

Across the square, cheerful and flourishing, the pharmacist's family grew. Everything was going well with him. Na-

poleon helped in the laboratory; Athalie embroidered a cap
for him; Irma cut out paper tops to cover the jam jars; and
Franklin could recite the multiplication table all in one
breath. He was the happiest of fathers, the most fortunate
of men.

But a secret ambition was gnawing at him. Homais wanted
the cross of the Legion of Honor. He did not lack the
proper qualifications:

1. He had displayed an unlimited devotion at the time of
   the cholera epidemic.
2. He had published at his own expense various works
   for the public welfare, such as (a) his memorandum
   Cider, Its Manufacture and its Effects; (b) his observations on the woolly aphis, sent to the Academy; (c)
   his volume of statistics, and even his pharmacist's
   thesis, not to mention his membership in "several
   scientific societies" (he was member of one).

"Were it only," he exclaimed, swiveling around, "my distinguished record as a volunteer fireman!"

Then Homais cultivated the powers that be. He secretly
rendered important services to the prefect during the elec-
tions. In short, he sold himself; he prostituted himself. He
even addressed a petition to the king in which he asked that
"justice be done." He called him "Our Good King" and
compared him to Henri IV.

Every morning the apothecary would tear open the newspaper to look for his nomination; it did not appear. Finally,
in his impatience, he had a star of the Cross of Honor de-
signed in his garden plot, with two small tufts of grass running off at the top to imitate the ribbon. He would walk
around it with his arms crossed, pondering the ineptness of
the government and the ingratitude of men.

Out of respect, or from a kind of perverse sensuality that
caused him to proceed slowly in his investigations, Charles
had not yet opened the secret compartment of a rosewood
desk that Emma had always used. But one day he finally
sat down before it, turned the key, and pushed the spring.

All of Léon's letters were there. This time, there could be
no doubt! He devoured them to the very end, searched every
corner, all the furniture, all the drawers, felt behind the
walls, sobbed violently, screamed, crazed with rage. He found
a box and kicked it open. Rodolphe's portrait stared out at

him full in the face, in the midst of a jumble of love
letters.

His depression astounded people. He never went out any
more, received no one, even refused to call on his patients.
It was assumed that he had "locked himself up to get
drunk."

Sometimes, however, some curious soul would look over the
hedge and gaze in amazement at this unkempt, bearded
man dressed in filthy clothes, crying aloud wildly as he
walked in the garden.

In the summer evenings he would take the little girl with
him and go to the cemetery. They would return at nightfall
when there was no more light in the square except for
Binet's window.

But he could not indulge his sadness to the full since
there was no one around to share it with. So he would visit
Madame Lefrançois to be able to talk of *her*. The landlady
heeded him with only one ear, however, having her own
troubles, as he had his. For Monsieur Lheureux had finally
set up *les favorites du commerce*, and Hivert, who had
earned a good reputation for running errands, was demanding more money and threatening to hire himself out to
her competitor.

One day when Charles had gone to the Argueil market
to sell his horse, his last asset, he met Rodolphe.

They paled, seeing each other. Rodolphe, who had merely
sent his card when Emma died, stammered out some excuses at first, then grew bolder, and even had the nerve
(it was August and a very warm day) to invite him to take
a bottle of beer in the tavern.

Facing him, with his elbows on the table, Rodolphe chewed
his cigar as he spoke, and Charles lost himself in daydreams
about this face that she had loved. In it, he felt as if he
were seeing something of her again. It was very strange. He
would have liked to be this man.

The other man continued to talk about farming, livestock,
manure, stopping up with conventional phrases all the gaps
into which an embarrassing allusion might have slipped.
Charles was not listening. Rodolphe noticed this and studied
the passage of his memories on his mobile face. It reddened
after a while, the nostrils twitched, and the lips trembled.
There was even an instant when Charles, filled with somber
fury, fixed his eyes on Rodolphe, who stopped talking out

of fear. But very soon the same mournful lassitude reappeared on his face.

"I don't blame you," he said.

Rodolphe remained mute. Charles, with his head in his hands, repeated in a muffled voice and in a resigned tone of infinite sadness: "No, I don't blame you, anymore."

He even added a rhetorical phrase, the only one he ever uttered: "Fate is to blame."

Rodolphe, who had manipulated that fate, found him much too easygoing for a man in his situation—rather comic and even a bit contemptible.

The next day Charles sat down on the bench in the arbor. Rays of light passed through the trellis; the vine leaves cast their shadows over the gravel, the jasmine scented the air, the sky was blue, beetles buzzed about the blossoming lilies. Charles was choking up like an adolescent in love in the vague flood of emotion that swelled his unhappy heart.

Berthe, who had not seen him all afternoon, came to fetch him for dinner at seven.

His head was thrown back against the wall. His eyes were closed, mouth open, and in his hand he held a long strand of black hair.

"Come, Papa," she said. Thinking he wanted to play, she pushed him gently. He fell to the ground. He was dead.

Thirty-six hours later, in response to the apothecary's request, Monsieur Canivet came. He peformed an autopsy but found nothing.

When everything was sold, there remained twelve francs and seventy-five centimes—enough to pay for Mademoiselle Bovary's fare to her grandmother's. The old lady died that same year. Since old Rouault was now paralyzed, an aunt took her in. She is poor and has sent her to work in a cotton mill to earn a living.

Since Bovary's death, three doctors have succeeded one another in Yonville without being able to establish themselves, so effectively does Monsieur Homais rout them. He has an enormous clientele. The authorities cultivate him and public opinion protects him.

He has just received the Legion of Honor.

The TRIAL
of "MADAME BOVARY"

The TRIAL of "MADAME BOVARY"

Opening Speech for the Prosecution
by the Imperial Attorney, Monsieur Ernest Pinard

Gentlemen, at the onset of these proceedings the prosecution is faced with a difficulty that it cannot conceal. It does not consist in the nature of the charge itself, although the terms offenses against public morals and religion are indeed a little vague, a little elastic, and it will become necessary to specify them. Yet, after all, when one is addressing upright and experienced minds, it is easy to come to an understanding in that regard, to determine whether a particular page of a book casts a slur upon morals or religion. The difficulty, then, is not caused by the charge, but rather by the length of the work that you will have to judge. For the work concerned is an entire novel. If it were an article in a newspaper, you would be able to see at once where the offense begins and ends: the prosecution reads out the article and submits it to your judgment. Here we are not concerned with a newspaper article but with a complete novel that begins on the first of October, ends on the fifteenth of December, and consists of six installments in the *Revue de Paris* of 1856. What is to be done in this situation? What is the prosecutor's role? Is he to read the whole novel? It would be impossible. On the other hand, to read only the passages under indictment would be to lay ourselves open to a most justified reproach. One could say to us: if you do not present the case in all of its parts, if you omit what precedes and what follows the particular passages, it stands to reason that you are stifling the argument by restricting the field of dispute. To avoid this dilemma, there is only one course to follow, and this is it: to tell you first the story of the entire novel without reading it to you, without referring to any incriminating passage; subsequently to read out to you these passages;

and finally to meet the objections that may be raised against
the general principles of this prosecution.

What is the title of this novel: *Madame Bovary*. It is
a title that tells nothing in itself. There is a second one in
parentheses: *Provincial Morals*. There again is a title that
does not reveal the author's intentions but that gives an inkling
of them. The author has not chosen to follow one or another
philosphic system true or false; he has chosen to paint a picture from life, and you will see what picture! The book
begins and ends indeed with the husband, but the most important portrait of the work, which throws light upon the other
painting, is certainly that of Madame Bovary.

I am now telling the story, I am not quoting. We find
the husband at school, and already, it must be said, the
child shows what the husband is going to be. He is extremely dull-witted and shy, so shy that when he arrives at
school and they ask him his name, he begins by answering
"Charbovari." He is so dull-witted that he works without
making progress. He is never the first, nor is he ever the
last of the class; he is a model, if not of incompetence, at
least of ridiculousness to the school. After finishing school,
he goes to study medicine at Rouen, in a room four flights
up, overlooking the Seine, which his mother had rented for
him in the house of a dyer of her acquaintance. It is there
that he does his medical studies, and where he manages
little by little to achieve not the degree of doctor of medicine,
but that of health officer. He went to the wine shops, he
missed some lectures, but when all was said and done his
main dissipation was playing dominoes. There you have
Monsieur Bovary.

He is going to get married. His mother finds him a wife,
the widow of a bailiff at Dieppe; she is virtuous and ugly,
she is forty-five years old and has an income of twelve
hundred francs. However, the notary who held the capital
of the income went off to America one fine morning, and
the younger Madame Bovary was so stricken, so strongly affected by this unforeseen blow, that she died of it. There
is the first marriage, there is the first scene.

Monsieur Bovary, now a widower, thinks of remarrying.
He consults his memories; he has no need to go far; at once
he recalls the daughter of a neighboring farmer who had
singularly aroused Madame Bovary's suspicions, Mademoiselle Emma Rouault. Farmer Rouault had only the one
daughter, educated by the Ursuline nuns in Rouen. She took
little interest in the farm; her father wished to marry her off.
The health officer presents himself; he is not difficult about
the dowry, and you understand that with such inclinations on
both sides, things move quickly. The marriage is celebrated.

Monsieur Bovary is at his wife's feet; he is the happiest of men, the blindest of husbands; his only concern is to anticipate his wife's desires.

Here Monsieur Bovary's role becomes dim; Madame Bovary's becomes the principal subject of the book.

Gentlemen, did Madame Bovary love her husband or try to love him? No, and at the very beginning there took place what one may call the initiation scene. From that moment another horizon stretched before her, a new life appeared to her. The owner of the château de la Vaubyessard had given a great fete. They had invited the health officer, they had invited his wife, and for her it had been like an initiation into all the voluptuous excitements of the senses. She had glimpsed the Duke de Laverdière, who had had successes at court; she had waltzed with a viscount and had felt an agitation she had never known before. From that moment she had lived for a new life; her husband, everything that surrounded her, had become intolerable to her. One day while looking through a drawer she had come upon a piece of wire that pierced her finger; it was the wire from her marriage bouquet. In an effort to get her out of the boredom that consumed her, Monsieur Bovary sacrificed his practice and went to settle at Yonville. It is here that the scene of her first downfall takes place. We are now at the second installment. Madame Bovary arrives at Yonville, and there, the first person she meets, the first person on whom she fixes her attention is not the local notary, but the notary's only clerk, Léon Dupuis. He is a very young man who is studying law and who is about to leave for the capital. Anyone but Monsieur Bovary would have become perturbed by the visits of the young clerk, but Monsieur Bovary was so naïve that he believed in his wife's virtue; Léon, inexperienced, shared the conviction. He departed, the chance was lost, but chances are easily found again. In the neighborhood of Yonville there lived a Monsieur Rodolphe Boulanger (you see that I am telling a story). He was a man thirty-four years old, of a brutal nature; he had had much success with women of easy virtue; at that time he had an actress as his mistress; he set eyes upon Madame Bovary, she was young, charming; he resolved to make her his mistress.

It was easily done; three opportunities were enough for him. The first time he went to the Agricultural Show, the second time he paid her a visit, the third time he took her riding, as her husband thought this necessary for her health; and it is here, on their first visit to the forest, that her ruin takes place. They have innumerable trysts at Rodolphe's château, or even more often in the health officer's garden. The

lovers attain the extreme limits of sensual pleasure! Madame
Bovary wants to elope with Rodolphe, Rodolphe does not
dare to say no, but he writes her a letter in which he tries
to prove to her with many reasons why he cannot take her
away. Prostrated by the receipt of this letter, Madame Bovary has brain fever; typhoid fever develops. The illness
kills her love, but she survives. This was the second scene.

I now come to the third. The affair with Rodolphe had
been followed by a religious reaction, but it had been short;
Madame Bovary was about to fall again. Her husband had
considered that entertainment would be helpful to her convalescence, and he took her to Rouen. In a box at the theater facing the one occupied by Monsieur and Madame
Bovary was Léon Dupuis, the young notary's clerk who had
completed his legal studies in Paris and had returned from
them remarkably learned, remarkably experienced. He goes to
see Madame Bovary; he proposes a rendezvous to her. Madame Bovary suggests the cathedral. On coming out of the
cathedral, Léon proposes that they get into a closed cab. At
first she resists, but Léon tells her that things are done in that
way in Paris, and so she opposes him no further. Her downfall
takes place in the cab. Their assignations multiply, first with
Léon, as with Rodolphe, in the health officer's garden, and
then in a room Léon had rented at Rouen. But eventually
she also grows tired of this second love, and it is then that
the scenes of desolation begin that form the last of the novel.

Madame Bovary had lavished presents on Rodolphe and
on Léon, she had lived a life of luxury, and in order to meet
such expenses she had signed many promissory notes. She
had obtained a power of attorney from her husband enabling
her to manage their joint resources; she had found a moneylender who had her sign the notes, and these, not being paid
when they fell due, were renewed in the name of an
accomplice. Then had come official notices, judgments, bankruptcy, seizure, and finally notice of sale of the furniture be-
longing to Monsieur Bovary, who was unaware of all of it.
Reduced to the most cruel extremity, Madame Bovary begged
for money from the whole world and obtained it from no
one. Léon does not have any, and he recoils appalled at the
idea of a crime she suggests as a means of obtaining it.
Reaching the last stages of humiliation, Madame Bovary goes
to see Rodolphe; she does not succeed; Rodolphe does not
have three thousand francs. For her there remains only one
way out. To apologize to her husband? No. To explain it all
to him? But this husband would have the generosity to pardon her, and that is a humiliation she cannot accept: she
poisons herself. Then come the painful scenes. We have the

husband beside the icy corpse of his wife. He has her wedding dress brought; he orders her to be shrouded in it and
for her remains to be enclosed in a triple coffin.

One day he opens her writing desk and there finds Rodolphe's letters and those of Léon. You think then that his
love will die? No, no, on the contrary, it is stimulated, it is
inflamed for this woman whom others have possessed, just
because of these mementos of passion that she has left to
him; and from that moment he neglects his practice, his family; he lets the last remnants of his patrimony be dispersed to
the winds, and one day they find him dead in the arbor of
his garden, holding in his hands a long strand of black hair.

There is the novel; I have told it in full, without suppressing any scene. It is called *Madame Bovary;* you may
give it another title and call it with justice *A History of the
Adulteries of a Provincial Wife.*

Gentlemen, the first part of my task is fulfilled: I have
told the story; now I am going to quote, and after the quotations will come the accusations on two counts—offense against
public morals, offense against religious morals. The offense
against public morals is in the lascivious pictures that I will
place before your eyes; the offense against religious morals is
in the mingling of voluptuous images with sacred things. I come
now to the quotations. I shall be brief, for you will read the
novel in its entirety. I will restrict myself to put before you
four scenes, or rather four pictures. The first will portray her
love for and her downfall with Rodolphe, the second a religious bout between the two adulteries, the third the affair
with Léon, and the fourth the death of Madame Bovary.

Before uncovering for you these canvases, allow me to
inquire about Monsieur Flaubert's tone and color, his brush-
work, for after all, if his novel is a painting it will be necessary for us to know to what school he belongs, what colors
he employs, and what manner of a portrait he has painted
of his heroine.

The author's general color, permit me to say to you, is a
lascivious color, before, during, and after these transgressions. Madame Bovary is a child, she is ten or twelve years
old, she is at the Ursuline convent. At this age where the girl
is still unformed, where the woman cannot feel the first excitements that disclose a new world, she confesses her sins:

> When she went to confession, she would invent trivial
> sins in order to prolong her stay there, on her knees in
> the shadow, hands clasped, her face at the grill as the
> priest whispered above her. The references to fiancé, hus-

band, heavenly lover, and eternal marriage that recur in sermons awakened unexpected joys within her.*

Is it natural for a little girl to invent trivial sins when one knows that for a child it is the smallest things that are the most difficult to tell? To show her at such an age inventing trivial sins in the shadows while the priest whispers, bringing to her mind the similes of fiancé, of husband, of heavenly lover, and of eternal marriage, which she feels like a thrill of pleasure—is this not to evoke what I have called a lascivious painting?

Now, do you want to see Madame Bovary in her simplest actions, in her natural state, without a lover, without a fault? I pass over the mention of "the next day" and over this bride "whose self-control gave no opportunity for conjecture,"† which is already a more than equivocal turn of phrase; but would you like to know what was the husband's state?

This bridegroom of the next day, "who could have been taken for the virgin of the night before," and this bride, "whose self-control gave no opportunity for conjecture."‡ This husband who gets up and departs, "his heart filled with the joys of the previous night, his spirit calm, flesh content," and who goes away "pondering his happiness like those who after dinner still savor the taste of the truffles they are digesting." §

I must insist, gentlemen, on showing up the hallmark of Monsieur Flaubert's literary brushstrokes. At times there are strokes that mean a great deal, and these strokes cost him nothing.

And then at the château de la Vaubyessard, do you know what draws the eye of this young woman, what strikes her most? It is always the same thing; it is the Duke de Laverdière, who was said to have "been Marie-Antoinette's lover between Messieurs de Coigny and de Lauzun" and at whom "Emma could not keep herself from staring, as on someone extraordinary and august. He had lived at Court and slept in the bed of queens!" ‖

That is only a historical parenthesis, one might say? An unfortunate and useless parenthesis! History may be able to authorize suspicions, but it has no right to elevate them to certainties. History has spoken of the queen's necklace in any number of novels, history has spoken of a thousand things,

* p.56
† p.51
‡ p.51
§ p.54
‖ p.67

but these are only suspicions, and, I repeat, I do not know that history has authorized anyone to transform these suspicions into certainties. And when Marie-Antoinette has died with the dignity of a sovereign and the calm of a Christian, the blood that has been shed ought to erase all faults, and even more so, suspicions. God knows, Monsieur Flaubert did need a striking image to depict his heroine, and he has chosen that particular one to express both Madame Bovary's depraved instincts and her ambition!

Madame Bovary is supposed to waltz very well, and here she is waltzing:

> They began slowly, then moved more rapidly. Everything was turning around them, the lights, furniture, paneling, and the floor, like a disk on a pivot. Passing near the doors, the hem of Emma's dress flared out against her partner's trousers; their legs intertwined; he looked down at her, she raised her eyes to him; a numbness overcame her, she stopped. They started again and the viscount, with a more rapid movement, swept her away, disappeared with her to the end of the gallery, where, out of breath, she almost fell and for one moment leaned her head on his chest. And then, still turning, but more gently now, he led her back to her place; she leaned back against the wall and put her hand before her eyes.*

I know very well that people do waltz a little in this way, but that does not make it any the more moral.

Take Madame Bovary in her most simple actions. It is always the same kind of brushwork, the same on every page. Even Justin, the servant of the druggist next door, is suddenly awestruck when he is received in the privacy of this woman's dressing room. He is haunted by his voluptuous admiration even in the kitchen:

> His elbow on the long board on which she [Félicité, Madame Bovary's maid] was ironing, he would look avidly at all the female garments strewn around him: dimity petticoats, fichus, muslin collars, and pantaloons with drawstrings, voluminous around the hips and tapering near the bottom.
> "What's this for?" the boy would ask, stroking a crinoline or fingering some hooks.
> "Haven't you ever seen anything?" Félicité replied with a laugh. ... †

The husband also wonders, in the presence of this sweet-

* p.70
† p.185

smelling woman, if the scent comes from her skin or from
her petticoat:

> ... every night he would come home to a glowing fire,
> the table set, the furniture arranged comfortably, and a
> charming woman, neatly dressed, smelling so fresh you
> wondered where the fragrance came from and whether it
> wasn't her skin lending the scent to her petticoat.*

Enough quoting of details! Now you know how Madame
Bovary appears in repose, when she is tantalizing no one,
when she is not sinning, when she is still completely innocent, when on her return from an appointment she is not
yet beside a husband whom she detests; now you understand the general color of the painting, the general appearance of Madame Bovary. The author has taken the greatest
pains, has employed all the marvels of his style to paint this
woman. Has he tried to show her from the point of view
of intelligence? Never. Of feeling? That neither. Of mind?
No. Of physical beauty? Not even that. Oh! I know very
well that there is a most brilliant portrait of Madame Bovary
after the adultery; but the picture is primarily lascivious,
the poses are voluptuous, the beauty of Madame Bovary is
the beauty of enticement.

I now come to the four principal passages; I shall quote
only four; I intend to limit my field. I have said that the
first concerns the love affair with Rodolphe, the second
the religious conversion, the third the affair with Léon, and
the fourth her death.

Let us look at the first. Madame Bovary is near to her
downfall, ready to succumb: "The domestic monotony"
pushed her to luxurious fancies, "the conjugal embraces
evoked adulterous desires. ... She cursed herself for not having loved him [Léon]. She thirsted for his lips." †

What had first captivated Rodolphe and put the thought
into his head? The billowing of Madame Bovary's dress and
its clinging to her bodice as she moved! Rodolphe has brought
his servant to Bovary to have him bled. The servant faints,
Madame Bovary is holding the basin:

> Madame Bovary picked the basin up to put it under
> the table. As she bent down, her dress (a yellow summer
> frock with four flounces, long-waisted and wide-skirted)
> billowed around her over the floor. She was slightly un-
> steady on her legs as she stooped and stretched her arms,

* p.77
† p.131

and the folds of the fabric collapsed in a few places in response to her gestures.*

Here also are Rodolphe's thoughts:

He pictured Emma in the room, first dressed as he had seen her and then nude.†

This is the first day that they speak together:

They were looking at one another. A supreme desire was causing their dry lips to quiver. Gently, without effort, their fingers intertwined.‡

Those are the preliminaries to her downfall. Now we must read the downfall itself:

When the outfit was ready, Charles wrote to Monsieur Boulanger that his wife awaited his convenience and that they were counting on his kindness.

At noon the next day Rodolphe arrived at Charles's door with two riding horses. One had pink pompons on its ears and a buckskin sidesaddle.

Rodolphe was wearing high soft-leather boots. He told himself that she had probably never seen their like. Emma was indeed charmed by his appearance when he appeared on the landing in his long velvet coat and his white tricot riding breeches. . . .

Emma's horse broke into a gallop as soon as it felt soft ground. Rodolphe kept alongside. §

And there they are in the forest:

He led her farther along, around a small pond where the green duckweed covered the water. . . .
"I shouldn't, I shouldn't," she said. "I'm mad to listen to you."
"Why? Emma—Emma—"
"Oh, Rodolphe!" the young woman said slowly, leaning on his shoulder.
The cloth of her habit clung to the velvet of his coat. She threw back her head, her white throat swelled in a sigh, and without resisting, tears streaming, with a long shudder and her face hidden, she gave herself to him.||

When she got up again, when, after having shaken off the languors of love, she returned home, to this home where she would find a husband who adored her, after her first trans-

* p.135
† p.137
‡ p.153
§ p.159
|| p.162

gression, after this first adultery, after this first fall, is it remorse, the sense of remorse that she feels in the face of this
betrayed husband who adores her? No! With head held
high, she returns home, glorifying adultery:

> ... when she saw her reflection in the mirror, she was
> astounded at her appearance. Her eyes had never been so
> large, so black, nor of such a depth. She was transfigured
> by some subtle change permeating her entire being.
>   She kept telling herself, "I have a lover! A lover!"
> relishing the thought like that of some unexpected second
> puberty. So she was finally going to possess those joys of
> love, that fever of happiness, of which she had so long
> despaired. She was entering into something marvelous
> where all would be passion, ecstasy, delirium... *

Thus, from this first transgression, from this first fall,
she makes a glory of adultery, she sings a hymn to adultery, to its poetry, its pleasures. There, gentlemen, is what I
find much more dangerous, much more immoral than the
downfall itself!

Gentlemen, all else pales beside this glorification of adultery, even the nighttime trysts several days later:

> Rodolphe would announce his presence by throwing a
> handful of gravel against the shutters. She would jump
> up. Sometimes she had to wait because Charles had a
> habit of sitting by the fireside and chattering interminably.
>   She would rage with impatience. If looks could have
> done it, she would have pushed him out the window. Fi-
> nally she would begin undressing, then pick up a book
> and start quietly reading with obvious pleasure. Charles,
> already in bed, would call to her.
>   "Emma, come to bed, it's late," he would say.
>   "I'm coming," she would answer.
>   But as the candles were too bright for his eyes, he
> would turn toward the wall and fall asleep. Then, holding
> her breath, she would sneak out of the room, a smile
> on her face and her heart pounding, half undressed.
>   Rodolphe had a voluminous cloak that he would wrap
> around her. He would wind his arms around her waist and
> lead her silently to the back of the garden.
>   They would stay in the arbor on the same bench of
> rotting wood where in the old days Léon had looked at

her so lovingly in the summer nights. She rarely thought
of him now.

The stars shone through the leafless jasmine branches.
They could hear the river flowing behind them and an
occasional crackling of dry reeds on the bank. Great
masses of shadow loomed up against the obscurity, and
sometimes, rising as if with a shudder, they would advance
like huge black waves ready to engulf them. The cold
of the night made them hold each other even more
tightly; the sighs emerging from their lips seemed louder;
their eyes, which they could discern only with difficulty,
seemed even larger; and in the midst of the silence, their
whispered words fell crystal clear on their souls and echoed
and reechoed with continuing vibrations.*

Gentlemen, do you know anywhere of a more expressive
language? Have you ever seen a more lascivious painting?
Listen further:

Never had Madame Bovary been so beautiful as now.
She had that indefinable beauty that comes from joy, enthusiasm, and success, a beauty that is but the blending of
temperament with circumstances. Her desires, her regrets, her experience of sensual pleasure, and the continually youthful illusions had nurtured her gradually, as
fertilizer, rain, wind, and sunshine nurture a flower, and
she finally blossomed forth in all the fullness of her being.
Her eyelids seemed purposely shaped for her long amorous
gazes, in which the pupils disappeared, while her heavy
breathing caused her delicately chiseled nostrils to flare and
raised the fleshy corners of her upper lip (which was
lightly shaded by a slight black down). One would have
said that some artist skilled in depravity had arranged the
coil of hair on the nape of her neck. It was wound
carelessly, in a heavy mass, and loosened every day by
the chance meetings with her lover. The inflections of her
voice became more languid, and also her body. A certain
penetrating subtlety detached itself even from the folds
of her dress and the instep of her foot. As he had during
the first days of their marriage, Charles now found her
delicious and completely irresistible.†

Until now this woman's beauty had consisted in her
grace, in her appearance, in her clothes; at last she has
been shown to you unveiled, and you can say if adultery has
not made her more beautiful:

* p.168
† p.191

"Take me away," she sobbed. "Take me away. Please!"
She kissed him passionately, as if to draw the unexpected consent from his mouth.*

There you have a portrait, gentlemen, as Monsieur Flaubert knows how to paint them. How this woman's eyes di-
late! What an enchantment has been shed over her since her
fall! Has her beauty ever been so dazzling as on the day
after her downfall, as on the days which followed her sin?
What the author is showing you is the poetry of adultery,
and once more I ask you if these lascivious pages are not
profoundly immoral!

I come now to the second passage. The second passage
is about a religious change. Madame Bovary has been very
ill, at death's door. She comes back to life, her convalescence
is marked by a transitory religious period:

Abbé Bournisien came to see her at that hour. He would
ask about her health, bring her the news, and try to nudge
her toward religion with some unctuous gossip that was
not without charm. The very sight of his cassock comforted
her. †

At last she is going to take Communion. I do not very
much like to find sacred matters treated in a novel, but if
they are mentioned, they must at the very least not have
been travestied by the language. Is there anything, in this
adulterous woman who goes to Communion, of the faith of
the repentant Magdalen? No, no, it is still the passionate
woman looking for illusions, and who looks for them in the
most sacred, the most august things.

One day, at the height of her illness, she believed herself dying and asked for Communion; and as the preparations for the sacrament went on in her room, as they
arranged the dresser with its clutter of medicine bottles into
an altar and Félicité scattered dahlia petals over the floor,
Emma sensed something powerful passing over her, freeing
her from all her pains, from all perception and feeling.
Her body, freed of its burden, no longer thought; another
life was beginning; it seemed to her that her being, ascending toward God, was going to be destroyed in that love
like a burning incense that is dissolved in smoke. ‡
In what language does one pray to God with the words

addressed to a lover in the effusions of adultery? We shall
doubtless be told of local color, we shall hear the excuse that
a romantic, fanciful woman does not, even in matters religious,
do things like the rest of the world. There is no local color
that excuses this mixture! Voluptuous one day, devout the
next, no woman, even in other countries, even under the sky
of Spain or of Italy, murmurs to God the adulterous endearments she gave to her lover. You will appraise this language, gentlemen, and you will not excuse these words of
adultery introduced, as it were, into the sanctuary of the
Divinity! That was the second passage; I come now to the
third, which is about the continuation of adultery.

After the religious period, Madame Bovary is again ready
to fall. She goes to the theater in Rouen. *Lucia di Lammermoor* was playing. Emma thought back on her past:

> Ah! If, in the freshness of her beauty, before the defile-
> ments of marriage and the disillusionments of adultery—
> [there are those who would have said "the disillusion-
> ments of marriage and the defilements of adultery"]—
> before the defilements of marriage and the disillusionments
> of adultery, she had been able to offer her life to some gen-
> erous, solid heart. Then virtue, tenderness, sensual delights,
> and duty would have mingled. Never would she have fallen
> from such high happiness.*

When she saw the actor Lagardy on the stage, "she wanted to run into his arms, to take refuge in his strength as in
the incarnation of love itself, and to say to him, to cry out:
'Take me away, take me with you, let us go! I am yours,
yours; all my passion and all my dreams are yours!'"
Léon was behind her:

> He stood behind her, leaning his shoulder against the
> wall of the box, and she quivered occasionally at the warm
> breath from his nostrils blowing into her hair. †

A moment ago you were told of the defilements of marriage; now again adultery is going to be shown to you in
all of its poetry, its ineffable charm. I have said that the
author might at least have modified the expressions and said
"the disillusionments of marriage and the defilements of adultery." Very often, when one is married, instead of the cloud-
less happiness one had expected, one encounters sacrifice

* p.217
† p.219

and bitterness. The word "disillusionment" may therefore be justified; the word "defilement" cannot be.

Léon and Emma made a rendezvous at the cathedral. They conversed there, where people do not converse. They went out:

A street urchin was playing on the pavement. "Get me a cab!" The child flew off like a shot . . .

"Ah! Léon, really—I don't know—if I ought—" she simpered. Then, with a more serious expression: "It's very improper, you know."

"How so?" answered the clerk. "It's done in Paris!" And that statement convinced her. It was an irresistible argument.*

We know now, gentlemen, that her downfall did not take place in the cab. Because of scruples that do him honor, the editor of the *Revue* suppressed the passage about her downfall in the cab. But if the *Revue de Paris* draws the blinds of the cab, it allows us to enter the room where their trysts take place.

Emma wants to leave, for she had promised that she would return the same evening. "Besides, Charles was expecting her; and she already felt in her heart that cowardly submissiveness that is, for many women, both the punishment and the atonement of their adultery."

Léon would keep walking along the sidewalk. She would follow him to his hotel. He would go up, open the door, and go in; and then, what a passionate embrace!

After the kisses came an outpouring of words. They told each other all the woes of the past week, their misgivings, their anxieties about letters; but now all that was forgotten and they looked at each other laughing with sensual delight and uttering terms of endearment.

The bed was a large mahogany one shaped like a boat. The red silk curtains that hung from the ceiling were bunched very low near the bell-shaped headboard—and nothing in the world was as beautiful as her dark hair and white skin standing out against the deep red when she covered her face with her two hands in a gesture of modesty and revealed her nude arms.

The warm room with its noise-muffling rug, its gay ornaments, and soft light, seemed exactly right for the intimacies of passion. †

* p.232
† p.250

You see what takes place in that room. It is another passage of great importance—as a lascivious painting!

How they loved that dear room filled with gaiety, despite its slightly faded splendor. They always found the furniture as they had left it, and sometimes even found hairpins beneath the base of the clock that she had forgotten the previous Thursday. They would sit and eat by the fire on a small table inlaid with rosewood. Emma would carve the food and put the pieces into his plate, chattering all the while, and she would laugh loudly and dissolutely when the champagne froth spilled over the fragile glass onto the rings on her fingers. They were so completely lost in each other that they actually believed they were living in their own house and would remain there until death like a couple eternally young. They said *our room, our rug, our armchairs;* she even said *our slippers.* They were a gift from Léon, in response to a whim of hers— pink satin slippers trimmed with swansdown. Her leg dangled in midair when she sat on his lap, since she was too short for it to reach the floor; and the charming backless little slipper was held on solely by the toes of her bare foot.

For the first time in his life he was tasting the inexpressible subtlety of feminine grace. He had never before encountered this refinement of speech, this quiet elegance of dress, these poses of a soothed dove. He admired the raptures of her spirit and the laces of her petticoat. Moreover, wasn't she "a woman of the world"—and a married woman? In other words, a real mistress.*

There, gentleman, was a description that will leave no doubt, I hope, as to the justification of our criminal charge? Here is another, or rather, here is the continuation of the same scene:

She offered tender words and kisses that drove him mad. Where, where had she learned this corruption, so deep and yet so disguised that it appeared almost disembodied? †

Oh! I can understand the disgust her husband inspired in her when he would embrace her on her return; I can understand perfectly that when meetings of this kind had taken

* p.251
† p.262

place, she felt a horror at night at having "to sleep next to him." *

This is not all; there is a last picture that I cannot omit; she had finally become wearied by passion:

> She kept promising herself a profound joy for their next meeting; then she would admit to herself that she had felt nothing extraordinary. This disappointment soon gave way to a renewed hope, and Emma would return to him more impassioned and avid. She would undress savagely, tearing at the thin lacing of her corset, which fell down around her hips like a gliding snake. She would tiptoe on her bare feet to see once more if the door were locked, then she would drop all her clothes in one movement—and pale, without speaking, solemn, she would fall against his chest with one long shudder. †

Here I point out two things, gentlemen: a painting which is admirable with respect to talent, but a painting which is abominable from the point of view of morality. Yes, Monsieur Flaubert knows how to beautify his paintings with all the resources of art, but without the circumspection of art. With him there is no reticence, no veil; he shows nature in all of its nudity, in all of its coarseness!

Here is another passage:

> They knew each other too well to feel those mutual revelations of possession that multiply its joys a hundredfold. She was as sated with him as he was tired of her. Emma was finding in adultery all the banalities of marriage.‡

Banalities of marriage, poetry of adultery! Sometimes it is the defilement of marriage, sometimes it is banalities, but always it is the poetry of adultery. You see, gentlemen, the situations Monsieur Flaubert likes to portray, and unhappily he portrays them all too well.

I have related three scenes: the scene with Rodolphe, and there you have seen her downfall in the forest, the glorification of adultery, and this woman whose beauty becomes all the greater because of its poetry. I have spoken of the religious period, and there you have seen prayer borrow its language from adultery. I have spoken of the second affair, I have unrolled the scenes which took place with Léon. I have shown you the scene in the cab—which was suppressed—but I have shown you the picture of their room and of the bed. Now that we believe that our case is estab-

* p.271
† p.265
‡ p.272

SPEECH FOR THE PROSECUTION

lished, let us come to the final scene, to the scene of torment.

Many cuts have been made here, apparently by the *Revue de Paris*. Here are the terms in which Monsieur Flaubert protests against this: "For motives that I have not been able to determine, the *Revue de Paris* has felt obliged to make a deletion in the issue of December first. Their scruples having been renewed at the time of the present issue, they have thought fit to remove several further passages. In consequence, I disclaim responsibility for the lines that follow; the reader is begged therefore to regard them only as fragments and not as a whole."

And so let us pass over these fragments and come to the death scene. She poisons herself. She poisons herself, and why? "It's really quite simple to die," she thought. "I'll fall asleep and it will all be over."* Then, without a regret, without a confession, without a tear of repentance for her present suicide and for her past adulteries, she is to receive the Last Sacrament. Why the Sacrament, when, in her thoughts just before, she is going into nothingness? Why, when there is not a tear, not a sigh of repentant Magdalen for her sin of disbelief, for her suicide, for her adulteries?

After this scene comes that of the Last Sacrament. These are holy and sacred words to us. It is with these words that we have closed the eyes of our forbears, of our fathers or our near ones, and it is with these same words that our children one day will close our own eyes. If one wants to reproduce them, it must be done exactly; at the very least they must not be accompanied by sensual images from the past.

You know it, the priest makes the holy unction on the forehead, the ears, the mouth, the feet, while pronouncing the liturgy: *Quidquid per pedes, per aures, per pectus,* etc., always followed by the words *misericordia....* Sin on the one hand, mercy on the other. These holy and sacred words must be reproduced exactly; if they are not reproduced exactly, at least do not introduce anything sensual.

She turned her head slowly and seemed suffused with joy at the sudden sight of the purple stole—probably rediscovering in this instant of extraordinary peace the lost ecstasy of her first flights of mysticism and beginning to have visions of eternal bliss.

The priest stood up to take hold of the crucifix. She stretched out her neck like one who is thirsty, and pressing her lips to the body of the Man-God, she placed on it, with all her fading strength, the most passionate kiss of love she had ever given. Then he recited the *Miserea-*

* p.294

tur and the *Indulgentiam,* dipped his right thumb into the oil, and began the unctions; first on the eyes, which had been so covetous of earthly splendors; then on the nostrils, avid for warm breezes and scents of love; then on the mouth, which had opened to emit lies, had groaned with pride, and had cried out in lust; then over the hands, which had reveled in sensual contacts; and finally on the soles of the feet, which had once moved so rapidly when she was hurrying to quench her desires and which now would walk no longer.*

Now come the prayers for the dying, which the priest recites very low, and where at each verse the words "Christian soul, depart for a higher region" appear. They are murmured at the moment when the dying man's last breath escapes his lips. The priest recites them, etc.

As the death rattle grew louder, the priest hurried his prayers. They mingled with Bovary's muffled sobs, and at times everything seemed to merge with the monotonous murmur of the Latin syllables that sounded like the tolling of a bell.†

The author has thought fit to alternate these words, to make them into a sort of reply. He allows the intervention of a blind man on the sidewalk below, chanting a song whose profane words are a sort of response to the prayers for the dying.

Suddenly there was a clatter of heavy clogs on the sidewalk and the tapping of a stick. Then a voice arose, singing raucously:

> Often the warmth of a lovely day
> Makes a girl dream of love....
> There was a strong breeze that day
> And her short petticoat flew away! ‡

It is at this moment that Madame Bovary dies.

Thus you have the picture: on the one hand the priest who recites the prayer for the dying, on the other the organ grinder who draws from the dying woman "a horrible, frenzied, despairing laugh—imagining that she could see the hideous face of the beggar standing out against the eternal darkness like a nightmare.... A convulsion pulled her back

* p.301
† p.302
‡ p.302

down on the mattress. They all drew near the bed. She was no more." *

And then afterward, when the body is cold, the thing that must be respected above all is the corpse that the soul has quitted. When the husband is there, on his knees, mourning his wife, when he has drawn the winding sheet over her, anyone else would have stopped short. And this is the moment when Monsieur Flaubert gives the final brushstroke:

The sheet sagged between her breasts and her knees and then rose again over her toes.†

That was the death scene. I have shortened and arranged it, as it were. It is for you to decide and to determine if this is a mingling of the sacred and the profane, or if it would not be something worse, a mingling of the sacred and the sensual.

I have told you the story of the novel, then I made my charges against it, and if I may say so, the style Monsieur Flaubert cultivates, and which he achieves without the circumspection but with all the resources of art, is the descriptive style: it is the realistic school of painting. And you see to what lengths he goes. Recently I happened to see an issue of *L'Artiste*; there is no question here of accusing *L'Artiste*, but only of learning Monsieur Flaubert's style, and I ask your permission to read you some lines that have no connection with the present trial, but that show to what extent Monsieur Flaubert excels in painting. He likes to paint temptations, above all those temptations to which Madame Bovary succumbed. Indeed I find a model of this style in the following few lines on the temptation of Saint Anthony, signed "Gustave Flaubert," in *L'Artiste* for the month of January. God knows it is a subject on which one can say many things, but I do not think that it would be possible to give more vividness to the image, more brilliance to the apollonian ‡ portrait of Saint Anthony: "Is this wisdom? Is this glory? Would you rest your eyes on dewy jasmine? Would you feel your body plunge into the sweet flesh of ecstatic women as if into a wave?"

It is indeed the same color, the same power of brush-work, the same vividness of expression!

I must now sum up. I have analyzed the book, I have told the story without omitting a page, then I made my charge, which was the second part of my task. I have speci-

* p.302
† p.306
‡ After Apollonius of Tyana.

fied a few portraits, I have shown Madame Bovary in repose, in relation to her husband, in relation to those whom she should not have tempted, and I have dwelt upon the lascivious colors of her portrait! Then I analyzed several important scenes: the downfall with Rodolphe, the religious period, the affair with Léon, and the death scene, and in all of them I found offenses against public morality and against religion.

I require only two scenes; for the offense against morality, will you not see it in the downfall with Rodolphe? Will you not see it in this glorification of adultery? Will you not see it, above all, in what takes place with Léon? And then, for the offense against religious morality, I find that in the passage about her confession (p.56), in the religious period (p.207), and finally in the last death scene.

Gentlemen, you have three defendants before you: Monsieur Flaubert, the author of the book; Monsieur Pichat, who accepted it; and Monsieur Pillet, who printed it. In such matters there is no offense without publicity, and all who have collaborated in the publicity should be equally penalized. But we hasten to add that the owner of the *Revue* and the printer are only secondary defendants. The principal person accused is the author, Monsieur Flaubert; Monsieur Flaubert, who, when informed by the editors, protested against the deletions made in his book. After him, in second place, comes Monsieur Laurent Pichat, whom you will call to account, not for the deletions he did make, but for those that he should have made; and finally, in third place comes the printer, who is the advance guard against scandal. In all other respects, Monsieur Pillet is a reputable man and I have nothing whatever against him. In regard to him we ask only one thing, that you enforce the law. Printers must read; when they have not read a book or had it read, they print at their own risk and peril. Printers are not machines; they are licensed, they take oath, they are in a special situation, they are responsible. Again I repeat, if you permit me the expression, that they are like an advance guard; if they allow the offense to pass, it is as if they allowed the enemy to pass. Mitigate the penalty as much as you wish with regard to Pillet; be just as indulgent with regard to the director of the *Revue*; but for Flaubert, the principal culprit, for him you must reserve all your severity!

I have performed my task; we must now expect or anticipate objections. As a general objection, the defense will say to us, "But, after all, is the novel not fundamentally moral, since the adulterous woman is punished?"

To this objection there are two replies: assuming a moral

work, hypothetically speaking, a moral ending could not pardon the lascivious details that could be found in it. And
therefore I say the book fundamentally is not moral.

I say, gentlemen, that lascivious details cannot be screened
by a moral ending, otherwise one could recount all the orgies
imaginable, one could describe all the depravities of a harlot,
so long as she were made to die on a pallet in the poorhouse. It would be permissible to study and to show all of
her lascivious attitudes! It would be running counter to all
the rules of common sense. It would be to place poison within
the reach of all, and the remedy within the reach of a very
few, if there is a remedy. Who is it who reads Monsieur
Flaubert's novels? Are they the men engaged in social or
political economy? No! The light pages of *Madame Bovary*
fall into hands that are even lighter, into the hands of young
girls, sometimes of married women. Well then! When the imagination will have been seduced, when this seduction
will have reached into the heart, when the heart will have
spoken to the senses, do you think that a very dispassionate
argument will be very effective against this seduction of the
senses and the feelings? And besides, man must not presume
too much on his strength and on his virtue; man gets his instincts from below and his thoughts from on high, and with
all of us virtue is only the result of an effort that is very
often painful. Lascivious paintings generally have more influence than dispassionate arguments. That is my reply to
this theory; it is my first reply, but I have a second one.

I maintain that the story of Madame Bovary, considered
from a philosophical viewpoint, is not at all moral. Doubtless
Madame Bovary dies poisoned, and it is true that she has
suffered much; but she dies at an hour of her choosing,
and she dies not because she is an adulteress, but because
she has wished to die; she dies in all of the glamour of her
youth and beauty; she dies after having had lovers, leaving a
husband who loves her, who adores her, who will find
Rodolphe's portrait, who will find his letters and Léon's, who
will read the letters of a wife who was twice an adultress,
and who after that will love her even more after she is dead.
Who is there in the book who can condemn this woman?
No one. That is the inference. There is not one character in
the book who might condemn her. If you find in it
one good character, if you find in it one single principle
by virtue of which the adulteress is stigmatized, I am wrong.
Consequently, if in all the book there is not an idea, not a
line by virtue of which the adulteress is shamed, then it is I
who am right: the book is immoral!

Might the book be condemned in the name of conjugal

honor? But conjugal honor is represented by a compliant husband who, after his wife's death, on meeting Rodolphe, searches the lover's face for the features of the wife he loves (p.321). I ask you this, can you stigmatize this woman in the name of conjugal honor when there is not a single word in the book in which the husband does not bow before the adulteress?

Would it be in the name of public opinion? But public opinion is personified by a grotesque being, by the druggist Homais, who is surrounded by ludicrous characters ruled by this woman.

Will you condemn it in the name of religious feeling? But you have this feeling personified in the Abbé Bournisien, a priest almost as grotesque as the druggist, who believes only in physical suffering, never in moral suffering, who is almost a materialist.

Will you condemn it in the name of the author's conscience? I do not know the opinion of the author's conscience, but in his Chapter IX, which is the only philosophical chapter in the book, I find the following sentence: "There is always a kind of numbness after a person's death, so difficult is it to understand this new state of nonexistence and to accept the fact that it has occurred. . . ." *

This is not a cry of disbelief, but it is at least a cry of skepticism. Doubtless it is difficult to understand and to believe it, but when all is said and done, why is there this stupefaction in the face of death? Because its coming is something that is a mystery, because it is difficult to understand and to judge it, yet one must submit to it. As for myself, I say that if death is the coming of nonexistence, if the compliant husband feels his love increase on learning of his wife's adulteries, if opinion is represented by grotesque beings, if religious feeling is represented by a ludicrous priest, then one single person is in the right, prevails, rules: she is Emma Bovary. Messalina prevails against Juvenal.

That is the philosophical inference of the book, drawn not by its author, but by a man who pondered and thoroughly studied these things, by a man who searched for a character in the book who might have ruled this woman. There was none. The only character who rules is Madame Bovary. Hence one must search elsewhere than in the book, one must search in that Christian morality that is the foundation of modern civilization. In the light of this morality, everything becomes explained and clarified.

In its name, adultery is stigmatized and condemned, not because it is an imprudence that exposes one to disillusion-

* p.303

ments and to regret, but because it is a crime against the family. You stigmatize and you condemn suicide, not because it is a madness, for the madman is not responsible; not because it is a cowardly act, for it sometimes demands a certain physical courage; you condemn it because it is the contempt for one's duty in the life that is ending and the cry of disbelief in the life which is beginning.

This Christian morality stigmatizes realistic literature, not because it paints the passions: hatred, vengeance, love (the world only lives by these, and art must paint them)—but because it paints them without restraint, without bounds. Art without rules is no longer art; it is like a woman who throws off all garments. To impose upon art the single rule of public decency is not to enslave but to honor it. One grows only by a rule. Gentlemen, there you have the principles we profess; there you have the doctrine we conscientiously uphold.

Counsel's Speech for the Defense
by Monsieur Marie-Antoine-Jules Sénard

Gentlemen, Monsieur Flaubert is accused before you of having written an indecent book, of having committed flagrant offenses in this book against public morality and religion. Monsieur Flaubert is beside me; he swears before you that he has written an honorable book; he swears before you that the intention of his book, from first line to last, is a moral and religious intention and that if it is not misrepresented (and we have seen for a few moments what a great talent can do to misrepresent an intention), it would be for you (as it will shortly become again) what it has already been for its readers: an eminently moral and religious intention that can be described in these words: the incitement to virtue through horror of vice.

I bring Monsieur Flaubert's statement here before you, and I fearlessly place it against the public ministry's charge, for this statement is important. It is important because of the person who made it, it is important because of the principles that guided the writing of this book that I am about to describe to you.

The statement is primarily important because of the person who made it, and allow me to say, Monsieur Gustave Flaubert was not someone unknown who would have needed to be introduced to me or to have given me information, I don't say as to his morality, but as to his position. I come here into this court after having read the book and after having felt in response the emanation of everything in me that is honorable and deeply religious to fulfill a duty to my conscience. But at the same time that I come to fulfill a duty to my conscience, I come to fulfill a duty to friendship. I remember— how could I forget—that his father has been my old friend. His father, with whose friendship I was long honored, honored until his last day; his father, and I may say his illustrious father, was chief surgeon at Rouen Hospital for more than thirty years. He was the patron of the great anatomist

Dupuytren; in giving his great teachings to science, he endowed it with great men of whom I need only cite a single one—Cloquet. He has not only himself left a great name to science, he has left great memories of immense services rendered to humanity. And at the same time that I recall my ties with him, I must tell you that his son, who stands indicted before this court for outrage against morality and religion, his son is the friend of my children, as I was the friend of his father. I know his mind, I know his intentions, and here the attorney has the right to stand as personal guarantee for his client.

Gentlemen, a great name and great memories impose their obligation. Monsieur Flaubert's children have not failed him. There were three—two sons and a daughter who died at the age of twenty-one. The eldest has been considered worthy of succeeding his father; now and for the past several years it is he who fulfills the same mission that his father fulfilled for thirty years. The younger one is here; he stands before your bar. In leaving them a large fortune and a great name, their father has left them the obligation of being men of understanding and courage, useful men. My client's brother is engaged in a career in which good works are an everyday occurrence. The son who stands before you has devoted his life to study and to letters, and the work that is now being prosecuted before you is his first work. This first work, gentlemen, which, according to the imperial attorney, excites the passions, is the result of long study and long meditation. Monsieur Gustave Flaubert is a man of serious character whose nature draws him to grave and painful things. This is not the man whom the public ministry, with fifteen or twenty lines bitten off here and there, has represented before you as a maker of lascivious paintings. No, I repeat, his nature contains all the most grave and most serious things imaginable in the world, but at the same time, these are also the most painful things. Just by restoring a sentence, by placing the few quoted lines beside those that precede and follow it, his book will at once reassume its true color, while at the same time the author's intention will be revealed to you. And from the too facile argument you have heard you will retain only a feeling of profound admiration for a talent that is able to transform everything.

I have told you that Monsieur Flaubert is a serious and a grave man. In accordance with his cast of mind, his studies have been serious and wide. They have embraced not only all the branches of literature but also the law. Monsieur Flaubert is a man who was not content with the observations afforded him by his own sphere; he has studied other spheres: *Qui mores multorum videt et urbes.*

After his father's death and the completion of his school studies, he visited Italy, and from 1848 to 1851 he traveled through the countries of the Orient, Egypt, Palestine, and Asia Minor, in which, doubtless, a traveler with his great intelligence might acquire something elevated and poetic —the colors and distinction of style that the public ministry have just cited in order to establish the offense they impute to us. The distinction of style and the literary qualities will remain; they will emerge brilliantly out of these proceedings, but they cannot in any way lend support to the accusation.

Since his return in 1852, Monsieur Gustave Flaubert has written and has tried within a wide frame to present the result of his attentive and serious studies, the result of all he had acquired in his travels.

What is this frame he has chosen, what is his subject and how has he treated it? My client is a man who belongs to none of those schools whose names I have heard just now in the indictment. God knows he belongs to the realist school in the sense that he is interested in the real nature of things. He belongs to the psychological school in the sense that he is prompted, not by the materialistic side of things, but by human feelings and the unfolding of the passions within their given sphere. He belongs perhaps less to the romantic school than to any other, for if romanticism does appear in his book, just as realism appears, it is only in a few ironic phrases scattered here and there, which the public ministry has taken too literally. What Monsieur Flaubert has desired above all has been to take a theme from real life, has been to create and embody true middle-class prototypes and to arrive at a useful result. Indeed it is precisely this useful purpose that has most concerned my client in the study to which he has been dedicated, and he has pursued it by producing three or four characters from present-day society living in circumstances that are true to life, and by presenting to the reader's eye a true picture of what most often happens in the world.

In summarizing its opinion on *Madame Bovary*, the public ministry has said: "The second title of this work is *The Story of the Adulteries of a Provincial Wife*." I emphatically protest this title. This alone would have proved what their constant preoccupation has been had I not already sensed it from beginning to end of the indictment. No! The second title of this work is not *The Story of the Adulteries of a Provincial Wife*; it is, if you must absolutely have a second title, the story of the education too often given in the provinces; the story of the dangers to which it can lead, the story of degradation, of villainy, of a suicide seen as the consequence

of an early transgression, and of a transgression that was itself
induced by the first misstep into which a young woman is
often led; it is a story of an education, the story of a deplorable life to which this sort of education is too often the
preface. That is what Monsieur Flaubert has wanted to paint,
and not the adulteries of a provincial wife; you will recognize this at once on reading the accused work.

Now, in all of that the public ministry has perceived,
above all, a lascivious color. If I could take the number of
lines that the public ministry has cut out and compare them
against the number of lines it has left in place, they would
come to a total proportion of one to five hundred, and
you would see that this proportion of one to five hundred is
not a lascivious color; it is nothing at all, for it exists only
in cutouts and commentaries.

Now, what is it that Monsieur Gustave Flaubert has
wanted to paint? In the first place, the education given a
woman that was above the station to which she was born
(as happens with us, it must be said, all too often) and the
resulting mixture of incongruous elements this produces in the
woman's understanding; and then, when marriage comes, as
the marriage is suitable not to her education but to the station into which she was born, the author has described all the
events that take place in the position that has been made
for her.

What else does he show? He shows a woman turning to
vice from an unsuitable marriage, and from vice to the last
stages of degradation and misery. Presently, after reading
various passages, when I will have revealed the book to you
as a whole, I will ask the court for liberty to state the question in these terms: if this book were placed in the hands
of a young woman, could it have the effect of drawing her
toward dissipation and toward adultery, or on the contrary,
would it show her the danger from the start and cause her
to shudder with horror? When the question is put in this way,
your conscience will resolve it.

I say this for the following reason: Monsieur Flaubert has
wanted to paint the woman who instead of trying to be contented with her given station, with her birth and her
birth, instead of trying to live the life that belongs to her, is
troubled by a thousand alien aspirations derived from an
education that has been too elevated for her; who instead
of adapting to the duties of her position, instead of being
the contented wife of the country doctor with whom she
spends her days, instead of seeking happiness in her home
and in her marriage, seeks it in interminable daydreams; and
who then, very soon, when she encounters a young man who

flirts with her, plays the same game (God knows they are inexperienced, the two of them!). She becomes aroused, as it were, by degrees, and she is appalled when, on resorting to the religion of her early years, she does not find sufficient strength in it—and we shall soon see why she does not find it. Nevertheless, the ignorance of both the young man and herself preserves her from this first danger. But soon she becomes acquainted with a man like so many others, of whom there are all too many in the world, a man who takes hold of her, poor spoiled woman, and seduces her. That is the essential, that is what one must see, that is the book itself.

The public ministry is angered, and I think wrongly, on the grounds of conscience and human decency because in the first scene Madame Bovary takes a sort of pleasure, a joy in having broken out of her prison, and returns home telling herself: "I have a lover." You think that there we have no first cry of human distress! The burden of proof is between us. But you should have looked a little further on, and you would have seen that if the first moment, the first instant of that sin arouses a sort of transport of joy, of delirium in this woman, a few lines further on came disappointment; and in the author's phrase, she feels humiliated in her own eyes.

Yes, disappointment, sorrow, and remorse came to her at the same instant. The man to whom she had entrusted and given herself had taken her only to play with for an instant, like a toy; remorse consumes her; it rends her. What has shocked you has been to hear this called the "disillusionments" of adultery; you would have preferred the writer to have said "defilements" for this woman who, not having understood marriage, had felt herself defiled by her husband's touch, and who after having sought elsewhere for her ideal had found instead the disillusionments of adultery. The court will judge. If it were up to me, I would say to her: "Poor woman! If you think your husband's kisses are something boring and monotonous, if you find in them—it is the word that has been pointed out—only the platitudes of marriage, if you seem to find defilement in this union over which love has not presided, beware; your dreams are an illusion and one day you will be cruelly disenchanted." The man who speaks out strongly, gentleman, and who uses the word "defilement" to express what we have called "disillusionment" uses a word that is true but vague, a word that does not help our understanding. I prefer a man who does not speak out strongly, who does not employ the word "defilement," but who warns the woman of disappointment and disillusionment, who says to her: "There where you think to find love you will find only libertinage; there where you think to find happiness you will find only bitterness. A husband who goes quietly about his affairs, who puts on his nightcap and eats his supper with you, is a prosaic husband who disgusts you. You dream of a man who loves you, who idolizes you, poor child! That man will be a libertine who will have taken you up for a moment to play with you. The illusion will occur the first time, perhaps the second; you will have returned home happy, singing the song of adultery: 'I have a lover!' The third time it will not have come to that; disillusionment will have set in. The man of whom you had dreamed will have lost all of his glamour; you will have rediscovered in love the platitudes of marriage, and you will have rediscovered them with contempt and scorn, with disgust and piercing remorse."

There, gentlemen, is what Monsieur Flaubert has said, it is what he has painted, it is what is in every line of his book; it is what distinguishes his work from other works of the same kind. With him the great failings of society figure on every page; with him adultery moves replete with disgust and shame. From the ordinary relationships of life he has drawn the most striking lesson that could be given to a young woman. Oh! God knows, those of our young women who do not find enough in honest and elevated principles or in a strict religion to hold them to the performance of their duties as mothers, who do not find it above all in that resignation, that practical understanding of life that tells us that we must make the best of what we have, but who turn their dreams outside, these most honorable and pure young women who, in the banality of their household, are sometimes tormented by what goes on around them, they will be made to reflect by a book like this one, you may be sure of it. That is what Monsieur Flaubert has done.

And note one thing well: Monsieur Flaubert is not a man who paints you a charming adulteress only to have her rescued by a *deus ex machina*. No, you have leaped too quickly to that conclusion. With him, adultery is but a succession of torments, of regrets, of remorse; and finally it reaches a final expiation that is appalling. It is excessive. If Monsieur Flaubert sins, it is through an excess of zeal, and I will tell you in a moment whose opinion this was. The expiation is not long in coming; it is here that the book is eminently moral and useful; it does not promise the young woman some of those wonderful years at the end of which she might say: "After that, let me die." No! From the second day, bitterness and disillusionments come. The conclusion in favor of morality is to be found in every line of the book.

The book is written with a power of observation to which the imperial attorney has rendered justice; and it is to this that I call your attention, for if the accusation is groundless, it must fall. The book is written with a power of observation that is truly remarkable down to the smallest details. An article in *L'Artiste*, signed Flaubert, has served as another pretext for the charge. Let the imperial attorney note first that this article is extraneous to the accusation; then let him note that we hold it to be most innocent and most moral in the sight of this court, on condition that the imperial attorney will have the goodness to read it in its entirety instead of cutting it into shreds. What is striking in Monsieur Flaubert's book is that a number of descriptions have called forth an almost daguerrean fidelity in their reproduction of all types of intimate things, of thoughts and human feelings —and this reproduction becomes even more striking through the magic of his style. Note well that if he had applied this fidelity only to scenes of degradation, you would be able to say with justice: the author has been pleased to paint degradation with all the descriptive power at his command. From the first to the last page of his book he applies himself without any sort of reserve to all the events of Emma's life, to her childhood in her father's house, to her education in the convent, and he omits nothing. But those like myself who have read from beginning to end will say something important for which you will be grateful and which not only will be his vindication but also must exclude him from any prosecution whatsoever: we will say that when he comes to the difficult parts, when he comes precisely to degradation, instead of imitating many classical authors well known to the public ministry (but whom they forgot while writing their charge and whose works I have brought, not to read aloud, but for you to read in the counsel room), instead of imitating our great classical authors, our great masters who have not failed to describe scenes of the union of the senses between man and woman when they have encountered them —there Monsieur Flaubert has been content with a word. There all of his descriptive power disappears, because his intention is chaste, because there where he could write in his own way and with all the magic of his style he feels that there are things that cannot be approached or described. The public ministry still finds that he has said too much. When I will have shown the men who have described these things in great philosophic works and when in comparison I show the man who possesses such a high degree of descriptive ability and who, far from using it, stops himself and abstains, then

I will have the right to demand satisfaction for the charge that has been put forward.

Nevertheless, gentlemen, just as he likes to describe to us the pleasant bower where Emma played as a child, with its foliage, with the small pink or white flowers that came to bloom and its scented paths—just so, when she will have left there, when she will travel other roads, roads that will be muddy, and when she will soil her feet, when the stains will have splashed even higher—then he must not say so! But this would be completely to suppress the book; more than that, it would be to suppress the moral element on pretext of defending it, for if the transgression may not be shown, if it may not be pointed out, if in a painting from real life that aims by its attitude to show danger, downfall, and expiation—if you would forbid him to paint all that, this would obviously remove all meaning from the book.

This book has not been the object of a few hours' distraction to my client; it represents two or three years of incessant study. And now I am going to tell you something more: you will see Monsieur Flaubert after so many years of labor and study, after so many voyages, after so many notes gathered from the authors he has read; you will see his sources, and God knows it is strange to have to justify them; you will see him—this author of the lascivious colors—entirely permeated with the writings of Bossuet and Massillon. And it is by examining these authors that we will presently discover him seeking not to plagiarize but to reproduce in his own descriptions the thoughts and the colors employed by them. And then, after all of this labor of love and his work was completed, do you believe that, filled with self-confidence and despite so much study and meditation, he wished immediately to be involved in litigation! Doubtless he might have done so had he been someone unknown to the world, had his name belonged to himself alone, had he felt he could dispose of it and betray it as he liked, but I repeat: he is one of those whom *noblesse oblige*; he is named Flaubert; he is the younger son of Monsieur Flaubert; he wanted to make his way in literature while profoundly respecting morality and religion, not by arousing the court (such an advantage would not occur to him) but by personal dignity, by not wanting his name to appear at the head of a publication had it not been thought worthy of being published by a number of persons in whom he had faith. Before delivering the pages to the printer, Monsieur Flaubert read them, in part and in whole, to a number of friends highly placed in the literary world, and I state to you that not one of them was offended by what now so strongly excites the severity of the imperial attorney. There was no one who even dreamed it. They simply examined and studied the literary merits of the book. As for its moral intention, it is so evident—it is written in every line in terms so far from ambiguous—that there was no need even to question it. Reassured as to the book's merit, encouraged as well by the most eminent men in publishing, Monsieur Flaubert thought only to deliver it to the press and to publicity. I repeat: the whole world was unanimous in rendering homage to its literary merit, to its style, and at the same time to the excellent intention that presides from first to last line. And when the book was prosecuted, it was not only he who was surprised and dismayed, but, allow me to say, it was also those of us, and myself first of all, who cannot understand this prosecution, we who have read the book with keen interest as fast as it was published and who are his intimate friends. God knows there are nuances that sometimes escape us in our daily lives, but they cannot escape women of great understanding, purity, and chasteness. I cannot mention any names in this court, but if I told you what has been said to Monsieur Flaubert, what has been said to myself by mothers of families who have read this book, if I told you their astonishment after having been so highly impressed that they felt obliged to thank the author, if I told you of their astonishment and dismay when they learned that this book must be considered as contrary to public morality, religious faith, and to the faith of their whole lives— good God! But in these many opinions there is enough to hearten even myself, if I needed to be heartened at the moment of contesting the public ministry's attacks.

Nevertheless, among all of these literary opinions there is one I wish to tell you of. Among them is a man respected for a fine and noble character, a man who fights courageously each day against adversity and suffering, a man famous not only for many deeds unnecessary to recall here, but famous as well for his literary works, which we must recall, for therein lies his authority—an authority all the greater for the purity and the chasteness that exist in all of his writings —Lamartine.

Lamartine was not acquainted with my client; he was unaware that he existed. Lamartine, at home in the country, had read *Madame Bovary* as it was published in each number of the *Revue de Paris*. Lamartine's impressions were so strong that they grew even greater with the events that I now describe.

A few days ago Lamartine returned to Paris, and the next day he made inquiries as to where Monsieur Gustave Flaubert lived. He sent to the *Revue* to ask for the residence of a Monsieur Gustave Flaubert whose articles had been published under the title of *Madame Bovary*. He instructed his secretary to go and present his compliments to Monsieur Flaubert, to express to him the satisfaction he had felt on reading his work, and to inform him of his desire to meet the new author who had been revealed by so fine a work.

My client went to see Lamartine and there he found a man who not only encouraged him, but a man who said to him: "You have given me the best work that I have read in the past twenty years." In a word, it was such praise as my client, in his modesty, hardly dared let me repeat. Lamartine proved that he had read all the installments, and he proved it in the most gracious way, by reciting entire pages. Lamartine only added: "At the same time that I read you without reservation down to the last page, I reproached you for the last ones. You hurt me, you literally made me suffer! The expiation is out of proportion to the crime; you have created a frightful, a hideous death! Assuredly a woman who defiles the conjugal bed must expect an expiation, but this one is horrible; it is an agony such as one has never seen. You have gone too far, you have unnerved me; such descriptive power applied to the last instants of death has caused me inexpressible pain!" And when Gustave Flaubert asked him: "But, Monsieur de Lamartine, do you know that I am being prosecuted before the Criminal Court for having written such a work, for offending the public and religious morality?" Lamartine replied: "I think that for all of my life, in my literary works as in other things, I have been the man who has best understood the meaning of public and religious morality. My dear boy, it is not possible that a court exists in France that would condemn you. It is already most regrettable that they should have so misunderstood the nature of your work as to have ordered the prosecution, but it is not possible for the honor of our country and our time that there exists a court that would condemn you."

That is what took place yesterday between Lamartine and Flaubert, and I have the right to say to you that this opinion is one that is worth consideration.

With this understood, may we now see how it is that my own conscience tells me that *Madame Bovary* is a good book and a good influence? And I ask your permission to add that I am not lenient toward this sort of thing; leniency is not my habit. I have seen some literary works that, although they came from our great writers, have never held my eyes for two minutes. Later in the counsel room you will be shown some of those lines that I have never cared to read, and I will ask your permission to tell you that when I came to the end of Monsieur Flaubert's book, I was convinced that a cut made by the *Revue de Paris* had been the cause of everything.

Here, gentlemen, is a portfolio filled with opinions about this book by all the literary men of our time, including the most distinguished, expressing the admiration they felt on reading this new work that was at once so moral and so useful!

Now, how could such a work have been liable to prosecution? Will you permit me to tell you? The *Revue de Paris*, whose editorial committee had read the work in its entirety— the manuscript had been sent to them long before publication— had found nothing to take exception to. When the time came to print the issue of December 1, 1856, one of the directors of the *Revue* became alarmed by the scene in the cab. He said: "This is not suitable; we are going to suppress it." Flaubert was offended by the suppression. He did not want it to take place unless a notice was put at the bottom of the page. It is he who insisted upon the notice. For his own pride as an author, not wanting his work to be mutilated, nor on the other hand, for anything in it to cause the *Revue* any uneasiness, he said to them: "Suppress if you think fit, but you must announce that you are suppressing." And then the following notice was agreed upon: "The Directors have felt obliged to suppress a passage here, on which the editors of the *Revue de Paris* could not agree; we hereby give notice to the author."

Here is the suppressed passage; I am going to read it to you. We have a proof of it that we have obtained with great difficulty. Here is the first part, which has not a single correction; one word has been corrected in the second part:

"Where to, sir?" asked the coachman.

"Anywhere!" Léon said, pushing Emma into the carriage. And the lumbering vehicle started off.

It went down the Rue Grand-Pont, crossed the Place des Arts, the Quai Napoléon, the Pont Neuf, and stopped short before the statue of Pierre Corneille.

"Keep going," cried a voice from within.

The carriage started off again, and as soon as it reached the Carrefour La Fayette, headed downhill, galloping toward the railroad station.

"No, straight ahead!" cried the same voice.

The cab emerged through the gate, and when it reached the boulevard, trotted gently beneath the large elms. The driver mopped his forehead, put his leather cap between

his legs, and drove the vehicle beyond the sidelines near
the meadow to the water's edge.

It traveled along the length of the river, moving over the
cobbled towing path and went for a long time in the direction of Oyssel, beyond the islands.

But suddenly it made a leap across Quatre-Mares, Sotteville, the Grande-Chaussée, the Rue d'Elbeuf, and made
its third stop before the botanical gardens.

"Will you keep going!" shouted the voice with greater
anger.

And immediately resuming its course, it passed by Saint-
Sever, along the Quai des Curandiers, the Quai aux Meules,
once more over the bridge, through the Place Champ-de-
Mars, and behind the poorhouse gardens, where the old
men in black coats were walking in the sun along a terrace
green with ivy. It went up the Boulevard Bouvreuil, along
Boulevard Cauchoise, then crossed the whole of Mont-Riboudet as far as the Deville hills.

Then it came back, and with neither fixed plan nor
direction, wandered about at random. It was seen at Saint-
Paul, at Lescure, at Mont Gargan, at Rouge-Mare, and at
the Place du Gaillardbois; in the Rue Maladrerie, the Rue
Dinanderie, in front of various churches—Saint-Romain,
Saint-Vivien, Saint-Maclou, Saint-Nicaise—in front of the
customs house—at the Basse-Vieille-Tour, at the Trois-
Pipes, and the Cimetière Monumental. Occasionally the
coachman on his box would cast looks of despair at the
cafés. He did not understand what kind of a rage for
locomotion inspired these people, who did not want to
stop. He attempted to a few times and immediately heard
angry outbursts at him from behind. Then he lashed his
two sweating nags even more furiously, without paying attention to the jolts, bumping into things here and there, not
caring, demoralized, and almost weeping from thirst, fatigue, and unhappiness.

And at the harbor, amid the wagons and the barrels
in the streets, the inhabitants at the corners were wide-
eyed with astonishment at this most extraordinary spectacle in a provincial town—a constantly reappearing cab
with closed blinds, shut up more tightly than a tomb and
tossing about like a boat.

Once, in the middle of the day, in the open country, at
a moment when the sun bears strongest against the old silver-plated lanterns, a bare hand reached out under the little yellow homespun curtains and threw out some scraps
of paper that scattered in the wind, to alight farther along
like white butterflies on a field of red clover in bloom.

Then, about six o'clock, the carriage stopped in a side street of the Beauvoisine section and a woman stepped down, walking away with her veil pulled down and without looking back.

Madame Bovary was surprised at not seeing the stage-coach when she reached the inn. Hivert had waited for her for fifty-three minutes and finally gone off.

Yet nothing forced her to leave except that she had promised she would come back that evening. Besides, Charles was expecting her; and she already felt in her heart that cowardly submissiveness that is, for many women, both the punishment and the atonement of their adultery.*

Monsieur Flaubert reminds me that the public ministry has taken exception to the last sentence.

THE IMPERIAL ATTORNEY: No, I only pointed it out.

MONSIEUR SÉNARD: What is certain is that if exception is taken, it will fall on the words: "both the punishment and the atonement of their adultery." And besides, that might be liable to exception as much as anything else, for in all to which you have taken exception there is nothing that could seriously support your case.

Then, gentlemen, this sort of fantastic drive, having displeased the editors of the Revue, was suppressed. This was an excess of caution on the part of the Revue, and most certainly it was not an excess that could have given grounds for a lawsuit; nevertheless, you will see how it has given grounds for suit. What one does not see is that a passage that has been suppressed in this way appears in a very strange light. People have imagined many things that do not exist, as you have seen from the reading of the original passage. My God, do you know what people have imagined? That there was probably something in the suppressed passage that was analogous to what you will be kind enough to read in one of the most marvelous novels to come from the pen of an honorable member of the Academy of France —Monsieur Mérimée.

Monsieur Mérimée, in a novel entitled La Double Méprise, describes a scene that takes place in a post-chaise. It is not the hiring of the carriage that is important, but, as in this case, it is the account of what takes place inside it. I do not want to impose upon you; I will have the book passed to the public ministry and to the bench. If we had written half or a quarter of what Monsieur Mérimée has written, I would be somewhat embarrassed in performing my task, or

* p.233-235

I would even have to modify it. Instead of saying what I have said and what I assert—that Monsieur Flaubert has written a good book, a book that is decent, useful, and moral—I would say: literature has its rights; Monsieur Mérimée has written a most remarkable literary work; one must not be fussy over details when the whole is irreproachable. I would not confine myself to that; I would forgive him, and you would acquit. Well! God knows it is not by omission that an author can give offense in such matters. And for the rest, you will have the details of what took place in the carriage. But since my client, Flaubert, was satisfied to show a drive and since what took place inside was revealed only by "a bare hand reached out under the little yellow homespun curtains and threw out some scraps of paper that scattered in the wind, to alight farther along like white butterflies on a field of red clover in bloom"; as my client was content to leave it at that, no one knew anything and the whole world imagined, because of the suppression itself, that he has said at least as much as the member of the Academy of France. You have seen that he said nothing.

Well then! The prosecution arises out of this unfortunate suppression because, in the offices that are so rightly charged with reviewing all writings that might offend against public morality, when they saw this cut it put them on guard. I am obliged to state, and the gentlemen of the *Revue de Paris* will permit me to say, that they started their scissors two words too late: the cut should have started before they got into the cab; to cut after that was hardly worth the trouble. The cutting has been most unfortunate; but, gentlemen of the *Revue,* if you have committed this small mistake, assuredly you will pay dearly for it today.

In those offices they said: we must watch out for what comes next; when the following number appeared, they fought over every syllable. These officials are not obliged to tell all, and when they saw written that a woman had taken off all her clothes, they took alarm without going any further. It is true that, unlike our great masters, Monsieur Flaubert has not taken pains to describe the alabaster of her nude arms, of her bosom, etc. He has not said, as a poet whom we love:

Je vis de ses beaux flancs l'albâtre ardent et pur,
Lis, ébène, corail, roses, veines d'azur,
Telle enfin qu'autrefois tu me l'avais montrée,
De sa nudité seule embellie et parée,
Quand nos nuits s'envolaient, quand le mol oreiller
La vit sous tes baisers dormir et s'éveiller.

He said nothing to compare with what André Chénier said. When all is said and done, what he said was: "She abandoned herself. . . . Her clothes dropped to the ground." She abandoned herself! What next! And so all description is to be forbidden? But when one makes an accusation, one must read all, and the imperial attorney has not read all. The passage he accuses does not stop where he stopped; there is an amendment that I now quote:

> Yet there was something wild, something strange and tragic in this forehead covered with cold sweat, in those stammering lips and wildly staring eyes, in the embrace of those arms—something that seemed to Léon to be coming between them subtly as if to tear them apart.*

They did not read that in the offices. The imperial attorney took no notice of it just now. He saw only this: "Then she would drop all her clothes in one movement . . ." and he cried: "Outrage against public morality!" Really, with such a system it is only too easy to bring charges. God save the authors of dictionaries from falling into the imperial attorney's hands! Who would escape conviction if, by means of cuttings, not of phrases but of words, someone took it into his head to make a list of all the words that might offend morality or religion?

My client's first thought, which unfortunately met with opposition, had been this: "There is only one thing to do, print the book immediately, not with the cuts but in its entirety, exactly as it left my hands, with the cab scene restored." I was entirely of his opinion; my client's best defense would have been the printing of the complete work together with a notation of several points to which we would have begged the court to give their special attention. I myself had titled this note "Statement by Monsieur Gustave Flaubert Against the Charge Leveled Against Him of Offense to Religious Morality." I had written with my own hand: "The Criminal Court, sixth chamber," and directed it to the president and the public ministry. It had a preface that included the following words: "They accuse me with phrases taken from here and there in my book; I can only defend myself with my book." To ask judges to read a novel in its entirety is to ask them much, but we are before judges who love truth and who desire it, and who in order to understand will not shrink from any task; we are before judges who desire justice, who desire it strongly, and who will unhesitatingly read all that we beg them to read. I had said to Monsieur Flaubert: "Send that to the press at

* p.266

once and place my name at the bottom beside yours: Sénard, attorney-at-law." They had begun printing; we had ordered an edition of one hundred copies; the printing was progressing with extreme rapidity, working days and nights, when we received an injunction against continuing the printing—not of the book, but of the notation in which the accused passages were coupled with explanatory notes! We appealed to the imperial attorney, who told us that the injunction was absolute, that it could not be lifted!

Very well, so be it! We have not published the book with our notes and our remarks, but, gentlemen, if your first reading will have left you any doubt, I ask you the favor of reading it again. You love, you desire, truth; you cannot be like those who, when one brings them two lines of a man's writings, are certain to hang him whatever the circumstances. You do not want a man to be judged on fragments, however cleverly chosen. You do not wish it; you do not wish to deprive us of the customary resources of the defense. Very well! You have the book, and although it will be less convenient than what we had proposed to do, you will make the distinctions, the comments and comparisons for yourselves because you desire truth and you wish it to be the basis for your decision, and truth will spring from the careful scrutiny of the book.

Nevertheless, I cannot confine myself to that. The public ministry attacks the book; I must take up the book itself in order to defend it; I must complete the quotations he has made, and for each accused passage I must show the nullity of the accusation. This will be my whole defense.

I shall certainly not attempt to outdo the public ministry by expressing more of the lofty, spirited, and touching opinions that surrounded all he said; the defense would not have the right to use such embellishments; it will content itself with showing the texts just as they are.

And at the outset I assert that nothing is more false than what has just been said about the lascivious tone. Lascivious tone! Just where have you found that? Has my client depicted that sort of woman in *Madame Bovary?* Eh! God knows it is sad but true, she is a young girl born decent as almost all of them are; but most of them, at least, are pretty frail when education, instead of strengthening, has weakened them or thrown them into an evil path. He has taken a young girl; has she a depraved nature? No, it is an impressionable nature, susceptible to highly charged emotions.

The imperial attorney has said: "This young girl has constantly been presented as lascivious." But not at all! He presents her as born in the country, born on the farm where she busies herself with all of her father's labors, and where no kind of lewdness could have entered her mind or her spirit. Then, instead of following the destiny that was naturally hers through being brought up for life on a farm or in a similar sphere, he shows her under the imprudent authority of a father who mistakenly has this girl—who must marry a farmer or a countryman—educated in a convent. And so she is placed in a convent, above her sphere. No remark coming from the public ministry is unimportant; therefore nothing must be left unanswered. Ah! You have spoken of her little sins in quoting these lines from the first installment: "When she went to confession, she would invent trivial sins in order to prolong her stay there, on her knees in the shadow . . . as the priest whispered above her." You are already gravely mistaken in your judgment of my client. He has not committed the offense to which you take exception; the error is entirely on your side—firstly, as to the age of the young girl. As she entered the convent only at the age of thirteen, it is obvious that she was fourteen when she went to confession. So she was not a ten-year-old child as you were pleased to call her; you have been materially mistaken there. But I am not talking about the improbability of a ten-year-old child's liking to remain at the confessional "as the priest whispered above her." What I wish is to have you read the lines that precede this passage, which will not be easy, I agree. But that is the disadvantage of our not having the notation; with the notation we should not have to search through six issues.

I drew your attention to this passage in order to restore its true character to *Madame Bovary*. Will you permit me to say what appears to me much more important—the thing Monsieur Flaubert has understood and has thrown into relief? There is a kind of religion that is generally preached to young girls and that is the worst kind of all. In this regard there may be differences of opinion. As for myself, here is what I flatly assert: I know of nothing more beautiful, more useful, and more necessary to support us on the path of life than religious sentiment; not only for women, but also for men, who have sometimes extremely painful trials to overcome. I know of nothing more useful and necessary, but the religious sentiment must be solemn and, allow me to add, it must be strict.

I want my children to understand God, not a God in the abstractions of pantheism, but a Supreme Being with whom they are in harmony, to whom they raise themselves in prayer, and who, at the same time, helps them to grow and gives them strength. This thought, do you see, which you

share with me, gives strength in evil days, strength in what
we call the world; it is the refuge, or better still, it is
the strength of the weak. It is that thought that gives a
woman the stability that enables her to bear the thousand
small burdens of life, to offer her sufferings to God, and to
ask him for the grace to fulfill her duty. That religion,
gentlemen, is Christianity; it is the religion that establishes
harmony between God and man. By allowing a sort of
intermediary power to intervene between us and God, Christianity makes God more accessible to us and makes our
communication easier. The mother of God also receives the
prayers of women, and this does not seem to me to corrupt the purity or the holiness of the religious sentiment,
but that is where the corruption begins. In order to adapt
religion to all natures, they interpose all sorts of wretched,
shabby, petty little things. The pomp of ceremonies, which
should be the great pomp that grips our souls, instead
degenerates into a little business of relics, of medals, of
good little Gods and Virgins. And what catches the imagination of curious and eager children—the imagination
of young girls above all? It is these weakened, diminished,
shabby images of the religious spirit. Then they invent
little religious practices, little pieties of tenderness and love;
and instead of having the sentiment of God and of duty
in their souls, they give themselves to daydreams, to little practices and little pieties. And then comes poetry, and
then, one is obliged to say, then come the thousand thoughts
of charity, of tenderness and mystical love, a thousand forms
that beguile young girls and that sensualize religion. These
poor children who are naturally credulous and weak are
caught by all that—by the poetry and daydreams—instead of
attaching themselves to something rational and stern. The
result is that you have many extremely devout women who
are not religious at all. And when chance pushes them out
of the path they should follow, instead of finding strength
they find only all sorts of sensualities that mislead them.

Ah! You have accused us of mingling sensualism with
the religious element in this picture of modern society! Rather
accuse the society in which we live; do not accuse the man
who, like Bossuet, cries out: "Awake and beware the
danger!" Go rather and tell the fathers of families: "Take
care, these are not good habits to give to your daughters;
in all these mixtures of mysticism there is something that
sensualizes religion." That would be to tell them the truth.
It is on that account that you accuse Flaubert; it is on that
account that I extol his conduct. Yes, he has done well to
warn families in this way of the dangers of emotionalism

to young girls attracted by petty practices instead of becoming attached to a strong and severe religion that would
support them in their day of weakness. And now, you are
going to see the purpose behind the trivial sins "as the
priest whispers above."

She had read *Paul and Virginia* and dreamed about the
bamboo cottage, the Negro Domingo, and the dog Fidèle,
but most of all about the sweet friendship of some dear
little brother who gathers ripe fruit for you in huge trees
taller than steeples or who runs barefoot over the sand,
bringing you a bird's nest. *

Is this lascivious, gentlemen?

THE IMPERIAL ATTORNEY: I have not said that this passage
was lascivious.

MONSIEUR SÉNARD: I beg your pardon. It is precisely from
this passage that you have plucked a lascivious phrase, and
you have been able to find it lascivious only by isolating
it from what precedes and follows it.

Instead of following the Mass, she looked at the pious
vignettes edged in azure in her book, and she loved the
sick lamb, the Sacred Heart pierced with sharp arrows,
and poor Jesus stumbling as He walked under His cross.
She tried to fast one entire day to mortify her soul.
She attempted to think of some vow to fulfill. †

Do not forget that; if she invents trivial sins to confess
and attempts to think of some vow to fulfill, as we now
find in the preceding line, evidently she has had her ideas
slightly warped somewhere. And I ask you now if I need
to dispute your passages! But I continue:

In the evening, before prayers, some religious selection
would be read at study. During the week it was a summary of Abbé Frayssinous's religious-history lectures and
on Sunday, for relaxation, passages from *Le Génie du
Christianisme*. How she listened, those first times, to the
sonorous lamentation of romantic melancholy being echoed
throughout the world and unto eternity! Had her childhood been spent in an apartment behind a store in some
business district, she might have been receptive to nature's
lyric effusions that ordinarily reach us only via the interpretations of writers. But she knew the countryside too
well; she knew the lowing of the flocks, the milking, and
the plowing. Accustomed to the calm life, she turned away

* p.55
† p.56

from it toward excitement. She loved the sea only for its storms, and trees only when they were scattered among ruins. She needed to derive immediate gratification from things and rejected as useless everything that did supply this satisfaction. Her temperament was more sentimental than artistic. She sought emotions and not landscapes.*

Now you will see with what delicacy the author introduces that good old maid and how he teaches religion by slipping a new element into the convent—the novels that are introduced by this person from outside. Never forget that when it comes to judging the religious morality.

There was an old maid who came to the convent for one week every month to work in the laundry. Protected by the archbishop because she belonged to an old aristocratic family ruined during the Revolution, she ate in the refectory at the good sisters' table and would chat with them for a while after dinner before returning to her work. The girls would often steal out of class to visit her. She knew the romantic songs of the past century by heart and would sing them softly as she plied her needle. She told stories, brought in news of the outside world, ran errands in the city, and would secretly lend the older girls some novel that she always kept in the pocket of her apron, of which the good creature herself devoured long chapters between tasks. †

This is not only marvelous from a literary point of view: acquittal cannot be denied the man who writes such admirable passages pointing out to everyone the perils of this kind of education and showing a young woman the dangers of the life in which she is about to embark. Let us continue:

It was always love, lovers, mistresses, persecuted women fainting in solitary little houses, postilions expiring at every relay, horses killed on every page, gloomy forests, romantic woes, oaths, sobs, tears and kisses, small boats in the moonlight, nightingales in the groves, gentlemen brave as lions, gentle as lambs, impossibly virtuous, always well dressed, who wept copiously. For six months, at the age of fifteen, Emma soiled her hands with these dusty remains of old reading rooms. Later, with Walter Scott, she grew enamored of historic events, dreamed of traveling chests, guardrooms, and minstrels. She wished that she had lived in some old manor, like those long-waisted

* p.56
† p.56

ladies of the manor who spent their days under the trefoil of pointed arches, elbows on the rampart and chin in hand, watching a cavalier with a white feather emerge from the horizon on a galloping black charger. During that period she had a passion for Mary Stuart and adored unfortunate or celebrated women. Joan of Arc, Héloise, Agnès Sorel, La Belle Ferronnière, and Clémence Isaure blazed for her like comets over the murky immensity of history, on which, still standing out in relief, but more lost in the shadow and with no relationship to each other, were Saint Louis with his oak, the dying Bayard, a few vicious crimes of Louis XI, a bit of the Saint Bartholomew Massacre, Henri IV's plume, and the continuing memory of the painted plates praising Louis XIV.

In the ballads she sang in music class there were only tiny angels with golden wings, madonnas, lagoons, gondoliers—gentle compositions that enabled her to perceive, through the foolishness of the style and the weaknesses of the music, the attractive fantasy of sentimental realities.*

What, you did not remember that? When, after returning to the farm and marrying a village doctor, this poor country girl is invited to a ball at the château—you did not remember that when you tried to draw the court's attention to the ball scene to show something lascivious in the waltz she was dancing! You did not remember her education when this invitation transported her from her husband's humble home to the château and the poor woman was dazzled by the sight of these handsome men and beautiful ladies and this old duke, who was said to have enjoyed good fortune at court. . . ! The imperial attorney indulged in a fine outburst on the subject of Queen Marie-Antoinette! Assuredly there is not one of us who does not share your thought. Like you, we trembled to hear the name of this victim of the Revolution, but the subject here is not Marie-Antoinette; it is the château de la Vaubyessard.

There was an old duke there who was the object of all eyes and who—so people said—had had relations with the queen. And when this young woman was thus transported into this world and saw the realization of all the fantastic dreams of her youth, you are astonished at the intoxication she felt; you accuse her of having been lascivious! But rather accuse the waltz itself that people dance at our large modern balls, and in which, as an author has described it, "the woman leans on the shoulder of her partner, whose leg clings to hers." You find Madame Bovary lascivious as Flaubert describes her. But there is not a man, and I

* p.57

do not except yourselves, who, having attended a ball and seen this sort of waltz, has not wished that his wife or his daughter would forego this pleasure that contains something so wild. If one counts on a young girl's purity to protect her and sometimes allows her to give herself to this pleasure that has been sanctioned by fashion, one must count very heavily on that protection; and however heavily one counts on it, she will very possibly show the same effects Monsieur Flaubert has shown in the name of morality and purity.

There she is at the château de la Vaubyessard; there she is gazing at this old duke, observing the scene with rapture, and you cry out: "What details!" Just what can that mean? Details? Details are everywhere when one quotes only a single passage.

> Madame Bovary noticed that several of the women had not put their gloves in their wineglasses.

> At the upper end of the table, alone among all the women, there was one old man eating, bending over the well-filled platter with his napkin knotted in back like a child, drops of sauce dribbling from his mouth. His eyes were bloodshot and he wore a small pigtail tied with a black ribbon. It was the marquis' father-in-law, the old Duke of Laverdière, once favorite of the Count d'Artois in the days of the Marquis de Conflans's hunting parties in Vaudreuil; it was said he had been Marie-Antoinette's lover between Messieurs de Coigny and de Lauzun.*

Defend the queen, defend her above all before the scaffold; say that her title deserves respect, but spare your accusations when all that has been said is that according to gossip, the duke had once been the queen's lover. Can you be serious in accusing us of having insulted the memory of this unfortunate woman?

> He had led a thoroughly debauched life, filled with duels, wagers, and abductions, had run through his fortune and been the terror of his entire family. A servant behind his chair was shouting into his ear the names of dishes that the old man would point to with his finger, mumbling. Emma could not keep herself from staring at the slack-mouthed old man as on someone extraordinary and august. He had lived at Court and slept in the bed of queens!

Although these descriptions are undeniably charming, you see that it is not possible to pick out a line here and there

* p.67

from which to create a kind of lascivious tone, against which one's conscience would protest. It is not a lascivious tone; it is the tone of the book that is at the same time its literary principle and its moral principle.

There she is, this young girl who has received this education, there she is become a woman. The imperial attorney has said: "Did she even try to love her husband?" But he has not read the book; if he had read it, he would not have raised this objection.

There she is, gentlemen, this poor woman; at the outset she will indulge in daydreams. On page 60 you will see her daydreams. And there is more, there is something of which the imperial attorney has not spoken and which I must point out to you: these are her impressions on her mother's death—and you will see if that too is lascivious! Now if you will be good enough to turn to page 58 and to follow me:

She cried a great deal the first days after her mother's death. She had a memorial picture made with the dead woman's hair, and in a letter that she sent to Les Bertaux, all filled with sad reflections about life, she asked to be buried in the same tomb when she died. Her father thought she must be ill and came to see her. Emma was inwardly pleased to feel that she had achieved at her first attempt this rare ideal of pallid existence that mediocre hearts never achieve. She let herself glide in to Lamartinian meanderings, listened to all the harps on the lake, to the songs of dying swans, to all the falling leaves, the pure virgins rising to heaven, and the voice of the Eternal reverberating in the valleys. She tired of this, didn't want to admit it, continued first out of habit, then out of vanity, and was finally surprised to find herself soothed and with as little sadness in her heart as wrinkles on her forehead.

Now I wish to reply to the imperial attorney's objection that she made no effort to love her husband.

THE IMPERIAL ATTORNEY: I have not objected to that; I said that she had not succeeded.

MONSIEUR SÉNARD: If I have misunderstood you, if you have not made this objection, that is the best reply that we could have. I thought I heard you make it; let us agree that I was mistaken. Moreover, here is what I find at the bottom of page 62:

And yet, in line with the theories she admired, she

wanted to give herself up to love. In the moonlight of the garden she would recite all the passionate poetry she knew by heart and would sing melancholy adagios to him with sighs, but she found herself as calm afterward as before and Charles didn't appear more amorous or moved because of it.

After she had several times struck the flint on her heart without eliciting a single spark, incapable as she was of understanding that which she did not feel or of believing things that didn't manifest themselves in conventional forms, she convinced herself without difficulty that Charles's passion no longer offered anything extravagant. His effusions had become routine; he embraced her at certain hours. It was one habit among others, like the established custom of eating dessert after the monotony of dinner.

On page 63 we will find a mass of similar things. Now we see the danger about to begin. You know how she had been brought up; this is what I beg you not to forget for an instant.

After reading these last six pages, there is no man who would not say, the book in his hand, that Monsieur Flaubert is not only a great artist but also a man of feeling, for he has diverted all of the horror and contempt toward the wife and all of the sympathy toward the husband. He is an even greater artist because he has not transformed the husband, because he has left him to the end just as he was: a good man, common and mediocre, performing his professional duties, faithfully loving his wife, but lacking in refinement, lacking in any aspiration of mind. He is the same at his wife's deathbed. And yet there is no other character one remembers with more sympathy. Why? Because he has kept his simplicity and his goodness of heart up to the end; because up to the end he performed his duty, from which his wife had strayed. His death is as beautiful and as moving as his wife's death is hideous. The author has shown the stains left on the wife's corpse by the vomitings of poison; they have soiled the white sheet in which she will be shrouded; he wanted to make it an object of disgust. But there is a man who is sublime; he is the husband beside that grave. He is a man who is great and sublime, whose death is admirable; it is this husband, all of whose remaining illusions were successively destroyed with his wife's death, who embraces his wife with his dying thoughts. Remember this, I beg you; as Lamartine told him, the author has gone beyond what is permissable in rendering this woman's death hideous and her expiation most ter-

rible. The author has known how to concentrate all sympathy
on the man who had not swerved from the line of duty,
who had kept his mediocre character, which doubtless the
author could not have changed, but who also kept all his
generosity of heart. And the author has heaped all horrors
upon the death of the wife who deceived and ruined him,
who gave herself to the moneylenders, who forged his name
to promissory notes, and who finally arrived at suicide. We
will see if this was the natural death for a woman who,
had she not found the poison with which to end it, would
have been crushed all the same under the weight of misfortune. That is what the author has done. His book would
not be read if he had done otherwise, if he had not been
lavish with the charming images and powerful pictures to
which the prosecution objects, but which were needed to
show where such a dangerous education as Madame Bovary's
may lead.

Monsieur Flaubert constantly emphasizes the superiority of
the husband over the wife, and what sort of superiority is
this? It is that of duty fulfilled, while Emma strays from
it! And then, placed as she is on the downward path of
that unsuitable education, there she is after the ball scene,
starting off with a young boy, Léon, as inexperienced as herself. She will flirt with him but will not dare go further;
nothing will happen. Then comes Rodolphe, and he will
take this woman. After having seen her for an instant, he
says to himself; "She is all right, this woman!" And she will
succumb to him because she is weak and inexperienced. As
for her downfall, you will reread pages 159-162. I have only
a word to say to you about this scene, there are no details,
no description, not one image that paints the agitation of
the senses; one single word indicates the fall: "She gave
herself to him." Again I will beg you to be good enough to
reread the details of the fall of Clarissa Harlowe, which
I do not believe to have been described in a bad book.
Monsieur Flaubert has substituted Rodolphe for Lovelace,
and Emma for Clarissa. You will compare the two authors
and the two works, and you will judge.

But here I meet with the imperial attorney's indignation.
He is shocked that remorse does not follow immediately upon
the downfall and that instead of expressing bitterness she
tells herself with satisfaction: "I have a lover." But the
author would not be right if, while the cup was still at her
lips, he made her taste all the bitterness of the enchanted
potion. A man who would write as the imperial attorney
expects might be moral, but he would be saying something
that is not in human nature. No, it is not at the moment

of the first transgression that the feeling of wrongdoing awakens; if that were so, it would not be committed. No, it is not at the moment when she is still under the intoxicating illusion that the intoxication itself may warn her of the immense wrong she has committed. She recalls only the rapture; she returns home happy and glowing, she sings in her heart: "At last I have a lover." But does this last for long? You have read pages 163 and 164. Two pages later, if you please, on page 165, the feeling of distaste for the lover has not yet appeared, but already she feels a sense of fear and anxiety. She observes, she considers, she wants never to leave Rodolphe:

Something stronger than herself was pushing her toward him, so that one day, seeing her appear unexpectedly, he frowned as if he were annoyed.

What's the matter?" she asked. "Are you ill? Tell me!"

He declared, very gravely, that her visits were becoming imprudent and that she was compromising herself.

Gradually Rodolphe's fears began to affect her. At first she had been so drunk with love that she thought of nothing beyond it. But now that it was so indispensable to her life, she was terrified that it might be disturbed or even destroyed, She would look around anxiously when returning from his house, stare at every shadow on the horizon and each attic window in the village from which she might be seen. She strained her ears for the sound of footsteps, shouts, the noise of plows; and she would stop short, more pale and quivering than the poplar leaves swaying above her.

You see clearly that she is not mistaken; she feels strongly that there is something that is not what she had dreamed of. Let us take pages 169 and 170, and you will be even more convinced:

When it rained, they took shelter in the consulting room, between the shed and the stable. She would light one of the kitchen candles, which she had hidden behind the books. Rodolphe would make himself as comfortable as if he were at home. The sight of the bookcase and the desk, of the entire room, intensified his gaiety; he could not refrain from making various jokes at Charles's expense, which Emma found embarrassing. She wanted him to be more serious and even more dramatic on occasion. Once, for example, she thought she heard approaching footsteps in the lane.

"Someone's coming!" she said.

He blew out the light.

"Do you have your pistols?"

"What for?"

"To—to defend yourself," Emma said.

"Against your husband? That poor fellow!" And Rodolphe finished his sentence with a gesture signifying: "I could crush him with a flick of the finger."

She was amazed at his courage, although she sensed in it an indelicacy and blatant vulgarity that she thought shocking.

Rodolphe thought a long while about this talk of pistols. If she had meant it seriously, it would be the height of idiocy, even odious, for he personally had no reason to hate good old Charles. Rodolphe was not a man "devoured with jealousy." Besides, in this connection Emma had made a solemn promise to him that, moreover, he did not find in the best of taste.

She was also becoming quite sentimental. They had had to exchange miniatures and locks of hair and now she wanted a ring, an actual marriage band as a sign of eternal union. She would often speak to him of the bells of evening or of the "voices of nature." She would talk to him about her mother and his.

In short, she bored him.

Then on page 170:

He [Rodolphe] no longer used words so sweet that they made her cry, as he had in the old days; nor were his caresses so ardent that they drove her mad. So the great love affair in which she had plunged seemed to diminish under her like the water of a river being absorbed into its own bed, and she began to see slime at the bottom. She didn't want to believe it and redoubled her tenderness. Rodolphe hid his indifference less and less.

She did not know if she regretted having given in to him or if she wished, on the contrary, to love him even more. The humiliation of feeling how weak she was where he was concerned turned into a resentment tempered only by sensual pleasure. It was not an attachment, but a permanent seduction. He was subjugating her. She was almost afraid of him.

And the imperial attorney fears that young women may read that! I am less frightened and less timid than you. For my part, I perfectly understand the father of a family who says to his daughter: "Young woman, if your heart, your conscience, your religious feeling, and the voice of duty do not suffice to show your the right path—look, my child, and see what anxiety, sorrow, pain, and grief await the woman who attempts to find happiness elsewhere than in her own home!" These words would not offend you coming from a father—very well then! Monsieur Flaubert has said nothing else; it is the truest, the most striking picture of what a woman immediately finds when she had dreamed of happiness outside her own home.

But let us go on; we are coming to all the disillusioning adventures. You object to Léon's caresses on page 250. Alas! Soon she will pay the price of adultery, and you will find it a terrible price, just a few pages after the passages you accuse. She has sought happiness in adultery, unhappy woman! But there, besides the disgust and weariness that the monotony of marriage may give the woman who does not walk in the path of duty, there she has found only disillusionment and the contempt of the man to whom she had given herself. Does anything mitigate his contempt? Oh no! Rodolphe, who has shown himself so base, gives her a final proof of egotism and cowardice. She says to him: "Take me away! Take me away! I am stifling, I can no longer breathe in my husband's house, which I have shamed and dishonored." He hesitates; she insists; finally he promises, and the next day she receives from him a crushing letter, under which she falls overwhelmed, annihilated. She falls ill, she is dying. The following installment shows her in all the convulsions of a struggling soul that may perhaps be drawn back to duty through the very intensity of its suffering. But unfortunately she soon encounters the youth with whom she had toyed when she had been still inexperienced. That is the progression of the novel, and then comes the expiation.

But the imperial attorney stops me and says: "Assuming that the work's intention is good from start to finish, would you be able to permit yourself such obscene details as those you have permitted?"

Most certainly I could not permit myself such details, but have I permitted them? Where are they? I come now to the most offending passages. I am no longer speaking of the adventure in the cab; the court has had satisfaction on that count. I come to the passages that you have pointed out as contrary to public morality and that constitute a certain number of pages in the issue of December first. And there is only one thing I need to do to demolish the entire support for your charge: I need only restore what precedes and what follows your quotations—in a word, to substitute the complete text for your fragments.

On page 265, Léon, after having been in touch with Homais the pharmacist, goes to the Hotel de Bourgogne, and then the pharmacist comes to see him.

She had just left in exasperation. Now she detested him. His failure to keep his promise about their rendezvous seemed an outrage to her. She kept looking for other reasons to break with him: he was incapable of heroism; weak, commonplace . . .

Then, calming down, she finally realized that she had probably unjustly condemned him. But the disparagement of those we love always erodes a bit of the affection. One must not touch idols; the gilt rubs off on one's hands.

From now on, matters apart from their love entered into their correspondence. . . .

My God! It is because of the lines I am about to read that we are being prosecuted before you. Listen now:

From now on, matters apart from their love entered into their correspondence. Emma's letters to him talked of flowers, poetry, the moon and the stars, naïve expedients of a weakening passion trying to revive itself by external devices. She kept promising herself a profound joy for their next meeting; then she would admit to herself that she felt nothing extraordinary. This disappointment soon gave way to a renewed hope, and Emma would return to him more impassioned and avid. She would undress savagely, tearing at the thin lacing of her corset, which fell down around her hips like a gliding snake. She would tiptoe on her bare feet to see once more if the door were locked, then she would drop all her clothes in one movement—and pale, without speaking, solemn, she would fall against his chest with one long shudder.

The imperial attorney has stopped there; permit me to continue:

Yet there was something wild, something strange and tragic in this forehead covered with cold sweat, in those stammering lips and wildly staring eyes, in the embrace of those arms—something that seemed to Léon to be coming between them subtly as if to tear them apart.

You call that a lascivious tone; you say that it will give a taste for adultery; you say that those are pages that can inflame, arouse the senses—lascivious pages! But death is in these pages. You do not think of that, Mr. Imperial Attorney; you are shocked to find there the words "corset" and "she would drop all her clothes," and you cling to these three or four words of corset and dropping clothes! Would you like me to show how a corset may appear in a classic, a most classic book? This is what I shall give myself the pleasure of doing in a moment.

"She would undress——" Ah! Mr. Imperial Attorney, how you have misunderstood this passage! "She would undress savagely"——unfortunate woman——"tearing at the thin lacing of her corset, which fell down around her hips like a gliding snake . . . and pale, without speaking, solemn, she would fall against his chest with one long shudder. Yet there was something . . . strange and tragic in this forehead covered with cold sweat . . . in the embrace of those arms. . . ."

It is here that one must ask oneself where is the lascivious tone? And where is the stern tone? And if the young girl into whose hands this book may fall might find the senses aroused, inflamed——as in the reading of a classic of classics, a book that I shall quote to you shortly, that has been reprinted a thousand times, and that no attorney, imperial or royal, has ever dreamed of prosecuting. Is there anything analogous in what I am about to read to you? Or, on the contrary, does not this "something tragic that seems to come between them as if to tear them apart" arouse a horror of vice? Let us continue, if you will:

He did not dare question her; but seeing how experienced she was, he told himself that she must have known all the extremes of suffering and pleasure. What had once charmed him now frightened him a little. He was also rebelling against the increasing encroachment upon his personality. He resented Emma for this permanent victory over him, even tried not to want her; and then at the sound of her footsteps he felt himself grow weak like an alcoholic at the sight of strong liquor.

And that—is that lascivious?
And then take the last paragraph:

One day when they had parted early, she was walking alone along the boulevard. She noticed the walls of her convent and sat down on a bench in the shade of the elm trees. How calm those days had been! How wistful she was about the indescribable ideas of love she had tried to imagine for herself from books.

The first months of her marriage, her horseback rides

in the forest, the viscount waltzing, and Lagardy singing —all of this passed before her eyes.

Do not forget that either, Mr. Imperial Attorney, when you would judge the author's intention, when you would absolutely insist on finding a lascivious tone where I can find only an excellent book.

And Léon suddenly appeared to be as far from her as the others. "But I love him!" she told herself. Nevertheless she was not happy, had never been happy. Why then was life so inadequate? Why did she feel this instantaneous decay of the things she relied on?

And is that lascivious?

If there existed somewhere a strong and handsome being, a valiant nature, imbued with both exaltation and refinement, the heart of a poet in the shape of an angel, a lyre with strings of bronze, sounding elegiac nuptial songs toward the heavens—why, why could she not find him? How impossible it seemed! And anyway, nothing was worth looking for; everything was a lie. Each smile hid a yawn of boredom, each joy a curse, each pleasure its aftermath of disgust, and the best of kisses left on your lips only the unattainable desire for a higher delight.
A metallic clang rang through the air and there were four strokes from the convent clock. Four o'clock! And it seemed to her that she had been there on that bench for eternity.

One must not search through one book for something to explain what is at the heart of another. I have read you the accused passage without adding a word to defend a work that is its own best defense. Let us continue our reading of this passage that has been accused of immorality:

Emma would stay in her room. No one went up. She would remain there all day long, in a torpor, only half dressed, burning incense that she had bought in Rouen in an Algerian shop. She managed by enough fussing to relegate Charles to the second floor so that she wouldn't have to sleep next to him. All night long she would read sensational books in which there were orgies and gory situations.

This makes one envy the adulteress, does it not?

Often she would be terrified by a sudden thought and scream. Charles would come running.

"Oh, go away," she would say.

At other times, burning violently from her adulterous passion, panting and shaking, throbbing with desire, she would open her window, breathe in the cold air, let down her heavy mass of hair, and stare at the stars, yearning for the love of a prince. She would think of *him*, of Léon. At that moment she would have given anything for just one of those meetings that sated her desires.

Those were her festive days—when they met. She wanted them to be splendid, and when he alone could not pay for them, she freely paid the difference. This happened nearly every time. He tried to make her understand that they would be just as comfortable elsewhere, in a more modest hotel, but she always objected.

You see how simple all of this is when one reads the whole, whereas with the imperial attorney's fragments the smallest word becomes a mountain.

THE IMPERIAL ATTORNEY: I have not quoted any one of those phrases, and even if you wish to quote what I have never accused, still you must not simply pass over page 270.

MONSIEUR SÉNARD: I am passing over nothing, I am stressing the phrases accused in the summons. We are indicted for page 271.

THE IMPERIAL ATTORNEY: I am speaking of the quotations made before the court, and I think that you are accusing me of having quoted the lines that you have just read.

MONSIEUR SÉNARD: Mr. Imperial Attorney, I have quoted all of the passages with whose aid you hoped to establish an offense that is now shattered. You developed your case before the court as you saw fit, and to you it was fair game. Happily, we have had the book; the defense knows the book—if we had not known it, allow me to say that our position would have been very strange. I was charged with defending such and such passages, and then in court other passages were substituted. Had I not the thorough knowledge of the book that I have, the defense would have been difficult. Now, I am showing you by careful analysis that far from having to be presented as lascivious, the book should, on the contrary, be considered as an eminently moral work. After having done this, I am taking the passages that inspired the criminal indictment, and after having reunited your fragments with what precedes and follows them, the minute that I read them to you the evidence becomes so weak that it shocks you yourself! Nevertheless I still have a good right to quote the same passages you pointed out as offensive an instant ago in order to make you see the nullity of your charge.

I now resume my quotation where I left it, on page 272:

> Now he [Léon] was bored when Emma would suddenly sob on his chest; and his heart, like people who can stand only a certain amount of music, languished with indifference amid the stridency of a love whose subtleties left him cold.
>
> They knew each other too well to feel those mutual revelations of possession that multiply its joys a hundredfold. She was as sated with him as he was tired of her. Emma was finding in adultery all the banalities of marriage.

The banalities of marriage. The man who plucked out this phrase has said: "What, here we have a man who says that in marriage there are only banalities! It is an attack against marriage, it is an outrage against morality!" You must agree, Mr. Imperial Attorney, that with artfully chosen fragments one can go far in pressing charges. Just what is it that the author has called the banalities of marriage? That monotony that Emma had dreaded and had wished to flee and that she had unfailingly rediscovered in adultery, and which was precisely disillusionment. And so you see very clearly that if one reads what precedes and follows instead of cutting out parts of phrases and single words, then nothing whatever remains of the accusation. And you will understand perfectly that my client, who knows his own intention, must be somewhat indignant to hear it misrepresented in this way. Let us continue:

> She was as sated with him as he was tired of her. Emma was finding in adultery all the banalities of marriage.
>
> But how could she break free? Though she felt humiliated by the base quality of such happiness, she clung to it out of habit or depravity. Each day she clung more desperately to it, thus destroying all happiness by demanding too much of it. She blamed Léon for her disappointed hopes as if he had betrayed her, and she even wished for some catastrophe that would cause their separation since she lacked the courage to bring it about herself.
>
> Nevertheless, this did not stop her from continuing to write him loving letters, in line with the idea that a woman should always be writing to her lover.
>
> But even as she wrote she perceived another man, a

phantom fabricated from her most ardent memories ...

What follows is no longer under indictment:

... Then she fell back to earth, broken, for her surges
of imaginary love tired her more than wild debauches.

She was now living in a state of chronic and complete
wretchedness. She would often receive summonses, official
documents she barely glanced at. She wished she were
dead, or continually asleep.

I call that an incitement to virtue by horror of vice, as
the author himself declares, and which the most casual reader
cannot but see unless he is unwilling.

And now something more to make you perceive the kind
of man you have to judge. In order to show you, not the
sort of justification I might make, but if Monsieur Flaubert
had any lascivious tone at all, and where he takes his inspiration, let me give you this book he has used that inspired him to paint the wantonness, the seductions of this
woman who seeks happiness in illicit pleasures and who cannot find it there, who seeks again, who seeks on and on, and
who never finds it. And where has Flaubert taken his inspiration, gentlemen? From the book you see here; listen:

The Delusion of the Senses

Whoever therefore becomes attached to the emotions
must necessarily wander from object to object and become
deceived, so to speak, in shifting position; thus concupiscence, which is love of pleasures, is always changing
because all its fervor languishes and dies with continuity
and it is only change that revives it. And so what else is
the life of the senses but the alternate movement from desire to aversion, and from aversion to desire, while the
soul hovers always uncertain between the abating and the
rekindling passion. *Inconstantia, concupiscentia.* Inconstancy, thy name is concupiscence. There you have the life
of the senses. Meanwhile, in this perpetual movement, one
never ceases to be diverted by the sense of a ranging
freedom.

There you have the life of the senses. And who was it who
said that? Who wrote the words you have just heard on its
excitements and unceasing fervors? What book is it whose
pages Monsieur Flaubert constantly turns and that was his
inspiration for the passages that the imperial attorney now ac-

cuses? It is Bossuet! What I have just read is a fragment of a discourse by Bossuet on *Illicit Pleasures*. I will make you see that all of these accused passages are, not plagiarized—a man who adapts an idea is not a plagiarist—but modeled on Bossuet. Would you like another example? Here it is:

On Sin

And do not ask me, Christians, how this great alteration of our pleasures into torments takes place; the thing is proven by the Scriptures. It is the true God who tells it; it is the All Powerful who does it. And yet, if you consider the nature of the passions to which you surrender your heart, you will easily understand how they may become an intolerable torment. In themselves they all contain cruel punishments, loathings, and bitterness. They all contain a boundlessness that rages at being unable to find appeasement; a rage that sweeps them away, that degenerates into a kind of frenzy as painful as it is unreasoning. Love, if I may so name it from this pulpit, has its incertitudes, its violent agitations and irresolvable problems, and the hell of its jealousies.

And further on:

Eh! What can be easier therefore than to turn our passions into the insupportable pain of our sins by removing from them, as is most just, that portion of sweetness by which they seduce us, thus leaving them only the cruel anxieties and the bitterness with which they abound? Our sins against us, our sins upon us, our sins surrounding us; an arrow piercing our breast, an insupportable weight upon our head, a poison devouring our entrails.

Is all of this not meant to show the bitterness of passion? I shall leave you this book, which is all annotated and worn by this studious man who took his ideas from it. And he who drew his inspiration from such a source, who has described adultery in the terms you have just heard—this man is prosecuted for outrage against public and religious morality!

I shall read a few more lines from Bossuet on *The Sinning Woman*, and you will see how Monsieur Flaubert, when he had to paint these passions, took inspiration from his model:

But as we are punished for our wrongdoing without becoming disenchanted, we seek a new remedy for our mistake in change; we wander from object to object, and if we are finally held by someone, it is not that we are content with our choice, but that we are sated with our inconstancy...

Everything in these creatures appeared to him to be empty, false, disgusting; his heart, far from rediscovering the first attractions against which it had been so difficult to defend itself, now saw in them only frivolity, danger, and vanity...

I do not speak of an engagement of passion; what terrors are unleashed by secrecy! What precautions to be taken for the sake of the proprieties and for glory! How many eyes to avoid! How many observers to deceive! What qualms of fear as to the fidelity of the chosen servants and confidants of one's passion! What rebuffs to endure from the man for whom, perhaps, one has sacrificed happiness and freedom, and of which one would not dare complain! To all of that, add those cruel moments when slackening passion leaves us the leisure to reproach ourselves and to feel all the humiliation of our position; those moments when the heart, born for more substantial pleasures, wearies of its own idols and finds its torment in its aversion and in its inconstancy. Ungodly world! If that is your vaunted bliss, grant it to your worshipers, and in giving such happiness, punish them for the faith they have so carelessly placed in your promises!

Let me tell you this: when in the silence of the night a man has meditated upon the causes of corruption in women, when he has found them in education, and when, to express them and mistrusting his own observations, he has gone to the sources I have just mentioned; when he has taken up his pen only after having been inspired by the thoughts of Bossuet and of Massillon, may I ask if there is a word to express my surprise and distress on seeing this man summoned to police court for some passages in his book that express precisely the most noble ideas and sentiments he could have assembled! I beg you not to forget this when you think of the charge of outrage against religious morality. And then if I may, I will place before you in comparison what I myself would call an attack upon morality: the satisfaction of passions without bitterness, without those *drops of cold sweat* that fall from the brows of those who have succumbed to it. I will not quote from one of those licentious books whose authors have tried to inflame the senses; I will quote from a book that is given as a prize in our schools; I will only ask your permission not to reveal the author until after I have read you a passage. I will now read the passage; then

I will have the book passed to you. And I would rather see this book committed to justice than Monsieur Flaubert's.

The next day I was led again to her apartment. There I perceived all that could enhance sensual pleasure. The most agreeable perfumes had been diffused in the room. She lay on a bed that was covered only by garlands of flowers. She appeared there in languid repose. She gave me her hand and made me sit beside her. Everything, including the veil that covered her face, had charm. I saw the lines of her beautiful body. A simple cloth stirred with her movements, by turns allowing me to lose and discover ravishing beauties.

A simple cloth, when it was drawn over a corpse, seemed to you to be a lascivious image; here it is drawn over a living woman.

She noticed that my eyes were occupied, and as she saw them glow, the cloth seemed to fall open of itself; I saw all of the treasures of a divine beauty. In that moment she grasped my hand; my eyes roamed everywhere. I cried out: "Only my beloved Ardasire is so beautiful; but I call the gods to witness my fidelity..." She threw her arms around me and pressed me to her. All at once the room darkened, her veil opened; she kissed me. I was utterly beside myself; a sudden flame throbbed through my veins and set all my senses afire. The thought of Ardasire receded. A trace of memory... but it seemed only a dream... I was going... going to herself rather than to the dream. Already my hands were on her breast; they roamed swiftly everywhere; love shows itself only by its passion; it rushed headlong to its victory; a moment more, and Ardasire could no longer defend herself.

Who has written that? It is not even the author of *La Nouvelle Héloise*—it is the president of the Academy of France: Monsieur de Montesquieu! Here there is no bitterness or disgust, all is sacrificed to literary beauty—and they give that as a prize to students of the classics, doubtless to serve as model for the exercises or the descriptions they are given to do. In *Les Lettres Persanes*, Montesquieu has described a scene that could not even be read aloud. It concerns a woman whom this author places between two men who contend for her. This woman placed thus between two men has dreams—which appear to her very agreeable. Have we not succeeded, Mr. Imperial Attorney! Must we still quote Jean Jacques Rousseau in *Les Confessions* and elsewhere? No, I will only say to the court that if Monsieur Mérimée were prosecuted for his scene in the carriage in *La Double Méprise*, he would be acquitted at once. One would see his book only as a work of art, of great literary beauty. One would no more condemn him than one condemns paintings or sculptures that express not only the beauties of the human body but all its ardors and passions as well. I am not finished: I want your acknowledgment that Monsieur Flaubert has not exaggerated his images and that he has done only one thing—to draw the scene of degradation with a most masterly hand. He emphasized disillusionment in every line of his book, and instead of ending with something charming, he shows us this woman, after her contempt, neglect, and ruin of her house, arriving at the most appalling death. In a word, I can only repeat what I said in opening my defense, that Monsieur Flaubert is the author of a good book—a book that is an incitement to virtue through the horror of vice.

I must now examine the charge of outrage against religion. Outrage against religion committed by Monsieur Flaubert! And in what does the charge consist, if you please? The imperial attorney has thought to see in him a skeptic. I can reply to the imperial attorney that he is mistaken. I am not here to make a profession of faith; I have only the book to defend, and so I am able to confine myself to this single work. But as for the book, I defy the imperial attorney to find anything whatever that resembles an outrage against religion. You have seen how religion was introduced into Emma's education and how this religion, warped in a thousand ways, could not hold her from the downward path to which she was lured. Do you wish to know how Monsieur Flaubert speaks of religion? Listen to several lines I take from the first installment, pages 119 and 120:

> One evening as she was sitting at the open window and watching Lestiboudois, the sexton, trim the boxwood hedge, she suddenly heard the Angelus ringing.
> It was the beginning of April, when the primroses are in bloom; a warm wind blows over the flower beds, and the gardens, like women, seem to be dressing for the summer holidays. Through the arbor lattice and all around beyond it, the river could be seen making its meandering way through the grassy meadow. The evening mist was passing through the leafless poplars, blurring their outlines with a violet haze, paler and more transparent than a fine gauze hung on their branches. Cattle were moving about in the distance; neither their steps nor their lowing was audi-

ble; and the bell, still ringing, continued its peaceful lamentation in the air.

At this repeated chiming, the young woman's thoughts strayed to her old memories of youth and school days. She remembered the candelabras, taller than the altar, the vases filled with flowers, and the tabernacle with its little columns. She wished she were still moving in that long line of white veils marked with black by the stiff coifs of the nuns kneeling on their *prie-Dieux.*

These are the terms in which religious sentiment is expressed. And yet, to hear the imperial attorney, it is skepticism that reigns from one end to the other of Monsieur Flaubert's book. And now I ask you: where can you find skepticism there?

THE IMPERIAL ATTORNEY: I have not said that it was in that passage.

MONSIEUR SÉNARD: If it is not in that passage, then where is it? In your fragments, evidently. But here is the work in its entirety; let the court judge that and it will see that religious feeling is so strongly stamped there that the accusation of skepticism is a real calumny. And now, will the imperial attorney permit me to tell him that it was not worth the trouble to accuse the author of skepticism with such a fuss? Let us continue:

When she lifted her head during Mass on Sunday, she would see the sweet face of the Virgin in the bluish clouds of incense that were rising. Then a tender emotion would suffuse her; she felt completely limp and abandoned like the down of a bird swirling in the tempest. Without being aware of what she was doing at that moment, she headed toward the church, prepared for any act of devotion as long as she could give her soul up there and make her entire existence disappear.

This, gentlemen, was the first appeal to religion to hold Emma from the downward path of the passions. She fell, poor woman, then was thrust down by the foot of the man to whom she had surrendered herself. She almost dies, she recovers, she revives; and now you will see what appears on page 207:

One day, at the height of her illness, she believed herself dying and asked for Communion; and as the preparations for the sacrament went on in her room, as they arranged the dresser with its clutter of medicine bottles into an altar and Félicité scattered dahlia petals over the floor,

Emma sensed something powerful passing over her, freeing her from all her pains, from all perception and feeling. Her body, freed of its burden, no longer thought; another life was beginning; it seemed to her that her being, ascending toward God...

You see in what terms Monsieur Flaubert speaks of religious things.

...it seemed to her that her being, ascending toward God, was going to be destroyed in that love like a burning incense that is dissolved in smoke. They sprinkled holy water over the sheets; the priest took the white wafer from the holy pyx; and she nearly fainted with a celestial joy as she offered her lips to receive the body of the Saviour.

I beg pardon of the imperial attorney and of the court for interrupting this passage, but I want to say that it is the author who is speaking and to point out the terms in which he expresses himself on the mystery of the Communion; before I resume reading, I want the court to have discerned the literary value derived from this picture; and I want to emphasize these expressions that belong to the author himself:

...and she nearly fainted with a celestial joy as she offered her lips to receive the body of the Saviour. The curtains of her alcove swelled out gently, like clouds, and the rays of the two candles burning on the chest of drawers seemed to her to be two dazzling haloes. Then she dropped her head, thinking she could hear the far-off song of heavenly harps and see God the Father on a golden throne in an azure sky, in the midst of saints bearing green palms, a God radiant with majesty, signaling to angels with flaming wings to descend to earth and take her off in their arms.

He continues:

This splendid vision remained in her memory as the most beautiful dream imaginable, so much so that she kept trying to recapture the sensation, which continued with the same sweetness, albeit less intensely. Her soul, aching with pride, was at last reposing in Christian humility; she relished the pleasure of having succumbed and studied the destruction of her will within herself, which was to allow free entry of heavenly grace. And so there existed greater joys than mere happiness, another love above all other loves, with neither interruption nor end, which would grow eternally! In her illusions born of hope she envisaged a state of purity floating above the earth, blending with the heavens, into which she longed to be absorbed. She wanted to become a saint. She bought rosaries and wore amulets; she wanted an emerald-studded reliquary at her bedside so that she could kiss it every night.

There you have religious sentiments! And if you would like to reflect for an instant upon the author's principal idea, I would ask you to read these lines:

She grew annoyed at the rules of ritual; the arrogance of the written polemics displeased her by their pitiless attacks on people she didn't know; and the secular tales, with their religious touches, seemed to have been written out of such ignorance of the world that imperceptibly they drove her away from the truths she was seeking.

There you have Monsieur Flaubert's manner of speaking. Now, if you please, let us come to another scene, the scene of the extreme unction. Oh! Mr. Imperial Attorney, how mistaken you were, when stopping short at the first words, you accused my client of mingling the sacred and the profane, when he has been content only to reproduce the beautiful phrases of the extreme unction at the moment when the priest touches the organs of our senses, at the moment in which he says, according to ritual: *Per istam unctionem, et suam puissimam misericordiam, indulgeat tibi Dominus quidquid deliquisti.*

You have said: "One must not touch upon holy things. By what right do you travesty these holy words: 'May God, in his holy mercy, pardon you for all the faults you have committed through the sight, through the taste, through the hearing, etc.'?"

Wait, I am going to read the passage to you, and that will be my entire vengeance. I dare to call it my vengeance, because the author must be avenged. Yes, Monsieur Flaubert must leave here, not only acquitted, but avenged! You will see by what readings he has been nurtured. The passage is on page 301:

Pale as a statue, his eyes red as coals, Charles, no longer crying, stood at the foot of the bed looking at her, while the priest, on one knee, was murmuring in a low voice.

This whole picture is magnificent, and it is irresistible in the reading; but set your minds at ease, I shall not prolong it beyond measure. Here now is the passage:

She turned her head slowly and seemed suffused with joy at the sudden sight of the purple stole—probably rediscovering in this instant of extraordinary peace the lost ecstasy of her first flights of mysticism and beginning to have visions of eternal bliss.

The priest stood up to take hold of the crucifix. She stretched out her neck like one who is thirsty, and pressing her lips to the body of the Man-God, she placed on it, with all her fading strength, the most passionate kiss of love she had ever given.

The extreme unction has not yet begun, but already they reproach us with this kiss. I will not search as far as Saint Theresa, whom you perhaps know but whose figure is too distant; I will not even search in Fenelon for the mysticism of Madame Guyon, nor the more modern mysticisms in which I find many more examples. I will not ask the explanation for this kiss from these that you term schools of sensual Christianity; it is Bossuet, Bossuet himself, whom I will ask:

Obey and strive moreover to enter into Jesus' feelings while taking Communion; these are the feelings of union, of possession, and of love: the whole gospel proclaims it. Jesus desires one to be with him; he desires to possess, he desires one to possess him. His holy flesh is the medium of this union and of this chaste possession: he gives himself.

I now resume my reading of the accused passage:

... Then he recited the *Misereatur* and the *Indulgentiam*, dipped his right thumb into the oil, and began the unctions; first on the eyes, which had been so covetous of earthly splendors; then on the nostrils, avid for warm breezes and scents of love; then on the mouth, which had opened to emit lies, had groaned with pride, and had cried out in lust; then over the hands, which had reveled in sensual contacts; and finally on the soles of the feet, which had once moved so rapidly when she was hurrying to quench her desires and which now would walk no longer.

The priest wiped his fingers, threw the oil-soaked bits of cotton into the fire, and came back to sit near the dying woman, to tell her that now she must unite her sufferings to those of Jesus Christ and give herself up to Divine mercy.

As he ended his exhortations, he tried to place a consecrated candle in her hands, symbol of the celestial glories with which she would shortly be surrounded. Emma was too weak to close her fingers, and had it not been for Monsieur Bournisien, the candle would have fallen to the floor.

But she was no longer so pale, and her face wore an expression of serenity, as though the sacrament had cured her.

The priest did not fail to point this out. He even explained to Bovary that the Lord sometimes prolonged people's lives when He thought it necessary for their salvation; and Charles remembered the day when, as now, she was about to die and had received Holy Communion.

"Maybe we shouldn't give up hope," he thought.

Now, when a woman is dying and when the priest is giving her extreme unction, when one makes a mystic scene of this, and when we reproduce the sacramental words with scrupulous fidelity—now they say that we are touching upon holy things. We have put a reckless hand upon holy things, because to the *deliquisti per oculos, per os, per aurem, per manus, et per pedes* we have added the sin that each of these organs had committed. We are not the first to have done the same. Monsieur Sainte-Beuve also places a scene of extreme unction in a book you know well, and here is how he expressed himself:

Oh! Yea then, first to the eyes, as the most noble and the most keen of our senses; to the eyes for what they have seen, for what they have looked upon in other eyes that was too tender, perfidious, and mortal; for what they have read and reread that were too interesting and too cherished; for the futile tears they have shed for worldly possessions and for unfaithful creatures; for the sleep they have so often forgotten at night while dreaming of them!

To the hearing also for what it has heard and has allowed itself to say that was too sweet, too flattering and intoxicating; for the sound the ear slowly draws from deceiving words and for the secret honey they have drunk from them!

Then for the sense of smell for the too subtle and voluptuous perfumes of spring evenings deep in the forest, for the flowers received in the morning and every day that were breathed in with such satisfaction!

To the lips for what they have pronounced that was too ambiguous or too open, for what they have not replied in certain moments or what they have not revealed to certain persons, for what they have sung in solitude that was too melodious and too full of tears, for their inarticulate murmuring, for their silence!

To the throat in place of the breast for the heat of desire according to the holy phrase (*propter ardorem libidinis*); yea, for the pain of affection, rivalries, and the many pangs of anguish in human love; for the tears that choke a speechless throat; for all that makes a heart beat and that torments it!

To the hands also for having clasped a hand with whom it had no holy tie; for having felt tears that were too burning; for having perhaps begun to write, without finishing, some illicit reply!

To the feet for not having fled, for having been capable of long solitary walks, for not having wearied soon enough in the midst of conversations that ceaselessly started afresh.

You have not prosecuted that. There you have two men, each in his own sphere, who have taken the same thing and who have added to each one of the senses the sin or the offense it had committed. Would you have forbidden them to reproduce the ritual form *Quidquid deliquisti per oculos, per aurem,* etc?

Monsieur Flaubert has done what Monsieur Sainte-Beuve has done, without becoming a plagiarist on that account. He has exercised the right, which belongs to all writers, to add to what another author has said, to complete a subject.

The last scene in the novel of *Madame Bovary* has been based, like any study of this type, on religious documents. Monsieur Flaubert has based the extreme unction scene on a book lent to him by a friend who is a venerable priest—a priest who later read this scene, who was touched to tears by it, and who has not conceived that the majesty of religion could have been injured by it. This book is entitled *Historical, Dogmatic, Moral, Liturgic, and Canonic Explanation of the Catechism, With the Answer to Objections Raised Against Religion by the Sciences,* by Abbé Ambroise Guillois, priest of Notre-Dame-du-Pré at Mans, sixth edition, etc., a work approved by His Eminence Cardinal Gousset and by Their Reverences the Bishops and Archbishops of Mans, Tours, Boulogne, Cologne, etc.; volume 3, printed at Mans by Charles Monnoyer, 1851. Now you will see in this book, as you have just seen in Bossuet, the principle and, as it were, the text of the passages the imperial attorney has accused. Now it is no longer Monsieur Sainte-Beuve, an artist and a literary fantacist, whom I quote; listen now to the Church itself:

> Extreme unction can restore health to the body if this is useful to the glory of God . . .

And the priest says that this often happens. Now here is the extreme unction:

> The priest addresses a short exhortation to the invalid if he is in condition to hear it to dispose him to receive in a worthy manner the sacrament he is about to administer to him.
> The priest then anoints the invalid with the stylus or with the tip of the right thumb, which he dips each time into the holy oil. These unctions must be made above all to the five parts of the body that nature has given man as the organs of sensation and knowledge: to the eyes, to the ears, to the nostrils, to the mouth, and to the hands.
> As the priest makes these unctions—

We have followed the ritual step by step.

—he pronounces the corresponding words [*To the eyes, on the closed eyelid*]: "With this holy unction and by His benign mercy, may God forgive you all of the sins that you have committed with the sight." At this moment the invalid must detest anew all of the sins that he has committed with the sight: so many indiscreet glances, so much guilty curiosity, so much reading that aroused a host of thoughts contrary to religion and to morals.

What has Monsieur Flaubert done? By uniting these two parts, he has placed in the priest's mouth the words that should be in his mind and at the same time in the mind of the invalid. He has copied purely and simply.

[*To the ears*]: "With this holy unction and by His benign mercy, may God forgive you all the sins that you have committed with the sense of hearing." At this moment the invalid must detest anew all the offenses of which he has been guilty in listening with pleasure to slander, to calumny, to unseemly talk, to obscene songs.

[To the nostrils]: "With this holy unction and by His benign mercy, may the Lord forgive you all the sins that you have committed by the sense of smell." In this moment the invalid must detest anew all the sins that he has committed by the sense of smell, all of the searching for subtle and voluptuous perfumes, all the sensualities, all that he has breathed of the odors of iniquity . . .

[To the mouth, on the lips]: "With this holy unction and by His benign mercy, may the Lord forgive you all the sins that you have committed with the sense of taste and by the spoken word." The invalid must, at this moment, detest anew all the sins that he has committed in uttering curses and blasphemies . . . in eating and drinking to excess . . .

[On the hands]: "With this holy unction and by His benign mercy, may the Lord forgive you all the sins that you have committed by the sense of touch." The invalid must at this moment detest anew all of the thefts, all of the wrongs of which he may have been guilty, all of the more or less guilty liberties that he has allowed himself . . . Priests receive the unction on the outside of the hands because they have already received it on the palms at the moment of their ordination, and other invalids receive it on the palms.

[On the feet]: "With this holy unction and by His benign mercy, may God forgive you all the sins that you have committed by your steps." The invalid must at this moment detest anew all the steps that he has taken in the paths of iniquity, so many shameful walks, so many guilty meetings . . . The feet are anointed on the upper part or on the sole, according to the comfort of the invalid, and also according to the usage of the diocese. The most common practice seems to be to do it on the soles of the feet.

And finally, to the breast. Monsieur Sainte-Beuve has followed this; we have not done so because here it concerned the breast of a woman. *Propter ardorem libidinis,* etc.

[To the breast]: "With this holy unction and by His benign mercy, may the Lord forgive you all the sins that you have committed by the ardor of the passions." The invalid must at this moment detest anew all the evil thoughts, all the evil desires in which he had indulged, all the feelings of hatred and vengeance that he had harbored in his heart.

And following the ritual, we might have spoken of something worse than the breast, but God knows what a holy wrath we would have aroused in the public ministry had we spoken of the loins:

[*To the loins (ad lumbos)*]: "With this holy unction and by His benign mercy, may the Lord forgive you all the sins that you have committed through the dissolute pleasures of the flesh."

Had we said that, with what eloquence would you not have tried to crush us, Mr. Imperial Prosecutor! And nevertheless, the ritual adds:

The invalid must at this moment detest anew so many shameful pleasures, so many carnal delights ...

There is the ritual, and you have seen the accused work; there is no mockery in it, everything in it is genuine and moving. And I repeat, the man who gave this book to my client and who saw the use he had made of it—that man clasped his hand and was moved to tears. You see therefore, Mr. Imperial Attorney, the rashness—not to use a more precise word that would be more severe—of your charge that we had meddled with holy things. You see now that we did not mingle the profane with the sacred in adding to each of the senses the sin committed by it, since that is the language of the Church itself.

Need I now dwell upon the other details of the charge of outrage against religion? Here is what the public ministry says to me: "It is no longer religion, it is the morality of all the ages that you have outraged; you have insulted death itself!" How have I insulted death? Because at the moment when this woman dies there passes by in the street a beggar she had met more than once demanding alms beside her carriage as she returned from her adulterous assignations—the blind man she had been accustomed to see, the blind man who sang his song as the carriage slowly mounted the hill, to whom she threw a coin and whose aspect made her shudder. This man passes in the street; and at the moment when Divine mercy forgives, or promises forgiveness, to the wretched woman who is paying for the transgressions of her life by this frightful death, human mockery appears to her in the form of a song that passes beneath her window. My God! You find outrage in that; but Monsieur Flaubert has done only what Shakespeare and Goethe have done, both of whom did not fail to let us hear some song of sadness

or mockery at the hour of death to remind the dying of some
pleasure he will no longer enjoy or of some transgression to
expiate.

Let us read:

> Indeed, she was looking all around her, slowly, like
> someone waking from a dream. Then, in a clear voice she
> asked for her mirror, and she leaned over it awhile,
> big tears trickling from her eyes. Then she threw her head
> back with a sigh and fell back on the pillow.

I cannot read it—I am like Lamartine: "For me the expiation goes beyond truth. . . ." Nevertheless, Mr. Imperial Attorney, I would not think I would be doing wrong in reading
these pages to those of my daughters who are married, virtuous girls who have been given good examples, good lessons,
and whom one has never, never by any indiscretion placed
outside the straight and narrow path, outside of the things
that can and must be understood. I find it too painful to
continue this reading; I will confine myself strictly to the
passages under indictment!

> He had taken her hands and was holding them tightly—

This is Charles, on her other side; Charles whom we hardly see and who is so admirable.

> —shuddering at each beat of her heart, as at the rever-
> beration of a falling ruin. As the death rattle grew louder,
> the priest hurried his prayers. They mingled with Bovary's
> muffled sobs, and at times everything seemed to merge
> with the monotonous murmur of the Latin syllables that
> sounded like the tolling of a bell.
>
> Suddenly there was a clatter of heavy clogs on the side-
> walk and the tapping of a stick. Then a voice arose,
> singing raucously:
>
>> Often the warmth of a lovely day
>> Makes a girl dream of love.
>
> Emma lifted herself up like a galvanized corpse, her
> hair undone, her eyes fixed and staring.
>
>> To gather up the corn
>> That the scythe has reaped,
>> My Nanette bends to the furrow
>> In which it was born.

"The blind man!" she cried. And she began to laugh—
a horrible, frenzied, despairing laugh—imagining that she
could see the hideous face of the beggar standing out
against the eternal darkness like a nightmare.

There was a strong breeze that day
And her short petticoat flew away!

A convulsion pulled her back down on the mattress.
They all drew near the bed. She was no more.

See, gentlemen, at the moment of death the reminder of her
transgressions and remorse made in the most poignant and
frightful way. This is not the fancy of an artist wishing only
to show contrast without useful purpose, without a moral;
this is the blind man she hears in the street singing the
frightful song he used to sing as she returned all sweating and
hideous from her adulterous assignations; it is the blind man
she saw at each one of these assignations; it is the blind man
who pursued her with his song, with his importuning; it is
he who comes at the moment when Divine mercy is
present to personify the human passion that pursues her at
the supreme instant of death! And they call that an outrage
against public morality! But I can say, on the contrary, that
there you have a tribute to public morality; nothing could be
more moral than that. I can say that in this book the defects
in education are brought to life as they really are in the living flesh of our society and that with every line the author
is putting to us this question: "Have you done all you should
in the education of your daughters? Is the religion you have
given them capable of sustaining them in the storms of life,
or is it only a mass of sensual superstitions that will leave
them unprotected when the tempest roars? Have you taught
them that life is not the realization of chimerical dreams, but
that it is something prosaic with which one must compro-
mise? Have you taught them that? Have you done what you
should for their happiness? Have you said to them: 'Poor
children, outside the road I show you, in the pleasure that
you pursue, only disgust awaits you, only neglect of your
home, only agitation, disorder, squandering, upheavals, seizure.'" And you can see if anything is missing from the picture: the bailiff is there, so also is the moneylender who
sold everything to satisfy the whims of this woman; the
furniture is seized, the public sale is about to take place, and
the husband is still unaware of it all. Nothing remains for
the wretched woman but to die!

But, says the public ministry, her death is voluntary, this woman chooses her own hour.

But could she have been able to live? Was she not condemned? Had she not already drained the last dregs of shame and degradation?

Yes, in our theaters they show fallen women who are graceful, smiling, and fortunate, and I will not say what they have done. *Questum corpore fecerant.* I will merely say this. When we are shown them happy, charming, wrapped in silk, offering a gracious hand to counts, marquesses, and dukes, these women who themselves often answer to the title of marchioness or duchess—that is what you call respect for public morality. And the man who shows you the adulterous woman dying in shame—this man commits an outrage against public morality!

In effect, I will not say that you have expressed an idea that is not your own, since you have expressed it; but you have yielded to a great pressure. No, I cannot believe it; it is not possible that you—the husband and father of a family, the man I see before me—would have come here without the pressure of the indictment and of a preconceived idea to say that Monsieur Flaubert is the author of an evil book! Indeed, left to your own inspiration, your opinion would be the same as mine; I am not speaking from a literary point of view—you and I could not differ in that respect—but from the point of view of morality and religious feeling as you and I both understand it.

They also told us that we had presented a materialistic priest. But we have taken the priest as we have taken the husband. This is not an eminent clergyman; this is a simple clergyman, a country parish priest. And just as we have insulted no one, just as we have expressed no feeling or idea that might be injurious to the husband, still less have we insulted the clergyman in this book. I have only a word to say about this.

Would you like to hear of books in which clergymen play a deplorable role? Take Balzac's *Gil Blas* and *La Chanoine;* take Victor Hugo's *Notre Dame de Paris.* If you want priests who are the shame of the clergy, you must look elsewhere—you could not find them in *Madame Bovary.* And what is it that I have shown? A country priest who in his duties as a country priest is just what Monsieur Bovary is—a simple man. Have I portrayed him as libertine, glutton, or drunkard? I have not said one word of that kind. I have portrayed him fulfilling his ministry, not with a lofty understanding, but as his nature called him to fulfill it. Next to him, and in a state of almost perpetual argument, I have placed a personality who will live—as the creation of Monsieur Prudhomme has lived—as other creations will live, for they are so well studied and true to life that there is no possibility of our forgetting them. This personality is the country pharmacist, the voltairian, the skeptic, the unbeliever, the man who is perpetually in dispute with the priest. But in these disputes with the priest, who is the one who is continually beaten, derided, and ridiculed? It is Homais who has been given the role that is the more comic because it is the more true to life, a role that best portrays our skeptical age —what we call a rabid priest-hater. Again allow me to read pages 91-92: The innkeeper's wife is offering a glass of wine to her priest:

"May I help you, Monsieur le curé?" the landlady asked, reaching for one of the brass candlesticks lined up along the mantelpiece. "Would you like something? A drop of cassis, a glass of wine?"

The priest refused quite politely. He had come for his umbrella: he had forgotten it the other day at the Ernemont convent. After asking Madame Lefrançois to send it to him at the parish house in the evening, he headed back to the church, where the Angelus was ringing.

When the pharmacist could no longer hear the sound of his shoes in the square, he began criticizing the curé's recent conduct. The refusal of a drink seemed to him the most detestable hypocrisy. All priests tippled in secret and were trying to bring back the days of the tithe.

The landlady came to the curé's defense.

"And anyway, he could bend four of you over his knee. Last year he helped our people bring in the hay. He carried six bales at a time; that's how strong he is!"

"Bravo!" said the pharmacist. "So send your daughters to confess to such healthy brutes. Now, if I were the government, I would want the priests bled once a month. Yes, Madame Lefrançois, an extensive bloodletting every month for the sake of law and order."

"Oh, stop talking, Monsieur Homais. You're blaspheming. You have no religion."

The pharmacist answered, "I do have a religion; and it's even deeper than all of theirs with their mummery and their tricks! On the contrary, I worship God, I believe in a Supreme Being, in a Creator whoever He is, it doesn't matter, who placed us here below to fulfill our duties to family and state, but I don't need to go into a church to kiss silver plates and fatten up a bunch of fakers who eat better than we do! You can worship Him just as well in the woods or in a field or even by studying the heavens, like the ancients. God, for me, is the God of Socrates, Franklin, Voltaire, and Béranger! I am for the *Savoyard Vicar's Profession of Faith* and for the immortal principles of eighty-nine! So I cannot accept a doddering deity who parades around in his garden with a cane in his hand, sends his friend up a whale's belly, dies with a shriek, and is resurrected three days later. These things are obviously absurd, and besides, they're completely opposed to the laws of physics; which incidentally shows us that the priests have always wallowed in a shameful ignorance in which they try to engulf their entire flock!"

He stopped talking and looked around for an audience. In his fervor the pharmacist had believed himself for a moment in a Town Council plenary session. But the mistress of the inn had stopped listening to him.

What have we there? A conversation, a commotion, just as there was every time Homais had occasion to speak of priests.

Now we come to something better in the last passage, page 300:

> Public attention was distracted by the appearance of Monsieur Bournisien walking through the marketplace with the holy oils.

> Homais, out of obligation to his principles, compared priests to crows attracted by the smell of death. The sight of a priest was personally distasteful to him: the cassock reminded him of a shroud and he cursed the one partly out of fear of the other.

Monsieur Flaubert's old friend, the man who lent him the catechism, was very happy with this passage; he told us: "That is strikingly true. This is truly the portrait of a priest-hater, whom 'the cassock reminded of a shroud and he cursed the one partly out of fear of the other.' " Homais was impious and he detested the cloth, a little because of impiety perhaps, but more because it reminded him of the shroud.

Permit me now to summarize my argument:

I am defending a man who, had he encountered some literary criticism on the form of his book, on some phrases, on the excess of details, or on some point or other, would have accepted this literary criticism with all his heart. But to see himself accused of outrage against morality and religion! Monsieur Flaubert cannot believe it; and here before you he protests such an accusation with all the astonishment and all the force at his command.

You are not the kind of men who condemn books on a few lines; you are the kind who judge the intention and the execution above all, and you will ask yourselves the question with which I opened my defense and with which I now close: Does the reading of such a book give a love of vice or does it inspire a horror of vice? Is not so terrible an expiation an inducement and an incitement to virtue? The reading of this book cannot produce in you any impression other than the one it has produced in us, namely: that the book is excellent as a whole, and irreproachable in its parts. All of classical literature holds our precedent for paintings and scenes which go far beyond what we have permitted ourselves. In that regard we could have taken it for our model, but we have not done so; we have imposed upon ourselves a moderation which you will take into account. If, in a word here or there, Monsieur Flaubert may possibly have overstepped the bounds he imposed upon himself, I would not only remind you that this is his first work, but I would have to add that then, even had he miscalculated, his error would be without damage to public morality. And in calling him before the Criminal Court—this man whom you now know a little through his book, whom you already like a little, I am certain, and whom you would like even more if you knew him more—he is already punished enough, he is already too cruelly punished. Now it is up to you to pronounce judgment. You have judged the book as a whole and in its parts: it is not possible that you will hesitate!

Verdict*

The court has devoted part of the hearing of last week to arguments in the proceedings entered against Messieurs Leon Laurent-Pichat and Auguste-Alexis Pillet, the director and the printer respectively of the periodical *La Revue de Paris*, and against Monsieur Gustave Flaubert, author, all three charged: (1) Laurent-Pichat with having committed offenses of outrage against public and religious morality and decency by having published parts of a novel entitled *Madame Bovary*, and notably the various parts contained in pages 73, 77, 78, 272, 273 of *La Revue de Paris* for the first and the fifteenth of December, 1856; (2) Pillet and Flaubert with having aided and abetted Laurent-Pichat with full cognizance in the acts that prepared, promoted, and accomplished the above-mentioned offenses as provided by Articles 1 and 8 of the law of May 17, 1819, and by Articles 59 and 60 of the penal code.

The case for the prosecution was pleaded by Monsieur Pinard, deputy imperial attorney.

After having heard arguments for the defense presented by Maître Sénard for Monsieur Flaubert, Maître Desmarest for Monsieur Pichat and Maître Faverie for the printer, the court postponed verdict until the sitting of Februa *j* 7, on which date the verdict was pronounced in these terms:

WHEREAS Laurent-Pichat, Gustave Flaubert, and Pillet are charged with having committed the offenses of outrage against public and religious morality and decency: the first as instigator in publishing a novel entitled *Madame Bovary* in the periodical entitled *La Revue de Paris* of which he is managing director, and specifically in the issues of October 1 and 15, November 1 and 15, December 1 and 15, 1856; and Gustave Flaubert and Pillet as accomplices, the former by furnishing the manuscript, the latter by printing the said novel;

AND WHEREAS, in the terms of the indictment before Criminal Court, the particularly cited passages of the said novel, which comprises nearly 300 pages, are contained in

* This material from the *Gazette des Tribuneaux*, February 9, 1857.

pages 73, 77, and 78 (issue of December 1), and 271, 272, and 273 (issue of December 15, 1856);

AND WHEREAS the passages under indictment, viewed in the abstract and singly, do in fact present, either by expressions or ideas, paintings at variance with good taste and of a nature to offend lawful and respectable susceptibilities;

AND WHEREAS the same observations may properly be applied to other passages not defined in the indictment and that at first reading seem to present theories as contrary to the morality and institutions which form the basis of society as they are contrary to the most august ceremonies of the church;

AND WHEREAS by these various titles the work submitted before the court deserves stern censure, for the mission of literature must be to enrich and to refresh the spirit by improving the understanding and by perfecting the character, far more than to instill a loathing for vice by offering a picture of disorders that may exist in society;

AND WHEREAS the accused, and in particular Gustave Flaubert, vigorously deny the charge directed against them, stating that the novel is eminently moral in intent, that the author has been concerned principally to expose the dangers deriving from an education inappropriate to one's station in life, and that, pursuing this idea, he has shown the woman, the principal character in his novel, aspiring to a world and a society to which she was not born, unhappy in the modest condition that was her proper sphere, forgetting first her duties as a mother, then neglecting her duties as a wife— successively bringing adultery and ruin upon her house and ending wretchedly in suicide after descending to the most complete degradation, even to the point of stealing;

AND WHEREAS this fundamental idea, moral no doubt in principle, should in its expression have been complemented by a certain austerity of expression and by a cautious restraint, particularly in the exposition of those pictures and situations that the author's plan obliged him to place before the public;

AND WHEREAS it is not permitted, under pretext of painting character or local color, to reproduce in all their immorality the exploits and sayings of the characters the writer has made it his duty to paint; and whereas such a system applied to the works of the mind as well as to products of the fine arts would lead to a realism that would be the negation of the beautiful and the good, and that in begetting works equally offensive to sight and mind would be committing continual outrages against public morality and decency;

AND WHEREAS there are limits that even the most frivolous literature must not overstep and that Gustave Flaubert and codefendants appear to have insufficiently understood;

BUT WHEREAS the work of which Flaubert is the author appears to have been labored over long and seriously from the viewpoint both of writing and character study; and whereas the passages challenged in the indictment are very few in comparison with the extent of the work; and whereas these passages, whether in the ideas they expound or in the situations they portray, all arise from the cast of characters the author wished to paint, while exaggerating and imbuing them with a coarse realism that is often shocking;

AND WHEREAS Gustave Flaubert protests his respect for decency and for all that pertains to religious morality; and whereas it does not appear that his book, unlike certain other works, has been written with the sole aim of gratifying the sensual passions or the spirit of licentiousness and debauchery or to ridicule the things that should be surrounded by the respect of all;

AND WHEREAS he has committed only the fault of sometimes losing sight of the rules that no self-respecting writer should ever break, and of forgetting that literature, like art, if it is to achieve the good work that is its mission to produce, must be chaste and pure in its form as in its expression;

In the circumstances, inasmuch as it has not been sufficiently established that Pichat, Flaubert, and Pillet have been found guilty of the offenses with which they have been charged;

The court acquits them of the accusation brought against them and dismisses the charges without costs against the defendants.

SELECTED BIBLIOGRAPHY

WORKS BY FLAUBERT
Mémoires d'un fou 1838
Novembre 1842
L'Education sentimentale (first version)
    1845 (Meridian Classic 0452-008522)
Madame Bovary 1857 (Signet Classsic 0451-522400)
Salammbô 1862
La Tentation de Saint Antoine 1874
*Trois Contes: Un Coeur Simple, La Légende de Saint Julien
l'Hospitalier, Hérodias* 1877
Bouvard et Pécuchet (unfinished) 1881

BIOGRAPHY AND CRITICISM
Auerbach, Erich. *Mimesis.* New York: Doubleday Anchor Books,
    1957.
Bart, Benjamin F. *Flaubert's Landscape Descriptions.* Ann Arbor:
    University of Michigan Press, 1956.
————, ed. *Madame Bovary and the Critics.* New York: New
    York University Press, 1966.
Brombert, Victor. *Novels of Flaubert.* Princeton, N.J.: Prince-
    ton University Press, 1966.
Culler, Jonathan. *Flaubert: The Uses of Uncertainty.* Ithaca, N.Y.:
    Cornell University Press, 1974.
Fairlie, Alison. *Flaubert: Madame Bovary.* London: Arnold, 1962.
Girard, René. *Deceit, Desire and the Novel.* Baltimore and Lon-
    don: The Johns Hopkins University Press, 1976.
Giraud, Raymond D., ed. *Flaubert: A Collection of Critical Es-
    says.* Englewood Cliffs, N.J.: Prentice-Hall, 1964.
James, Henry. *The Future of the Novel.* New York: Alfred A.
    Knopf (Vintage Books), 1959.
Levin, Harry. *The Gates of Horn: A Study of Five French Real-
    ists.* New York: Oxford University Press, 1963.
Lubbock, Percy. *The Craft of Fiction.* New York: The Viking
    Press, 1963.
Man, Paul de, ed. *Madame Bovary.* New York: W. W. Norton
    and Co. (Norton Critical Editions), 1965.
Nadeau, Maurice. *The Greatness of Flaubert.* La Salle, Ill.: Open
    Court Publishing Co., 1972.
Spencer, Philip. *Flaubert: A Biography.* New York: Grove Press,
    1953.
Starkie, Enid. *Flaubert.* New York: Atheneum, 1964.
Steegmuller, Francis. *Flaubert and Madame Bovary: A Double
    Portrait.* Chicago: University of Chicago Press, 1977.
———— tr. and ed. *Selected Letters of Gustave Flaubert.* New
    York: Farrar, Straus and Cudahy, 1954.
Thorlby, Anthony. *Gustable Flaubert and the Art of Realism.* New
    Haven: Yale University Press, 1957.